TRUE LIES SERIES

# TRUE
# DECEPTIONS

# VERONICA
# FORAND

Untrue Colors Copyright © 2015 by Veronica Forand. Updated March 2024.

Cover design: The Killion Group, Inc

Published by: SolVi Press LLC

Manufactured in the United States of America

# BOOKS BY VERONICA FORAND

### *TRUE LIES SERIES*

*Untrue Colors*

*True Deceptions*

*True Peril*

*Snowed*

*London Calling*

*Christmas Blizzard Rescue*

———————— ❧ ————————

*Sign up for my* newsletter *and be the first to receive information about new releases, sales, and bonus materials.*

*www.veronicaforand.com*

*To Mom.*

*Your love, advice, and inspiration challenge me*
*to work hard and reach for the stars.*
*Thanks for being my biggest cheerleader and my best friend.*

# CHAPTER 1

───────────── 🌀 ─────────────

Simon didn't want to know what the future held, and he didn't want to acknowledge the past. At this exact moment, however, he wanted Anna Marie from Wisconsin, an all-American blue-eyed, blonde pharmaceutical sales representative looking to experience everything life offered. During dinner, he'd given her his usual warning that people weren't always what they seemed, but she'd ignored his words and stroked the length of his leg with her foot, requesting some private time with him.

"Listen love, I think we should call it a night. I'm leaving Bermuda soon and so are you, and, at this point, I don't have room in my life for a relationship."

She laughed and reached across the table for his hand. "I'm looking for company for one night only. I have to return home tomorrow, and so far, I have nothing to take home with me but memories of business meetings and a tour of the local hospital."

She caressed the top of his hand and weaved her fingers between his. How could he turn down such an offer?

He lifted her fingers to his lips and kissed them. His gaze rested on full lips painted blood red to entice and seduce. "I'm sure I can provide you with some far more interesting memories to take home."

"Good." She stood up and encouraged him to the door of the restaurant. "I bet I can leave you with a few as well."

Once they were alone in his hotel suite, Anna Marie poured them each some champagne, bending over enough to reveal an amazing pair of breasts about to cascade out of her floral sundress. Biting her bottom lip, she lifted her gaze to peek at him through golden hair. Seductive energy swirled around her. Simon read her intentions like the cover of a tabloid.

He stood on his balcony. The view overlooked Castle Harbor at night, but he faced his dinner companion who continued to pour them each a drink. Dinner had dragged for two hours, and he was ready for dessert. Her eyes lifted from her task. Her smile reminded him of the carefree and happy life he'd enjoyed before Nicola had died in a blaze of heroism.

"This is the most luxurious hotel I've ever seen. It's four stars up from the hotel I'm staying in." Looking like a child in a candy store, she'd probably sacrifice everything to live in Simon's world. She had no idea how costly it could be. And he'd never allow her to find out.

"I'm glad you like it." He sat on the couch and stretched his legs under the bleached wood and glass coffee table.

"Wisconsin is beautiful in April, but there's no ocean breezes like here. Even the smell of the water is nice. Bermuda must be totally different from England, too."

"True."

"Have you ever met anyone with a title?"

Besides his father and half brother? "No. The British aristocracy doesn't lower itself into my social circles."

She laughed and whipped her hair over her shoulder. "I love the royal family. The dresses. The hats. It's all so glamorous."

"Come here." He had the perfect cure for her prattle.

She carried the crystal flutes to the couch and handed him one. He placed it on the table and focused his attention on her. Her blue eyes could swallow a man whole and keep him hypnotized. He had difficulty looking away.

She sipped the champagne too fast, without seeming to enjoy the taste, only the exclusivity of the beverage. "I haven't had champagne since my sister's wedding. I usually drink cosmos. What do you usually drink?"

"Vodka."

"Most of the guys I know drink beer." She took a few more sips. Her eyelashes fluttered, and her tongue peeked out of those perfect lips to lick a leftover drop of her beverage.

Simon reached his conversational limit. He took her glass and placed it next to his. Her smile became demure, but seductive. She placed her hand on his leg, both an offer and an acceptance. That was all he needed. Tonight, nothing mattered but the beautiful woman in his arms. He pulled her toward him, his hand caressing her back. Straight blonde hair fell across her shoulders. He brushed it aside in order to taste the salty air flavoring her neck. A sigh escaped her lips. He wanted all of her, all night.

When he pulled the straps of her dress down and claimed an exposed breast, she sighed again and spurred him on by brushing her fingers though his hair. His thumb played with her nipple until her sighs turned into moans. Soon he had her sprawled across the couch, topless and begging for attention. He complied with her wishes and provided her with pleasures small town farm boys had probably never shown her.

His kisses moved up her neck, stopping to nibble her earlobe. She turned toward him, demanding his attention on her soft, full lips. His mouth feathered over hers until she parted her lips, and their tongues met. She tasted like champagne mixed with nuts. Almonds. Bitter almonds. *Shit.*

Her eyes widened, and she gasped for breath. He pulled away just before her body began to convulse. Five to ten minutes since the last sip—someone must have spiked the hell out of the champagne for the poison to hit her so quickly. It didn't help that she'd spent dinner flirting instead of eating. She had nothing in her system to stop the cyanide from killing her.

Simon turned away from Anna Marie and spit out her saliva. He wiped his tongue on his shirt and then spit again. He'd be fine, but she wouldn't be. He knelt next to the couch and brushed her hair back. Her body rocked, and he held her steady by her shoulders, whispering stupid nothings, but the horror reflected in her eyes didn't subside. Her convulsions had slowed, and tears fell fast down her cheeks. She would die in the arms of a stranger who didn't know her, love her, or have the capacity to mourn for her.

Anger rushed through him. *Another woman dies because of me.* "I'm so sorry. I didn't know."

Struggling to breathe, she stared at him as though he was a monster, until her eyes shut, and she faded away from Bermuda and the glamorous life she'd never have.

No one was supposed to know his location. He'd stayed hidden for the past eight months. It was time to relocate and hide somewhere new.

The next few hours involved moving her body to a vacant room in his hotel. The task was easily handled with the help of a laundry cart and knowledge of the security cameras. He cleaned off the champagne bottle and left it by her side for the local authorities to play with.

When he returned to his suite, he had a visitor. An unexpected and unwanted visitor.

"Simon Dunn. On a stakeout, are you?" Dressed in white trousers and a pink polo shirt, Tucker Magee looked like a pretty boy on a modeling assignment instead of a spineless intelligence officer.

"I'm on vacation."

"For eight months?"

"How the hell did you find me, Tucker?"

"The problem with shagging every sexy woman on the island is their love of social media. The boys at headquarters have had the facial recognition program scanning for you for months."

"Glad to know the vast resources of the Secret Intelligence Service are used for employee retention instead of actually protecting the commonwealth. You could simply offer more vacation time and a better benefits package."

Tucker glanced at the back of his hand. No doubt he'd just had a manicure and was admiring the handiwork. His image had always taken priority over his actual job requirements. "Her name was Sarah, here on break from university."

"I don't remember her."

"A picture of her in a bar with her friends showed your ugly face in the background. They tagged you 'hot guy.'" He smiled, the snotty prat.

"What the hell do you want?"

"My assignment is to bring you back to London."

"I'm not ready."

Tucker's eyebrows rose. "Word on the street is you killed Luc Perrault after he stole away your latest piece of ass. They even say you snuffed Nicola in a rage of passion."

His accusation fueled Simon's anger. "I didn't kill her."

"Doesn't matter. The rumor will increase your influence brokering arms deals. Everyone's going to mind you now that you're a known murderer, and that makes it even more important that you return to your post."

"I'm done."

"I don't think you understand your options. Come back immediately or stay here and face a murder conviction. Your choice." Tucker tapped his fingers together beneath his chin and grinned. "Choose wisely."

Simon's heart accelerated to full speed, drugged by adrenaline and fury. The bastard had framed him, killing a beautiful someone in order to punish him for leaving a job that burned away his soul. He stormed over to Tucker's chair, intent on ripping his heart out. Before he reached him, Tucker pulled out a 9mm Ruger and pointed it directly at Simon's crotch. His eyes narrowed, and he waved Simon back with the barrel of the gun.

"What makes you so sure I won't disappear again?" Simon asked.

"You've always hated collateral damage. It's your biggest weakness. We don't have time to insert anyone else into the game right now. Return to work or we'll create a bloody trail behind you so deep you'll drown in it." Tucker rose from his seat and strode to the door. "I expect to see you back in your flat by tomorrow." He left the room without looking back.

# CHAPTER 2

One transatlantic flight later, Simon paused in the hallway outside of his flat. Nicola had lived with him there for five years as his pretend lover. He'd spent too much time working there, hoping she'd become his real lover. It never happened. She'd died first.

The muscles in his face tightened. He needed a strong drink to get through the night. Alcohol and women were his panacea. Female companionship, however, would only remind him of Anna Marie, and that was a memory best left alone for a while.

He flicked the lights on and made his way to the kitchen. The flat smelled like window cleaner and furniture polish—too clean after being vacant and locked up for months.

Fresh food and beer filled the refrigerator. Probably compliments of the lying rat bastards at MI6 who were blackmailing him to return to his former position. He grabbed a bottle and went to decompress in an old leather recliner. One refreshing sip cooled his throat. He shut his eyes to filter out the lingering memories of his former partner who gave everything for her country and received permanent anonymity in return.

The click of a gun and a tap against the back of his head woke him up. Usually, he'd be prepared to counterattack. This time, however, he didn't care. *Go ahead, asshole. Kill me.*

"Don't move." A voice, soft and unsure, revealed all Simon needed to know. *How wonderful, more estrogen.*

"If you're going to kill me, do it now. If not, get the hell out of my flat."

She hesitated. The fool.

He reached behind him, grabbed her hair, and pulled her over the back of the recliner. She squeaked as she flipped forward into his lap. The gun flew out of her hand and skidded across the floor, landing under the coffee table. His fist kept a secure hold on her hair, and he tugged her face where he could see it—as wholesome and innocent as Anna Marie's. Blonde hair, blue eyes, American accent. She looked exactly like the future collateral damage Tucker had warned him about. Beautiful until poisoned with cyanide and left to die.

Maybe this was a nightmare and the blonde would disappear after a few minutes.

"Simon?" she whispered.

"Have I ever shagged you?" He brushed his hand over her jeans to the top of her thigh. Her rock-solid muscles tensed.

She shook her head.

He would have remembered. Model pretty, but not as thin. Long denim covered legs ended in bare feet with blue nail polish decorated with daisies.

His hand slid over her shoulder and rubbed the back of her neck. Her shiver shot across his limbs and into places Simon didn't want awakened. "Will I ever?"

She shook her head again and proved how useless she was to him at the moment. He pushed her off his lap, sending her to the floor.

"Then get the hell out of my flat." If someone wanted him dead, they'd hired an imbecile to handle the job.

His aggressive actions sent her fleeing from the room. She had five minutes to pick up her things and leave before he picked her up and tossed her out the door. Distractions would delay him from finishing his assignment and disappearing again permanently. His hand rested on his holster in case she decided to try to kill him again. Part of him hoped she'd succeed.

A minute later she returned from the kitchen with a glass of wine instead of her suitcase. Why the hell would she stay if he'd threatened her? The liquid rippled in her shaky hand. She wore a brave face—chin tilted up, lips closed and frowning—but if he yelled "boo," she'd hit the floor face first. He was certain of it.

"Why are you still here?"

"I'm Cassie Watson." She sat on the couch, all six feet something of her, dressed in loose jeans and a pink T-shirt. "They told me you'd be a jerk, but I thought they were kidding. They weren't." She took a deep breath and a swig of wine. "Anyway, I'm your new partner."

"I work alone."

She took another sip. "I was told to report to your flat and wait. They said it would be weeks until you arrived." She frowned, probably in response to *his* frown. "I understand if you don't want me, but—"

"I *don't* want you."

She ignored him and drank more wine. "I have no place to live except here. I was told that, once embedded, I wouldn't be coming out for a while. So if we're not colleagues, perhaps we can be roommates?"

"You want to be my chum? Are you daft?"

She swallowed hard. "The service won't let me return to my old job until I complete whatever assignment they placed me here to do."

She was right. In his world, you succeeded and moved to the next assignment or you died.

"You're American."

"No. I'm British. My father and mother divorced when I was

five. Mom moved me to Southern California soon after. The service said sounding American would be better, because you wouldn't want an English woman after your last partner died."

He overlooked her comment about Nicola. It was in the past—a past he wanted to forget.

He phoned a contact at MI6 to confirm her identity, and that she had, indeed, been assigned as his new partner, on an assignment the service wasn't ready to reveal. She remained on the couch, drinking wine and trembling. It was like they were now recruiting Sunday school teachers to be spooks. She spoke too softly, acted too timid, and drank her wine as though it was soda. She had nothing on Nicola, who was focused, smart, and sexy as hell. There was only way out of this situation—murder Tucker. He must be laughing his ass off. If Simon didn't accept this Cassie person, they'd eliminate her and send over some other annoying neophyte.

He stood up and stretched to his full six feet, five inches. In two steps he stood over her. Her earrings sparkled the same color as her eyes. Aquamarines. He leaned forward and rested his hands on the back of the couch, one on each side of her shoulders. She tried to pull back, but the couch kept her blocked in. His nose stopped an inch from hers.

"*If* you insist on staying here, you are under my control at all times. You do as I say, go where I tell you to go, and *never* talk to headquarters without my permission. Screw with me once, and I'll throw you and all your pretty things onto the sidewalk, embedded or not." Obedience and perseverance were the two most useful skills a new agent could possess, especially when lacking competence.

She nodded and held her glass almost steady. "I understand. I've trained for months. I'm ready."

Her gaze focused on his chin. Neophyte. She'd never convince anyone they were lovers. Her training must have consisted of watching James Bond movies and playing Risk, the game of world domination.

"How many assignments have you worked on?"

"Including this one?"

"Sure."

"One."

"You have a lot of catching up to do." He could smell merlot on her breath. So damn tempting, but thoughts of Anna Marie and her final kiss stopped him cold.

"I learn fast." She lifted her glass to take another sip, forcing him to pull his face away from hers. "Do you have our assignment?"

Even if he knew, he wouldn't tell her until she'd earned his trust. "I have no idea. I'll be told within the week. Can you stay out of my way until I learn why you're here?"

"Absolutely." She placed her hand on his chest to push him back. Her confidence growing. "I guess I'll be going to bed now."

He didn't move. He hadn't thought this far. "There's only one bed, and I don't sleep on the couch. Ever."

"Fine. I'll sleep on the couch," she said, making him feel like a callous idiot.

But he couldn't back down. She'd think he cared. He didn't.

"Fine." Pushing away from her, he stormed out of the room.

———————— ✆ ————————

*Oн. My. God.*

Cassie exhaled all the stress she'd hidden from her new superior. Or maybe not *actually* hidden. If he was as good as everyone had told her, he'd have seen how scared she was. After three years as a technology specialist, she received an order to do field work. They insisted her skills were necessary for the success of the assignment. Although she didn't want to leave her post, the request came with an ultimatum. Take it or find a new job. She couldn't blow it, no matter how hostile Simon had turned out to be. The sooner she finished, the faster she could return to the work she loved.

Retrieving her weapon from under the coffee table, she placed it on the couch and stared at the black finish. The gun still had the safety on, to prevent her from accidentally shooting someone. Guns killed. They shouldn't be issued to people who refused, for ethical reasons, to eat animal products.

She rubbed behind her ears, trying to ease the sore spots. Simon had pulled her hair hard, but what choice did he have with someone threatening his life? If only HQ had told her he'd be arriving so soon. On the other hand, he could have simply turned around and seen she wasn't a real threat.

She wasn't a threat to anyone. She hadn't even argued when they'd reassigned her. After months of intense training, she still hesitated to shoot at inanimate objects and had never developed the calm, cool demeanor necessary for undercover work. She acted like a spacey schoolgirl from Southern California. No wonder he'd shown her no respect. Secret agent stuff didn't appeal to her. She much preferred working at her desk over this grungy apartment.

Her ineptness became clear when she'd failed the firearms training and barely made it through one-on-one combat. Her only skills aside from computer science were her ability to memorize a hundred different faces shown to her in random order and her speed through the obstacle course. Not exactly skills Simon seemed to care about.

Several times in the training process, she'd argued with her superiors about her lack of ability. They'd disagreed, insisting she'd be an asset in the field. By the time she'd entered her third month of training, they refused her request to go back to her old job until she successfully completed her mystery task. She could accept her new position or leave the service. It was like they'd removed her from her job permanently. She wasn't even allowed to speak to her old colleagues in her department.

Instead of dwelling on the negatives of the situation, she needed to get practical. Her suitcase with her pajamas and toothbrush sat on the floor in the bedroom. *His* bedroom.

She got up and went to the bedroom, then opened the door and tiptoed into the dark room. The light from the hall illuminated a path from the door to the center of the bed. Simon was stretched out atop it, wearing boxer shorts and nothing else. His jeans and T-shirt lay in a heap on the floor. He watched her in silence, hands resting behind his head.

If the devil came to tempt her, he'd arrive in the form of Simon Dunn.

She'd seen hundreds of hot guys while surfing the beaches in Southern California. Simon, however, was not only graced with abs of steel, arms of well-defined muscle, and a handsome face, his body appeared molded by Roman gods for purely hedonistic activities. His expression conveyed a bored resignation with life. His tightly cropped hair gave him a military appearance, and his eyes were the bluest eyes she'd ever seen, even bluer than her own.

"Are you standing in my room for any particular reason, or simply sightseeing?" His deep voice caused her insides to vibrate as though standing near a subwoofer.

"Suitcase. I need my suitcase." She turned away from him and grabbed it. "I'll leave it in the hall closet."

"Fine."

She paused at the door, waiting for him to say "good night," "nice to meet you," or even "I hate your presence in my flat."

"Cassie?"

She turned around and smiled. "Yes?"

"Shut the door when you leave." He rolled onto his stomach and pulled the pillow over his head.

"Sure thing, boss." She waved at his back then closed the door and sighed.

This was so far over her comfort zone. Like sky diving was to a person who preferred strolling through a park at dawn.

She wouldn't make it one week with him. She'd gladly work with someone less scary. No, scary wasn't the word to use for

Simon. Overwhelming. He overwhelmed all of her senses and made her feel naked and vulnerable.

She moved into the bathroom and remained staring at the wall until her heart slowed to a steadier beat. Stripping off her jeans and shirt, she jumped into the shower and let the hot water ease her stress. Washing her hair with orange blossom shampoo and feeling the lather slide down her body placed her close to nirvana. She turned the water off and tried to be positive. She'd survive as she'd survived the death of her mother—one day at a time.

Her arm stretched across the room for her towel at the same moment the door opened. Simon stared directly at her uncovered chest and then moved his glance down her body. The only part hidden was her backside.

*What the…*

She flung the towel around her and stepped over the edge of the tub. Heat covered her face like a crimson veil.

"Hey," she hollered. "The door was locked."

He leaned against the wall, looking almost bored. "I'm locked out of nothing here. Do you understand?"

The calming effect of the shower disappeared. All of her fears and insecurities emerged. They'd said the assignment would push her boundaries, but she'd never thought the mission through. This wasn't a challenge. This was hell on Earth.

"I have no bed, my previous existence has been erased, I'm assigned to the devil, and now I have zero privacy? Wrong." Her voice lifted to an octave below a screech. She stepped toward him and poked him in the chest. He didn't move. "I will have privacy. Unless you are stopping terrorists bent on killing me in the shower, you will never, and I mean *never*, enter this bathroom while I'm inside."

Simon smiled. A dimple emerged on his cheek and laugh lines appeared around his eyes, the kind that only formed after decades of happiness. It was so unexpected, it frightened her.

"Glad to see you have your limits. You appeared too timid to survive in the field. I refuse to work with someone like that. Too much fear will make you do inept things, causing one or both of our deaths. Goodnight." His gaze drifted across her bared body parts before he turned and left the room.

# CHAPTER 3

S imon never woke up because he'd never fallen asleep. He spent his night staring at walls and trying to rid himself of the image of Cassie's body. He couldn't. Her perfect breasts and the blonde curls between her legs had been tattooed on his brain. And those long legs would look amazing on top of his sheets. Her sex goddess appearance, however, was only part of the problem with her. She embodied everything he didn't want in a partner—inexperience, clumsiness, and a body he'd obsess over. Tucker must have planted her here as a joke. Simon didn't appreciate the humor. The idiot had no respect for human life, only for outcomes.

Throwing on running shorts and a black T-shirt, he slipped into the small office next to his bedroom, sat at one of the two desks, and logged into his computer. Without knowing his target, he had no idea how useful Miss Cassie Watson would be. He didn't have time to play around, so he entered a little-known database that held the personnel files of MI6's most valuable assets and located Cassie Watson. Her file was only a few weeks old. Ms. Watson, formerly known as Catherine Wallace, was thirty-one, was born on the second of January at Bristol General

Hospital, and had a PhD in Computer Science. A brain in a centerfold's body.

She'd taken a position at General Atomics, arriving at MI6 a year later. A robotics specialist with a focus on software development, and also a very capable hacker, she'd never experienced fieldwork. That was obvious. Despite remaining calm after he'd yanked her down, she didn't respond defensively until he invaded her shower. She showed too much weakness. If he'd wanted to extract every bit of information in her head, he'd have had it in under two minutes.

He needed food. Slipping past the living room without a glance toward his new partner, he headed to the refrigerator. Orange juice, iced tea, beer, fruit, vegetables. No eggs? Milk was missing as well. Who stocked a fridge without eggs?

"You're up early." Her morning voice was deeper than the night before and sexy as hell.

Temptation stood next to the couch with tousled hair and sleepy eyes, wearing a short nightshirt—emphasis on the short part. Holy hell. Distractions killed, and her looks could disarm a man even if her fighting skills couldn't.

"Did you do the shopping?"

She nodded and padded into the kitchen in bare feet and daisy toes.

"You forgot eggs and milk."

"No, I didn't. I don't eat animal products."

"Why not?" he shot back at her. His hunger had killed any small desire he might have to respond diplomatically.

"It's just wrong." She slipped past him without meeting his gaze and poured herself a glass of orange juice.

He tried to keep the scowl off his face, but her nonchalance pissed him off. The do-gooder attitude would screw up his work *and* his meals.

He stepped toward her to see if she'd back up. She did. "Milk is not an animal."

"It comes from an animal."

He stepped forward again, and she coughed into her hand. Either the orange juice or his presence didn't agree with her.

*This isn't a game, pretty girl. This is a billion dollars, enough weapons to start an army, and a group of power hungry dealers who care more about profit margins than human—or animal—life*

She didn't back away when he pretended to pick something off her shoulder. It was a start. Perhaps the shrinking violet thing was all an act. Doubtful.

"Do you drink coffee?" Simon tried to be pleasant to her, but her apprehension bothered him.

She nodded, yet her eyes never met his.

"Good. Make the coffee. I'll be back with a proper breakfast in an hour." Some exercise and real food would help him empathize with this puzzle of a woman.

"You're leaving?" Tension surfaced in her jaw, and she sucked in her bottom lip. She had amazing lips. Probably the most distracting thing about her, besides her legs.

He headed to the door and turned back toward her. "I work out every morning. I suggest you do the same. We'll be busier in the afternoon and at night."

"I plan on doing yoga this morning." She opened a cabinet. "Don't worry about the coffee, it'll be ready when you return."

Her nightshirt lifted up as she reached for the coffee, exposing pastel pink knickers. Four steps and he'd be next to her. He shook his head. He had an assignment to complete and a retirement to plan. Even if she were willing, which didn't seem the case, mindless sex with this gorgeous blonde would solve not one of his problems. It would only create a myriad of new ones.

An hour later, he returned with proper provisions. Cassie sat in the kitchen, dressed in a long turquoise skirt and white T-shirt. Her hair was twisted into a bun, and not a spot of makeup marred her perfect complexion. The poster child for the all-American girl.

She leaned on the table, reading a book while picking at a steaming plate of sweet potatoes and a mix of green vegetables.

He'd had girlfriends who ate like rabbits, but he'd never had to rely on them to save his ass on a mission. She'd better keep up.

"Coffee?" he asked with an attempted smile.

"All done." She tried to maintain eye contact. Despite her bravado, she wouldn't last a week. Men with inverted moral codes would break her in one night, but it wasn't Simon's job to second-guess why she'd placed herself in the middle of a battlefield.

"Can I pour it for you, boss?" A sliver of her smile emerged.

He sighed and then laughed at his own hesitation to give her a break. "Only if your ethics allow you to add cream."

"I'll make an exception this time."

He pulled out two pans and prepared himself an omelet with cheddar cheese, ham, sweet peppers, and mushrooms. Cooking was no hardship. It provided him a chance to relax and focus on one thing. When not in the kitchen, his thoughts needed to process transportation logistics, appraisals of non-cash collateral, technical information, and international arms treaties.

She handed him some coffee. The old black mug felt funny in his hand. It belonged in Nicola's. He preferred the large white one from the Hard Rock Cafe, which was situated next to Cassie. The temptation to take it back from her almost overtook him, but he suppressed it.

Sitting at the table again, she glanced toward him. "You don't seem the type to cook."

"I hate stereotypes, don't you?" He took in her earthy outfit. Her hippie persona was definitely not going to work when they went to meet his contacts. Which brought him to his next question. "What's your specialty?"

"Robotics." She shrugged, as though every bombshell of a blonde majored in robotics.

"Any languages?"

"I know about forty computer languages."

"Good. You can speak to all the computers we encounter. What about foreign languages?"

"Spanish and French."

"Fluent?"

"Mexican Spanish fluent, not so much in French. Since I don't know my role, I'm unsure what skills I'll need."

They must have chosen her for a purpose. She'd be the technical expertise, while he handled the practical logistics. "You're supposed to be my lover. Are you comfortable with that?"

He watched her reaction. She nodded, swallowed hard, and then dropped her eyes to her potatoes. He'd take that as a no.

---

FORTY-EIGHT HOURS LATER, Cassie still hadn't received any information on what her role would be. Simon treated her as though she didn't exist. He cooked for himself and spoke to random people on his phone. In response to her questions, he gave one-word answers. A few times he'd asked her to get out of the way because his body took up so much more of the hallway than hers did. He also refused to let her near the computers. Searching some of the case files would tell her something, and any bit of information would calm her nerves better than the nothing she knew presently.

She'd looked Simon up on her work computer, one day before her office had been stripped of her things. That attempt to find out about him, however, had left her confused. Simon Dunn didn't work for MI6. He didn't seem to work anywhere. His record in the Driver and Vehicle Standards Agency held a minimal amount of data: his name, Simon C. Dunn; date of birth, 29 May 1980; and his address in some other part of London. Yet she couldn't track down where he was born or any record of his education.

She headed to the office and stationed herself behind him. He stared at the computer screen, sitting in the same position he'd been in all day. He'd only left his chair to eat, sleep, and exercise. Maps and papers covered the desk. He'd written most of his notes in a shorthand she didn't recognize.

The previous evening, he'd found his way to the living room to watch a soccer game. Stretched across the couch, also known as "her bed," he yelled at the television until well past midnight. She'd fallen asleep on the recliner with a pillow over her head. When she woke, her back ached, but Simon's blanket from his bed covered her. He only seemed to acknowledge her existence while she was sleeping.

At the moment, she was awake. Therefore, he ignored her. Tapping his shoulder, she waited for him to look at her. He didn't. She cleared her throat, but he still didn't acknowledge her. "If we're going to be stuck together, we should at least get to know each other," she said.

He continued typing. "I know everything about you. You received your PhD from the University of Southern California, placed third in your age group in a triathlon in Los Angeles, and have had no friends since arriving in London three years ago."

"And yet I know nothing about you." Ten minutes in one of his computers might provide her with enough details to satisfy her curiosity, but he guarded them as though she were a plant from an enemy organization.

"You know everything a girlfriend of mine would know, except my favorite position in bed." He spun his chair around to face her and raised his eyebrows. "Curious?"

Yes, very curious, but men like Simon unnerved her. She tended toward computer geeks who liked to watch old black and white films while drinking organic lemonade.

"I don't think that's necessary." Perhaps bothering him wasn't such a great idea after all.

"As you wish. Do you mind if I return to work now?" Without waiting for an answer, he faced the screen.

She turned to go, but a faint echo of her mother's voice caused her to stop.

*Fight for what you want. Being the nicest kid in the room isn't enough.*

Years of struggling through the tech world, justifying her

ability over and over and over again, should have toughened her. Years of watching younger men with less experience and expertise take positions she'd applied for, just because they went to the same college or were in the same fraternity as the company president, should have pushed her to step up and demand what she deserved. Instead she'd always slipped into a background role and never made waves.

*No more.*

Her life would not be defined by a man's inability to see her worth beyond her blonde hair. Simon's attitude toward her needed to change. He had to see her as a contributing member of the team. Headquarters couldn't have pulled her out of her office to sit in a colorless apartment and do nothing. Did her education and training mean anything? Was she really hired to be arm candy to a man who didn't show any respect toward her?

She blocked his monitor with her hand to grab his attention. "There must be something I can do."

He moved so fast, she didn't have time to react. His hand manacled hers, and he pulled her in front of him, down to his level. She almost fell forward onto his lap. When his movements stilled, he stared at her like a cobra lulling its prey. His thumb caressed her palm and calmed the fright caused by his action.

His mouth hovered over hers. She could smell alcohol and something else, which she couldn't describe, but craved. He remained completely still except for his breathing. Garnering all the self-control she could, she held her breath to avoid his tempting scent.

"Have you ever brokered an arms deal with rebels in Sierra Leone?" He spoke as though he were propositioning her with things unrelated to weapons caches.

She inhaled deeply, having held her breath a second too long. "No."

"Then you're not needed at this time." He released her hand and repositioned her away from the front of the screen.

Her nerves flew around in a vortex of emotional, sexual, and intellectual frustration, distracting her until she forgot everything she'd ever learned about confidence and strategic alliances. Dating surfer dudes and computer geeks hadn't prepared her for Simon Dunn. Not even her arrogant thesis advisor intimidated her the way Simon did.

She returned to the living room and flopped on the couch, wishing she could leave. Anywhere on the planet would be preferable to being in the same apartment as Mr. Simon Dunn. But if she walked out the door and out of Simon's life, she'd lose her job and possibly her chance at moving to another position either in the U.K. or the U.S. She was stuck. She had limited funds, a small suitcase of clothes, and a 9mm handgun she refused to use.

The doorbell saved her sanity. She leaped off the couch to answer it. Before she reached the front entrance, though, Simon, gun in hand, grasped her shoulder to halt her.

"Overkill?" She pointed to the weapon.

"Always. That's why I'm not dead." He motioned her to stay back as he checked the monitor hidden in the hall closet. "Okay. You can open it."

Now she was his butler? She almost refused, but the person on the other side of the door rang the buzzer with impatient or desperate frequency. Simon didn't budge. He remained by the closet with his gun by his hip and waited for Cassie to do his bidding.

When she finally cracked the door open, a black-haired woman in a flirty yellow dress strutted through. Her posture revealed more confidence than a supermodel on a catwalk. Even with heels, however, the woman was tiny compared to Cassie in bare feet. Her facial features were dark and sensual. Her coloring and petite stature allowed her to shift from suburban housewife to line cook to marketing executive with ease. Not Cassie. She'd always stood taller than most men, and her hair hung like a neon banner announcing her presence. Blending in was not her specialty.

"Cassie, I love your new place." The woman kissed her below each cheek as though they knew each other from way back.

It was like Cassie had stepped into in a parallel universe where her life was a game in progress, but she didn't know the players or the rules.

The second the door closed, the woman dropped her friendly act. Turning away from Cassie, she strolled straight into Simon's arms, lifted up onto her toes—making her even taller than the three-inch stilettos allowed—and pulled his head toward her until they were kissing hello. One hell of a nice hello. Okay, to be fair, she was on the giving end and he was receiving, but he wasn't exactly rejecting her advances.

"Simon," she purred, "I haven't seen you in so long. We need to catch up."

He grinned, and Cassie's stomach tied up in knots. He was gorgeous wearing a scowl, but when smiling he was seductive and sweet and sexy, all rolled into a body a woman would love to own. Apparently, the woman in the yellow dress owned at least a piece of him.

"Aren't you a beacon of sunlight in an otherwise drab afternoon." His hand draped over her shoulder. "I'd like to introduce Cassie Watson. Cassie, this is Pauline Hall, the best handler in the business."

"Nice to meet you, Cassie." Pauline dropped her hand to Simon's rear end, and her eyes remained focused on his face.

"Handler?" Cassie stared at the back of Pauline's head.

Simon looked over at Cassie and then glanced at the woman, his smile a bit more restrained.

"I'm here to help you prepare for your trip." Pauline stepped further into his arms. Their bodies seemed comfortable in that position, as though they'd been together a hundred times.

"My trip?"

"Our trip," Simon corrected.

"I don't understand."

Pauline laughed. "She really hasn't a clue what she's doing, does she?"

Cassie could tolerate a lot of things, but she hated when people equated her looks and hair color with a low IQ. "*She* is standing right next to you and *doesn't have a clue* because no one has bothered to give her one. If you'd like to discuss mobile manipulation platforms in personal robotics applications, I'd be more than able to hold an intelligent conversation."

Simon raised his eyebrows but didn't say anything.

Pauline, however, smirked. "That's a bit over my head. If you don't mind, I need to... *discuss* a few things of a more pedestrian nature with Simon." She pulled him in the direction of his bedroom, not the office. "We'll be back in a little while."

They disappeared behind the bedroom door.

Cassie stood alone for a few minutes, feeling like the annoying little sister. Yet, she wasn't a little sister, she was a professional woman who had more education than the two individuals making out in the room next to her. Her temper, which had barely simmered during the past thirty years, now boiled over.

# CHAPTER 4

———————— ❧ ————————

As soon as the door locked Cassie out, Pauline began her pursuit. She wrapped her arms and one flexible leg around Simon. A hand dropped between his legs, sending his neurons firing. Damn, she was sexy. But today wasn't the day to reignite their old flame—a remnant of his wild days before Nicola and her professional ethics.

Nicola had never tolerated Simon's workplace trysts while she was his partner. According to her rules, he couldn't have her or anyone else at the service. Although his heart had craved her over anyone else, he made do with local beauties who didn't care if he never called them again. Despite his chronic blue balls at work, Simon and Nicola's relationship functioned perfectly. They'd made more deals and stopped more arms shipments from reaching their targets than any other team from the U.K., U.S., France, or Germany. Nicola had been one of the most competent women he'd ever known. Yet she still ended up burned.

He kissed the top of Pauline's head as he unwound her from his body. "As much as I'd love to throw you on the bed and explore how many ways I can send you over the edge, I need to focus for a few hours, and I'm hesitant to anger my new partner during our 'get to know each other' period."

Pauline shifted away from him to the cheap mirror above his dresser. She arranged her hair, touched up her makeup, and then sat in an armchair by the window. Her beauty and sophistication transformed the barren bedroom into the luxurious boudoir of an imperial palace. Today, however, Simon wasn't in the mood to play with the glamorous princess, and he sensed she'd be having his head for his rejection. Her fingers tapped on her leg, and her exhalation sounded like hissing.

Simon remained standing. He wanted a break from women but was being inundated with them. One very tall blonde tempted him to hell and back with her looks alone, and the other, a gorgeous brunette, would be willing to break the law, crush a few moral codes, and be excommunicated from a few religions all for an afternoon tryst.

Her face had fallen into a frown. Pursed lips never looked good on anyone, especially annoyed women. "I thought you'd be more willing, since Nicola's gone."

The comment ripped at his gut. He moved past the end of the bed, as far from Pauline as possible. "I'm already knee deep in shit with the service, and compromising one of their best handlers won't endear me to headquarters."

She stood. That spitfire confidence returned with his compliment. She followed him across the room. "Remember your first year in the field? I handled *all* your needs, and you had no complaints."

"As much I enjoyed our close ties, I'm older and wiser. Go on with your task."

Just one hand touched his arm, tempting and seductive. "You should take advantage of the personal service required since that Russian group attacked our network and Headquarters wants the most secure data hand delivered. It makes the job much more interesting."

"Pauline." His tone came out as a warning. "Spill it."

"Fine." She backed away and sat on the bed, leaning across the pillows in a provocative pose. "Cassie, as you know, is absolutely green when it comes to anything outside her little cubicle on the twelfth floor. She hasn't had a boyfriend since moving to London. She's one of those workaholic types. Anyway, she needs a bit of softening around the edges. Your job is to make sure she looks like your lover and not some skittish little mouse."

His phone vibrated in his pocket. Looking at the video, he couldn't help but chuckle. "I'm not sure if little or skittish is the best way to describe her. Unpredictable, yes."

Cassie had tensed while Pauline snogged him near the front door. Was his partner jealous of Pauline on a professional or a physical level? *Interesting.* Either could work in his favor. If she did feel some attraction toward him, perhaps he could manipulate her into breaking her non-violent stance in order to do their job. Otherwise, she'd be like an appendix about to burst. Useless and deadly.

Too bad he couldn't switch out Pauline for Cassie. The woman could probably kill without guilt, plus lie, cheat, and steal as well as he could. She didn't, however, have the skill set necessary for his purposes.

"Simon, you have your work cut out for you. She needs to be more sophisticated when it comes to all aspects of her assignment. I've never seen someone who didn't want this job be placed in such a high risk position."

"She didn't want the job?"

Pauline shook her head.

That didn't make sense at all. Usually, new agents craved adventure and took chances that placed them in the line of fire. If she didn't want to be here, Simon had no idea how she'd perform. He also had no idea what they were supposed to do together. "As of this minute, you haven't told me *what* I'm supposed to do except seduce a surfer girl. Not an incredibly challenging assignment. What's next?"

"You have to reestablish yourself. People think you're dead or in hiding. It's time to make an appearance. Tucker mentioned a deal brewing to arm rebels in Sierra Leone. Do you think you can get in on it?"

She crossed her legs, allowing the hem of her yellow dress to lift to the top of her thigh. Her Cheshire cat smile told him she was still on the prowl. Annoyance replaced attraction. Only Nicola had ever made Simon lose focus on his job. Pauline was wasting her time trying to break him down. He wouldn't repeat his past mistakes.

"Already arranged. As for Cassie, tell Tucker I'll obtain the results he wants using my own methods. Next."

She leaned back on the bed, posed like a centerfold about to get naked. "Some businessmen in North Korea are looking to arm a few soldiers with suicide drones near the DMZ."

*Drones in the Korean Demilitarized Zone?* Cassie's role clicked into place. Plenty for a robotics expert to do there.

"How do I make contact?"

"They'll be at SOFEX Jordan in two weeks."

"I'd better get busy then." He'd skipped the Special Operations Forces Exhibition & Conference the year before, but every major player in the world of legal and illegal arms deals would be there. He needed to return and get back in the game.

He glanced at his phone for a peek at his new partner. Between Pauline's failed seduction and Cassie's lack of composure, the wrong women surrounded him. At least he could send Pauline away. Cassie, on the other hand, he was stuck with until this was done. The woman exhibited zero patience—the most important quality to have in this job. The inadequate training new agents received made them overconfident and a risk to themselves and others. He'd seen eight colleagues perish in the first six months of their assignments due to rookie mistakes. And, unlike Cassie, they'd never hesitated to fire a gun.

---

CASSIE TIPTOED to the bedroom door and listened. She heard nothing. Grabbing a glass from the kitchen, she tried to listen through the door and then the wall. Not a sound. The door had a heavy rubber seal on it. In fact, every door in the flat was sealed. So much for eavesdropping.

They'd been planted in the bedroom for forty-five minutes. If they were having sex, they would have finished by now. Maybe. Although by the looks of Simon, he could probably carry on all night.

Pacing for several minutes did not calm her nerves. The more she thought about her unknown role, Pauline's open acceptance into Simon's world, and their mutual love fest going on behind a closed door, the more Cassie's frustration bubbled to the surface.

She wanted professional respect. Was that too much to ask? To be included in the plans and to understand her role in whatever they'd be doing and where ever they'd be going. Tension mounted in her gut, spread into her throat, and expanded to create an intense throbbing behind her eyes. She'd been sweet and nice and respectful, and they'd both ignored her. What if she *demanded* answers?

Her knock on the door to ask how long they would be went unanswered. They could, at least, acknowledge her existence. She knocked again and called for Simon. Nothing. This was ridiculous. She spoke in a loud voice and received no response. How could they not hear her?

Despite her actions, the lovebirds remained locked in his bedroom. She supposed the walls were indeed soundproof. If someone punched in the front door to kill her, Simon would never know.

She picked up the blanket from the couch and sat in the recliner. Her outburst would accomplish nothing—only distract her from the mission. Whatever that was. She hated being angry and frustrated. After several deep-breathing exercises, her stress decreased, and she nodded off.

Sometime after the sun fell below the horizon, Simon and

Pauline emerged, fully clothed. Pauline's makeup was intact, and her dress appeared wrinkle-free. Still, Cassie didn't want to acknowledge them. The exclusion hurt too much.

She needed to get a grip. She didn't have the experience to make demands.

Simon immediately went to the office and closed himself in.

Pauline, smiling like a woman who'd spent hours in the arms of a hot, sexy man, waved to Cassie with all the sincerity of a cheerleader toward the school computer geek. "I'll see you in the morning."

"You will?"

"We're going shopping. It'll be fantastic, you'll see. When I'm done with you, you'll feel like a million pounds. Don't worry, Simon's paying."

Wearing clothes picked out by Simon's lover would *not* be fantastic. "What time should I expect you?"

"Nine o'clock sharp. Don't stay up all night with Simon."

Cassie smiled, trying to act more confident and saucy than she felt. "I'll try, but he's insatiable."

"Isn't that the truth?" Pauline laughed, but for some reason it came across as artificial.

When Cassie finally shut the door on Pauline's back, she headed for the office. Before she reached it, the door opened and he stepped out. He was no longer smiling. With his tight black T-shirt, fitted jeans, and sullen expression, he looked like a bouncer ready to remove a troublemaker. She caught her breath and almost turned to flee.

His rigid gaze, however, froze her in place. "I don't care who placed you on this job, if you can't control yourself or respect my need for privacy, then you need to be replaced. Immediately."

"Excuse me?"

He held up his phone and played a video—with accompanying sound—of her sneaking around the flat and putting her ear to the door.

"You could see me?" She appeared incredibly foolish on the video. Why couldn't she have taken a walk or made dinner?

"I told you before, nothing happens in my world that I don't know about. And if I ever catch you trying to listen to a conversation you do not have the authorization to hear, I will pull you from this assignment faster than you can throw yourself on the floor and cry."

"How will I complete the assignment if I don't know what it is?"

"You need to do what I tell you, and you will know only what I determine you need to know. With too much information, you'll endanger yourself and everyone around you. Trust me when I say clueless suits you."

"I'm sorry. I thought Pauline would tell us our task together."

"Pauline is not permitted to speak to anyone but *me* about the logistics. If she did, she would be terminated. She takes her job seriously, and so do I. As for you... Why the hell are you here? You obviously don't like violence, and you have the seductive ability of a Teletubby. I've honestly never encountered an operative like you in all my years working in the field."

He took a beer from the refrigerator and returned to the office, leaving her behind to feel even more useless and incompetent.

# CHAPTER 5

*hy the hell are you here?*

Simon's words played in Cassie's head over and over. She had no idea, and apparently, he didn't either.

She didn't sleep that night. Her mind rewound and replayed the events with Simon and Pauline again and again. Neither one had done anything wrong. She, on the other hand, had decided to promote herself to the moral authority. With zero field experience, she'd challenged her superior's judgment. Instead of showing her preparedness, she'd proven her ineptness.

Simon had left for some unknown place before she could rouse herself from the couch. No matter. He probably wouldn't speak with her anyway. She took advantage of the solitude and gained some perspective during a five-mile run along the Thames. By the time she returned to the flat and showered, she was ready to deal with Pauline again.

She threw on a pale pink knit dress and flat canvas shoes. Pauline arrived dressed in a sophisticated black skirt and ivory silk blouse. With her dark features and petite frame, she carried herself with a cool elegance Cassie envied.

Pauline embraced her in the same cold manner as the day before. "Ready?"

"I guess."

"Trust me." Her dark eyes perused Cassie's tall frame. "You'll be beautiful when I'm done with you. I haven't failed yet."

They left for Bond Street in a chauffeured car. Pauline ignored her and spoke on the phone, setting up appointments for the day. At their first stop, she hustled Cassie into a day spa.

"Is this necessary?"

"Simon only dates women of a certain caliber." She lifted Cassie's nails, bitten down to the quick during crunch times at work. With a shake of her head, she waved over a manicurist. "She needs acrylic tips, medium long, and make the color blood red. Same color on the toes. Get rid of the daisies." The words came out as a command, not a suggestion.

"Red?"

"Trust me. You're not going anywhere that pink or blue would be appropriate."

According to the stylist, Cassie's hair color—golden blonde with natural sun-kissed highlights—was perfect, but Pauline told the woman to remove two inches from the ends and add some layering at the bottom.

"Trust me. This is what I do." Pauline said "trust me" so often, she sounded like a philandering husband.

As a treat, Pauline arranged for Cassie to enjoy an hour-long massage—her first massage since leaving California. When she emerged, her calm and relaxed state evaporated when she couldn't find either her clothes or shoes. The salon staff wasn't talking, except to tell her to wait for Pauline to reappear.

After Cassie had waited twenty minutes dressed in only a terrycloth robe, Pauline strolled in with several bags. "These are for you. They should fit."

"I don't understand. Where are my things?"

"Cassie, do you think Simon would date a hippie girl with sensible shoes?" She shook her head and sighed. "No. He requires sophistication. *Your* things, however, scream folk music and country fairs. I promise to replace everything I took, both here and in the flat, but you must start over."

Her meager property just became nonexistent, as did the size of her confidence. "You took everything?"

"Trust me. You didn't have anything worth keeping." Easy for Pauline to say. She had a complete wardrobe and a credit card. Cassie had nothing. All her possessions had been confiscated. And who would own the clothes Pauline had bought for her? Simon? The British government?

Pauline pushed a few bags into Cassie's hands. "Stop acting like a child. This is strictly business, not anything against your style. Not really."

For all Pauline's faults, most of which were related to her relationship with Simon, she had an amazing fashion sense. Cassie emerged from the dressing room in a long black Donna Karan cashmere sweater and a tight wool skirt that conformed to her every curve. Even her underwear had been replaced. No more cotton comfort. Everything under her clothes was decorated with silk and lace. Every bit of her clothing had been harvested from some sort of animal.

"Shoes?" She lifted her pedicured red toes toward Pauline.

"In the large white box." She pointed to a box marked "Jimmy Choo," a designer Cassie could never have afforded on her past salary without foregoing food or heat.

Inside the box, long black leather boots with shiny gold heels —tall enough for Cassie to look Simon in the eye without tilting her head—peeked out of tissue paper. "These are beautiful, but I don't wear leather."

"Simon's girlfriend does. That's you, by the way. You need to make a fashion statement and be unforgettable in a short amount of time. This should do it."

Her job required her to take on a new persona, but in the process, her essence was being systematically stripped away and replaced by someone functioning according to a different paradigm. Her insides began to tighten, twist, and moan, one part in hunger and the other part in fear. She didn't like the new Cassie. She wanted comfortable clothes, a desk job, and a bed. But she resigned herself that once the assignment was over, she'd sprint back to her roots. And her Birkenstocks.

The day continued at a fast pace. Despite her earlier misgivings, she enjoyed Pauline's company. How could she complain? The woman acted cordial the entire day and was carrying an unlimited credit card she used exclusively on Cassie's purchases.

They shopped at the best shops in the Bond Street area. Not only did Pauline not question the moral or economical wisdom of paying three thousand pounds for a pair of flimsy leather stilettos, she also decided Cassie should have the handbag to match.

They skipped lunch to visit Burberry. No time to eat for the fashionable. Cassie's stomach, however, protested. Pauline tried to help by offering her fruit at the Chanel boutique. It wasn't enough, but she carried on with the hope she'd be back in the apartment in the next few hours.

After hitting every major designer in the area, she'd accumulated enough clothes to open a small boutique of her own— Versace gowns, Chanel suits, shoes with long Italian names, and every accessory possible.

By six o'clock, Cassie needed a break. Pauline, it seemed, had had enough as well. With a wave of her hand, she summoned their car. They traveled toward Notting Hill. When the car pulled up in front of *Assaggi*, a small Italian restaurant, Pauline prodded her out the door.

"Go. Find some food. I'll bring your purchases to your flat."

Cassie remained in her seat. "You don't have to go through the trouble. I can go home to eat. I'm pretty tired."

"This isn't a suggestion. It's an order. Have a great time on your trip. I'll stop in when you return." An elegant finger pointed to the door.

She wanted to hug Pauline, because she'd been the closest

thing to a friend Cassie had known since leaving California. Pauline, however, seemed to prefer a quick exit.

When Cassie emerged onto the sidewalk, she ducked her head back inside the car for a final good-bye. "Thank you for everything."

"Go."

At the order, Cassie shut the door. Before the car sped out of sight, she remembered she had no money and no phone with her. Stranded across town, hungry and broke, she'd have to carry her killer boots on the walk back to the flat.

"Amazing." Simon's baritone voice wrapped around her and pulled her back from the edge of the busy road.

Cassie spun around. For the first time since they'd met, Simon wasn't dressed in jeans, workout clothes, or boxer shorts. He wore a black suit rivaling her new designer clothes. His white shirt was open at the neck, but the total effect made him seem overdressed. She strode toward him, but the boots had created quarter size blisters on her feet, and her sexy strut turned into a wounded man's limp. Simon held her around her waist and steadied her gait. She sank into his embrace—almost melted into it when he kissed her cheek and murmured in her ear how much he liked her new outfit.

Some of the crowd behind them had turned to look. They must be staring at Simon. His presence diminished everyone else's. Cassie couldn't keep her eyes off him.

She straightened to her full height plus three inches, rising above the crowd. Together they must have appeared like two well-dressed giants. "How did you know I'd be here?"

"I know everything. Have you forgotten already?" His breath tickled.

She tilted her ear into his shoulder to brush off the sensation. "Apparently I did."

"I decided Italian food would be perfect for dinner."

"That's fine. I can have a salad."

"No. You need more to eat than that. Consider this our first date as a couple. I'll be acting the part of a domineering boyfriend and will pick your meal for you. You'll eat everything on your plate and enjoy it. That's an order." His expression did not allow for resistance, so she nodded.

Her acquiescence brought a slight grin to his face, revealing a dimple in his right cheek. Darn, it was sexy. If she had to follow someone into hell, he might as well look like Simon.

The maître d' embraced Simon and led him past a line of impatient people, to a private table in a corner of the dining room under a large orange and gold contemporary painting. "Mr. Dunn, we're glad you've returned. It's been a long time."

"Too long, Tony." Simon pulled out Cassie's chair and waited for her to be seated, then took the seat next to hers. "Please bring me a bottle of the 2000 *Famiglia Anselma Barola*."

"Certainly." The man hurried away in search of whatever Simon had just ordered.

A few patrons stared in their direction, but Simon ignored them all, focusing his attention on Cassie. He reached out and covered her hand. *So it begins. Our playacting.* She couldn't let him down, so she allowed her hand to rest comfortably under his. Acting as lovers wasn't so bad.

His thumb rubbed the top of her hand absentmindedly... or maybe on purpose. "I'm glad you met me here tonight. I need to go somewhere, and I thought you'd like to drive with me."

Did she have a choice? "Sure. I need a field trip. It'll be fun."

"If everything goes as planned, you'll wait in the car while I pick up what I need."

"Not so fun."

"I'd prefer to have you bored in the car rather than transported to the morgue. Although more exciting, it's not quite as satisfying."

*Nope. Not fun at all.*

Cassie hated death. She'd spent months by her mother's side as cancer slowly killed her. Would a quick killing be any less horrifying? Her nerves curbed her appetite. She didn't want to eat. She'd never wanted a career in subterfuge and violence, but her only choices had been early retirement or spy school.

The maître d' returned with a bottle of red wine, uncorked it, and poured them each a glass. Simon didn't touch his, so Cassie left hers sitting in front of her as well and smiled at the waiter who had arrived to take their order.

"We'll each have a garden salad, then the venison." Simon squeezed her hand and smiled.

Cassie forgot to smile in return. He squeezed a little harder until she acknowledged him.

"Sounds good." *Venison? Bambi? Darn him. Why couldn't we start with scallops?*

He nodded to the waiter, who hustled away.

Trying to pose as an attentive lover, Cassie leaned toward him to whisper in his ear. "I can't eat deer meat."

"Yes, you can," he whispered back before biting her earlobe.

The moan leaving her mouth was not part of the act. If he continued to seduce her with his teeth, he'd have her on the floor, begging for him, before the salad arrived. She backed away and sighed.

Lifting her wineglass, Simon sniffed it, and then handed it to her. An odd gesture, but endearing anyway. "Drink."

He picked up his glass and toasted to a successful mission. He savored his wine, but never let his eyes leave hers. She took a sip. The wine ran over her tongue, allowing the flavor to emerge slowly. Simon gave her an imperceptible nod. She must have passed one of his tests.

Headquarters had provided so little background on her new identity that she was unsure what to say to fill in the gaps in conversation. "This is a so romantic. Remind me again where we met?"

"At a party in Miami," he replied.

"I love Miami." She did love Miami and had spent a few months there for General Atomics.

"I know."

"That's right, you know everything about me. What's my favorite ice cream flavor?"

"You don't eat ice cream...but you do allow me to coat you in it and lick it off." His voice deepened as though he could taste it, taste her.

In response, her stomach fluttered, making her want to skip dinner and go straight to dessert. She bit her lip to keep her feelings at bay. She could fall hard for this controlling, hard-edged hulk of a man, despite knowing every seductive word and action toward her was business as usual for him.

Simon refilled her wineglass to three quarters full, leaving his glass half empty. She wanted to slow down with the alcohol, but Simon was very persistent. No one had ever ordered her to drink more than a glass of anything before. At least the wine was a good vintage. The salad came and went without complication, despite the cheese and the buttermilk dressing. Her hunger and her need to prove her professionalism trumped her ethics. That would have bothered her normally, but Simon's overpowering presence and a bloodstream full of whatever red wine she was drinking won out over her principles.

Simon bumped his hand into a water glass. Cassie's hand shot out to stop it from spilling.

"Good catch," he said, but he didn't look too apologetic about his mishap. Perhaps men like him didn't feel the need to apologize for klutzy moves. Women like Cassie, on the other hand, over-apologized for things that weren't even their fault. She needed to act more like Simon.

The waiter presented their main course with a flourish. He even stood over the table waiting for them to take a bite of their food.

The thought of venison, however, destroyed her appetite.

"Eat, angel." Simon cut her a piece and held the fork in front of her mouth.

"I'm not hungry, *honey*."

The waiter glanced at Simon and then at their water glasses. If he could have fled, he probably would have sprinted away.

Simon smiled and reached out with his other hand to beckon her closer to him. "Let's just say it'll make me really happy to see you eat and enjoy what's on your plate." His expression became earnest with a minor threat mixed in. "Seriously."

Cassie silently apologized to the deer for being involved in its slaughter and promised to donate more funds to PETA next Christmas. Then she took a bite. The meat, covered in a heavy mushroom sauce, melted in her mouth. She wanted to hate the flavor, but continued to chew until the piece disappeared. Simon handed her the glass of wine, waited for her to swallow, and then encouraged her to take another bite. The waiter smiled at Simon and departed.

She sipped wine in between each successive bite and ignored the gorgeous man next to her, who was busy devouring his own meal, no doubt content in his manipulation of her cravings. In less than ten minutes, her dish was empty.

Their waiter stood next to her to clear the plate. "Did you enjoy the meal, madam?"

She really did, and hated herself for it. "Yes, thank you. My compliments to the chef."

Simon didn't acknowledge her comment, but focused on the waiter. "Two cappuccinos and one of your chocolate tortes, Martin."

"Coming right up, Mr. Dunn," he said before rushing away.

If Simon Dunn leaned over and kissed her, she'd kiss him back. Yep. How could she resist? How could any woman resist him? She sighed and took another sip of her wine, probably her fourth glass.

Simon turned his blue eyes toward her. A self-satisfied smirk graced his face, like a vampire who was watching his victim's first kill. "You liked it."

"Only because you ordered me to enjoy it."

He brushed her hair back behind her ear. "That's a good enough reason...for now."

# CHAPTER 6

———————————— ✆ ————————————

Dinner was a test. Simon had pushed Cassie's boundaries as far as he could. She did what he'd told her, even as it went against every fiber of her being. Her willingness to follow his orders proved he might be able to keep her alive after all.

He lifted her into his Range Rover and buckled her up. He'd carefully observed her limit with alcohol. Two glasses. After that, her reflexes and attention faded. Three glasses put her at risk of doing something stupid, and four took her over the edge, too easily seduced. Simon, however, preferred women who were sober and consenting.

He'd monitor her intake from now on to make sure she never exceeded her "stay alert—stay alive" limit. It wasn't Cassie's inability to say no worrying him. It was his colleagues' desire to diminish the capacity of those around them.

"Thanks." She rolled her head toward him but never lifted it from the headrest. Her eyelids fluttered, then closed. She was out cold within a few minutes of the drive from Notting Hill. A restless sleep, but at least she wasn't singing pub songs and asking him personal questions. Not that he would have answered.

The trip to Oxford would take an hour or two depending on

traffic. Driving provided him time to think and plan the next few weeks in their assignment...as long as he didn't glance at the blonde beauty passed out next to him. She could break the concentration of a Tibetan monk.

Even seven sheets to the wind, she was captivating. Every male in the restaurant had focused on her alone when she'd walked by their tables. Yet she didn't have a clue how her appearance affected the men around her. Pauline deserved a lot of credit. She'd transformed an innocent surfer girl into a sexy companion every man in Simon's world would love to possess. Her looks would both help his assignment and hinder it. He'd have to watch her everywhere they went. The men Simon did business with had no problem taking what they wanted, consequences be damned.

Forty-five minutes into their journey, Cassie stirred.

"Simon?" She swiped at his shoulder, missing it. Her hand fell between them, motionless.

"I'm here." He reached out, rested his hand on her thigh, and squeezed, more to comfort her than to seduce her.

"My stomach hurts," she whispered.

"You ate a lot tonight." And drank a lot.

She sat up with a jerk and covered her mouth. "Pull over."

"Now?" In the middle of the motorway?

"Now."

Fifteen minutes later, Cassie, cleaned up from their emergency stop, was drinking a ginger ale to settle her rebellious stomach.

"I'll never eat like that again." The strain in her voice gave Simon pause, but once on this path, she'd committed to going all the way. No U-turns permitted.

"When you and I are finished together, and you're safely tucked back in your little office, you can live on lettuce and potatoes." He left his hand resting on her leg. She needed to become comfortable with him. She needed to trust him. "Until then, you eat what I eat."

She shrugged as though she didn't have a say in the matter

anyway. She didn't, so her cooperation was a bonus. "Can I ask where we're headed?"

"Oxford. I have some business to take care of. You'll wait in the car."

"That's fine." Her eyes closed again, and silence returned.

His job would be easier if she remained asleep. He cut the engine, double-checked his gun, and looked over at her one more time. Her innocence and beauty made him ache for something he swore he'd never desire again.

"Goodnight, angel." He kissed her on the forehead and headed toward the familiar brick house.

Two white cameras pointed into the yard to warn intruders of the security system. If they were smart, and they were, they'd have two hidden cameras near the others. The large ones warded off people with no bravery or brains, and the hidden cameras recorded the movements of those who assumed the destruction of the visible cameras would cover their crimes.

He tossed a small stone at one of the cameras. It hit the lens, but didn't shatter it. He waved in the same direction and then used his key to open the back door. With a minimal amount of noise, he slipped into the kitchen.

He strode past the large stove where he'd cooked hundreds of breakfasts and countless dinners and stopped at the refrigerator to grab a beer. Home. Or as close to a home as possible for a person who had stayed off the radar most of his life. This place had always been a haven away from his work, but now he needed to find a way to convince the people he cared most about to assist him with a quick transaction. A simple arms transaction would reassure his suppliers and potential buyers of his ability to deliver after such a long absence.

The kitchen light flashed on. A small woman with the face of a fairy, dressed in an oversize men's flannel pajama top, ran toward him, zipping up her jeans. Her brown hair and pink streaks fluttered behind her.

He braced for his deserved pounding.

"You bastard. How dare you disappear and not tell us?" Her booming American accent ricocheted across the room, yet her frown quickly transformed into a smile. She propelled herself into his arms and gave him a hug.

He pulled her close, relieved to see her healthy and safe. "You look good. How are you feeling?" he murmured into the top of Alex's head. Last time he'd seen her, she'd been beaten into unconsciousness and had broken bones and bruises in every part of her body. From the way she sprinted toward him, her leg must have healed as well.

"Fine. What about you? Henry's been worried."

"I wasn't worried." Henry, wearing the flannel pajama bottoms that matched Alex's top, leaned against the doorframe and smiled. "I figured you'd headed to a beach somewhere with a beautiful woman in one arm and a bottle of vodka in the other."

"Something like that." Simon released Henry's wife and went over to him, extending his arm to shake hands and then slapping him on the shoulder. "Congratulations on your wedding. Sorry I missed it."

"It would have been nice to have my brother there, but I had enough to deal with that day with Alex's father. He insisted she was lowering her standards to marry me."

"Understandable. You are only a professor and an earl. He could probably buy both Oxford University and your castle in Ripon without making a dent in his cash flow." As Simon recalled, Henry and Mr. Northrop's first meeting had begun with a fight between Henry and his future father-in-law's security guard.

Alex hopped up to sit on the island and crossed her legs. "We appreciated the gift."

He'd returned a painting he'd taken from Henry for a sting operation—an action he'd always regret, as it put his family in danger.

"Something borrowed and something blue." If he could make it up to them, he would. Now, however, he needed to borrow something even more important to Henry than the painting. "I'm really sorry. About everything."

"Apology accepted. Right, Henry?" Alex stated.

Henry just shook his head and headed across the room to stand next to Alex. "You're a bloody idiot sometimes. We all could have been killed."

"But we weren't." She pulled him closer to her and caressed his shoulders. "No harm, no holding grudges."

Her leg bounced up and down as she continued to hold her husband. Henry had picked a hyper wife, but a truly good one. Simon envied him.

Henry focused on Simon. "Are you home for a while? You're always welcome here."

"There's no way I'm moving back here and disturbing this love fest. I have a flat in London."

"Are you still with Nicola?" Alex asked, peeking around Henry. It was her way of finding out what had happened to her. She wasn't authorized to find out, and he hoped she wouldn't push for information.

"No. She left me." He'd kept his former partner's identity hidden from Henry by referring to her as a long-term girlfriend. He'd never gotten around to introducing them. Alex, however, had met her the week Nicola had died. His failure to save her still ripped at his soul and numbed his heart. Only the bleak remnants of a one-sided love story remained.

He pushed his thoughts away from his past and focused on his present, and the sleeping beauty in the car. He'd never fall for a partner again. The pain wasn't worth the benefits.

Alex jumped down from the island and grabbed sparkling water for herself and a beer for Henry. When she looked back at Simon, she gave him a slight nod. She'd respect his wish to keep Nicola a secret.

Simon threw them his trademark grin, the one he barely used anymore. "I've replaced her with a gorgeous blonde named Cassie."

"Will we ever meet her? Or will she be another phantom girl-friend?" Henry asked.

"It depends." He hoped she'd stay sleeping in the car. Bringing her here had been a stupid idea. If she met Alex and Henry, she'd be one step further entwined in his life. He didn't want or need attachments. He needed sex with a nameless beauty, one who didn't work with him, and a solid business relationship with his partner.

They spent several minutes sharing details of the wedding and non-details of Simon's time away. Between Henry's classes at Oxford University and his and Alex's work with the Ripon Women's Group, a charity for battered women and their families, they'd settled into their marriage with ease.

Simon should really take more interest in the Ripon's Women's Group. Henry had founded it to pay homage to their respective mothers. Their father had beat the shit out of both his wife, Henry's mother, and his mistress, Simon's mother. The women had made excuses about why they needed him in their lives. The abuse ended after the boys had discovered each other's existence in their teenage years and joined forces. They'd met up with their father late one night and gave him some advice. If either of their mothers showed up with even the slightest bruise on any part of her body, the boys would inflict triple the pain on their father.

When Alex finished her detailed description of their wedding, Simon refocused on business. Keeping his attention on her, he leaned forward, resting his elbows on his knees. He needed her and had only a few minutes to convince her to come with him. "Do you still appraise art since becoming a countess?"

She nodded. "I hire myself out as an independent consultant, so I can work as much as I'd like and escape up to Ripon with Henry when I need a break."

"Are you currently engaged?"

"Why?" Henry interrupted. Damn. He knew where Simon was headed with his questions.

"I may have a short-term project for her."

"No." Henry's eyes narrowed. Simon couldn't blame him. His work was never benign.

Alex stopped Henry from continuing by flashing him the palm of her hand. "Henry, you have no say over my professional life."

"Right, but I have a lot of say regarding your health and safety, and his assignments tend to involve guns. Lots of them."

Alex's expression brightened. She loved challenges, and Simon was more than willing to provide her one.

"This doesn't involve art. I'm doing a simple trade with several hundred diamonds. I just need an appraiser," he told her.

Henry shook his head. "She's not a jeweler."

Simon glanced at the heirloom ring on her finger. "She can tell the difference between a black diamond and a black sapphire with her naked eye. I think she qualifies."

"When?" Alex ignored Henry.

"Next weekend."

"Where?"

"Sofia."

"No." Henry stood and walked over to him. "Simon, don't mess with our lives anymore."

His younger half brother's face turned an unflattering shade of crimson, and his hands tightened into fists, but he wouldn't swing. Henry had never bested Simon in a fight. What really caught Simon's attention, however, was how Henry's anger had been directed at him. In fact, he hadn't once tried to influence Alex's decision. *Interesting.*

Simon took a casual sip of his drink and leaned back, as though the assignment would be risk free. "It's one favor. I'll even let her choose a diamond to keep, if they are indeed real."

"What are you exchanging for the diamonds?" Henry asked.

Enough guns to supply a rebel militia in Africa. "You don't want to know."

Alex stood and headed to the hallway. "Sure. Sounds fun."

"If you go, I'm going too." Henry called out after her. "Someone needs to look out for your safety. Lord knows Simon's focus will be elsewhere." His mouth curled into a snarl. "If one pink hair on her head is harmed, I'll rip out your heart and use it for target practice."

His threat was weak. Henry had used his tactical skills from his days as a sniper to rescue Alex. For his efforts, someone had blown off a knuckle in his right hand. His aim had to be as off as his crooked finger.

"I'll take care of her."

"Damn you, Simon." Henry's shoulders sagged. "I can't lose her again."

He had a point, and yet Simon was a selfish son of a bitch. He knew it. If he used Alex just this once, he'd be back in the game and able to save thousands of lives by keeping guns from the enemy. He'd return the countess to Henry within a few hours.

Several minutes later, Alex called out from the other room, "Simon, you left the light on in your car. I'll get it."

*Damn. Cassie is awake.*

He leaped toward the door and sprinted out the back, only to watch Alex introducing herself to his new partner. The women walked back to the house together. Cassie still wore her skyscraper boots and towered over Alex by more than a foot.

Henry approached Simon from behind. "Cassie?" His tone had softened, but he still sounded aggravated.

"Yeah."

A smile curved his mouth up, and he smacked Simon on the shoulder. "Wow. I'm impressed."

*Wow* pretty much described the Amazon goddess walking into the kitchen. Even tired and a little wobbly in her sky-high boots, she dominated the space.

"Cassie Watson, I'd like to introduce Henry and Alexandra Chilton, the Earl and Countess of Ripon." He left out the family ties.

Cassie lifted her eyebrows at the mention of the title, but otherwise held it together. "Nice to meet you both."

"Call us Alex and Henry." Alex clasped her hand. "Would you like a drink?"

"Water would be great."

Alex buzzed around the kitchen and asked her a thousand personal questions. Cassie answered like a pro with her fake story —meeting Simon at a party, never finishing college, moving to England for a change of pace. She'd led an interesting fictitious life, although Simon preferred her real history.

When they all settled at the table, Alex and Cassie fell into a longwinded discussion about living on the East Coast of the United States versus living on the West Coast. Benign enough. Simon ran up to his room to pack a few of his things, including a tuxedo, three suits, and a briefcase containing several guns and ammunition, which had been hidden under the floor in his closet. This had been his primary residence before Alex attached herself to Henry, and before Nicola died. He placed the clothes in a suit bag and carried everything downstairs.

When he arrived back in the kitchen, Henry was sitting at the island, nursing his drink. Alex and Cassie remained at the table, completely engrossed in each other.

Simon sat on the stool next to Henry.

"She's not your usual type," Henry said with a smirk.

"Yes, she is. All the women I date are gorgeous."

"Maybe, but Cassie seems more intelligent than the women you used to bring around. She mentioned her preference for the Ninth Doctor, knew Sofia is the capital of Bulgaria, and laughed when we told her how lucky she was to be with you."

Simon froze. "You mentioned my assignment to her?"

"Alex said she was excited to travel to Sofia. She never told Cassie why she was going."

"Do not speak to her about my work. Do you understand?" His voice came out threatening. He didn't want Cassie in Sofia. She was assigned to work with him on the drones, not on an unre- lated arms deal in Bulgaria.

Henry raised his eyebrows. "You're taking my wife into a

dangerous situation. God knows why I trust you, but I do. I'd appreciate you reciprocating the feeling. Calm down."

How could he calm down? The more she knew about assignments that didn't concern her, the more vulnerable she'd be later. He needed her safe in the flat until SOFEX Jordan. Not because he cared about her, because he didn't. Yet her expertise made her a valuable commodity.

He turned away from Henry and approached Cassie, his suit bag slung over his shoulder. "Time to go, angel. We have a long drive."

Henry followed Simon to the table and placed his hand on Alex's shoulder. "Call me later. I want details."

"Will do." Simon waved to Alex, then clasped Cassie's hand and led her to the door before she had a chance to make plans with her new friend.

His arm gripped her elbow to prevent her from falling over in the boots.

"I like your friends," Cassie said, strapping into the SUV. She turned toward him, her expression skeptical. "They don't act very dangerous."

"You'd be surprised."

"How do you know them?"

He fired up the engine. "Old acquaintances."

She sighed, crossing her arms over her chest. "You're not going to tell me anything, are you?"

"You know everything you should. Don't try to make this relationship personal." He didn't want to like her, but he did. If only he could erase all the pleasant memories of the evening—the romantic dinner, meeting his family. This was just a job, and she was merely the hired help.

They rode in silence.

She closed her eyes and remained quiet until they arrived in London. Why did she have to be so beautiful? And trusting? And nice? If he took her to Sofia, Teodor would follow her around like a teenage boy with his first hard-on and screw up Simon's ability to focus on the deal. She was better off in London for the time being.

He opened her door and shook her shoulder. "Get up."

Blonde hair covered her face. She shifted, and her hair fell over her shoulders. "I'm up."

She arched her back and stretched her legs. Part of her makeup had smudged around her eyes. The slight imperfection annoyed him. He licked his finger and rubbed it smooth.

Yes, she was intelligent and articulate, but she'd never develop into a competent field agent. In his experience, people either had street smarts or not. She didn't. She'd probably take a bullet rather than harm someone. The urge to protect her overrode his instincts. Nicola took care of herself and would think nothing of slitting a man's throat if he attempted to hurt her. It was one of her best qualities. Cassie wouldn't be able to fend off a mosquito. Simon shouldn't lose sleep over her inevitable demise. She wasn't his responsibility. In fact, he'd transfer her back to MI6 headquarters at Vauxhall Cross if he could. So why the hell was he so conflicted about her?

He helped her inside the flat and almost came undone when she faced him to say good night. She stared at him, and her lips curved up. It wasn't meant to be seductive, but the gesture brought his focus to her mouth. He turned without a word and headed to bed.

Several hours later, a vibration on his phone woke him. Someone was at the front door. He grabbed his gun and headed to the monitor in the closet to see who thought a five a.m. visit was a good idea. A sharp intake of air, a high-pitched squeak, and a deep laugh greeted him as he left his bedroom.

*What the hell?*

In the foyer, a man wearing a delivery service uniform and a ball cap pulled over his eyes pointed a gun at Cassie, who stood against a wall with wide eyes and a pale complexion.

*Son of a bitch.*

"Put the gun down, Tucker."

"Tucker?" Cassie asked in a faint voice. She appeared unable to function and, may God strike him dead, enticing as hell wearing a low-cut pink nightgown, probably one of Pauline's purchases.

Tucker noticed. His eyes lingered on her breasts as he aimed the gun at her. Nicola would have held her head up and spit in his face, but Cassie wasn't the spit in the face type. She was the "die while pleading for her life" type.

Tucker carried a large envelope in one hand and continued to train his gun at Cassie, who stood several inches taller than her assailant. He turned toward Simon and tipped the brim of his baseball cap back, revealing his pretty boy face. "I'm impressed with your ability to recognize me. Cassie thought I was with DHL, not the man she'd had lunch with two months ago."

Simon aimed at Tucker's forehead. "I have an innate ability to spot an asshole, even one in disguise. Put the gun down."

Tucker chuckled. "I wanted to see how she's doing. Not very well. I could have been an assassin." He faced her. "Didn't you learn anything in training?"

Cassie backed into the table behind her and clenched her hands together, tight enough to turn her knuckles white. Her breathing sounded shallow and rapid. Not the reaction expected of a field operative.

Simon sealed his emotions inside and pointed his Glock toward the floor. "Go ahead, shoot her. I could care less, but don't get blood all over the flat. By the way, you suck at choosing competent agents. Next time, send me someone at least as good as Nicola."

Tucker smirked and lowered the gun. "Same cold bastard as always."

Leaving Tucker with Cassie, Simon headed to the kitchen for a shot of something strong. Cassie's unique knowledge of robotics applications, particularly as they applied to drones, would protect her from Tucker's threats for a little while, until Simon could locate a safe position for her, away from fieldwork.

"Don't get me wrong. I think Miss Watson here is quite necessary," Tucker called out to him. "Apparently, no one else is as capable in her minuscule area of expertise. I just hope she doesn't get you killed before you complete your objective."

By the time Simon had returned to the foyer, Tucker had wrapped his arm around Cassie and pulled her in close. She focused her gaze away from him. Rushing to comfort her would give Tucker too much ammunition to use against them. Humiliation was his specialty.

Simon took a sip of the vodka, his temper almost at the boiling point, and focused on his guest, ignoring the trembling woman in his arms. "Where's Pauline? I don't recall inviting you into my home."

"I prefer a more personal approach lately, so I reassigned her."

Cassie straightened up to her full height, a good three inches taller than Tucker. For a moment, Simon thought she'd fight him, but she remained passive. Tucker held her tight, his gun tucked into her side.

"Too bad. She's more competent than you and has better legs."

"This is for your *partner*." Tucker released her and then threw the large envelope in his hand at Simon's head.

Simon caught it with ease and opened the package. A U.S. Passport and a California driver's license for Cassie Watson. They'd made her an American. He'd prefer she was British, but wouldn't challenge Tucker. Not yet.

Tucker holstered his gun. "I want her to accompany you on the Sierra Leone transaction. She'll benefit from the experience."

"She's not ready."

"If she's not ready now, she won't be ready for Jordan, which means she's expendable." Tucker had enough authority to hamper Simon's efforts as well as to pull Cassie out of his operation and place her in some even more dangerous assignment.

A deep-rooted desire to protect her from the asshole overwhelmed Simon, despite the professional instincts that urged him to let this beautiful weak link in his team fade into obscurity.

"On the other hand," he said, "I could use a beautiful woman to accompany me."

She wasn't ready. She'd never be ready. Beautiful, smart—and at the same time stupid enough to open the door for a stranger with a gun. She'd be a liability. Maybe Henry could watch her while he and Alex made the exchange. On a good note, Tucker had no idea who Simon worked with when he made the transactions, and he never would. The service didn't want a direct connection to him, or to know too much about how he structured his deals. The arrangement protected him and the SIS.

He passed Tucker and placed his hand on the doorknob. "I have all I need. You'll hear from me after the exchange."

As soon as he was out the door, Simon locked it.

"I'm so sorry. He woke me up, and I forgot the protocol." Cassie's words came out between heavy breaths that bordered on sobs.

Anger at Tucker ignited his temper. Fury at Cassie's passive personality fueled it further. Most of all he was mad at himself for wanting to protect her. He stormed toward her. "You forgot to think? You forgot to pause before allowing a potential enemy with a gun into our fortress? You forgot you're working and not taking an extended vacation?"

"He woke me up and had a package. I didn't think it should be left in the hall." Her voice trembled and revealed just how unprepared she was for this assignment. The skittish voice put him over the edge.

He tried to contain his snarl, but he could feel his lips tighten and curl. "I have two days to fix you before we leave for Bulgaria." He needed a new plan to keep them both alive.

"Fix me?"

"You're broken." He shook his head. "Don't leave the flat. And change into something less like that." He pointed at the nightgown he wanted to rip off her body, then headed to the bedroom to put on some running clothes. He needed more self-discipline, she didn't need to do anything. After a few kilometers, he'd regain control of his emotions.

An hour later, when he returned from his run, sweaty, but still tense, Cassie sat in the middle of the floor in tight black shorts and a jog bra.

She lifted her head up and rolled onto her back with her arms overhead. "I agree with Tucker. I'm not ready for this. If I can be reassigned back to my desk job, I swear I'll be out of your hair by lunch."

"You're too naive." He knelt next to her and placed a hand on the ground by her waist. "Do you understand how serious this is? If you try to leave, they will kill you. They won't think twice about it in order to protect my cover. The only way I can help you through this is by having your complete trust and obedience. Don't do *anything* without asking me, including opening the door. I'm sorry if that sounds dictatorial, but I don't want either of us to die."

She shook her head. "I don't know why they picked me. I'm useless. Would you really have let him shoot me?"

The worse she felt about herself, the more ineffective she would become. He lowered his voice. "Tucker likes to test people. If I show I care about you in even the most benign professional manner, then threats against you will become more frequent. We'll make it work. You have your strengths."

"Like what?"

He brushed his hand through her hair, calming her, inflaming himself. "You appear too beautiful to be intelligent. Men will assume you have nothing of substance in your head. That's great for intelligence gathering. They'll say things in front of you they shouldn't."

"Great. I look like a bimbo."

He ignored her complaint. "From what I've read from our sources in the States, you understand drone technology better than some of the top computer scientists at the Pentagon."

"They're catching up. There are a few new languages only a

handful of people have had access to. Is that why I'm here?" She swallowed hard, bringing his attention to her swanlike neck.

He nodded. "I don't know how drones work. I'll need to rely on you when it comes to choosing the right type for an as yet unnamed buyer."

"So I'm not useless."

"No."

"And you don't mind me being your partner?"

He minded. He'd have to use every precaution available to protect her. It made the assignment twice as dangerous. "Not at all."

A smile blossomed on her face. Not a big smile—a slight smile, revealing a renewed ounce of confidence. The doubt still lingered in her eyes.

*Make her more confident, Simon. Get her head back in the game.*

He leaned in to kiss her lips, but veered off and kissed her cheek. She tasted salty and sad. He kissed her again on the corner of her mouth. Second thoughts stalled him from continuing until she lifted her head and rested her hands on his shoulders. She looked at him with too much trust, too much faith. His hands caressed the back of her neck as he traced her lips with his tongue. Her moan called to him. He needed more. Just a little more. He stretched out next to her, but never let her go. His tongue touched hers, tasting her fading fear and her renewed spirit. She pulled him closer, but Simon's control had perched itself on the edge of a very dangerous cliff. If he continued, they'd be naked within minutes.

He groaned and pulled away, leaving a soft kiss on her cheek. "Like I said, you're beautiful, desirable, and have a brilliant mind. I'm lucky to have you with me."

After he released her, she remained on the floor and shut her eyes. "Thanks."

"Go take a shower. We'll reconvene at breakfast. I need to prep you for our Bulgaria trip." His extreme hunger for her took him by surprise. She was cocaine to a junkie, calling to him, luring him into an addiction he didn't want and knew he wouldn't be able to handle. He tried to return his thoughts to the logistics of the next arms deal. All he could think about, however, was kissing her again. After she left the room for the bathroom, he headed outside for another run around Battersea Park.

# CHAPTER 7

⚬

During college, Cassie had traveled across Europe with a backpack and a group of friends. They'd stayed at youth hostels throughout France, Germany, Austria, and Hungary, and consumed cheap wine, local cheeses, and fresh bread. The experience had created lifelong memories. Nothing, however, equaled traveling with Simon.

They flew first class from Heathrow Airport directly to Sofia. Wide seats, champagne, and endless little luxuries made the trip easy and fun. A driver picked them up in a black Bentley to transport them to the Opera Sofia Hotel. Once in the car, the driver poured them each more champagne. As always, Simon sniffed both glasses before handing one to Cassie.

"Will we have time for sightseeing?" she asked.

"No."

"How long will we be here?"

"As long as it takes."

He remained silent the rest of the drive, but she didn't care. There was so much to see out the window. Every once and a while, her mouth dropped open at the sheer opulence of everything around her. The National Theater was all lit up. She'd read about it in the tour book she'd purchased on one of her walks up and down the Thames. The urge to say "wow" raced through her, but she held back, as a professional should. Simon, on the other hand, acted as though he traveled like this all the time. He probably did.

During the flight and the ride from the Sofia airport to the hotel, Simon had kept one hand on her at all times. A solid and secure hand. He'd even wrapped an arm around her as someone carried their luggage up to the hotel suite. What would it be like to really attract a man like Simon? Would he be possessive and overbearing? Yep. On the other hand, he'd never be needy. He just didn't seem like the type. Just now he held her like she was his possession. His control felt comforting, but confining. Cassie didn't want to be owned, just appreciated.

Back at his flat, Simon had provided limited details of her role in Sofia, but never offered anything specific. Her expertise wouldn't be necessary, but her presence would. That would have to be good enough. She'd do exactly what he asked of her and become an asset to the team. She refused to let him down again.

When the bellboy opened the door to their huge suite, Cassie tried to appear bored at the Egyptian motif, glancing at her nails to check for chips in the manicure. Yet the sight of the biggest hotel suite she'd ever seen—with a living area, a dining area and two bedrooms—made her feel like a child on her first visit to Harrods.

As soon as the door shut, Simon let her go. The warmth of his arm faded away, leaving her with a chill at her waist. He walked around the room scanning the light fixtures, the television, and the furniture.

"I need to make a few phone calls. Stay out here, order us some dinner, and don't open the door for anyone without me next to you." He disappeared into one of the bedrooms.

"Okay," she spoke to the closed door.

What was the assignment? Would someone point a gun at her again? Fear coiled in her stomach. Despite the interesting sights, she wanted to go back to the office. Action adventure movies made this look exciting. In reality, the tension made her sick.

After ordering a steak and a beer for Simon and a salad and some orange juice for herself, she called out to him, but he didn't answer. Listening at his door wasn't an option, so she sat on the couch and turned on the television. There was only one channel in English, showing a documentary about farm subsidies. She turned the television off, stared out the window, and sighed. The lights at night created a warm, golden glow over the city. She longed to meander through the streets. It would be easier to handle her imprisonment in the luxury hotel if she had a task to focus on.

Boredom almost knocked her unconscious, but she revived at the knock that sounded on the door to the suite. She tapped on Simon's door, telling him they had visitors. The memory of Tucker's armed entry squeezed her gut. Her fear subsided a bit when Simon emerged from the bedroom with his gun in his hand. Thank God for overkill.

He remained a step behind her with a relaxed expression in his face. Wearing black tailored pants and a black button down shirt, he looked like he owned half the city. Like a person who feared nothing. "Go ahead and ask who it is."

She peered through the peephole. Henry, Simon's friend, stood directly in front of the door and Alex, his wife, stood partially in view as well. Despite the refraction of the small glass hole distorting their faces, they still appeared too perfect for words.

"It's Henry and Alex," she said to Simon.

He nodded to her, and she opened the door. Henry and Alex walked in, aristocrats to the core. It was obvious they'd been born to wealth and privilege. At least Henry was—she wasn't sure about Alex's background. Dressed in jeans and a navy blazer, he carried a small Louis Vuitton suitcase and placed it next to the coffee table.

"Nice to see you again, Cassie." Alex's hair had no pink now. Instead she'd colored it a rich, dark chocolate. Her outfit, loose fitting pants and a silk blouse, matched her title more than the ripped jeans and oversize shirt she'd worn when they'd first met.

Alex gave her a friendly hug, but Henry just stared with an eyebrow raised. Was he shocked to see her?

Simon walked up behind Cassie and held her waist with one arm. "I needed some companionship on this trip."

He kissed Cassie's neck and showered her with the affection he showed only in public. Her body, however, didn't understand that the tender actions meant nothing to him. Heat slithered down her limbs, and she pressed closer, her head resting on his shoulder. She wanted him, especially since the other night on the floor. His kisses had been heaven, whether they were real or not. She'd love to read his mind and know if he had feelings for her or if he was merely a master in artifice. Probably the latter.

"Nice location," Henry said as he and Simon shook hands.

"It's convenient."

Alex flopped on the couch. "What are the plans for dinner? I'm starving."

"I ordered room service for the two of us, but maybe we can go to a nearby restaurant?" Cassie asked, glancing at Simon.

He shook his head. "I don't want to be seen until the meeting." Apparently, arriving in a Bentley at the most expensive hotel in the city wouldn't get them noticed, but slipping into a small restaurant would.

Alex picked up the phone on the table next to her and ordered what sounded like a pantry full of food, but she was speaking in another language, so Cassie wasn't sure.

"I ordered you grilled chicken and salad," she told Henry, who nodded and went to the minibar to pour himself a drink.

When all the meals had arrived, the four sat around the dining room table. Alex had a pile of food in front of her. Pasta, steak, some green beans, and a large slice of fruit torte. For such a little woman, she ate like a linebacker.

Simon turned toward Alex. "We leave at five a.m. We should return by eleven."

She nodded. "I'll be ready, as long as room service delivers some tea by four forty-five."

"Tea?" Henry asked.

Alex shrugged. "Trying to acclimate to life as a British countess."

Simon had moved closer to Cassie and clasped her hand, but focused on Alex.

"I don't care what you drink, just be ready." Simon then turned to Henry, ignoring Cassie, except for the slow, sensual circles his thumb was making in the center of her palm. "If you don't hear from us by noon, leave without us."

Henry glared. "You better not be late. In and out, an easy transaction. I swear, Simon I'll kill you if she gets hurt."

Alex laughed. "I'll be fine. I'm so excited. I've spent too many months in museum basements. Do I get a new identity?"

Simon flashed Alex a smile that lit up his face, a smile he'd never directed toward Cassie. "You're Italian and a gemologist. You'll only speak to me, and your hair and face will be partially hidden. *Capisce?*"

"*Si, caro.*"

Henry frowned. "Don't *caro* him."

"It's all a game. Relax. You're my only *caro.*" Alex leaned forward and kissed him. He held her close and deepened the kiss until watching them became uncomfortable.

Simon interrupted the newlyweds "It's not a game, and I expect everyone at this table to take it seriously." He stared directly at Cassie as he said it, like she believed the whole thing was a joke.

"What about me?" she asked.

"You stay in the hotel with Henry."

She didn't want to sound insubordinate, but what was she doing in Sofia if her assignment involved sitting in a hotel room with a stranger? "I'm not leaving the hotel?"

"No." He looked as though he wanted her a hundred miles away from Sofia.

Great. Alex had transformed from fun friend to capable opera-tive, and Cassie still got treated like arm candy. A knot formed in her stomach, caused by frustration and jealousy. Lots of jealousy.

*Stop whining and do the job, Wallace, or Watson, or whoever I am.*

As Simon and the countess discussed more details for the next hour, Cassie poured herself some wine. She didn't want to be on the assignment, yet she didn't want Alex replacing her. Alcohol would calm her down. Just a glass. When their meeting ended, Simon disappeared into the bedroom.

Alex and Henry sat together on the couch, unable to keep their hands off each other. They eventually took their groping into the second bedroom. Cassie sat in a chair by the window, looking out over the city. Simon approached her and lifted the half empty wineglass from her hand. After taking a sip, he placed it on the bar, out of her reach.

"You'll be safe with Henry. I trust him with my life." He rubbed her shoulders and eased her stress.

"I guess." Confusion swirled through her brain, making every-thing unclear. "Why am I here? Tucker made it sound like I needed to accompany you."

"Tucker needs to feel necessary, and he does that by messing with other people's lives. I usually travel with a female compan-ion, and Henry doesn't like Alex acting as my lover. You'll have your moment, but this trip doesn't involve anything more tech-nical than some diamonds, assault rifles, and ammunition." His thumbs pressed into the spot between her neck and shoulder blades. Heaven. Her head fell back into his solid chest, and she closed her eyes, enjoying a few minutes of his attention.

He stepped back and took her hand. "Come on. It's time for bed, and you can't sleep on the couch when we have guests."

Helping her stand, he led her to their room. Was he going to continue his seduction behind closed doors? She wanted him, but knew deep down he'd overwhelm her. She simmered, and he blazed.

After slipping inside the bathroom to change into her nightgown, she froze at the door to the bedroom. Simon, hands behind his head, torso exposed, lay on the bed wearing only his boxer shorts. One muscular leg hid under the sheets. The other hung off the bed, with his boxers pushed up his leg an inch below exposure. Not one tattoo on his body, just smooth tan skin stretched over well-developed muscles.

She climbed under the covers and tried not to touch any body parts, especially the unclothed ones. The scent of minty toothpaste and some lethal combination of soap and Simon drew her face in his direction. The temptation was too great. Her foot stretched toward his. As soon as she felt his leg, he pulled her to him. Her head tucked into his shoulder, and his hand caressed her hair. She tried to sleep, but his presence aroused her. What would a more competent agent do? Have sex and enjoy Simon's company with no commitment or regrets, or fall asleep next to the hottest guy she'd ever met and act as though he was her brother?

She opted for the latter. By morning, she'd counted three hundred and twenty-eight ceiling tiles on the right side of the room.

---

CASSIE'S BODY fit Simon's perfectly. He fell asleep holding her in his arms, her blonde hair draped over his shoulder. His successful sleep technique included reciting the countries of the world in alphabetical order and picturing Nicola's dead body, a single bullet hole in her chest, flames all around her. The memory made him sick and cut off the lust he felt for her replacement. He awoke alone.

Quickly dressing in jeans, a black T-shirt, and a black leather jacket to hide his Kevlar vest, he strode into the living room. Cassie, wearing a blue dress that made the most of her long legs, stood next to Henry. They each held a glass of orange juice.

Her bare feet, the ones that rubbed against his legs all night, caught his attention. She wore bright red polish on toes begging to be sucked. If that didn't destroy his concentration, nothing would. Why couldn't they pair him with a middle-aged bloke with bad breath and a beer belly?

"Morning. Coffee?" she asked.

"Please. Where's Alex?"

He heard her enter the room and turned to see a mysterious woman in a loose black sheath dress and high black heels strolling toward him. The vest he'd provided her was barely noticeable. Her hair was hidden under a long white scarf and large round sunglasses covered part of her face. Her lips drew the most attention, covered in a crimson red lipstick. Cassie seemed like a country cousin next to her.

"*Sono pronta.*" Alex, the faux Italian beauty, moved with poise and control. She'd better be on her game so they could keep the transaction quick and simple. Teodor had met her a year before when she'd worked as an art appraiser for her dead husband, may he rot in hell, and Simon didn't want her new life as his brother's countess exposed.

"Perfect." He meant it. She never failed to create a unique persona and personality. If he could recruit her full-time, he would in a heartbeat. She knew over twenty languages, could appraise art and jewels quickly and accurately, and kept calm in the most stressful situations. Her only imperfection was Henry's love for her. A love that often curbed her lust for adventure.

Cassie handed Simon some coffee and kissed him on the cheek. He kissed her back and rested his cheek against her damp hair. She smelled like the hotel shampoo, a citrusy scent. A scent he'd never inhale in the future without thinking of his California girl. One last kiss and then he guzzled his coffee, retrieved his briefcase, called down for his car, and headed to the door.

"Eleven. Be here," Henry barked at Simon.

Alex hugged her husband, but didn't kiss him, probably to keep the lipstick from smearing. "We'll be fine. See you in time for lunch."

Cassie would be safe with his brother. Henry, a former

member of the British equivalent to the U.S. Navy SEALs, could extricate them from some of the most extreme situations. In this case, all he needed to do was keep her in the hotel and take her back to the U.K. if Simon and Alex were delayed.

During the hour's drive out of the city, Alex stared out the window, hummed a French folk song, and tapped her hand on her leg. When she bit her bottom lip, Simon's gut told him he'd screwed up in using her. Something was wrong. She never acted anxious. The car pulled down the dirt road leading to the exchange area. The point of no return.

"What's wrong? Are you nervous?"

She lifted her eyebrows and tried to smile. "Me? Nervous? Never."

"It's too late to go back, but I get the feeling you shouldn't be here with me."

"It'll be fine. Really." Her smile struggled to stay in place.

He lifted her chin to force her to look into his eyes. "Everything that affects this assignment is my business. What's wrong?"

She tried to shift her face away from his, but he held her chin and wouldn't let it go until she talked. The forest and farmland flew by outside the window, and Alex remained silent.

Enough. She wasn't in control of this transaction, he was. "Spill it, or I abort the mission."

"It's not a big deal. I'm just pregnant."

The statement pole-axed him. He released her chin for fear he'd hurt her. "You're pregnant with my brother's child, and you decide to travel to Bulgaria for an arms deal. Are you out of your mind?"

She faced the window and refused to turn toward him. "I need this. One more adventure before the baby's born. Looking at diamonds is safer than drinking coffee according to all my mum-to-be manuals."

"Baristas, however, aren't armed and willing to gun down people who change their orders. Does Henry know?" Of course he didn't. He would have tied her down if he knew, although it wouldn't have been necessary. Simon would never have asked her to come had he known about her condition. *Damn.*

"I didn't want to stress him out." She shook her head. "He's going to kill me."

"No. He's going to kill me."

She stared at her hands clasped together on her lap. "I'm sorry for putting you in such a lousy situation. The past few months with Henry have been wonderful, but professionally, I don't feel challenged, and then you offered me an adventure. I should have told you my limitations sooner."

"Let's get you safe. Then I'll lecture you on the benefits of honesty and loyalty."

The entire plan needed to change. He didn't give a damn what it cost him in terms of his reputation or money. He had plenty of both to cut this transaction short if needed. MI6 refused to place him on the payroll, in order to keep all connections with this operation outside the law. He'd pocketed the profits from the arms deals he'd arranged over the past seven years, but had never received a penny from the government. The set up provided him enough money to handle huge transactions with high profile players, including medium size nations looking to acquire arms not otherwise available because of treaty restrictions.

"When you appraise the diamonds, approve them if they are, in fact, diamonds. I don't care about the quality. I'll cover any shortfall. I don't want to wait around and argue values. In and out."

She shook her head. "I'll cover any shortfall. It was my decision that changed everything."

"I'm responsible for everyone who works with me, especially the mother of my niece or nephew." When he placed his hand over hers to assure her he wasn't mad, he felt another pang of jealousy toward Henry. Not for his wife, but for his growing family and a life that would involve football games on Sunday afternoons and children and eventually grandchildren gathered around a dinner table. A real family. Something Simon had never experienced.

The car slowed at the side of a field large enough to fit two helicopters with room to spare. They'd arrived at the transfer site before Teodor, but a black Mercedes was idling nearby. The location in the hills outside of Sofia protected the transfer sites with open fields surrounded by lush forests.

The door opened in the other car. Arif Tejen Bio, the buyer from Sierra Leone, exited the vehicle with two huge bodyguards holding AK-47 rifles. The man had reason to be paranoid. He'd lost several family members to assassins in the past two years, including his father.

Simon stepped out and shook his hand. Several minutes later, Teodor's Maybach came down the dirt road.

"Simon, my friend, where have you been?" Teodor approached with Jarek, his head of security.

"Busy."

"I'm glad you're back. Things go more smoothly with you involved."

"Let's hope it stays that way." Simon approached Bio, nodding his head to the guns pointed in his direction. "I need to confirm the authenticity of the diamonds. Once Teodor has them in his possession, he'll arrange for the arms to arrive. We'll transfer them to your boat upon receipt of the cash. Any questions?"

Bio shook his head. In Bio's world, gunning colleagues down for economic gain was an acceptable option. He'd have to respect the rules in this larger international game if he wanted to remain a player. His men stood down with their weapons.

Simon waved Alex out of the car. She strode to his side, completely at ease amid assault weapons and leering men. Thinking about the safety of his niece or nephew would only make him do something stupid, so he tried to focus on the deal. "Gentlemen, this is my colleague from Rome. She'll be appraising the diamonds."

They didn't need to know anything about her, so he didn't provide her name.

Teodor stared at her as though appraising her for value. A slight smile appeared on her face, but she didn't speak. Her eyes were hidden behind the large sunglasses, and the scarf covered her hair. The disguise should work, because no one cared about her, only that she approved the value of the diamonds.

When one of Bio's men handed her a black metal box, she placed it on the hood of the Bentley and pulled a jeweler's loupe from her pocket. She opened the box and lifted a silk cloth to reveal hundreds of diamonds of varying size and color. She peered at several of them through the loupe, although she didn't need it to do her job.

"Well?" Simon asked. Everything should be perfect. Everything needed to be perfect.

She nodded. She tapped the side of her glasses three times and then shrugged. The diamonds were all real. Good quality. Excellent. It should be an easy transaction.

"Repackage them, and let's go." He shook hands with Bio. "Your cargo will be delivered through Greece. Expect the shipment in twelve hours."

"Your thoroughness is appreciated. I will contact you when we need more shipments." Bio jumped in the back of his car with his bodyguards, and the car sped away.

Covering the remaining gems with the cloth before sealing the box, Alex handed it to Teodor. Never one to ignore a beauty, he lifted her hand and kissed it.

"Thank you, my dear."

She graced him with a smile that tolerated his advances, but did not invite them.

"Come here, *cara*." Simon ordered her to his side and away from Teodor's attempts at seduction. He touched her back in a possessive move. Alex never flinched. She stood stable and confident, waiting for Simon's next order. The perfect spook.

Within five minutes, Teodor's Arpia Black Hawk thundered to

a landing in the field. Simon called his own pilot. Ten minutes later, his team's Mi-17 landed. The Mi-17, a Russian transport helicopter, was one of several aircraft Simon used to ferry merchandise around the world. Simon always preferred a less flashy mode of transportation than Teodor.

The transfer of the green boxes filled with arms and ammunition lasted twenty minutes. One of the men on Simon's team gave him a thumbs-up, indicating the correct contents in each of the boxes. By nightfall, the weapons would reach their destination in the middle of Africa. Teodor always came through, which was why he worked so well with Simon. They trusted each other more than normal business associates would in this field.

Still standing near their cars, Jarek, his phone to his ear, strode over to Teodor, speaking in Ukrainian with a sense of urgency. Simon had no clue what he was saying, but Alex understood Ukrainian. He'd rely on her translation.

When Jarek hung up the phone, he turned back to Simon, ignoring Alex. "We have a problem. Bio's been detained by Ground Forces patrolling the area. They may be moving in this direction."

Alex gave Simon a subtle nod, affirming what he'd said.

Shit. Someone must have alerted the authorities to extra activity in this normally quiet area of Bulgaria. Alex, in her condition, wouldn't do well spending even a day in a prison cell. The risk was too great.

"Thanks for the heads-up. I'll be in touch." As a safety precaution, he needed to fly Alex away from here with the cargo, instead of driving her back to the hotel. He called Derek, the pilot of the Mi-17, and told him to wait. They had two more passengers. "Care to see Greece this afternoon?"

Alex shrugged, as though deciding on a restaurant for lunch. They trotted across the field. She moved well despite the heels. Both ducked under the rotors. Two of his men assisted them into the back of the helicopter.

Once inside, she yelled over the noise. "Henry is going to kick your ass for the delay."

"This is the safest way home. He'll respect my decision." Simon leaned back on the bench and buckled in. Alex was wrong. Henry wasn't going to kick his ass. He was going to murder him.

---

THE DEAL HAD NOT GONE ACCORDING to plan. At one p.m., Cassie and Henry boarded a plane for Heathrow without Alex and Simon. Where was he? She didn't want to worry, but her entire existence had become braided into Simon's life. Without him, what would she do? Where would she go? Watching Henry attempt to contain his anger toward Simon didn't help calm her frazzled nerves.

"I will never allow that irresponsible pain in the ass to so much as talk to Alex again, never mind see her, and if he dares to show his face in Oxford—or Ripon, for that matter—he'll need a wheelchair to leave." Henry raged on and on and on. He provided gory details on the torture he was going to inflict upon Simon, and cursed more than an English gentleman should.

Several passengers stared at him, and it wasn't with admiration or respect.

"Shhhhh. If the flight attendant asks you to leave the plane, I'll say I never met you before in my life."

He glared at her for a split second and then his expression softened, and the furrows between his eyebrows almost disappeared. "I'm sorry for taking this out on you. You did nothing wrong except fall for the wrong man."

Fall for Simon? Ha. He was her boss. And yes, he was gorgeous, smart, full of confidence, and endlessly fascinating, but he had too many secrets, was too much of a control freak, and… a ton of other stuff that made him completely inappropriate for her.

Falling back to the story they used in public, she shrugged and sighed. "I've always thought he was kind of sweet. A true romantic."

"You must not get out much." He then went back over all of Simon's faults and never once mentioned Alex. Perhaps he was focused on Simon to keep himself from worrying about his wife. It made sense, because the question of Simon's safety clouded Cassie's thoughts and made her sick to her stomach.

When she and Henry finally arrived in Oxford, they received a text message from Simon. He told them he and Alex had been delayed but were on their way. That was it. No other details. She and Henry sat in silence in his study. Although happy that Simon and Alex were safe, they weren't back home. So, more waiting. Cassie drank wine, and Henry drank Scotch. The sun faded, the moon rose, and Cassie's fear destroyed her attempt to appear rational.

Henry gripped the armrest as though he had someone by the neck. "I hope you're not too attached to Simon. His life expectancy is now down to about two hours."

"Do you think they're all right?"

His mouth twisted into a frown. "Although Simon is one of the most competent people I know, there's always danger in what he does."

"If you're so mad about Alex taking part in the assignment, why did you let her go with him?"

Henry snorted. "I couldn't control her anymore than I could alter the orbit of the moon." He took a sip of Scotch, tapping the glass with his index finger. "Regrettably, marriage doesn't give me ownership of her person. She had a reason for going with Simon, and I trust her. Simon, on the other hand, has his own agenda."

She wanted to assure Henry of her own trust in Simon, but what did she really know of him? He never showed fear. He hated incompetence. His inner and outer strength provided her security and protection, but if he had to choose between her safety and finishing an assignment, would he pick her? Probably not.

Henry led Cassie to Simon's room to sleep. Why would Simon

have a room at his friend's house? The men must be closer than she realized. She remembered he'd gathered a few things from the room when they'd first visited. His black and steel furniture created a forbidding environment, the complete opposite of the warm colors in the rest of the house. Some black and white cityscapes decorated the walls, but nothing personal. No photographs, no books, nothing that revealed Simon's essence. Or maybe it did. Even the bland, beige walls of the London flat had more warmth than this place. Cassie preferred colors.

Someday she wanted to buy a small farmhouse and fill it with bright blue and white furniture and colorful quilts. She could work in a small office that doubled as a guest room and watch her children grow up in a peaceful environment. The man she married would have to prefer a simple life and not one filled with guns. Although Simon's image popped into her head, he didn't fit in her dream future. His world was too stark and cold for her and, although she melted when he touched her, she couldn't see him wanting such a domestic situation with her or anyone else. The image of him in a colorful kitchen, cooking some wonderful meal, however, soothed her mind as she fell asleep.

In the morning, Henry made her breakfast. She didn't want the bacon or eggs, so she picked at some toast and drank two cups of coffee. As she helped Henry with the dishes, the Range Rover arrived. Simon opened Alex's door and walked to the house at a slow, methodical pace. He wore the same dark outfit as the day before. Alex, now dressed in sneakers and jeans, held on to Simon's arm. As they came closer to the house, the fatigue from their journey became apparent. Alex had dark circles under her eyes, and Simon needed a shave. Despite their disheveled appearances, the cloud over Cassie's mood lifted. He was safe.

"Thank God." Henry ran out the back door.

He hugged Alex tight and gave her a quick kiss on the lips. It was a lovely sight—until he pivoted and punched Simon in the gut with his left fist. Simon didn't move to block the hit. His face tightened, however, and he winced. The two men exchanged tense words with each other. Simon nodded at Henry and continued walking past him into the kitchen, his right arm tucked into his stomach.

He went straight to Cassie, looking like a soldier returning home from war. She was unsure what to say, so she remained silent.

His hands rested on her shoulders. "Are you all right?"

"Me? What about you?" Was he really worried about her?

"I've been better." Those beautiful blue eyes rotated away from her. "I'll grab our things. We're leaving."

"Do you want some coffee or breakfast?"

"No. We need to leave and give Alex and Henry some space."

Henry and Alex remained in the backyard embracing each other and talking. When they finally came in through the backdoor, their conversation became more animated and hostile.

Alex crossed the threshold first. "Stop worrying. I won't go with him again. I promise. Not my best idea, but I needed one last adventure before the baby arrived."

"You want an adventure? I'll give you enough thrills to last a lifetime. You don't need to fly all over Europe, risking your life." Henry followed her to the table, where she snagged a piece of bacon. His face suddenly whitened, and his eyes widened. "You're pregnant?"

"And you're going to be a dad." Alex whipped around, stood on her toes and kissed Henry on the chin.

*Terrific.* Alex was brave and calm under pressure, fluent in a million languages, an expert on art and gems, married to an earl, pregnant, and Simon's first choice for a partner. Nothing could have made Cassie feel more inadequate.

Henry's face colored again, this time into a flaming red. For the first time since Cassie met him, he sounded angry with Alex. "You took off on a dangerous adventure when you're carrying our child. Are you insane?"

"I want to be a responsible mother, so I'd never go off like that after the little guy arrives. Simon's timing was perfect. How could I turn him down?"

She stopped him from answering by tugging his lower lip with her teeth until he lifted her off the ground. They kissed long enough to make Cassie agree with Simon's decision to leave as soon as possible.

"God, you're going to drive me crazy for the rest of my life, aren't you?" Henry dropped Alex on her feet and kissed her on the top of the head.

"I hope so."

Simon came back in the room with their suitcases and prodded Cassie toward the door. "Let's go, angel. Now."

Alex ran up to Simon and hugged him, her head not reaching his shoulder. "Bye, Simon, and thanks for everything."

He backed away as though pregnancy was contagious, or perhaps he was afraid Henry would take another swing at him. "Go take care of your husband. He's going to need a shot of something strong to get him through this. And for the record, you're fired for hiding important information from me."

"Agreed. At least until Earl, Jr. is old enough to fend for himself."

On the drive home, Simon stared out at the highway in silence. Cassie needed to know. "Did you know she was pregnant?"

"She mentioned it to me yesterday."

A tightening in her throat made her pause before asking the question she didn't want the answer to. "And you didn't stop the mission?"

His eyes narrowed, and he glared at her. "I'm not her keeper. Besides, she has better survival instincts than most agents in the field. If Henry weren't her husband, I'd use her as back up any day. Pregnant or not." His adulation of Alex never faltered. The woman could do no wrong in his eyes. He seemed to adore her like a precocious little sister.

And that's when she formed the idea. Cassie could connect to Simon in a way Alex never could. She'd become his lover.

# CHAPTER 8

Simon jumped in the shower as soon as he arrived in the flat. He was tired from the trip and his unwarranted worry about Cassie. The warm water sprayed over his back and eased his tension. He passed several languid minutes leaning against the wall and thinking about how prepared Alex had been for the trip, yet even the queen of cool found herself in a potential minefield for herself and her unborn child. Cassie, on the other hand, didn't have any of Alex's reserves. Would she panic when trouble unfolded for the first time, or would she stand her ground and adapt? From her reaction to Tucker's gun, she'd probably shut down.

He stepped out of the shower, dried off, and shaved. If they were to succeed, it was time to use some of Cassie's expertise. She could research the types of military UAVs on the market, the cost, and the ability of a subcontractor to retrofit what they purchased to the specifications of their buyers. Then she could educate Simon. They had barely one week to get him knowledgeable enough to set up the transaction.

He made his way toward his bedroom with only a towel covering his bottom half. Cassie blocked his way. She'd changed into tight jeans and a low cut blouse. Sweet and sexy.

"Can I talk to you?" The hesitation in her voice didn't bode well for the conversation.

"Now?"

She nodded and sucked in her bottom lip. He'd give up everything to spend one night with free access to those lips. She must have noticed his focus on her mouth, because her hand touched her lip in an attempt to remove a nonexistent crumb from the corner.

"I'm embarrassed to say I doubted your ability. But you not only succeeded, you also brought Alex back unharmed." Cassie inched closer to him as though she'd abandoned veganism and was starved for a steak.

Was his pretty California girl coming on to him?

"So you'll trust me from now on?" he asked, maintaining his position in front of her.

"I don't have a choice."

"Cassie, you always have a choice. Be decisive. React. Don't second-guess every move you make. If you want something, take it." He bated his breath to see what she would do.

Stepping forward, she placed a hand on his chest. He brushed his fingers across her cheek and felt her lean into him. The tilt of her head against his palm short-circuited his normal control.

"What if I want you?" she whispered.

He should refuse her. She was his subordinate, and sex could screw up their already delicate relationship. Or it could strengthen it. Maybe give her more confidence. And then what? When the assignment terminated, they'd each go their respective ways with fond memories. Perhaps.

"Like I said. If you want something, take it."

She wrapped her arms around his shoulders and stepped forward, her mouth poised for a kiss. Who was he to deny her? He leaned in and pressed his lips to hers. She tasted of grapes. His gorgeous health fanatic. He deepened the kiss, indulging in her warmth, her feel, and her subtle reactions. Her mouth demanded more of him, and he complied. The connection tethered him to her.

Her hands dropped to the bare skin of his waist. A low moan left her lips, as her fingers tucked under the edge of his towel. Her touch sent his nerves firing.

Not fair.

He wanted his hands on her naked skin. Lacking the patience to unbutton her blouse, he yanked at her shirt until the threads holding the buttons broke. Buttons sprayed across the floor, tapping the hardwood as they scattered. The shirt followed. She stood an inch away from him, wearing only jeans and a white lace bra.

"That blouse was five hundred dollars." Her gaze followed the flight of the shirt until he lifted her chin back up to look at him.

"I'll buy you five hundred more to replace it. That way I can rip them off you whenever I want."

They remained entwined as they stepped into the bedroom.

He cupped her breasts and nuzzled the spot where her neck flowed into her collarbone. Her groan vibrated through him and reached a part of him he'd never known existed. Snippets of time with random women had never been this satisfying. Never fed anything more than physical desire. Cassie, however, needed to be claimed and protected. The thought should have scared him, but he felt her claiming him as well. He'd deal with the consequences later.

He lowered his mouth to her chest and moved the lacy fabric of her bra aside. Her body—its feel, its taste, its scent—had occupied his thoughts since their first encounter. And here she was offering herself to him.

Her new red nails dug into his back until the pain intensified. He bit her nipple in return. She moaned. Her amazing lips tickled his neck until some very vampish teeth scraped his skin.

How had this woman turned his libido upside down and twisted his desires in knots? Control went out the window when her hand yanked the towel from his hips, and she rubbed his inner thigh.

If she wanted to find his weakness, she had. One of her hands caressed his full length, while the other slid over his ass. She'd better not be bluffing, because she'd succeeded in making him out of his mind with need.

He led her over to the bed, reached into the dresser, and grabbed a condom. This would be a first for him. He'd never had sex in this flat, although he'd left the condoms there with the hope Nicola would eventually come around. Destiny, however, favored Cassie in his bed, here and now.

Her jeans were a definite barrier. She tried to sit up, but he placed a hand in the middle of her chest, tracing the edge of the lace covering her breasts, and forced her onto her back. She would undo him in less than a minute if she gained the upper hand.

He pulled her jeans past her ankles. Lying on the bed in a virginal white bra and knickers, the angel reached out to massage him. His body covered hers in an instant. Grasping each of her wrists and holding them over her head, he dropped his forehead to hers.

He was barely able to speak, but he needed to have her permission. "Say you want me."

"I want you." No hesitation, just lust and need.

"Perfect answer." He'd never craved a woman the way he craved the blonde currently in his bed. She drove him insane with worry and crazy with frustration, but he loved being in her presence.

"Now." Her legs wrapped around his waist. She pressed herself into him until his sanity deserted him.

His mouth covered hers, and they kissed. Her taste merged with his, her sweetness overpowering all the bitterness around him. He almost pulled away, knowing that Cassie had attached herself to him, and in the process linked him to her in ways that would tangle their lives.

His blood heated to a burning inferno. She tugged her hands

free and began assaulting his back again with her new red finger-nails. He'd be bloody soon, but he didn't want her to stop. He pulled down her knickers. The bra could stay, for now.

"Please, Simon." Her hands pressed into his back. She deep-ened their kiss and sent his hormones into a frenzy he hadn't felt since adolescence.

Hearing his name on her lips scraped away the last of the ice from his heart. He set a speed record for sliding the condom on and moved between her legs, shifting back and forth until he was sure she was ready. He entered her faster than expected, and she cried out with a low moan.

Her nails dug into his back again. Shit. It hurt, but he refused to ask her to stop. This aggressive side of her was wild, passion-ate, and driving him crazy. Then her hands dropped to his ass, and she forced him faster and deeper. He felt her tighten under him. Her pleasure took priority. With every move of his hips, he pressed into her, feeling her body react to his.

Her pleas for more urged him to go faster, harder. She arched her back and shuddered in complete surrender to him. The cries were no longer low and sexy—they were higher pitched and animalistic. They both came together, as though their bodies had each been design to pleasure the other.

He hugged her close, then rolled off her in a state of bliss. Everything felt perfect.

His breathing slowed and the frenzy dissipated and the erotic mist cleared. She was the type of woman capable of filling the voids—voids created by a broken youth and a bloody adulthood.

Blood, violence, deception. His dreams of a life with Cassie disappeared amid the reality of a blackmailing employer and a bunch of gunrunners. He couldn't steal her away. Happy-ever-afters didn't happen to men like him.

As his blissful thoughts receded into a pile of regrets, a wet spot under his thigh torpedoed the comfort he'd momentarily found in the here and now and blew it to smithereens.

"Shit."

"What?" Her question was whispered into his neck and would have been sexy as hell if he didn't want to shoot himself.

"The condom broke." When had he ever done something so stupid? Never. "Are you on birth control?"

"Sort of."

What the hell did that mean? "That's not an answer."

"I'm on the pill, but I was late with one when Henry and I fled Bulgaria. It shouldn't be a big deal. I'm the most regular person ever, and this is in the beginning of my cycle."

Simon turned his face into the pillow and exhaled. He couldn't afford to mess up like this.

"Seriously, it's no big deal." She sounded irritated.

Tell that to Henry and Alex who were right now making plans for a nursery at Ripon Manor, their castle.

---

SHE'D FAILED AGAIN. She couldn't shoot a gun, face danger head on, or control her jealousy and immature outbursts. Now, she could add failed seductress to her list. Although she did manage to get him naked, she was never in control. And now he'd be freaked out by the possibility of her pregnancy. So much for him having any respect for her.

He'd jumped out of bed and fled to the bathroom so fast he left a cool breeze behind him, ridding the room of any warmth they'd shared. He was probably on the phone that very moment trying to obtain a new partner.

Cassie pulled the covers over her head. *I should just stay here and hide for the rest of the assignment.*

"Cassie?"

Sure, now she'd be branded a coward. She flipped the sheets off her face, and they fell to her shoulders. Simon appeared in the doorway to the bathroom. Completely nude. Like the statue of David, only more masculine, and more muscular, and more real.

"Are you okay?" He sounded sincere, but he was trained to

show no real emotions. Everything was fake. He excelled at the skill. She rarely saw him smile, and even his frowns had an element of strategy behind them. She'd never been with a man who dominated every aspect of her life, including what to wear, what to eat, and the tempo and rhythm of any sex they had. She wasn't complaining. He took her to a level of satisfaction she'd only read about in her mother's stash of romance novels.

"Fine. Why wouldn't I be?" She lifted her arms over her head and yawned, as though she'd slept with a million guys.

"Because my bedside manner sucks. I overreacted."

She didn't want him to get all sentimental. "Simon. This is a professional relationship only. I need to be intimate with you so we're convincing lovers to the rest of the world."

"Is that so?"

"Absolutely."

His eyebrows lifted, and the corner of his mouth almost made it into a half smile. "And now we can just sleep together whenever the need arises, without any emotional attachment?"

"Sure." Sleeping with Simon on a regular basis would not be a good idea. She could name about thousand reasons to keep her distance, but her body craved him like it needed air.

"Interesting. By the way, how many men have you slept with? I'm only asking in my capacity as your professional lover."

"You first."

"Forty seven. And I've never had a johnny break on me before."

"A what?"

"A condom. And you?"

"The same. I've never had sex when the condom broke."

"That's not the question."

"Does it matter?" she asked.

"Yes. Strictly on a professional level, I need to understand your level of experience."

"You do not. It wouldn't matter if I was a virgin or had slept with a hundred men."

"You are so wrong." He stood over the bed, staring down at her. Intimidating as hell, but in a really erotic way.

She didn't want to answer and should probably bluff to make herself seem more sophisticated, but he didn't seem to find her sophisticated in the least. She covered her face with the blanket to her nose and whispered, "Four."

He stalked closer until he was leaning directly over her.

"Come again?" He tugged the sheet to fall just below her chin. "Four."

His face came even closer to her, and she could feel his breath tickle her skin. "When was the last time?"

"Twenty minutes ago. Fantastic, by the way. Those forty plus women must have been thrilled to be one of your conquests."

He didn't even smile. "Before that?"

She tried not to alter her face, but her mouth automatically tightened as though hiding something. The worst field agent ever. "I'm not a prude or anything. But I prefer to date guys a few times before I sleep with them. Not many stick around long enough."

He lifted his brows and waited for the direct answer to his question.

*Fine.* "The last time happened about five years ago in graduate school. A drunken night on the beach, a bonfire and a sleeping bag, and then in the morning trying to forget it ever happened." She lifted the covers again to hide the flames heating her cheeks, but he pulled them away from her face.

He sighed. "You deserve better than that. And this."

"You don't think I'm harboring feelings for you, do you? No offense, but you're not really my type."

His hand pushed a piece of her hair behind her ear, and she struggled to restrain herself from moaning at his touch. "What is your type?"

"Less violent, more of an equal in bed. Don't get me wrong, I enjoyed being manhandled, but usually I like more control." She turned away from him and tried to hide the tears threatening to form.

"I think you had too much control in bed this time."

"I did?"

He turned around, displaying wide shoulders tapering into a tight rear end and muscular legs. His perfectly shaped back, however, was marked by several red streaks. They seemed raw and painful.

"I did that?"

"I prefer the short blue daisies to the red daggers." He spun around and grinned, and she almost melted into a puddle of lust.

"I'm so sorry."

By the time he crawled back onto the bed, he was fully erect and ready to continue this new aspect of their working relationship. Did she want this? *Yes.*

He pried the edge of the sheet from around her body and pulled it down to her knees. "The bra has to go this time. And we're using something that isn't expired." He tossed a new condom onto her chest, and reached between her breasts to unsnap the bra, letting it open in front.

"I don't want you to feel obligated."

"This has nothing to do with obligation. You seemed unhappy with my technique last time, so I'm giving you the chance to take control." With a quick twist, he stretched onto his back and placed his hands behind his head, the same position he always slept in. "Do whatever you wish. No restraints, however. If someone comes in to kill us, I need to be able to reach my gun."

Cassie closed her mouth. Her jaw must have dropped the moment the huge, naked god stretched out beside her and offered himself to her to do anything she wanted. Could she really take him on? She did proposition him, and he did accept. Sure. She could take control of this situation and prove to him she wasn't some wilting violet.

Slipping the bra straps off her shoulders, she knelt beside the confident guy staring at her with a blaze in his eyes that incinerated any hesitation she might have felt. "First, I need you to promise not to move, unless an armed gunman breaks down the door."

He grinned. "I promise."

"Good. I'm not the best agent in the field, so I need to know you are. This is a test of your self-control." She bent toward his feet and pulled her finger across the arch of his foot. His muscles tensed, but he remained in place. "Very good."

She rubbed his feet and then massaged his ankles and calf. As she moved up his leg, his muscles twitched, every intimate one of them. Instead of showering him with attention, she sat back and stared. He was not enjoying himself, if the creases in his forehead and the clenching of his jaw told the truth. Too bad. He'd given her control.

She placed her hand in the middle of his chest. His heartbeat thumped against her fingers, but he remained with his hands tucked behind his head. A light dusting of dark hair covered his pectoral muscles, and she rubbed her hands over them then finally gave in and allowed her tongue the opportunity to enjoy tasting his chest, from the bottom of his sternum to the top. She took her own sweet time, until she needed more from him.

Straddling him, she reached for the condom and opened it. Simon's thigh muscles twitched as though he wanted to jump up, but he remained where he was.

After rolling it over him, she placed herself slowly on top. A position of control. Or so she'd heard. She leaned forward, and her hands rested on his shoulders. "You can use your hands, if you want."

"You trust I won't take control?" His hands wrapped around her waist.

She rocked forward and back, taking the time to experience every bit of him. His groans made her feel even more powerful.

Minutes passed as pleasure and ripples of ecstasy pulverized her senses, and then Simon tightened his grip on her waist, lifted her off him, and forced her back down. Hard. The axis of the universe shifted into something so amazing, she could have died right then with a smile on her face and zero regrets.

"Should I move my hands back behind my head?" he asked, almost in a challenge.

Cassie's head fell back as she experienced the best ride of her life. "I'm granting you control for this one task. Don't stop. Ever."

They continued until she was coming apart, and he was dominating the situation. She didn't care. The pressure built, and the unrelenting pounding took her higher than she'd ever gone. He controlled them right to the end, until he fell back on the pillow, and she fell forward onto his chest, exhausted and completely sated.

Simon's arms felt like home. Her plan to prove how capable she was as a field agent only proved how vulnerable her heart was where Simon was concerned.

"I could stay here forever," she mumbled to herself.

He turned his head away from her and exhaled. "This isn't the life for you, angel. You need to finish the assignment with me and then move on to someone who will be a forever type of guy."

"Trust me, I know."

After Simon, forever with another man seemed impossible to fathom.

# CHAPTER 9

E ach night, Simon watched Cassie sleep and wished he could tether her to him—for both her safety and his happiness. By morning, however, reality would kick its way into his psyche. She deserved so much better than him. Yet how could he ignore her blushing rose-colored cheeks after a night in bed, or the way she feathered her fingers over his hand when she wanted his attention?

He'd once prayed that Nicola had cared about him in a similar way. Nicola, however, had been a different bird, more like a hawk than a sparrow. And the hawk had focused on avenging her brother's death to the exclusion of everything else. The sparrow, however, seemed content just to be in Simon's presence. No alternative agenda. No plan for world domination. Her innocence dug deep into his skin.

Late one afternoon, as he stared at his computer screen and tried to concentrate on the meeting in Jordan, he heard the patter of Cassie's bare feet.

"I made dinner." She'd slipped in behind him and was pressing his shoulders with her thumbs in a move that could start as a massage but escalate quickly into something that involved the edge of his desk and the disappearance of her clothes. He dropped his head back and looked up at his biggest mistake to date. Blue eyes, blonde hair, and lips that felt perfect on his own.

He swung around in his chair and faced her. "If you're offering lentils, you'll have to eat alone. I'll head down to the pub for a burger."

"It's linguine with vegetables. Not a lentil on your plate."

"Don't get me wrong. I'm grateful for the lack of lentils, but what are we having for protein."

"I have chickpea salad to go with it." She led him to the kitchen.

"I'm shocked you're not anemic."

"I'm shocked your arteries aren't completely blocked with all the meat you eat."

"It's necessary. Meat builds muscle."

"I do appreciate the muscle." She clasped his shoulders and gave him a quick kiss.

He appreciated her.

She'd set the table with a single candle, a small vase of flowers she'd picked up at the market, and his old white dishes. With the lights low and the candle flickering, the room had a rustic and romantic charm. Two glasses of red wine perfected the peaceful setting. He could eat like this every night, meat be damned.

Cassie strolled over from the counter with a bowl containing the main course. "I eat better than you and take a multivitamin to make up for what I miss."

Before he could educate her on the problems with multivitamins, his phone rang.

"Dunn."

"Teodor. We have a problem."

Their last transaction involving the diamonds had wrapped up fine. Even Bio had walked away unscathed.

Simon clasped Cassie's hand and pulled her into his arms. "*We* don't have a deal brewing presently, so *I* don't have any problems."

"I arranged this deal with Grisha before you came back."

"So let Grisha finish it." As a middleman, Simon brought buyers and sellers together and made sure everyone received what they'd ordered. He also handled transportation logistics and methods of payment. Failure to work cooperatively resulted in negative economic—or other more creative—repercussions.

Grisha, born within walking distance to the Kremlin, hated Teodor's Ukrainian blood and the money he made from his corrupt practices. The Russian would rat out his mother to save his arse.

"Grisha was arrested outside his flat in Moscow this morning. They've already seized his assets and have sent a team of inspectors to claim my cargo for Russia. I emptied the warehouse as best I could, but the FSB is in pursuit. Our plane hasn't touched down yet. If they reach us, they'll claim we stole everything in our hold from their weapons cache."

"You did."

"Semantics. These are the guns we've been selling for three years. No one has claimed them before. Just help me split up the cargo and hide it for a few months."

*Shit.*

If Teodor went down, half of Simon's European operation would falter. He needed him in the game for at least another year or two until Simon could secure a more permanent retirement. Teodor's words had definitely screwed up Simon's plan for a quiet night with Cassie.

"Land your plane as soon as possible. Find a field if necessary," he demanded.

"They refuse. France is safest when it comes to extradition."

"Don't kid yourself. The Russians make deals with France all the time. Land in Austria. It'll be safer."

"They won't let us land."

"Where's the transfer site?"

"The Paris location."

There was nothing else he could do but go save the idiot's ass.

"You owe me, Teodor. My price is double, plus you pay for the gas in my bird."

"Fine."

"I'm on the way." He hung up and ignored Cassie's confused expression. Then he dialed up Fitz, his head of operations, and gave him the details of the meeting. "I need a car to the heliport. And a full crew. Thanks."

Cassie was still holding his hand and waiting with a thousand questions.

"You're leaving right now?"

"I need to change first." He kissed her cheek and then let her go.

"Oh." She picked up the bowl of pasta and vegetables and placed it back on the counter. "When will you be back?"

If things didn't go as planned, he'd need someone on a computer to assist. Someone with a PhD and a need to please. And if things went well, there was always an evening in Paris to look forward to. He tipped back half his glass of wine and made a decision, for better or worse. "Get dressed, angel. You're coming with me."

"I am?" A slow hesitation laced her words, but the spark of excitement in her eyes told him he'd said the right thing.

"You need a cocktail dress, preferably black. And heels so high you'll intimidate every man who comes near you." *Except me.*

Her eyes scanned her table setting.

"The helicopter leaves in twenty minutes. Dinner can wait."

"Helicopter?" she asked.

"Battersea to Paris. We'll be in the air about an hour and half. Can you handle it?'

"Yes."

"Then get ready. I need an international model at my side, and you look like I've dragged you from a farm somewhere." Actually, she looked like she just fell out of his bed, in soft gray sweatpants with hair that he'd held tight as they kissed.

"Okay." She headed off to the bedroom.

He followed, but ignored her so he could think clearly about kicking Teodor's ass for bringing him in at the last moment. It only took ten minutes to throw on a black Armani suit and the appropriate accessories. Cassie took a bit longer. The extra time was worth it. She wore a short black dress that exposed her legs to mid-thigh, and heels that took her height to the stratosphere. Her hair was secured in a twist, leaving her neck exposed…and very vulnerable to his lips.

"Is this all right?" she asked.

He pulled her in to his arms. "Perfect. Just make sure to stay by my side at all times. And act sort of clueless."

"That shouldn't be hard, according to Tucker."

"Tucker's an imbecile." He grazed her skin with his teeth and held back on letting his hands drift down to her thighs. They needed to leave.

When he pulled away from her, she sighed. At that moment he would have sold his soul to steal her away to the countryside and live out their lives with a million kids and a vegetable garden. To hell with Tucker and MI6.

But they'd find him again. And Cassie. And fuck everything up.

"Wait here." He went to the safe in the front closet and took out a ruby necklace and earrings—the same color as those blood red nails of hers. "If you're going to be seen as my date, you need to look like I spoil you rotten."

Her eyes widened with admiration and some hesitation. "Thanks. I promise I'll take care of them for you."

She put the earrings on and allowed him to drape the necklace around her neck. After he clasped the necklace, he lingered at an earlobe, biting at the earring. Then he pulled away before he carried her to the couch and forgot about Teodor.

"They're yours to keep. Consider them a hardship bonus."

Her hand touched the ruby on the necklace. "I can't take these."

"Angel, no one deserves them more. Come on, our car is waiting."

———————— ⌖ ————————

CASSIE HAD no idea what to expect on this trip to Paris, but it was already more exciting than the journey to Sofia and back. She touched the ruby in her necklace. The stone alone was worth more than all of her current assets combined. It would be the perfect souvenir for her time with Simon. The thought of leaving him after her assignment shot a pain straight through the center of her chest, but Simon didn't seem the type to settle down to an office job, long commute, and only one woman. He seemed more prone to one-night stands and moving from hotel to hotel.

He helped her into a chauffeured car, and they were whisked away to the heliport at Battersea, just across the river from Simon's flat.

"Remember. You're a receptionist at Sainsbury's main offices. You dropped out of university, and you live with me." Simon's words came out as a command, as though he were speaking to one of his men on the phone. "And don't talk to anyone, about anything."

"Then why do I need to memorize my background information?"

His eyebrows furrowed, and his mouth pinched. His threats, however, didn't work on her anymore. He was egotistical, a control freak, and a demanding boss, but he was also protective, considerate of her feelings—when work wasn't involved—and an amazing lover. "I need you to know who you are for when someone guns me down and kidnaps you. If you don't reveal your skill set, they won't torture you for hours trying to gain any information you may be holding. It matters."

She batted her eyelashes. "My favorite bubblegum is grape, and I have real issues with Virgos."

He didn't smile.

They arrived before she finished batting her eyes. No wonder he liked the location—easy access. Her outfit felt completely inappropriate for the jump seat inside the helicopter's large cargo hold. This was not a luxury transport—it was made to transport goods. The large black headphones she'd been handed pulled at her hair. Simon buckled her in, and then they were airborne over London.

The lights of the city faded quickly when they flew past the countryside and headed over the English Channel. Simon's hand rested on her knee, but he otherwise ignored her. Instead, he called out orders to the crew. Did they work for MI6 or were they part of an even more clandestine operation? She might never know. He didn't share much, if any, information with her. She was still on a need to know basis.

The initial excitement of the flight faded. The loud drone of the rotors through the earphones dulled her senses and lulled her into a brief nap. When she woke, Paris greeted her in a yellow haze of light. Old, new, elegant, chic. The city was breathtaking from the air. Were they headed to some sophisticated hotel or restaurant filled with the rich and powerful? Her stomach, still empty from a missed meal, lurched as the helicopter descended into a far corner of what looked like a huge airport. Charles de Gaulle?

"Be alert, angel. For anything."

"Okay." She had no idea what dangers could possibly harm her, because he skimmed work related conversations to the bare minimum.

He handed her a Fendi black leather tote bag, sleek and feminine. "Don't let this out of your possession at any time."

"What is it?"

"My back up plan." Evasion. Again.

The rotors slowed, but never stopped after the helicopter touched down. The airport covered a huge area, but they hadn't landed near the activity swarming around the commercial jets. Instead, they'd landed by a line of hangers a mile or two from the main terminals. The only people in sight moved between a huge transport plane and a Black Hawk helicopter. Men carried large wooden crates from the plane and loaded them into the helicopter.

Simon jumped out with his men and left her behind. A heavyset man dressed in a black, fitted suit strolled over to him. After they shook hands, Simon motioned a few of his team to assist with moving the crates.

She watched through the window, disappointed that she was a mere observer again. Simon took his job seriously and wouldn't use her at all if he didn't need her. Part of her was content to remain in the background. Another part of her wanted to show off her skills and impress the man who made her heart and body sing.

*I should leave my heart out of it.* As much as she wanted to, it was tough. There was something about the man that drew her to him. More than the sex. And it meant heartbreak eventually, because Simon wouldn't quit handling arms deals for her. On the other hand, she might not live to move on to another assignment.

Simon and his counterpart continued to call out orders on the tarmac while everyone else hustled between the plane and helicopter. It felt like an hour had passed since they'd landed. She leaned back in her seat and mentally walked through the first twenty numbers in the Fibonacci sequence. Her mind woke up from its weeks-long hibernation as the numbers populated her brain.

The cargo hatch in the back opened up and cool air surged into the hold. The numbers in her head blew away as a team dressed in black invaded her space. The small army of men carried crate after crate into the space. They stacked and bolted them to the floor in front of her. A few men glanced at her. Well, not her exactly. Her legs. They otherwise ignored her. Simon was still standing next to the only other guy in a suit. Their conversation was becoming more animated.

She hated waiting and was beginning to regret being Simon's brainless *model friend.*

A few minutes later, he arrived through the sliding door close to the pilot. He sat next to her and placed his headphones on again. "Looks like I need a computer expert. Up to the challenge?"

*Finally.*

"I'm dying for a challenge. What do you need?"

"I need you to delay a flight coming in from Moscow."

*Delay a flight?*

"I don't understand."

He unbuckled her from the harness and lifted her black tote. "Follow me."

With his arm tight around her waist, he rushed her into a black Mercedes, driven by a man in a uniform of black jeans, a black T-shirt, and black boots.

"Mr. Dunn, everything is set," the driver said while glancing into the rearview mirror.

"Thank you." With that, Simon closed the partition between the driver and the back. "We need to transfer the cargo from this plane to the two helicopters before Russian authorities arrive and drag us into a customs nightmare. Stall the plane and we'll have time to finish and leave."

"How can I delay a plane from landing? Streak across the runway."

He shook his head as though trying to rid his mind of that image. "As much as I'd love to see you naked, I'd prefer if you remained in the car. Clothes optional. Get into the website for the European Aviation Safety Agency. There's an override to the tower and approach voice communication system for every airport in the EU. It was an experimental program. France protested the intrusion on its autonomy, but the system was never completely eliminated. Mess things up enough so no one can land. Nothing big, just a short delay. There aren't many planes coming in at this time of night anyway."

"How much time do I have?"

"Ten minutes."

*Ten?* She'd need more than that to locate the program, never mind override it. She'd hacked into many government agencies and found information for MI6 without leaving a trace of her presence, but she'd never had such a small window of time. What if she did it wrong?

She shook her head. "I can't do this."

Simon lowered his eyebrows. "You can't do the first major task I give you?"

"I...ah...don't have a computer."

"Here." He handed her the black tote.

Sure enough, inside was a small laptop with a satellite link. "You don't understand. I could mess this up."

"Remove the computer from the bag and turn it on." His voice lulled her into compliance.

When she had everything set up, he touched her chin. "EASA. And I need this completed in seven minutes now."

She typed in the website he provided to her and then looked for a backdoor. Nothing obvious.

The man in the black suit rapped on the window. Simon opened it a crack.

"Where are they?" Simon asked.

"They're on final approach, and we have about twenty cases left." The man spoke in a strong Eastern European accent. Russian?

"Give me five minutes."

*Five minutes?* Her stomach twisted, but her concentration remained focused.

She finally made her way inside. Everything was organized. She located the specific program, which listed over a hundred airports, and then paused. In reality, she had no idea how to shut down the communications of one airport in one specific European country and prayed there were alternate operations that would prevent planes from crashing into each other. And then she found CDG on the list, the acronym for the Charles de Gaulle International Airport.

"I found it."

"Scramble everything."

"But—"

"Now."

With shaking hands, she disrupted the control tower communications. "Done."

"Good. Keep everything down for five more minutes. I'll be right back." Simon followed the other guy to the transport plane, and they both began giving orders to their men again.

A plane descended low into the airport. What the heck was it doing? Nothing should be landing now. Her chest tightened until she had to struggle to inhale. She watched in horror as the landing was aborted, and the engines thundered into a lift off. It was a commercial jet. Normal people who had nothing to do with guns. She couldn't do it. She couldn't watch innocent people die by her hands. She released the program and slammed the cover of the computer as though it was burning her hands. Her work at Vauxhall never seemed to harm anyone, but she'd never sat under a starry sky filled with potential victims of her handiwork.

Anger shredded her composure. Did Simon have any respect for human lives? How could he be so callous? Why did she keep making him into a good guy?

The rotors of both helicopters started up. Even from inside the car, the noise was deafening. Within seconds, both helicopters lifted off.

Her body wouldn't stop shaking. Perhaps it was the cool wind on bare arms and legs, but most likely it was fear. This was not an office job, where she was cloaked in a cubicle among a hundred colleagues. This was one woman and hundreds of lives.

Simon hopped back in the car and tapped the divider for the driver to move. He then placed his arm over her shoulder. "Mission accomplished."

"What mission? Why did I risk those innocent lives?"

"You delayed the flight and prevented the Russian authorities from tracking those guns to Teodor, my main supplier. And you allowed forty-eight crates of weapons and ammunition to move to their final destination." Not the slightest bit of regret crossed his face.

An icy chill stabbed at her chest. "I almost killed a plane full of people to save a few crates of guns that will be used to kill *more* people."

"Your job isn't to question why you do something. It's to do it and then move on to your next task."

"But—"

"You wanted a job using your expertise. You wanted to be useful. Congratulations. You finished the job perfectly. I would have preferred that you shut down the system for the entire time I'd requested, but I won't punish your insubordination this time."

"My insubordination?" Her voice rose into a yell. "Are you serious? I don't think Tucker—"

He placed a hand over her mouth and closed the gap between them, his mouth an inch from hers. "Do not ever mention his name, or the name of anyone else from there, outside the flat. Do you understand?"

She nodded.

His lips remained too close to hers. "Ever kill anyone, Watson?"

"No. Never."

He lifted his eyebrows. "Are you sure of that? It's easy to justify all your activities in a nice building in the center of London. Don't kid yourself. My job may involve an unfortunate amount of fatalities, but I'm putting my own life on the line as well. Hiding in a cubicle while drones bomb far away locations based on information you've provided doesn't make your victims' deaths any less your fault. You've done more damage from your desk than I ever did on the ground."

He was right. She'd never really thought about how her work assignments affected a larger operation—a potentially deadly operation. Her face felt hot and her lungs weighed down with regret. Was she helping the world or hurting it?

"You're one of a kind, angel. I hope you can keep some of that innocence you possess, but you need a reality check. Headquarters likes to gloss over the ugly parts of the job, but you should always think about the end result." He lifted her chin, waited for her eyes to meet his, and then kissed her. A deep, straight-to-the-heart kind of kiss.

She bit his lip and shook her head. As much as she enjoyed kissing him, this wasn't the time.

He backed away, but kept his hand touching her cheek in a comforting move. His breathing was heavy. "Dinner, hotel, or home?"

A night in Paris with a hot dude. Normally, she'd beg him for the adventure, but not right now. "Home."

# CHAPTER 10

———————— ✆ ————————

C assie's rose-colored view of her world had turned more of a blood red. This career was not Disney sweet, and she was not the pacifist she wanted to be. She'd taken the job with SIS for the challenge and the money. Then she'd blindly handled her job never thinking of the far-reaching consequences.

If Simon knew she'd been deceiving herself for years about her *benign* assignments, why hadn't she realized it herself? It would take her time to figure out if she even wanted to return to her old position. Was she helping the world or hurting it? Lives lost versus lives saved—that was one bit of calculus she didn't care to learn.

Simon's views tended to be black and white about their work. Nothing, not the death of a plane full of people, or threats against his life, seemed to bother him. And yet, he displayed acts of kindness and a moral center all the time. Although he never apologized for placing her in such a horrible position, he provided her with comfort and strong arms to fall into after the storm.

She spent the next week studying the newest lightweight portable drones. Without a full description of why they were needed, she could only teach Simon the basics about the different options available. The man was smart. He picked up enough knowledge of robotics and remote flight systems to speak intelligently to most people in the field. He relied on her for more detailed issues, like software applications and GPS guidance.

And when their work was done, they continued on with a relationship that scorched her inside and out and was guaranteed to break her heart. It didn't matter. Being with Simon felt completely right. When she returned to office work and a life alone in a flat, she'd remember this period in her life as crazy and passionate and eye-opening.

After a week of feeling cherished, however, he'd returned her to the background upon entering the Middle East. The cold environment in the middle of the desert provided ample opportunities to feel worthless. Men, thousands of them, moved around her with no time to acknowledge her existence either as a colleague, a woman, or a human being. Life in Jordan was about rank and power. Cassie's rank, however, hovered at the bottom of the food chain.

Making things worse, Simon halted his carnal pursuit of her. Instead he treated her like a business colleague. Public displays of affection were frowned upon in Jordan, so the few times he touched her were to lead her somewhere or stop her from going somewhere he didn't want her to go. He never held her hand and barely spoke to her. Her sexy lover had disappeared, and a cold, calculating arms dealer had taken his place.

After they'd checked into their hotel in Amman, Simon's leased black Mercedes took them into the desert. Several other cars, some with diplomatic flags, followed. Soon, an entire complex of buildings rose up from the horizon. Colored banners and a large white sign with a golden winged sword welcomed them to SOFEX Jordan. SOFEX—Special Operations Forces Exhibition.

Moving through security involved a series of checkpoints, each one more strenuous than the last. Finally, the car pulled up to a large cement exhibition hall. Cassie and Simon entered the air-conditioned building through two large doors. She'd been to high tech conferences in the past where the companies touted their wares with over the top displays and large plasma screens showing how their technology beat that of their competitors, but the scale was not the same as at SOFEX. In addition to the sheer size of the convention, the complex housed weapons, ammunition, aircraft, rockets, and so much firepower someone could begin and end the next world war without calling for reinforcements. Companies displayed the latest in attack helicopters near the next generation of warplanes. Every major defense company with weapons to sell had a display area.

That afternoon they mingled with the throngs of other attendees and perused what felt like a thousand displays. Simon needed to touch every weapon he encountered. He talked prices and workmanship and guarantees. Cassie was permitted to linger in the background. He occasionally introduced her to men who stared at her in a predatory manner, but otherwise discounted her existence.

The phrase *boys and their toys* replayed over and over in her head as groups of men in camouflage, military uniforms, long flowing robes, and power suits handled pistols, rifles, and a thousand other things that could kill innocent children. Once in a great while, she'd see a conservatively dressed woman either displaying products or accompanying a delegation through the main areas. A rarity. Cassie's navy blue suit and sturdy heels helped her blend into the surroundings, although her hair, even pulled tight into a bun, was about as a subtle as a golden turban in the crowd of somber colors.

"Are you hungry?" he asked.

"I'd love a cup of coffee."

They purchased two coffees at a small cafe tucked in between a handgun manufacturer and a company that made night vision goggles. They never sat. Instead, they strolled through the main building from display to display. Her feet were not loving all the walking, not in the two-inch pumps she'd worn to appear professional.

"Let's make our way to the North Korean booth. We need to get things started."

Simon picked up his pace without looking back at Cassie. She stayed with him, trying to keep her limping to a minimum.

They must have walked a half a mile through thick crowds, occasionally stopping to meet someone of some importance to Simon. The North Korean booth seemed fairly deserted compared to other displays. Simon stepped up to the platform and shook the hand of one of the four men in dark suits lingering around the booth. The man waved Simon and Cassie both into a back room behind their video screens.

"Mr. Dunn, it is nice to finally meet you."

"And you, Mr. Lee. This is my assistant, Cassie."

Mr. Lee gave her a very succinct bow. "Let us go for a walk."

They strolled for another half mile or so and exited the building next to a small outdoor display area for Pelican Technologies, a relatively new manufacturer of drones.

Simon, his hands behind his back, meandered along, nodding and shaking his head to various questions. He pointed to several mini-drones on display. Mr. Lee focused his full attention on Simon.

Cassie tried to listen to the main parts of Simon's conversation, but the two men spoke low amid a thousand competing sounds, and she could only understand every fifth word or so. Simon gave Mr. Lee his most reserved smile, the one that said he'd take everything into consideration, but offered no guarantees. Mr. Lee glanced over at her with a frown, obviously not wanting the assistant within hearing range. Simon simply ignored her.

She left them, and their secrecy, to get a better look at the new generation of Pelican drones. Three different models were on display. Two were quadcopters, and the third looked like a large model airplane. Fairly basic, nothing game changing, but if they handled the tasks the buyers required, then no one would complain.

"Beautiful machines, aren't they?" a friendly American male voice said from behind her.

Cassie turned around. One of the most handsome men she'd seen in her life, wearing faded jeans and a moss-green golf shirt, stood at her height and had a lean build. His face could be on the cover of GQ, no Photoshop necessary. Not cute, not rugged like Simon, but more debonair, with a five o'clock shadow emerging several hours before dinner. His short brown hair fluttered in the breeze revealing blond streaks, like a halo.

"Yes. My father flew model airplanes."

"These are a bit more sophisticated than a model airplane, but if you're game, I'll let you chose one. We can fly it together."

"That one?" She pointed to her favorite, the black quadcopter with the remote viewing goggles. It allowed the controller to enter a virtual flight simulation from the perspective of the camera mounted on the drone. She'd already flown similar models extensively while in San Diego.

He lifted it and moved to a launch circle. Then he walked over to a table and picked up the hand held controller and goggles.

His smile was so welcoming, she had a feeling he had no problem with women.

"I'm Dane, the sales representative for Pelican."

"I'm Cassie."

She glanced back to Simon who sent a warning in her direction, but didn't budge from his conversation with Mr. Lee. Fine, she could have some fun while waiting for him.

"It's nice to meet you. It's not easy to find beautiful women here." The salesman's eyes crinkled as he smiled, and Cassie felt appreciated for a moment, even if it was only for her looks. At least it was something. He handed her the remote and the goggles, which looked like high-tech sunglasses.

When Dane powered up the copter, he provided a brief description of the controller and how to operate the machine. She could see a full visual field from the perspective of the small camera mounted at the bottom of the unmanned aerial vehicle, or UAV .

With a soft touch on her shoulders as a heads-up, Dane's arms reached around her. He placed his hands over hers to control the flight pattern and took control of the machine. He *helped* her guide it around the display area as though she hadn't flown one like this for several hundred hours in war game simulations.

She laughed at the absurdity of her cover. "Thanks. You make it look so easy."

"You just need a little practice. You're doing great." He pressed closer into her back and continued to control the drone, only pretending to give her any freedom to fly it—similar to Simon's technique in bed.

After a few minutes, Dane brought the drone back and parked it in the landing circle.

"What did you think?"

"Fantastic." She removed the goggles and handed them back to him. "I'd love your job, demonstrating how to fly these machines."

He laughed as though his job were a big joke. "It's great. The job permits me to travel all over the world and meet people like you." He remained in her personal space. "What brings you out to the desert?"

"She's *my* assistant." Simon arrived and stretched his hand out to shake Dane's hand. Mr. Lee had disappeared into the crowd.

"Lucky you. And you are?"

"Simon Dunn." He almost growled the words.

"Dane O'Brien," Dane replied, with a smirk that contained hostile undertones.

They shook hands. Both men seemed to tighten their grips in an almost adolescent struggle before they let each other go. In terms of might and brutal force, Simon had Dane by inches and width. Dane, however, acted as though he wasn't intimidated.

When they backed away from each other, they transformed into friendly business associates.

"Mr. O'Brien, just the man I'm looking for. I seem to be in need of about twenty micro-drones with vertical take off and landing capabilities."

"No problem. *Your* Cassie seemed quite capable of handling our base model quad." Dane clasped Cassie's shoulders from behind her. She couldn't see Dane's face, but Simon's scowl returned.

"Fine. If she can fly it, a ground unit of soldiers would be able to learn to operate them quickly. What temperatures can they fly in?" Simon leaned toward them almost daring Dane to continue holding her.

Cassie nodded, pretending to be a party to the conversation, although she hadn't been informed what the drones would be used for and where they'd be flown.

"Do you need to handle extreme temperatures?" Dane asked.

Simon nodded. "And wind and rain patterns."

"Then you'll need the Pelican Quad 680. It's capable of handling wind up to a ten on the Beaufort scale and will work fine in temperatures from minus twenty-nine degrees Celsius up to forty-three degrees. It can fly by remote control or autonomously with the aid of a GPS navigation system. The other is a mere toy compared to this one. I'd be happy to explain more during dinner." He turned his focus to Cassie with more attention than Simon had bestowed on her since they'd arrived in the desert.

"Sorry, I have plans. Maybe we can meet later," Simon said in a voice that revealed not one ounce of pleasure.

"Send me the time and location." Dane turned back to Cassie. "Will you be joining us?"

"I hope so."

"Cassie, we need to go." Simon walked away, and she hustled to catch up, leaving Dane behind.

———————— ❧ ————————

THE SOONER SIMON could finish the task and remove Cassie from Jordan, the better. There were too many things that could go wrong—risks he'd accept for himself, but not for her. In addition, their inability to share a room while here drove him batty. Not only did he miss her in his bed, he missed their long conversations about everything from world politics to the best running paths around London.

When she arrived in the lobby for dinner, Simon's powers of speech disappeared in a fog created by the woman he shouldn't want so much. She wore a white gown that covered from her clavicle to the pulse point in her wrist and then flowed down her body, pooling on the floor. Modest, yet the material made the most of her subtle curves. She was sexy as hell. She'd twisted her hair up to reveal that swan's neck, and ears that begged to be sucked on. Everyone in the restaurant, men and women, stopped and stared at her entrance. The queen herself would not have garnered as much attention.

Simon escorted her to a table on the garden terrace. A thousand stars against a black sky provided the ambiance. The table contained three small candles and a vase of black irises. Cassie observed the restaurant with wide eyes. Her enthusiasm made treating her to the best a pleasure.

"A bottle of Saint George Reserve Cabernet Sauvignon 2009, if you have it," Simon ordered.

"Excellent choice, sir." The waiter departed.

Cassie seemed enthralled by everything in the room except him. No doubt she was frustrated, but he refused to reveal her expertise to anyone. She needed more patience.

She stared across the restaurant, never meeting his gaze. "We can drink wine in Jordan?"

"Yes. And they're especially happy about this bottle, because Saint George is a Jordanian vineyard. Several vintages have been rated in the exceptional range."

"Nice." Her frown, however, chilled the mood.

Why did his chest ache when she made such a sad face? He wanted to reach out and touch her, comfort her. Would the world end if he did? No. But could he stop at just one touch? Doubtful. They weren't married, and she was supposed to be his assistant. In other parts of the world, a businessman could flaunt his relationship with his assistant, but here it would draw unnecessary attention to them.

"Trust me, angel. Your time is coming. Patience."

"And then what? After all this?" She gestured around the room. "When we're done. Are *we* done?"

If he could keep her with him indefinitely he would, but life never worked in his favor. "You don't belong here. The quicker I can move you to a safer job, the better."

The waiter returned with the wine and poured them each a glass. Simon sniffed his glass as though a sommelier, except he was looking for deadly impurities. It wasn't foolproof, but it might prevent another Anna Marie incident. The thought of Cassie harmed in any way tormented his conscience.

"Could we have your mezze dishes without meat, but served with *shrak*?" he ordered.

"Yes, sir." The waiter took off again, leaving an open mouthed Cassie at the table.

"We're finally eating normal food today?"

"No, normal would involve meat, but I thought you'd prefer something lighter."

"If I didn't know any better, I'd think you cared."

He did care, but he wished he didn't. "A healthy partner doesn't complain as much."

"Have you ever had a complaining partner?"

"The biggest wimps I've worked with tended to be young men who thought they could handle life and death situations. They couldn't. When they had to make the big decisions, they toppled like a house of cards in a tornado. So far I've been impressed by your calm and your patience."

"Thanks." Her smile arrived at the same time the waiter brought eight small dishes of food including fresh olives, vegetables, hummus, tabbouleh, and dolmas, perfectly prepared stuffed grape leaves. Her smile brightened even further. A man could become lost in that smile. Simon needed to remember that and take precautions.

"What did you think of flying the drone today?" he asked.

"It was fun."

Using a slice of cucumber, she scooped up some hummus and popped the entire piece into her mouth. A small moan escaped her throat. A tiny bit of hummus remained on her lip, and she used her tongue to lick it off. If she continued to eat her meal in such a sensual manner, he'd be tempted to clasp her by the hand and drag her up to his room.

He tightened his fist and pictured her walking around the exhibition hall, all business. The environment in Jordan at this time of year would be intimidating for most people, but Cassie had handled it like a pro. Tons of military brass, diplomats, and businessmen either looked through her or at her most intimate body parts, and not many spoke to her as an equal. Things had changed in the world since Simon had started his arms business under the umbrella of MI6. Women were more and more accepted as players. Cassie's beauty, however, blocked her from the good old boy's club. They didn't want a woman at their table distracting them from the millions to be made.

His hand inched over to touch hers, but he held back. Jordan's mores were more liberal than the rest of the Middle East, but he couldn't be too forward with her in public. "Does Pelican meet your expectations?"

"Depends on what their final use will be." A small spark of intelligence and confidence flickered in those blue eyes of hers.

"According to Mr. Lee, we need long distance drones capable of carrying five extra kilograms."

"That shouldn't be a problem."

"Good. The UAVs will be operated by ground personnel."

She remained silent for a few minutes, completely lost in her thoughts. After a sip of wine, she continued. "There are drones that can hover without having the operator constantly maintain the controls, allowing the operator to multitask. Depending on their purpose, that might be a better option."

As she spoke about her specialty, her confidence rose. He needed to bring her up to speed with what Mr. Lee had requested in their meeting. "We'll ask Mr. O'Brian if the more advanced one has that capability."

She nodded. "Good. What are the add-ons?"

"I'll tell you later." He couldn't tell her yet what the drones would be required to carry, or she might back out. He sipped his wine.

"I hope it includes a small winch or hook. They're useful, especially in smaller UAVs."

And then the night took a nosedive. Dane, aka "Satan with a West Coast attitude," stopped at their table.

Acting as though he didn't know Dane's actual position with the CIA took all of Simon's control. Cassie would only see the friendly salesman instead of the cold-blooded killer he really was. And his old friend would use that cover to try to win Cassie away from him.

"Mind if I join you?" Dane asked Cassie.

"Yes," Simon replied.

His words were futile as Dane had already pulled up a chair and waved at the waiter for another wineglass.

"How are you enjoying your visit to Jordan, Cassie?" He ripped off a piece of the *shrak* and scooped up some of the eggplant and tomato dish.

"So far, all I've seen is the SOFEX complex, but I hope to see Petra before we leave."

"If I have time on Wednesday, I'd be happy to escort you around. Petra is breathtaking. There's a small café there that serves the most amazing pizza. I bet your favorite toppings are black olive and peppers."

"I love black olives," she responded with an uncharacteristic giggle.

Dane flashed his best smile directly at Cassie and ignored Simon. She responded with a welcoming laugh.

*Damn.*

The waiter set a new glass on the table, pouring Dane too generous an amount for a person who was about to be evicted.

He raised his glass in a toast to Cassie. "To amazing pizza and beautiful women to share it with."

Simon took a sip of his wine in order to keep from punching Dane in the face. His timing, as always, provided the maximum disruption in Simon's evening.

The eyes that had nearly stopped Simon's heart a minute ago now focused exclusively on Dane. "I haven't had a good pizza since leaving the States."

Dane gave a mock show of surprise. "Where have you been living, under a rock?"

"She's been living with me. Don't you have someone to meet with tonight?"

"Nope. I was hoping to enjoy the company of a surly Englishman and a beautiful blonde. Where were you before finding yourself stuck with such a stick in the mud?"

"California."

"So am I. I have a place in San Francisco."

"I grew up in San Diego." She beamed at Dane as though she'd been introduced to a long lost relative.

"We're practically neighbors. I've been down to San Diego for work. Where did you live?" Dane leaned on the table, all elbows and bad manners, but Cassie didn't seem to mind.

"Solana Beach. Just a small condo, but two blocks from the ocean." Memories of her home must be flooding her mind, because she appeared dewy-eyed. San Diego was one part of her fabricated history that held a link to Catherine Wallace.

"A great place. Less crowded beaches, good restaurants. We should travel there together sometime."

"Dane," Simon growled a warning.

The worm grinned and continued his pursuit of Simon's date, as he'd done with many of Simon's companions in the past. He pulled out a business card and handed it to her. "If you ever want to get together, call me."

She took it.

Mission accomplished, Dane downed the rest of his wine, paid for by Simon, clasped Cassie's hand, and kissed her good-bye on the cheek. Cassie stared after him, her smile still lingering. Simon tightened his hand into a fist and took a long slow breath. He required Dane's assistance to finish this job...and then he could kill him.

# CHAPTER 11

T he next morning, Simon met with a few suppliers he'd used in the past. Cassie was less than enthusiastic to return to the exhibition site. He tried to include her in some of the more benign conversations, but most of his contacts didn't trust anyone they hadn't known for years.

Her fidgeting hands never rested, tapping at her leg and pulling at the edge of her blazer. She had to be bored. She wanted more responsibility. Her role, however, would be more effective if she didn't give away her background. At least, not yet. Her eyes shifted to the clock in one of the displays. Perhaps this was for the best. He needed to get rid of her for an hour or so in order to meet with Dane in private. The less she knew about certain players in this world, the safer she'd be later on.

"Cassie, would you run over to the Omnicore Explosive Site? I need the price for thirty-five pounds of gray smokeless powder. They have a special exhibition price list that offers discounts if I order the supplies while the conference is in session."

"What about lunch?"

"You can grab something on your way there. It's in Hall C. I have a fairly long meeting to attend. We'll reconvene in two hours by the Raytheon platform."

"Have a good meeting." She strode off, catching the attention of several nearby men, who grinned at her hasty exit. She'd caught the attention of the entire conference. Many of his associates had asked about her status. He was firm in saying she was off-limits to everyone, especially to Dane. In another lifetime, she'd be free to find someone else. As long as she worked with Simon, however, she'd remain his companion and, hopefully, his bedmate.

He walked over to one of the more exclusive private dining spots in SOFEX and met up with his old rival.

Clasping Dane on the shoulders with more of a punch than an embrace, Simon focused his thoughts back on business. "What the hell are you doing on this side of the world?"

They walked through flowing silk curtains into a room filled with dark wood tables and chairs and were seated at a table covered with crystal glasses, silver pieces, and red linen napkins.

"I'm selling drones, and it appears you're buying. How interesting."

"Are you trying, but failing, to be undercover at Pelican, or did you lose your position at the agency?" Simon asked, ignoring his questions.

Dane, an embedded CIA agent who monitored the world of arms deals as carefully as Simon participated in it, refused to answer, which told Simon exactly what he needed to know.

A waiter brought them to a private table.

Simon focused on the waiter without a glance toward Dane. "We'll have the *mansaf*."

"You remember my love of lamb." Dane smiled and placed an order for wine as well. The waiter nodded and left them alone.

"You're entirely predictable, which is why I'm always a step ahead of you," Simon said with a laugh.

"Someday, you may be stuck at a desk job, a mere speck of who you once were." Dane, leaning back in his chair with a smirk, seemed amused by the prospect.

"I'll be retired before then."

"Actually, I thought you *had* retired. Last I heard, you'd flown the coop and found a few island girls to hide out with. Facebook never lies."

"Perhaps I planted those photos. My life is an open book. Currently my love of technology trumps my need for beaches and bikinis." *Except for one extra long beach body with a love of robotics.*

"Interesting. And you want my drones?"

"Maybe. I need prices and availability."

Dane tapped his fingers on the table. "About fifty thousand a piece. Also, I have people who can arm them for remote detonation for a price."

"Not necessary."

His brows lifted. "Interesting. Even more interesting is your new assistant. You always had fantastic taste in women, although she seems a bit out of your league."

"Stay away from her." Simon recognized Dane's hormones reacting to a potential conquest. They'd often competed for the same women. Dane tended to gain an upper hand with his pretty boy face and easygoing attitude. Although Simon trusted Dane with his life, he wouldn't trust him with any female over the age of twenty.

Dane laughed. "You never did like to share, did you? Remember lovely Valeriya? She chose my refinement over your depraved self-importance. Pissed you off to no end."

Simon's serious facade cracked, and he felt a smile emerge. "You bribed her away from me with a bottle of red wine and some asshole singing in Italian. You're welcome to any woman willing to leave for that fluff. Besides, your endgame was a bit more sinister than mine. I just wanted to move Tucker out of Russia."

Dane's face hardened. "Can't go back, so I move forward."

Tucker, a brand new operative posing as a student in Moscow, became swept up in the local culture, including a sexy coed named Valeriya. After they moved in together, she created an international incident when she stole laptops from two low-level American diplomats and turned them over to the FSB. It was all caught on tape. Tucker refused to believe her guilty. He'd been fucked over by love and was probably still in denial today that he'd done anything wrong.

Dane and Simon had been sent in to cleanup the mess, neither government trusting the other to get the job done. SIS directed Simon to expose her and remove Tucker before he was arrested for spying. Dane's job was to eliminate her... permanently. It was his last documented role as an assassin.

Dane completed his task, but not before Tucker learned his identity. Furious that the American had killed an *innocent* woman, Tucker contacted the Russian authorities to have him arrested. Before Simon could shut Tucker down, the git was arrested and questioned. He sang like a bird on crack to the Russian authorities. He'd not only revealed Dane's link to the CIA, but he'd also hinted at several other students who might be working with MI6. He was sent home in an embarrassing spy swap.

After claiming PTSD and begging for a second chance, he was permanently removed from the field and placed in a rather boring office building away from Vauxhall. Being a mid-level bureaucrat suited him far more than any field position.

The waiter returned with a large platter of lamb in a plate of rice, almonds, and pine nuts, and covered in a fermented yogurt sauce. A plate of flatbread accompanied it. A perfect way to shift the mood at the table.

Dane scooped up some of the meat in the bread and moaned as he chewed. "This is almost to die for. How is old Tucker these days?"

"He's no longer allowed to come out and play. And he probably hates you more than he hates me."

"The world is a safer place since his reassignment."

They clinked their wineglasses in agreement and laughed. Simon dug into the meal. The chefs had outdone themselves.

Leaning back in his chair, Dane smirked. "The shithead gave away everything he knew because he didn't want to spend the night in a Russian jail. His dick must be less than a half-inch long.

He should never have been allowed in the field. You English need better recruitment techniques."

And Dane should be back out in the world doing what he did best instead of hiding from the past.

---

A FOOD COURT had been set up in the northernmost area of the main conference center. Cassie had some tea and a falafel while she people-watched. It was not relaxing. Crowds caused her more tension than just about anything else, even guns and spiders. But once she exited the building to walk over to Hall C, and her tension lifted. Despite the heat, Jordan was beautiful, and the people had been nothing but nice to her. Perhaps she could return someday without the restrictions placed on her by Simon and her assignment.

A mere hundred yards from the massive crowds in the main area, Hall C was a calmer, quieter place. She strolled past the displays of some companies that didn't have the clout of the ones in the Main Hall. Massive HD screens with cinema quality videos broadcasted demonstrations of the awesome power contained in these weapons. She stopped at a manufacturer of gas masks and noticed a few samples small enough to fit an infant. She pictured a family huddled up together, praying for salvation with their masks on. The falafel she'd eaten turned into a lead weight in her gut. War stunk. Cassie, however, could make a difference. If she performed her job to the best of her ability, she could avert war around the world. And where she couldn't, she could try to minimize casualties. That was her goal.

Omnicore Explosive was located in the furthest corner from the entrance. Huge posters showing detonations and fireballs covered the back wall of the booth. Not a warm and fuzzy marketing approach. In addition, the salespeople had proven to be as obnoxious as all the other people Cassie had to deal with.

They wanted to know why she needed the explosives. She had

no clue. They wanted to know the grade, the preferred place of origin, and preferred packaging of the product. No clue, no clue, and no clue. She did know that Simon had requested thirty-five pounds. That's all he'd told her. Nice.

She took a price sheet from them and started back to the Raytheon exhibit to find Simon. So what if she was an errand girl right now. Last week, she'd been a vital part of the team when she'd taught Simon some fundamental information on drones. He asked the right questions and listened to her explanations with interest.

Her steps lightened. She couldn't wait to go back to London and have Simon's attention focused again on her, even for only a few hours a day, even if it wasn't permanent.

Back outside, she turned her head to avoid the bright glare from the windshields of the parked cars. Her stress evaporated as she walked past some storage areas. The silence, marred by an occasional helicopter or distant car, soothed her nerves. The heat sizzled on everything in sight, yet she slowed her pace in order to embrace the hot dry air. When she turned a corner, a breeze kicked sand into her face, and she squinted as she tried to protect herself. The sand burned. She pulled sunglasses from her pocketbook and tucked herself between some buildings until the wind died down. The sound of strangled cries, like those of a baby, echoed from a place farther into the alleyway.

The picture of the gas mask for the infant was still fresh in her mind. Her goal of protecting the vulnerable of the world could start here and now. She walked closer to the noise.

Situated behind a Dumpster, a man dressed in long black and white robes with a white Arab headdress tied with a black leather strap held a woman on the ground. One hand covered her mouth, and the other crushed her windpipe. The woman's eyes bulged in desperation. She tried to pull the man's hands away, but he held her on the ground. Her long black robe had a few rips in it and dust faded the color to gray in spots.

Two other men dressed in similar outfits stood nearby watching, without helping either the man or the woman. A chill ran through Cassie. She should run to get help, but despite her instincts prodding her in the opposite direction, she moved closer. The woman's face reddened.

"What are you doing? You could kill her." Her heart battered her chest as though telegraphing her a warning to turn away, but she ignored it. She pushed at the man harming the woman and started shaking his shoulders. "Stop. Please stop."

One of the other men grabbed her arms and pulled her away from the man assaulting the woman. Someone took Cassie's cell phone and her purse. She struggled and screamed. A thick, strong hand covered her mouth. She couldn't break free.

Two Jordanian soldiers arrived, but neither spoke English. The man who beat the woman yelled and pointed at both the slowing waking woman and Cassie. The woman shook her head, tears rolling over her cheeks.

How could someone be treated so poorly? What had she done?

A soldier pulled her to her feet. They secured the defeated woman's arms behind her back with handcuffs.

Then the soldiers stepped toward Cassie.

# CHAPTER 12

S imon left Dane and went to meet up with Cassie. She'd be excited to find out she was finally a player. Her expertise would be the game changer in this assignment. They could buy the drones from one source, probably Dane, and completely retrofit them to the needs of the North Korean businessmen, keeping the new and improved capabilities developed by Cassie off the radar of international groups looking for serious destructive power.

When he arrived at the Raytheon display, he couldn't locate her. He called and texted. No response. Toying with some of the exhibits, he kept one eye and one ear on the crowds at all times. Thirty minutes passed while he was waiting. *Was she lost?* He called her phone again and received no answer. She knew never to turn her phone off. *Ever.* He texted her again and even sent her an email. No reply. Perhaps she'd gone to the restroom.

A tall, blonde woman among mostly dark-skinned men in uniforms should not be difficult to find, but the only blonds he saw as he pushed through the crowds on the way to the restroom were several male members of the Swedish military. He stood outside the restroom door for several minutes before asking a woman to check for her inside. A minute later, the woman emerged with no news.

Where was she? A woman who never veered from the rules and, who followed his orders at least ninety-nine percent of the time, would not take off without telling him. Not here. He clenched his fist. If one person, any person, harmed her, he'd regret his decision a million times over.

He needed a plan. He returned to the Raytheon display and asked them to contact him if she came back. A few U.S. and German companies he'd done work with in the past also promised to contact him if they saw her.

Three hours turned into four hours, which turned into six. Where the hell was she? The hotel had been contacted, but he hesitated before calling in the SOFEX security team. He and Cassie didn't need that much exposure. Something happened to her. Something bad. He wanted to believe everything would work out, but if something smelled like shit, it generally was.

Cassie's disappearance didn't merely annoy him like the times he'd lost partners to South American jails or Russian hit squads. She was more important to him than a typical partner. And that made this whole situation even more frustrating. If he didn't know where she was, he couldn't help her.

After going over every possibility, no matter how remote, he contacted the one person who would give him the most crap —Tucker.

"When did you last see her?" Tucker sounded as angry as Simon felt.

"She left me while I spoke to one of my contacts." No way in hell was he mentioning his lunch with Dane.

"This assignment must be completed, and you lost our most valuable asset?"

"The same one at whom you aimed your Walther P99? Yes. Can we go through diplomatic channels to find her?"

Simon could hear Tucker's exhalation through the phone. "One major problem. She's American."

"That was your call. Why the hell would you make her American and tie our hands."

Tucker paused a few moments before responding. "It was necessary for the assignment."

"You're an idiot. Your cool maneuvering may end the assignment before it begins, unless you either locate her or find me a replacement." The idea of someone replacing Cassie stuck in his throat and made him want to reach through the phone and kill Tucker. "Help me find her. If you have to involve the Prime Minister, do it."

"I'm not your puppet, Dunn. Don't threaten me."

"Let me rephrase, then. If she's not located in the next twenty-four hours, I will drop my assignment, fly to London, and personally rip your heart out and shove it up your ass."

The line went dead.

A fear swept through Simon, as big as a tsunami, threatening to completely derail his control. He couldn't lose her. He wouldn't lose her. His heart would burst if the woman he cared for even more than Nicola disappeared from his side. He'd never survive it.

At the hotel in Amman, he questioned as many colleagues as he could without drawing too much attention to himself. No one had seen her. Sitting in the bar, he watched Dane arrive with a few U.S. military officers. If Cassie was acting as an American, he'd better start using his American contacts.

"Dane, do you have a minute?"

"For you, anything." He looked over Simon's shoulder. "Where's your companion?"

"Missing." Simon didn't have time to play games with Dane. He explained how she hadn't met at their designated spot after lunch.

Dane raised his eyebrows. "She's not exactly the easiest person to hide around here. Are you sure she didn't take off on her own?"

"She wouldn't leave without telling me. She's American and

has been gone almost eight hours now." He frowned. "Can you contact the embassy and see if the authorities have located her?"

"Give me some time, I should be able to find her." Dane pulled out his phone and began to dial.

---

CASSIE DIDN'T UNDERSTAND why she'd been arrested. No one spoke English. She only knew a man was abusing a woman, two bystanders did nothing to help, and the military had arrived. Instead of receiving assistance, both she and the woman were put in handcuffs and pushed into a police van, while the men walked away laughing. The woman had regained some of her energy and sat with her hands together, chanting something to herself over and over.

Cassie didn't cry. She didn't fight. A fog covered her senses and drugged her into a stupor. At first all she'd wanted was Simon, and she'd called out to have someone contact him. After the van doors had closed and they'd driven for what seemed like hours, she'd stopped asking. They'd ignore her anyway.

The van arrived at a white stone building surrounded by a large black iron gate. Guards in military uniforms, carrying assault rifles, stood at the entrance. Two women in black uniforms with white scarves covering their hair pulled the beaten woman out of the van and then grabbed for Cassie. She tripped. Her knee plowed into the asphalt. Pain tore through her leg. A jagged hole ripped in the fabric of her dress exposed a bloody wound. No one, however, rushed to her aid.

She lifted her skirt to look more closely at the wound, but a security guard yelled at her and yanked the skirt back down. Blood seeped through the material and oozed from the rip. She remained sitting, unsure of putting weight on her leg. Her throat felt like she'd swallowed a large stone and it was stuck halfway down her windpipe, making her breathing difficult. She rocked her body back and forth, but she didn't cry. Not yet. Not in front of the guards who had placed her in this hell. They left her on the ground, standing over her with large rifles at the ready. Did they think she'd run? She was too much of a coward.

Several other women, some in shabby robes and others in more Western clothes, arrived in police cars and vans. The police pushed them toward Cassie and the woman from the SOFEX compound. One newly arrived woman had a deep gash on her forehead. Blood smeared across her face and her right eye was swollen shut. Two of the women sobbed and pleaded in Arabic. Others remained silent, their heads bowed in submission.

When the group grew to seven, they were led into the building through heavy doors and then down long gray hallways. In a small empty room, female guards began to strip the prisoners. Several women cried out as guards pulled their clothes off and left them standing naked. One older woman, marked by deep lines and blemishes on her face, wore a constant scowl. She stripped off her clothes and stood completely naked with her shoulders back and saggy breasts thrust forward.

Although Cassie towered over the guards and the other prisoners, she tried to minimize her presence by slumping forward and standing in the back of the room. She didn't understand the orders, as she didn't understand Arabic. Instead, she followed the example of the women around her. The humiliation of the situation almost broke her, but she carried on without complaint. She removed her skirt, her blouse, her bra, and her panties. One hand automatically dropped over her crotch and the other covered her breasts.

The guards lined the women up against the wall. Six medium to short women with dark hair and dark complexions lined up next to Cassie. Standing there, at least six inches taller than the next tallest woman in the room, with her long golden hair shining brighter than the darker hues of the other woman, she'd never felt so alien and alone in her life.

A black beetle crawled across the floor and over one of the women's feet. The woman either didn't notice it, or didn't care.

Cassie stepped back, away from the path of the bug and stopped short of leaning on the dirty wall. One by one, the guards forced the women into showers and scrubbed them until their skin became red and sore.

When Cassie stepped under the spray, her body shivered at the cold water. Someone sprayed a bottle of something gross toward her. She shut her eyes against the onslaught. The taste of melted cardboard dripped into her mouth. Her stomach rebelled. She tried to rinse it out in the shower water, but the water was worse than the soap. A guard held a large brush on the end of a long handle and began to scrub her skin. When the brush scraped her injured knee, Cassie gasped and tried to cover it. The guard smacked her other leg with the back of the brush until she stood straight again.

After the torture of the shower, they moved to an examination room, still dripping wet. The scrape on Cassie's leg stung. She limped across the floor and waited. A chill shot through her. Her limbs trembled, and she lifted her hand to her mouth to keep from being sick. The stone wedged in her throat still made it hard to breathe. Did anyone speak English? If they did, they refused to acknowledge her.

A woman in a lab coat arrived, her hands already gloved. One prisoner went before Cassie. The woman searched between the prisoner's legs, in every possible crevice and when the nude prisoner cried and tried to push the guard's hands away, she received a slap across her cheek to stop her protests. The guard did not change gloves between prisoners. Bile rose up from Cassie's knotted stomach, knowing whatever disease the first woman had would be hand delivered to her. She prayed the woman was healthy. Whoever went last would fare the worst.

Another woman in a lab coat, older and carrying an iPad, rushed into the room and started to argue with the first. The older woman must have won the argument. She took over the exams with a calmer demeanor... and a box of gloves to change into between each patient.

As fingers pushed into her most vulnerable places, Cassie tried to shut out the humiliation. The cavity search, however, cracked her composure and darkened her soul. She bit her tongue until the coppery taste of her own blood rid her mouth of the lingering nastiness of the soap.

All the prisoners were directed into the shower again to clean up after the examination. As they walked by the new lab coated woman, she spoke softly to each prisoner. She nodded to Cassie. Her lips were pressed shut, but there was empathy in her eyes. And for a moment, Cassie felt some of her tension dissipate. Someone in the prison seemed compassionate. It would have to be enough for now. The woman not only protected them from cruelly indifferent contamination, but she gave them another consideration as well. Warm water. It sprayed over them, uncramped tense muscles and took away a bit of the fear, even though the water still smelled, and the soap was still nasty.

Cassie received a blue dress to wear. The material scratched her sensitive, scoured skin, but it was better than the shame of being naked in a room of strangers. The guards led her down another gray hallway and through three sets of locked doors. No other prisoners followed.

She noticed everything around her. The cracks in the wall with white sodium deposits leeching through. The water stains on the gray cement floor. The women dressed in the blue prison garb, who sat quietly in their cells, some with a cellmate, other times alone. Their heads lifted when she walked by, and they stared at her, an obvious foreigner. A few called out to her in a foreign and unsettling wail. She didn't know if she was being cursed or prayed for.

The guard stopped at a small, empty cell at the far end of a hallway. When she motioned for her to enter, Cassie froze. This was jail, in a foreign country where she didn't speak the language, didn't understand the culture, didn't know what her options included, if she even had options. The guard patted her arm to coax her in. Once Cassie crossed the threshold, the guard slammed the door. The echo thudded through her chest and knocked out any remaining emotion.

The cell contained a bed with a beige blanket and a navy blue pillow. The pillow was stained white. From tears? From something more insidious? A toilet and small sink sat in the corner, rusty and cracked. She sat on the bed, numb, staring through the bars into the hall. There was no cell across from hers, only a gray wall with no window. She heard shuffling in the next cell, but otherwise the only noises were hollow and industrial sounds from another part of the building.

Her knee hurt and her body shuddered from a chill that emanated from the inside and spread through her until jerky tremors shook her limbs. She curled into a fetal position and allowed her tears to fall.

# CHAPTER 13

———————— ❧ ————————

For what seemed like a day and a night, Cassie sat in solitary confinement. No one spoke to her or acknowledged her existence. Guards dropped off food she didn't recognize and warm glasses of water. The water tasted salty, as though they'd taken it from a dirty fish tank, but it was better than the water from her sink.

Her skin itched constantly. The only thing to observe in the cell was the comings and goings of the bugs crawling around the floor and walls. They didn't bother her, and she didn't bother them. If one crossed her imaginary boundary, she flicked it away, but refused to kill it.

When she woke from a long, uncomfortable sleep, a middle-aged man, dressed in black, was standing outside of her cell, staring at her through the open door. She'd only seen female guards since arriving behind the walls of the prison. The man leered at her. His dark, narrowed eyes examined her body head to toe. She shifted back in the bed to the corner of the cot. Her stomach, sick from the food they'd given her, contorted into a punch-in-the-gut type cramp. She wanted to escape, but that was impossible.

He left the door open and walked toward her, his posture becoming straighter, his pace quicker.

"Stay away from me. Please." She raised her hands to hold him off, but he moved them aside with ease.

"Help. Please. Help," she called to the empty hallway as, she struggled to push him away.

"Stop! Please!" Her cries became hysterical, frantic.

He grabbed a fistful of her hair. For a moment, he stood still, fingers caressing the long strands as though they were made of silk. Then he pulled her toward him. The position was awkward and vulnerable. A chill slithered over her body when his mouth descended on hers, forcing his way inside and destroying her hope for an easy way out of this hell. The violation caused her normal demeanor to snap.

Grabbing his hair and pulling, she attempted to free herself. He tightened his grip on her shoulders and shoved her back on the bed. Ripping at her shirt, he exposed her breasts. Humiliation and terror clouded her thoughts. She struggled to get away, but he had her pinned under him.

His hand went to push up her skirt, but she evaded him by shifting her hips side to side. He pulled her hair again until her scalp burned. Rage replaced fear. She kicked off the wall with every ounce of her strength. They both fell to the concrete floor, Cassie landing on top of him.

Hostile words launched at her from snarling lips. With solid punches to her gut, he knocked the wind from her lungs. Her stomach ached, and she felt dizzy. He lifted her up and shoved her into the wall.

Her shoulder struck the concrete, but she remained standing, despite the agony pervading her beat-up body. Rushing toward escape, she flung the door open wider and almost made it. He kicked her leg out from under her. Her forehead scraped against the bars as she fell to the ground. Her chin hit the floor first, with only the slightest bracing by her hands to soften the blow. Pain radiated across her jaw, her cheeks, and her ears. She ignored her injuries and pushed up to continue fighting.

She mule-kicked her legs behind her, hitting something several times. With effort, she managed to stand…and then she let loose with a ferocity she'd never felt before. After twisting around to face her attacker, she punched his face, using her long arms and her combat training. Rage and fear combined into an adrenaline-filled rush. Her growing fury guided her movements, inflicting on her attacker as much pain as she could unleash.

Her fist hit him in the nose. She felt the bone snap and heard his cries while blood sprayed across his face and onto the nearest wall. When he grasped his face with his hands, she kicked him in the balls, holding nothing back and forcing him onto the bed. Then she flew through the cell door and slammed it behind her. Her attacker bellowed like a wounded rabbit, but couldn't follow. But he still threatened her. Locked on the other side of the bars, he pulled a gun from his waist and pointed it toward her.

She ran to the other end of the hall past the cries of the other prisoners and crouched down by the door. Out of breath and shaking, she remained in a tight ball, wrapping her arms around her knees. She didn't cry and refused to whimper, but her body trembled, and a chill fell over her like a fog on a cold autumn night. As she took a few deep breaths, she vowed to never place herself in a position of weakness again.

The door unlocked and soon a bunch of guards, both male and female, surrounded her. They pulled her to her feet and forced her down the next corridor. She struggled against them. One grabbed her hair and tried to restrain her movements, but her arms shot out to strike anything nearby. Her height and arm length worked in her favor as she left a path of injured people behind her. The petite woman who had pulled her hair received a bloody mouth after coming into contact with one of Cassie's fists. She then kicked a male security guard in the knee so hard he fell to the floor. She fought everyone who came near her. No more sitting passively and allowing anyone to harm her ever again. It took several guards to wrestle her to the ground. They cuffed her hands behind her back, yet she still tried to fight. When they had her seated in a chair near the front of the building, a large man with a sober expression and a face covered in pockmarks squeezed her chin and stared into her eyes. Blood trickled from her cheek onto her lap.

"Stop," he insisted. *English. Finally.*

"Let me go. I didn't do anything wrong." She felt no pain, but could feel her jaw clenching and her eyebrows narrowing.

His face remained impassive. "Stop," he repeated.

*He didn't know English. No one did.*

The kind woman in the lab coat she'd seen before yelled something at the male guards, who had linked Cassie's handcuffs to her chair. The son of a bitch who had attacked her appeared in the room, escorted by two men. He was bloody and limping. Good. She prayed he received a harsh punishment for everything he'd put her through.

When the men left the room, hollering at each other, two females in black stood on each side of Cassie, with guns drawn. Anger and fear swallowed up her normally optimistic outlook and provided her with all the justification in the world to hit and punch and scream. The woman touched her scraped and bloody chin, but Cassie tried to pull away from this nightmare. It was too late to be friends. No one protected her. The only person she could rely on was herself. When the woman moved to examine under her uniform, Cassie fought her off, spitting in her face and growling. Peacefulness made her vulnerable. She wanted to live, to survive. She wanted to fight.

A large needle pricked her arm, a painful reminder that she had no control. Her fight evaporated within seconds.

She awoke in a cleaner cell, with an armed guard outside her door. Her head hurt. Her chest felt tight and her stomach ached as though a car had driven over it. She felt a bandage on her chin. The rest of her injuries were covered in an ointment reeking of Bengay and garlic. She lumbered to the sink and rinsed off her hands. Then she spit out whatever taste was leftover from the animal who had attacked her.

A black cloud lingered around her. She was alone in a prison where no one spoke her language. She'd been in a fight against a team of guards, and she'd survived.

She'd never been in a fight before, except in her training classes for this mission. And even in those, no one truly wanted to harm her. As an only child, she'd grown up fairly protected. The surf had battered her down at times, but the sea held no animosity toward her. The man who had attacked her, however, spewed hatred and a dirty lust. She wasn't sure if it was because she looked American, was a woman, or was a foreigner in a strange land. He'd wanted her to fear him, wanted to hurt her. She'd hungered to hurt him back. The pain she'd inflicted on him made her feel strong. Stronger than she'd ever felt.

She stood up and paced the floor. The movement hurt, but she wouldn't sit and wait in fear. She was tired of being afraid, of living in a protective cocoon of sunshine and moonbeams. Simon had told her in so many words and actions that she was incompetent. And here she was in the middle of hell. She continued walking seven steps in one direction and seven steps the other way.

*I can survive if I just make it another step. And another. Something will happen soon. Some idea will come to me, and I'll get free.*

Time stopped. She strode back and forth in an unending march, her thoughts focused on how she could escape. After what felt like hours, the doors down the hall opened. She peered through the bars to see who had arrived. Strolling toward her cell was a modern day hero, dressed in black pants and a billowy white cotton shirt. Dane. But he was too late. When his eyes focused on her, he seemed to struggle to maintain his faint smile. Probably disturbed by the sight of her bandage, and the swelling, and the cuts on her face.

Next to him was an armed escort and a red-headed woman in a black pant suit.

"Miss Watson. I'm Eileen Smith from the U.S. State Department. We've secured your release." She stepped into the cell and reached out to clasp Cassie's hands, but Cassie backed away. She didn't want to touch anyone.

Dane placed his hand on her shoulder and spoke in a calm voice, but pulled his hand off her when she shot him a glare of revulsion. "It's all right. You're going home."

*Home? Where was that?*

Ms. Smith returned to the corridor.

Dane pointed to the door. "Let's go."

No one spoke as they walked away from hell. The guards opened secure doors, and then led them into the courtyard in front of the white building. A U.S. soldier opened the back door to a tan Humvee.

Once everyone was inside, Ms. Smith handed her a new passport. "Do you need any medical attention?"

"No." She couldn't handle more poking and prodding.

The woman nodded. "Mr. O'Brien has offered to escort you back to the States. You can stay at one of the rooms in the embassy until your flight."

*The States?* Her American passport. She'd forgotten. The British government had no jurisdiction over her. Would they allow her to walk away from the assignment and return to California? Maybe they didn't want her back. This could be her way out of the limbo MI6 had placed her in.

Dane sat quietly for the first half of the long ride, then he attempted to counter all the violence Cassie had experienced. She ignored him at first, but he spoke so gently.

"You're safe with me. No one can hurt you now," he whispered.

It was enough. For the first time in days, she took a deep breath.

When they arrived at the embassy, he led her to a small apartment. She remained on the couch, listening to him make plans for them to fly to the United States. Perhaps she could stay there with him, hidden away from her enemies and her memories and Simon. Where the heck was Simon? She'd placed all her trust in him, and he never came.

She'd believed he cared about her. What a stupid childish fairy tale. Fairy tales didn't exist. Her mother's cancer existed, rape and torture existed, but happy-ever-afters didn't.

"Do you need anything?" Dane approached her, looking concerned but not touching her.

"No, thanks. I'm all right."

"Why don't you go into the bedroom and lie down."

She nodded.

Sleep would be wonderful. She wandered toward the bedroom, but the knock on the front door stalled her movement. Could someone be here to return her to the prison? She clasped the doorframe and placed her hand over her stomach. An empty feeling roiled through her.

Dane peered through the peephole. "Don't worry. It's Simon. Do you want to see him?"

Where had he been when she needed him?

She shook her head. He'd make everything worse. His presence in her life tended to upheave all her beliefs and expectations. He'd remind her that she was the one who'd screwed up, and he'd be right. She wanted to go back to California, live by the beach, and never set foot near Simon Dunn again.

"Open the damn door, Dane," Simon yelled. He wasn't calm. He wasn't peaceful. He was violence and anger. Part of her wanted to see him and yell and scream and fight him. The other part couldn't deal with him.

She walked into the bedroom and locked the door in case Dane let him in, or he crashed through the wall. She entered the bathroom and locked that door, too. Running water to fill her bath muffled the argument taking place in the living room. Simon had to have gained entry into the apartment because Dane probably wouldn't holler, "bastard," "asshole," or "son of a bitch," and he didn't have an English accent. Simon, however, swore like a man from the worst sections of London. Where Dane was light and comforting, Simon was dark and unstable.

She slid into the tub. The bruises on her face and torso still hurt, but the warm water would help her aching muscles. With soap and a washcloth, she tried to scrub off the grime and the memories, but everything was still too raw. She wrapped her arms around her chest and took some deep breaths. Her lungs couldn't take in much air. The large imaginary stone remained lodged in her throat and never released her from the feeling of suffocation. Would she ever be able to breathe without exerting herself?

Shutting her eyes, she tried to will herself to the bungalow of her youth, a place where she'd lived and laughed with her mother. They'd sit on the couch every Sunday afternoon, watching romantic comedies and eating popcorn. In the evenings, her mother would take her to the beach to say good night to the sun. The colors of the sunsets on the Pacific coast glowed as brightly as her mother's love. She wrapped herself in those thoughts and colors until she fell asleep chest deep in the warm water.

A few hours later, or maybe just a few minutes, she heard a distant knock on the bedroom door. The knock was soft and unde-manding. Simon must have left. He was never soft and unde-manding.

She dried off and wrapped the towel around her torso. She couldn't wear the awful prison outfit again. Dane's suitcase rested on the top of an armchair in the bedroom. Locating a large maroon sweatshirt and some sweatpants, she changed and answered the door.

Dane leaned against the doorframe and wore a carefree smile on his face. No worry, just peaceful concern. He glanced at her outfit, and his smile grew. "I thought you might like something to eat. Any requests?"

"French fries and tea?"

"Sounds good. I'll have the same."

He reached out, clasped her hand, and led her to the couch. When she sat, he placed a large blanket over her lap. No expectations. No demands.

The knock on the door a half hour later twisted her stomach into knots. Dane strolled to the door with confident strides. Dinner. He didn't let them in. He just took the food cart.

"French fries and tea, as you requested." He lifted the cover off the plate. The aroma of hot oil and salt floated over to her, making the room feel more like the United States than the Middle East.

"Thanks." Placing the plate on her lap, she picked at the fries. Her appetite hadn't returned, but she knew she needed to eat something. French fries and tea wouldn't settle her stomach, but she'd enjoy them in small amounts.

"Can you tell me why I was arrested?"

Dane sat next to her on the couch. "Prostitution."

"Seriously?" She had an ID badge for the exposition, and she'd been dressed in a conservative suit.

"For the past few years, some enterprising young ladies have come to Jordan to make some extra money. They'd conned some military buddies into obtaining them guest passes and then tried to score a lot of money in a short amount of time. When you helped the prostitute outside the exhibition hall, they assumed you knew her."

Someone working undercover and didn't want to create an international incident should not have become involved in a local matter. "I feel like an idiot."

"I heard what you did to the guard who came to visit you. That was incredibly brave. You're strong and amazing, Cassie. Don't ever let anyone tell you differently. The man has been removed from his post. I doubt he'll be prosecuted, but he won't be able to harm vulnerable women in prison anymore. The Jordanian government is embarrassed. They aren't known for hostility toward foreigners and would prefer this incident be buried." He sat closer and proceeded to devour the French fries.

"When is our flight?" she asked.

"In two hours. I found one at 1:30 a.m. I'll have you on the beach in California by lunchtime tomorrow."

She took a few bites of the fries, taking an occasional sip of tea.

"I can't thank you enough for everything. You're my hero."

His soothing smile emerged. "I take that title very seriously."

And then someone knocked on the door again.

# CHAPTER 14

S imon stood in the hallway at the U.S. embassy waiting to
see Cassie. If Dane refused him access to her this time,
he'd break down the door. She needed to see him, if only
to know that he cared. She probably didn't feel safe with him.
He'd failed to free her.

His *friend* had filled him in on all the details, before barri-
cading himself in the apartment with her. The Jordanian government refused to acknowledge they'd ever had custody of an
American woman named Cassie. The embassy wouldn't comment
on the case either. Everyone wanted it to go away. The prick who
had hurt her, however, would not go free. Simon's men were
already tracking him down.

According to Dane, Cassie was physically sound, but emotionally a mess. He recommended staying away from her. That would
be convenient for Dane, who had come to her side like a damn
white knight. Why did she have to be American? Simon would
have had her out in half the time if she'd been a British citizen.
His connections had strength in international diplomatic channels, but not in the United States. If Tucker had done his job better,
she would have been listed as a Brit from the start.

When the door finally opened, Dane blocked his access. "I think she needs more time."

"Bullshit. You need more time alone with her. Let me in."

He backed up, finally, and Simon saw Cassie. She looked like shit. Bandages covered her chin and the right side of her face. Her complexion was pale, and her eyes slightly sunken. When she saw him, she scrunched up her swollen lips as though tasting something foul.

He needed all of his control to restrain his anger toward her attacker and to bear the crushing of his heart at her rejection. His stomach roiled at the thought of a man assaulting her in a jail cell. Not only was her outer beauty marred, but her expression held a hardness he'd never seen before. Whatever happened must have affected her to the core.

"Cassie." He sat at her side. "Are you okay?"

She looked away from him. "No."

Dane sat on her other side and clasped her hand. "She needs some rest before our flight."

"Flight? What are you talking about?"

"I'm taking her back to California." Dane sounded so sure of himself. And yet he had no clue what he was doing or who he was dealing with.

"She doesn't live there anymore. She lives with me in London. And that's where she belongs." *Forever, if possible.*

"I think you should let her decide where she feels the safest. Now is not the time to push your own agenda on her."

Dane held her hand. The bloody hero. He could have contacted Simon earlier. Instead, he isolated her and came in like the cavalry, making Simon appear as though he didn't give a damn. And damn it all, he *did* give a damn.

When Simon looked toward her for a response, her gaze turned to the window.

Dane had erected a solid wall separating her from Simon. A wall that needed to be flattened. She probably thought mild mannered Dane shared her non-violent beliefs. She was wrong.

After several silent minutes, he needed to do something other than beg, so he ordered some eggs, toast, and a cappuccino from the kitchen. Dane ordered a salad. Cassie ordered nothing.

She wouldn't lift her eyes to acknowledge him. Her rejection ripped at his heart and left him momentarily hollow, but then she glanced in his direction. It was subtle, a quick peek from her blue eyes. A crack in the wall.

When the food arrived, she sipped her tea and pushed around a few leaves in Dane's salad, sharing food with him as though they were lovers.

"You should eat more," Simon said.

She shrugged and looked over to Dane for support.

"I'm fine." She wasn't. She'd stashed her emotions in a box and left them there to fester.

Simon pushed his plate in front of her.

"Eat something. The eggs, especially."

"Simon, she's a vegan. She–"

He shut Dane up with a wave of his hand. "She needs to eat something to build her strength." He turned to Cassie. "Eat two bites."

"Honey, you don't need to do anything you're not comfortable with." Dane's hand covered hers. "Do you want some fruit?"

"I'm okay." She slipped her hand out from under Dane's, leaned toward Simon's plate on the coffee table between them, and picked up a piece of toast. She ate it without a glance toward Simon.

He refused to acknowledge the small victory. He sipped his cappuccino and waited. She took another bite and then grabbed her tea.

She still trusted him. He had to make Dane disappear.

Patience. Simon had more than enough for the both of them.

"We should head to the airport soon." Dane stood and put out his hand to help her stand.

Simon remained seated. "Come home with me. You only had a

few days off from your job, and your colleagues will be worried if you don't return."

That comment lifted her eyes toward him. "Maybe I could look for a new job in the States."

"You seemed pretty happy in London."

Dane gave an all-knowing smile. "I'm sure she could find a position in San Francisco. In fact, I could put in a good word with my employer. I bet you'd love it there, sweetheart. And you could stay with me until you're settled."

Cassie sat in silence as Dane pushed every button he could to convince her to leave Simon.

There was no way in hell, however, that Simon was ready to let her go. "I thought you were helping your boss on a big project," he told her. "Sounds like he needs you. Are you ready to throw that away?"

"He doesn't need me."

"Maybe you should talk to him about it and give him a chance to convince you. It probably wouldn't take more than a few days. If you think you're not needed after speaking to him, then quit and find a new position."

She glanced at Dane, who had sat next to her again and was stroking her hand with his thumb. He was about a minute away from getting his arm ripped from the socket.

"I guess I shouldn't just leave my work without a word."

"Are you sure you need the stress of working right now?" Dane asked.

"I appreciate everything you've done for her, but this is her decision to make." Simon stood, a move that would either propel Cassie to stand as well or to remain with Dane. "You can walk away from everything in London, including us, but I think you're stronger than that."

In a final play to her emotions, Dane wrapped his arm around her shoulder. "You've been through a traumatic event. It takes time to get over something like that."

Her head fell onto his shoulder. She took in a deep breath

and closed her eyes. "You've been so wonderful to me, Dane. But I should return to London and take care of things there before moving on. Maybe we can meet in San Francisco sometime?"

He rubbed her shoulder and smiled, never pushing her. A smart call from a very competent player. "Call me the minute you arrive in the U.K. so I know you're safe."

"I will." Her smile let Dane down easy, and now Simon had no one but himself in the way of his relationship with Cassie.

———————— ✿ ————————

THEY FLEW first class to Heathrow. Simon kept his distance, which Cassie appreciated. She didn't want to talk right now. She didn't have a clue what she wanted in her life. Whatever it was she'd desired in the past had been left to rot in the prison cell.

She stared out the window for much of the flight, as Simon slept at her side. She glanced over at him. He'd folded his hands in his lap, and rested his chin on the center of his chest, as though he could wake up and handle anything with a split second's notice. Those magnificent blue eyes hid under closed lids and long lashes. The hard expression he tended to wear was softer now and more approachable. An urge to curl into his arms overwhelmed her. Would he take care of her? No. It was time she stood on her own. When everything had fallen apart, it was only her wits and her meager strength that had saved her. And even that hadn't been enough to free her from the hell she'd been locked in.

Simon's chest rose and fell in steady deep breaths. A man in control of everything, except the disaster of a woman beside him. How could she ever work with him again? She'd failed. Arrested, confined, attacked, and in need of the U.S. embassy to rescue her. He must think she really was too stupid to live. He probably wanted her to finish the assignment so they could go their separate ways.

When they arrived in London, Cassie needed privacy. "I'm taking the bedroom," she said.

He didn't argue.

She crawled into bed, burrowed under the covers, and fell asleep dreaming of soldiers in black carrying submachine guns.

What felt like only moments later, a loud knock yanked her from the nightmare of the ugly man leering over her.

She had no desire to talk to anyone, least of all the one man who thought she was the world's biggest idiot.

*Why won't he leave me alone?*

She threw on some clothes and sneakers and pulled the door open.

"Breakfast?" Simon, dressed in jeans and a loose, black, collared shirt, slipped his hands into his pockets and leaned against the wall. His expression stayed serious except for his eyes. They invited her into his arms.

She couldn't. Not yet.

"I'm going to go for a walk. I'll be back in a little while." She headed to the door.

He stepped back. "We should talk first."

"Is that an order?"

"No."

"Then I'm going out."

# CHAPTER 15

I t had taken every ounce of will Simon had to let her walk out of the flat. She needed space, and he wasn't doing a very good job of giving it to her. He'd had one of his men follow her. Never again would he leave her alone. He'd been an idiot to do so in Jordan.

She came back from her walk and locked herself in the bedroom again for several hours. When she finally awoke, she wandered out wearing jeans and Dane's sweatshirt and sat in the corner of the couch with her feet tucked under her. She should lose the sweatshirt, an ugly reminder of how much he owed his friend for getting her out of jail. If he let her run to Dane, would she go?

Damn. How could a woman completely hijack a man's life in a matter of weeks? And instead of being able to tell her how he felt, he needed to pussyfoot around her, hoping she wouldn't leave.

He poured himself some vodka and wandered over to the couch. "Where did you go?"

"I went to the Orangerie in Kensington Gardens."

He took a large swallow of his drink and placed the glass on the table beside her. Then he sat by her and clasped her hand. "Feel better?"

"I'm fine." Her eyes focused on their intertwined hands.

"You don't seem fine."

She shrugged. "Does it matter? I'm back on the job, as you requested."

"I don't give a bloody fuck about the job. I'm worried about you. It matters a lot."

In the face of his blowup, she shrugged. "Don't worry. I'll handle the assignment as I've been trained to do."

"This has nothing to do with the assignment. I need to know you're okay."

She pulled her hand until he let it go. "Please, don't act like you care. You're the coldest, most arrogant bastard of all. A perfect operative, because I've never seen the real Simon. You have only one personality, and all it cares about is where the next mission takes you."

"You have me all wrong."

"Don't. I'm already feeling foolish enough for my stupid crush on you. You must have thought it was so funny to see me so smitten, while you stayed focused on work. I'll finish the job, and then I'm done. I'm done with this work and with you. You can then forget about me like you did in Jordan."

Her gaze dropped away from him, leaving him with a void so deep, he'd never climb out without her help.

He stood and walked to the window, waiting for his frustration to subside. A cargo ship motored down the river. The waves rocked a few smaller vessels, but they stayed afloat. When the boats steadied, he turned back to Cassie.

He struggled to keep his frustration tamped down. Anger would only push her away. "I waited several hours at the Raytheon booth. I called every contact I trusted, asking them to keep an eye out for you. A mini army of at least twenty guys from eight countries searched for a tall blonde woman. I risked my cover and a lot of goodwill to locate you, but I failed. You'd vanished, and Tucker wouldn't help. I have no diplomatic immunity and no channels within the U.S. government. I couldn't find you."

"Whatever." Her tone offered no forgiveness.

"What do you want me to say? If you're looking for a perfect hero, I'm not your guy. I'm not the type to send flowers or fly over tall buildings. I never will be, but I'll do everything in my power to keep you safe. This time, however, I didn't have the power to get you out of jail."

Tears streamed down her face, but she focused on him with a cold stare that had replaced the beautiful innocence of the Cassie he'd once known. "Never once have you shown compassion for anyone. You walked away when Tucker pointed a gun at my head. You took a pregnant woman into a dangerous situation and then carted her all over Europe to get home. You left me in jail. You're heartless." She stood and walked up to him. An arm's length away in distance, a million kilometers in understanding.

"As I stated before, Tucker would have found a way to torture you if I'd shown the slightest partiality toward you. I had to be cold, because I won't put you at more risk than the assignment already entails. And as for Alex. She didn't tell me she was pregnant until we were at the field making the exchange. When our exit was compromised, I flew her out and left the car to keep her safe. And as for you." He gripped her shoulders. "I would have ripped the city apart to find you. I contacted Dane and begged him to engage his embassy's contacts. I'm not an American, so they wouldn't have released you to me. I needed to rely on Dane. Contrary to your ever-lowering opinion of me, I sure as hell was not going to let you rot in prison. You're out, you're safe, and I care. I care a whole hell of a lot. More than I should if I want to keep you safe."

"Don't touch me." She brushed his hands off her shoulders. "I'm not your plaything unless there's an audience in front of us, and right now, it's just us."

The darkness she'd experienced in that prison was eating her up. There was only one thing to do.

"Blame me if makes you feel better, but I need to know what happened to you. Everything."

"Poor Simon. Unable to handle the fact that you don't, in fact, know *everything*."

He clasped her arm, holding it firm.

She struggled to pull free but couldn't. "Let me go."

"Not until you tell me what happened at the prison."

"No." Her leg connected to his shin. It hurt like hell, but not enough to make him release her. She hadn't hesitated to use violence. Definitely not the old Cassie.

"Tell me."

She tried to slap him with her free hand. He moved out of the way with a millisecond to spare. Then he grabbed her free arm.

"I won't let you go until I know every detail from the time you left my side at the Expo." This technique wouldn't win him points at a meeting of abuse survivors, but his in-your-face method had worked for many of his men who had lost either comrades, limbs, or the desire to survive until tomorrow.

She pulled hard, but he held tight. His focus remained only on her. Whether she realized it or not, she had to talk.

"I don't want to talk about it. I want to go home and start over, but since I have no home anymore, I'm simply going to try to forget about Jordan. And I can't if you keep demanding I tell you." The volume of her voice rose. "Don't worry. I intend on finishing whatever my task is."

He dropped his forehead to hers despite the knowledge that she could slam into it. His voice softened. "I need to know what happened, and you need to tell me."

She'd never get through this if she held the memories inside to fester and destroy her. Although he'd been through the painful aftermath of missions gone wrong before, with other partners, this time, it felt more personal, as though *his* only hope at survival was making Cassie whole again.

Through tears and clenched teeth, she pulled out of his hold, but remained standing inches from him. "Debriefing me? I forgot.

You have a need to get the mission accomplished. And how can you complete it if your technical expert falls apart?"

"I need you, angel." His arm encircled her waist.

"You only need my knowledge." She dropped her head onto his shoulder.

He lifted his other hand under her chin, careful to avoid the bandage, and brought her lips close to his. "I need *you*."

He kissed her. A soft, sweet kiss that made no demands, only sought to comfort her. He didn't stay away from her split lip. Instead, he brushed his lips across the swelling and licked the wound. She didn't pull away. He kissed her again and again until her tears fell more quickly, and she began to return the kiss. He lifted her in his arms and carried her to the couch.

Her beat-up face rested on his chest, and her sobs came louder and faster. The agony of her nightmare finally surfaced. He held her tight as her body shook in uncontrollable waves. All he could do was rub her shoulders and let her mourn the end of her innocence. The Cassie of his dreams, the one with a permanent smile and a vegetarian pantry, had been lost to this brutal occupation.

He kissed the top of her head and gently brushed back her hair. Bruises across her cheek and the fat, split lip made her seem tougher than she was. He was tempted to strip her down to see the extent of her other injuries, but he needed her permission and her trust, and at this point he had neither.

She faced the window. Soft lights glowed over the river at dusk. When her breathing became slower and more controlled, she spoke. "I grabbed some lunch and then went to Omnicore Explosives and obtained the price list. Darn. I lost it in everything that happened."

Information he didn't need, and a task she hadn't needed to go on. It was his fault. One hundred percent his fault. He squeezed her more tightly, thinking about what could have happened. "That's okay. I'll call them later."

She sighed against him, and then she started talking. She told him everything. When she reached the part of her story about the guard, he had to force himself to stay calm for her sake.

"In the end, he didn't do anything. I fought back and escaped." She rested her head back on his shoulder.

"Did he touch you?"

"Yes."

"On your face?"

She nodded. "He punched me and pulled my hair. I've never been so scared."

"You said you fought him off." He held her tight and comforted her so she could continue.

He made her describe in detail what the man did. She tried to brush over the more intimate details, but eventually, through tears and anger, she told Simon everything. She'd escaped. She'd saved herself like the heroine she was, but didn't believe herself to be.

A half hour later, his beauty slept in his arms. He looked down at her bruises and rubbed his thumb across her lips. She needed him and, by God, he needed her.

---

Cassie awoke to an overcast skyline. Still dressed in her jeans and Dean's sweatshirt, she was stretched across the couch, entwined in Simon's limbs. He seemed like a safe haven, but, as always, looks could be deceiving and often were. She slipped out from under his arm and used the bathroom. When she returned, Simon, wearing only a pair of shorts, was sitting up, typing on his phone.

Why couldn't she hate him? Because he still held her trust, and he held her heart. She'd been unfair to blame him for what happened. Her actions, her consequences. It was time to stop blaming everyone else and take responsibility for her own life.

"Good morning." A warm smile broke across his face.

She lifted her arm in a lame wave, unsure how to proceed after pouring out the humiliating details of her incarceration.

"Hi." Her throat burned as she spoke. The outburst from the night before had strained it.

"You should take a shower. You'll feel better after the long night."

"In a few minutes." She sat next to him. "I'm sorry for causing you so much trouble. You always told me to think before I acted, and I didn't."

His fingers brushed through her hair, lingering by the base of her neck. "You cared about another human being. You did what any decent person—at least one with a core of gold—would."

"Not gold, iron. And it weighs me down. I've always felt in control of my life, but now I'm drowning. I can't understand how you've lived this way for so long. I heard about Nicola. Some people in the office said she'd do whatever it took to finish a job, including sex and murder. I'm not sure I could sleep with a person I wasn't attracted to, and I'm not sure I could kill anyone. And look at Alex, traveling around the globe with a husband following and a baby on the way. This life isn't for me."

He tugged on Dane's sweatshirt and slid it over her head, leaving her in a white tank top. He'd made no secret of his hostility toward Dane, so she let him remove the article of clothing. His hands traced a pattern across her back and shoulders, occasionally lifting the back of her shirt—nothing sexual, but more clinical, as though looking for injuries. When his hands stopped moving, she leaned back against his chest. Two powerful arms encircled her waist, and Simon's chin rested on her head.

"Don't compare yourself to Nicola or Alex," he said. "Nicola lived for her job and nothing else. She fought demons, both real and imaginary. Death never scared her. She lived with the motto "kill or be killed." She was killed. And Alex? She has more innate skills than any one person should have and remain sane. Trust me, there are times when Henry needs to bring her back down from the ledge. No one is perfect. In fact, you have skills they would have bartered away limbs for. Neither one of them was great with computers, especially Alex. She barely uses her laptop, except for an occasional report she needs to file."

"But my skills haven't been necessary so far."

"They are now. I'm still buying twenty drones from Pelican. I'll need you with me in San Francisco when I do. And there's a team of specialists meeting us in France to add explosives, making them suicide capable. You can outfit them. I can't."

His words landed hard. Suicide implied someone would die. "Like a suicide bomber, but the drone is unmanned? What about the other side? Will the explosives hurt people?"

"Cassie, this game we play is so much bigger than the two of us. I try to keep casualties to a minimum, but I'm not perfect. My job is to prevent most arms from getting to the people who ordered them, but to be effective undercover I need to have some shipments go through. Otherwise, who would use my services? We track the shipments closely and most of the time, we prevent the guns from getting through to non-allies. But this game makes for strange bedfellows. Several groups I assisted years ago now have a different diplomatic arrangement with Great Britain, going from friends to foes. Everything changes, all the time."

"Who are the drones being sold to?"

"The North Korean businessmen we met in Jordan. They're impatient with the ruling party, because they haven't seen the profits they were promised years ago, although they see large amounts of wealth flowing past them to the president's friends and family. They're hoping to start a war with South Korea by flying the drones over the DMZ to strike some South Korean, or even better, U.S. military targets. They figure they can make more money during a rebuilding of a united Korea, rather than wait for the current North Korean regime to share some of the wealth."

The muscles across her shoulders and up her neck tensed. She shifted to face him. "We're starting a war?"

He kissed her forehead. "It'll look that way, but you'll reprogram the drones so they detonate on the North Korean side of the border, thus averting disaster. The trick is to have the detonation linked to someone other than you and me. Perhaps faulty circuits."

The tension in her shoulders eased. She could actually avert a disaster in this job. "That's brilliant."

"Ironically, it was Tucker's idea. He's better working strategy than he is in the field."

"He was a field agent?"

"He was in the field, but was incompetent."

"As bad as me?"

"Worse." Simon's warm smile cracked into a full-fledged grin.

She shook her head in feigned shock. "Impossible."

"Believe it. He would have given away the keys to MI6 if they hadn't taken him out of the field." He squeezed her tight, as though he'd never let her go. "I'd take you on my team over Tucker in a heartbeat."

"Thanks. I'm sorry about spending time with Dane. He was so nice to me, I couldn't just ignore him after everything he did for me."

Simon kissed her again on the forehead, so gently it felt more like the draft from a butterfly wing. A strange but sweet gesture coming from such a giant of a man. "I'm not threatened by Dane in the least."

"You're not?"

"He's always brought out the worst in me."

"You know him?" That would explain the almost friendly hostility they shared.

"We've met a few times in the past and have battled over women. He usually won, but he always cheated."

"Are you afraid he has a shot with me?"

Simon laughed. "Not a chance."

"Really?"

"You're mine." His voice lowered, and his gaze burned though her.

As much as she liked the idea of being Simon's, the newly

emerged warrior in her stopped a full surrender to him. "I'm not property, Simon."

"Let me finish. When I lost you in Jordan..." He paused and swallowed hard. "Let's just say I never you want to lose you again. Ever."

He tightened his grip on her as if she would leave if he let go. He shouldn't worry, because she was staying put.

She kissed his cheek and tried, but failed, to curb the rush of tears from her eyes.

He moved his lips over the scratches on the side of her face, down over the bandage on her chin, and returned to her mouth where he soothed the pain with a lick of his tongue.

She pulled back, her heart beginning to beat out a rushed and panicked rhythm. "I don't think I'm ready for anything more than your sweet kisses."

He laughed. "I agree. You have full control over whether or not we resume being lovers. And I'll be more than happy to resume where we left off when you come to me begging on hands and knees. Only that will convince me you're ready." He stood up, leaving her alone on the couch. "You better shower and get dressed. I'm moving back into the bedroom. We can share it."

"I thought I was the one in charge of this relationship?"

"I never said that. You're in charge of when we have sex again. I'm in charge of this operation. Since you've recovered from being pissed at me about your time in jail, you need to be close to me for several reasons. First, we both should sleep in the bed for a better night's sleep. Second, I don't want you out of my sight any longer than necessary."

She couldn't help but laugh. Nothing stopped Simon from getting what he wanted.

He pointed to the bathroom. "Go, we have a lot to do to prepare for our trip."

She left the room and enjoyed a warm shower.

His unique way of caring for her made her feel competent and strong, not dependent and helpless. And although Dane had helped her, he acted more like a shoulder to cry on. Simon offered his shoulder for only a moment and then sent her back into the world. His confidence in her bolstered her own beliefs that she could handle the job assigned.

After the shower, she put on a salmon colored dress that fell to mid calf and located Simon in the office working on his laptop. She walked over to him and sat on his lap, certain he wanted her there. His hand slid up her dress an inch, stopping on her knee. The tease.

"So what's my task, boss?"

His hand remained on her leg, caressing her thigh. "In order to reprogram the drones, you need the security codes. And Dane has them."

---

A WEEK LATER, Cassie stood in the suite at the Fairmount hotel and stared out the window. The million dollar view overlooked San Francisco and, in the distance, the Golden Gate Bridge. When the bedroom door opened, she turned to see an even more amazing view. Simon.

"Nice outfit."

"Thanks." She spun around in her black high-heeled sandals. The black and white floral dress swooshed out from her legs. Black fit her mood. It also matched the remaining black and blue marks all over her body.

"Too bad you can't join me on my date," she said.

"Are you sure you're ready for this?" He raised his eyebrows. "If you need more time, I can arrange it. I'll hire someone Dane's type who can pull him away from his desk for a few hours."

"What's the likelihood he'll choose this week to date a random woman during normal office hours and not figure out she was a paid escort or a spy?"

"Slim." His hand balled into a fist, and he paced around the room for a few minutes. "It'll be quicker and easier if you pull

him away, but you are *not* dating him. You're going for lunch and
to speak with him about your future. That's all."

"I'll be fine."

"Maybe we should delay for a few days, and I can think of
another plan."

"We need to get back to work. If you want to hold hands and
sing 'Kumbaya,' find someone else. I'm not interested."

He rubbed his hand over his face as though thinking up a new
strategy for getting his partner in line. "Call me if, at any time,
you feel overwhelmed. Is that clear?"

"Perfectly. What do I need to do?"

"One of us has to infiltrate Dane's office. He must store the
security information on the drones somewhere near there. You
keep him at the restaurant, and I'll try to gain access to his desk. If
I can't, we'll have to call the whole operation off."

Part of her felt uncomfortable with the assignment. The other
part wanted to dive head first into the information she needed to
gather.

"Why would we call it off?" she asked.

"Without knowing the security codes, we won't be able to redo
the software."

"I could bypass a few security codes."

"I doubt it. Not these."

"What if *I* go into Dane's office?" she asked.

"Impossible. He won't be leaving your side today. He's
waiting for the opportunity to comfort you in bed. You're not
ready for that. You never will be, because after this, you're retiring
from the field. Just grab a bite to eat, talk, and make him think he
stands a chance."

"Let me try. I can find the codes."

"Sneaking into an office building without being caught is not
in your skill set. The only way we could get you inside is with
Dane next to you. And then he'll have you alone in his office. A
man tried to rape you. You need time and perspective. And
Dane's not a bad guy, but given the opportunity, he will make a

move on you. And I'm sorry, but I'm not going to let that happen."

Another strike against her? "No. I can do this. I will not let that jerk at the prison rule my life. And who are you to tell me what I can and cannot do?" she demanded.

"You're hurting. You need time. Don't do something you'll regret."

"Would Nicola or Alex have retrieved the codes for you?"

"One of them is dead. The other is happily married and would never feign attraction to another man to complete a task, at the risk of alienating her husband."

"Then I guess I'm your only option."

Simon stared out the window for a few moments. Tension showed in his stiff posture. His focus then shifted entirely to Cassie. "If you get into the building, you'll probably end up on a video feed."

"How will I know if there are cameras around?"

"You won't. So don't do anything that makes you look guilty." He sat on a fancy chair in the living room, dwarfing it. "And you can back out at anytime. I'm serious. Just get up and walk out of wherever you are."

This protective side of Simon comforted her, although she wouldn't tell him that. And the jealous side? It was nice to not be the only possessive person in the relationship. With his support, she'd be able to handle the assignment. Partly for her country, but mostly for herself.

With him seated, she towered over him with the three-inch heels. He looked up at her. Such a masculine face. No one would ever call him a pretty boy, even when he smiled and those dimples appeared and a boyish laughter reflected in his blue eyes. She leaned down, completely aware that her low-cut dress exposed a tad bit too much of her breasts, and placed her hands on his knees. His eyes dropped to her chest, as she'd predicted. She could do this job. How hard would it be to convince Dane that she was attracted to him?

"Thanks for the heads-up." She turned to leave the hotel suite.

"Cassie."

She looked back at him over her shoulder, with a newfound confidence in her role. "Simon."

"Be careful, not everything is what it seems."

"Whatever that means."

He stood up and walked over to her. "It means I can't tell you everything, but I need you on your guard."

"Fine." She sent him a quick wave and left him standing in the doorway as she headed to the lobby.

Wearing navy pants and a pale yellow golf shirt, Dane strolled into the hotel like a cover model for a golf magazine.

He greeted her with a friendly hug and a soft kiss on her cheek. "Wow. You look amazing."

She hugged him back and plastered on a casual smile. He'd taken such good care of her in Jordan. One of the good guys. It was clear he wanted her. Although he was gorgeous and sweet, and a strong shoulder to cry on, she didn't want him, because her heart belonged to the stubborn guy up in their hotel room.

Her hand remained around Dane's waist. "You look ready to take on the links."

"My plan is a casual stroll around Sausalito, and then we can grab some lunch. Simon isn't begging to come with us? I'm surprised."

"He's busy with work stuff. He's keeping me close, but giving me space too. Does that make any sense? I don't want to be pushed in any direction yet. And that sort of goes for you, too. I need to take things slow."

His eyes perused her outfit, and he smiled as though he'd won a prize. "I can take all the time you need, beautiful."

A resort area on the far side of the Golden Gate Bridge, Sausalito catered to affluent crowds and tourists. Seeing Dane's car, a new red BMW M8 convertible, Cassie placed him with the affluent crowd and not the tourists. The car, designed to be noticed and admired, fit him just as the rugged black Range Rover suited Simon.

He left the car with the valet at a waterfront restaurant.

"Care for a stroll before lunch?" he asked.

"Sure."

They walked in silence along the marina and past houseboats decorated with colorful planters full of flowers in full bloom. Cassie allowed the salt air to calm her soul. The ocean had always been therapeutic. When Dane slipped his hand into hers, she took it. Simon's hands overwhelmed hers, but Dane's felt comfortable. He wasn't as complicated as Simon. He wanted sex, and she wanted information. A simple transaction as long as she could retrieve the information and bail before the sex.

"Are you still living with Simon in London?"

"Yes." Dane's piercing eyes did nothing to calm her nerves, but she'd get through. *Think like a professional. Get rid of all emotions.*

"Are you going back?"

What could she say? That she had to because she worked there? "I don't know."

A few months ago, Dane would have been the man of her dreams. But Simon was it for her. Complicated. Difficult. It didn't matter. There would be no other man for her. But she was playing a part today. She was every bit as competent as his former partners.

"Stay. If only for an extra week or two. Give me a chance to win your heart. You've already won mine." He leaned in to kiss her, but she turned toward the city skyline across the bay so that the kiss landed on her cheek.

Dane's phone rang. He pulled the cell out of his pocket, his hand gripping hers close to his chest.

"What?" He spoke as though he wanted to kill the person on the other line. "I can get them for you this afternoon. What's the rush?"

She couldn't hear the person on the other end, but whoever it was clearly had the power to push all of Dane's buttons. He sent a half smile and a wink toward Cassie, but his frustration was clear.

"Fine. I'll have the pricing to you by noon. Gotta run. I have my hands full."

When he replaced the phone in his pocket, he returned his attention to Cassie.

"Sorry about that, some of my customers are more demanding than necessary. I need to run over to work for a few minutes. Do you mind coming with me?"

Getting into his office without having to ask. Perfect.

"Will you let me play with the little helicopter again? That was the most fun I had in Jordan." She'd hated flying the UAV with him. He'd wrested control of it from her because he thought she'd crash it.

"Absolutely. Maybe I can teach you a few tricks."

She smiled at his ignorance. "I'd like that."

# CHAPTER 16

Pelican Industries was headquartered in a large, modern building with palm trees lining the parking lot and a fenced-in area the size of a college stadium for demonstrations and research and development. The place was a hive of activity. People, dressed in casual business attire, holding coffee cups and tapping on electronic tablets, crowded the lobby.

A perky young redhead sat at the reception desk, waving to the employees and greeting visitors as they arrived. Dane spoke to her the way a politician greeted a potential voter, all smiles and artifice. It unnerved Cassie. He seemed too good to be true, too perfect in his world, too good at his job, too smooth an operator. Without the rose colored glasses she'd always worn to paint the world in a rainbow of good intentions, Cassie saw duplicity as clearly as she could see the ambition in the twenty-somethings milling about in the hallway. Dane was not simply a salesman.

He led Cassie down a maze of corridors and into his small office. With its floor to ceiling glass and stainless steel furniture, it was the perfect design for a high tech salesperson. Functional, organized, cold. He had nothing personal in the space except a coffee cup from the Carnegie Deli. Cassie had eaten there once when she'd visited New York.

"Are you a native of San Francisco?" she asked, hoping to get a better glimpse at the real Dane.

"No. I'm an East Coast transplant." He eyed the coffee cup and then sat at his desk and began typing on his computer, complete with an HD flatscreen monitor. She wanted to get a better view of what he was typing, but didn't want to approach that side of the desk yet.

"Where did you go to school?" She strolled to the window and looked out at the parking lot full of electric and hybrid cars.

"MIT. Computer science major, although I prefer sales. And you?" His eyes strayed from the screen to glance at her face, but he wouldn't see a reaction to the question. Without emotions to deal with, she could be anyone she wanted to be. She decided to be a surfer girl.

She embraced her new identity. "I was homeschooled and then tried college, but it wasn't really for me."

"So you hang out with Simon."

"Not all the time. I'm a receptionist at the Sainsbury's head-quarters. It's a grocery store chain in England." She shrugged, all while scanning the contents of the room for information on the drones Simon wanted to purchase.

"I've heard of it. I'm sure we could find you a better job over here. You'd have more fun hanging around me." He continued to type into his computer, as though her leaving Simon was a done deal. He didn't even know her. Why would he try to steal her away from Simon?

"I'm not sure I'm ready for a big change. I've had enough excitement to last a lifetime."

He stopped typing and gazed at her. "Do you really think Simon can provide you with a stable life? The man travels more than anyone I know."

"How do you know Simon so well?" She watched him formulate his answer.

He shrugged, revealing no emotion. "He just seems like the type that travels around, making deals and never settling."

"I'm not looking for forever. For now, Simon seems nice." And all consuming and terrifying. But still, he held her heart.

"Come here. I can help you decide." He waved her to his side of the desk. When she arrived at his side, he patted his lap.

The thought of kissing Dane again didn't appeal to her, but she needed information on the security codes for the drones. She smiled and pretended she was an actress. This was only a scene in a movie. Nothing real. She sat and placed an arm around his neck to stabilize her tall body. Her long limbs stretched out under his desk, and her chin rested on the top of his head. A completely awkward position.

She giggled. "I'm a bit too big for you."

"Never. You're perfect." He stayed away from her face, which was for the best. She had too many black and blue marks to avoid, from her chin to her forehead. Instead, he touched her neck with his lips and continued toward her ear. She focused on her job, ignoring the knots forming in her stomach.

"I—uh, remember, I'd like to take it slow."

"If anything makes you feel uncomfortable, you can tell me to stop," he said against her neck.

Her location on his lap provided the perfect view of his desktop. She gave him an encouraging moan and glanced over every paper she could. Sales numbers and invoices and sales meeting minutes and what looked like a British phone number. She committed it to memory and continued to allow playful sounds to escape her throat to encourage him to remain in the same position.

His computer screen had a blue bouncing ball blocking her view of the program running. She shifted in his lap and bumped his mouse. The screensaver disappeared, leaving a breakdown of the drones Simon ordered. Simon must have made the call when they were at the marina. Had he seen Dane kiss her? Probably. His timing had been too perfect. He could be looking in the window from the parking lot below right now.

He probably wasn't very happy with her right now, but that

made it even more necessary that she came back with the information he wanted.

Dane's hands started moving up her back. She placed a kiss on the top of his head and then saw exactly what she needed. A yellow Post-it on the far side of his desk with the word "NETOPS-35." Under the SPAWAR Integrated Cyber Operations Pillar Contract, AC4S provided Network Operations—NETOPS—support to Department of Defense customers. Cassie understood their systems, especially the thirty-fifth protocol. They were one step behind the security systems she'd been working on. If this was the security system on the drones they were ordering, she could reprogram them without too much trouble. That was all she needed to know.

She leaned away from him and kissed the tip of his nose. "I need to use your bathroom."

His breathing was heavy, and she felt his hardened attraction to her when she shifted off his lap and stood.

Ugh. She had to leave this situation before he asked for more than she cared to give.

"I have everything I need. I'll walk you to the Ladies' Room. We can leave from there. Why don't we go back to your hotel so I can drop this off with Simon?"

"Simon asked for it?" She tried to sound surprised.

"He seems to have the best timing of anyone I know."

More likely the best surveillance.

He pulled her back for a moment and whispered within an inch of her mouth, "Dinner?"

If they were making out in the daylight, they'd be in bed together at night. "I can't. I promised Simon we'd talk about where our relationship was headed tonight."

"I hope he's headed to London, and you remain here."

She brushed one of her fingers across his angled cheek. "You don't know anything about me."

"I know you grew up in San Diego. You won a surfing competition at age thirteen and have only lived in London for two years."

"Did the State Department give you that information? Or did you Google me?" He had her fictitious story down pat.

"A little bit of everything." He had a devilish gleam in his eyes she'd never seen before.

---

SIMON PURCHASED a beer and waited in the lobby for Dane and Cassie to return from their *date*. He hated feeling so out of control with his emotions. Cassie was a liability at work, his Achilles heel. He couldn't dampen his attachment to her, so he had to make sure she was safe. And the idea of Dane's hands on the woman he loved was more than any man should have to bear.

Dane returned Cassie to the hotel at a quarter past noon. His arm encircled her waist. They both looked too happy and comfortable together. Although Dane's poaching of Simon's girlfriends in the past had never bothered him, the man needed to stay away from Cassie. His kiss on her cheek had almost forced Simon to storm Sausalito like a platoon at Normandy, but Cassie had handled herself perfectly. How could she use her body as a tool after being assaulted at the prison? Was it an act? Or was she falling for Dane?

No. She cared for him, not Dane. He could feel it in her actions and words. That didn't fade so easily, and she wasn't the type to shift her attention. At least, he didn't think she was.

*Dammit. She has me tied up in knots.*

She took the furthest spot at the table from Simon's chair. Dane sat between them, grinning like the winner he wasn't.

He handed Simon a large envelope. "Here's the information you requested. We'll send everything to the address you provided."

The envelope would contain a few sheets of useless paper that provided no important details of the actual transaction. Simon would send an encrypted email to him later to confirm all the details, including the shipping logistics to a transfer location in France.

"Did you kids have a nice lunch?" Simon asked, not wanting the details, but craving them anyway.

Dane placed a hand over Cassie's. "It would have been better if we didn't get sidetracked."

"Business comes first."

Cassie visibly gritted her teeth at his comment. She still had no clue how much more she mattered to him than any assignment. Right now, however, was not the time to tell her.

"For you maybe. I enjoy the occasional moment of pleasure." Dane rubbed her hand and looked at her as though they were lovers.

She tilted her head and narrowed her eyes at Dane, but she didn't deny anything. And she shouldn't. Dane had marked her neck like an adolescent boy with zero control—more to piss Simon off than to claim Cassie. Simon swallowed his anger. Dane never made it past her neck. That was obvious from her unruffled demeanor.

Simon couldn't be mad at either one of them. He'd directed Cassie to find the information in Dane's office about the security codes. This was her first chance to help in the assignment. She didn't deserve him second-guessing her work tactics.

It still didn't make him feel better. He had murderous intentions where Dane was concerned.

If she found something they could use, she should display Dane's sloppy hickey as a kill mark. Right now, however, she looked as though she needed some fresh air away from both of them.

"Cassie, why don't you go relax after the long flight and what appears to have been a *boring* morning. There's a spa on the third floor. They'll fix your hair, nails, and give you a massage. We have dinner reservations at seven. I'll meet you in the suite at five."

She nodded to Simon with a half smile twisted by a bit of attitude. Her smile brightened toward Dane. "Thanks. You still owe me some time to play with those remote control airplanes."

"Call me anytime." When she stood to leave, Dane rose as well and moved to kiss her. She turned her head so his lips landed on her cheek again.

His frown lifted Simon's spirits. With a brief wave, she breezed out of the lobby.

Dane called the waitress over and ordered a beer. "Interesting tactic, following us. Your timing was perfect."

"I enjoy it. Besides I needed the paperwork more than you needed to molest my girlfriend. She's paid you back enough for your kindness. Now leave her alone. She's confused, and she's been through hell."

"She's confused, because she doesn't want to hurt your feelings when she leaves you for me." He smirked as though he'd already won her.

"Let me make myself clear. If you ever go near her again without my express permission, I'll set up a Twitter account for Dane O'Brien, CIA prick, and provide detailed stories of our exploits together." Their friendship had survived a lot of hardship, especially working for competing agencies, but it wouldn't survive anything to do with Cassie.

"That's the best you can do? Because I can think of at least five ways to make you suffer and none of them involve lame Internet games."

"Try me. I'm full of ideas."

Their friendly competition had always ended in a round of drinks at the closest bar in whatever part of the world they'd been in. Now, however, hostility boiled through Simon's pores. Cassie was not a prize. She was his destiny.

# CHAPTER 17

Simon needed several more days in San Francisco to determine the modifications necessary to provide the North Koreans with their requested specifications. Dane offered to take care of Cassie while Simon worked with the engineers on specifications that Cassie had secretly drawn up. Simon would let him watch over her again when the polar vortex reached into hell.

After a beautiful dinner overlooking the bay, they returned to the hotel suite. She seemed happier than she had since the incident in Jordan. She snuggled into his arms on the sofa. The light in her eyes shined brighter again, and even her bruises were fading. He lifted her chin and pulled at the small bandage covering her stitches.

"What are you doing?"

"I'm removing your stitches this evening."

"You? Do you have training?"

"Sure." He'd taken a required medic course several years ago. Nothing in depth, but he could remove stitches easily enough. "Let's keep ourselves out of the local hospital database. Admit it, you could easily hack into it and find medical records on anyone you want."

She shrugged. "Who would want my medical information?"

"You'd be surprised."

She tried to pull away, but he caught her before she could stand up. "Let me go, Simon."

"I thought you trusted me."

"With things you have training in. Not with cutting out stitches."

From the panicked look in her eyes, he'd bet his offshore accounts she'd never given blood because of the involvement of needles. "Wait here. That's an order, not a suggestion."

He released her.

She crossed her arms over her chest, but remained seated. "If you hurt me—"

"It might hurt a bit. Stop being a baby." He rummaged through his suitcase and found his first aid kit—a little more advanced than a kit found in a normal household. He pulled out small scissors in a sterile package and a pad of alcohol.

"Come over here. Sit on the bed so you're lower."

She sat on the edge of the bed, and he pulled the chair over to face her. Two tiny stitches held her skin together just under the curve of her chin. The wound had healed well. He gave credit to the medical personnel at the jail. If they'd just bandaged it, she would have ended up with a deep scar.

"Do you want me to distract you, or are you tough enough?"

"I'm okay. Go ahead." She glowered at him but remained seated.

He dabbed the alcohol over the stitches, causing her to take a swift inhalation of air.

"Shit." She hissed.

"Nice mouth."

"I'm sorry. It burned more than I expected. Can we do this later?" She bit her bottom lip and swallowed hard. The actions focused his gaze and his hunger on her mouth.

He leaned in and kissed her. Her sigh caught him off guard.

Any further and he'd forget all about her chin. "Suck it up, Watson."

"Easy for you to say."

Like the trouper she was, she let him do it.

Then she examined his work in the bathroom mirror. "I guess you did okay," she said with a frown.

He kissed her and then tucked her into bed.

Just minutes later she was asleep, and he was contacting his men in Europe about transporting the drones into France under the radar of any customs officers.

---

ONCE THE ORDER WAS COMPLETE, Dane invited them to the demonstration area outside the Pelican headquarters. He set up the UAV and handed Cassie the controller.

He wrapped his arms around her again, for *safety* reasons. She struggled to fly it straight, pitching it toward the wall of the building. He brought it down and let her try a different type of drone, but kept her close to him while she flew.

Simon could see Cassie's frustration rise, but he didn't step in. She needed to shut down Dane's advances on her own for him to back off permanently. The machine ascended several times straight up and hovered over the parking lot.

He tried to control the machine while she worked the remote, but he underestimated her abilities. A faint smile flitted across her face. Dane, however, was unaware of this change in her confidence as he was still holding her from behind. Somehow, she managed to take it over the harbor, dive bomb a boat, and crash it into the sea, from what Cassie described later in a play-by-play account of the accident. Her view of the scene through the goggles ended when the UAV smashed into the waves.

"Enough." Dane pulled the controller out of her hands. "Stop. You broke a fifty thousand dollar machine." He finally lost his magically cool demeanor.

Cassie moved to Simon's side. Her head rested on his shoulder.

"You're the idiot that allowed her to fly an expensive model without proper training. I'd fire your ass if it was my company." He wrapped an arm around her. He could feel the vibrations of her laughing uncontrollably into his shoulder. "It's okay, angel. Dane is an ass."

Dane's phone rang, and he began apologizing to someone. The apology was cut off every few words by someone screaming in the other phone. When he hung up, his eyes narrowed on Simon. "You owe me, Dunn. If you'll excuse me, I need to smooth the feathers of the Coast Guard commander driving over here with what's left of the machine. I'll be surprised if we don't receive a fine and a citation for illegally flying over civilian airspace."

Cassie's face remained tucked in Simon's shoulder. "I'm so sorry. I didn't know what I was doing."

Dane waved her apology off with a flick of his wrist. Game over. He wouldn't be going after her after this performance. He liked his job and his ability to track arms deals from the comfort of a corporate expense account.

"Come on, I'll buy you some lunch." Simon led her back to the parking lot. They drove away in a rented black Expedition.

As soon as her door closed, Cassie started laughing again—a huge laugh coming from the deepest center of her lungs and reverberating throughout the car. "Oh my God, that was the most fun I've had since I was a kid."

"You do understand that you're now stuck with me. I don't think Dane will ever want you near him again."

"That makes it even more perfect. He gave me a hickey for your benefit, not caring what it did to my personal reputation *or* my psyche after being molested in jail. I have zero guilt."

"Good. What did you think about the handling of that quadcopter, before you kamikazed it?"

"The rotors are set up in a diamond layout. That's preferable to a square. They're similar to Aeryon Scouts. Those babies can hover in place so quietly, you wouldn't know one was there until it smacked you in the head."

"Any problems?"

"It had a slight balance problem, but I could fix that by tweaking the channel entries. I'll have to fly all twenty to make sure they're stable."

"No problem. There's a lot of room on my farm."

"Your farm?"

"I bought it a few years ago. Don't get too attached. I'll need to sell it after this transaction. Too many people are learning about it."

"Do you own any other properties?"

He paused. What could he tell her? Everything. "About ten."

"Ten houses?"

"Houses, land, an apartment in New York. It enables me privacy wherever I am in the world."

"All paid for by the British government?"

"I'm independently financed. I can eat what I kill." And he ate well. Really well.

"What about me?"

"Technically, you're my employee."

"So you can give me a raise?" She lifted her eyebrows and smiled, like a child begging for an ice cream.

He leaned over and kissed her. "If you're successful in programming the drones to our buyer's specifications, I'll give you the property in France as a bonus, although I recommend selling it and finding something more remote."

"Deal."

---

AFTER SEVERAL DAYS of making final demands on the Pelican transaction as prescribed by Cassie, Simon transported her to Europe, away from Dane and back to his own turf.

They arrived at his isolated French farmhouse near the Swiss border on a sunny spring morning. The mountains around them provided an elegant backdrop to their dangerous job.

Simon had purchased the four-hundred year old stone building a few years before in order to guarantee privacy in his transactions. The British government had promised he could keep the spoils of his secret war, and after investing some away for retirement, he reinvested most back into his cover. His operation could out price and out maneuver any other dealer in the world. Even his nearly eight-month absence did little to affect his net worth or his ability to obtain clients.

Life in France held simple charms for Simon. While they waited almost a week for the shipments to arrive, he and Cassie went for daily walks through the countryside and spent hours sitting side by side, either reading or just enjoying each other's company. He cherished this down time as the plans began to take shape for the transfer to the North Koreans.

The four explosive experts from Israel arrived with a shipment of potassium chlorate to arm the drones. Simon had used dealers of ammonium nitrate fertilizer in the past, but countries monitored the export and import of that chemical, making it impossible to move without an international incident. Potassium chlorate was shipped in smaller quantities and had more stable properties. The odorless white powder became an explosive when combined with a fuel, cutting off several steps necessary to make ammonium nitrate into an explosive.

While the men set up their lab in the farmhouse, he checked on Cassie. He found her sitting at a small writing table in the bedroom, with a teacup on one side and a laptop on the other. Her fancy dress clothes had been discarded in favor of faded jeans and a gray T-shirt she'd picked up on the drive from Paris. Her hair was tied into a braid—one Simon wanted to pull back into him when he took full possession of her again. But she hadn't begged, and he wouldn't cross the line until she wanted him as much as he wanted her.

He strolled across the floor and sat in a chair next to her. "You look comfortable."

She lifted her legs and rested them across his thighs. "I am now. When are the drones arriving?"

"Tomorrow. Which gives me time to work with our Israeli friends."

"Have they loaded explosives onto a UAV before?"

"No, but they've impregnated missile heads. I'm hoping the concepts are similar enough, and that your expertise will help us protect the Alps from an unfortunate incident."

She shuddered. "Don't joke about something like that."

"I've worked with these guys for the past seven years. They're the best. Are you ready?" He rubbed her legs.

"I can reconfigure the program to allow remote access and then place it behind a hidden firewall so the buyers won't notice it." She glanced back at the computer. A program in a language he didn't understand appeared next to a schematic of the drone he'd purchased from Pelican. One of the many things she had in her old computer.

"You're sure?"

"Don't you trust me?" She grinned with a confidence he'd never seen in her before. Perhaps it came from working in her area of expertise.

He kissed her. "With my life."

"Wow. That's a lot of trust to place in an incompetent agent."

"You convinced Dane you have nothing to do with my work, all while collecting data right under his nose. Impressive. Don't downplay your skills. You make a great spook."

"Coming from you, that's the highest compliment."

They kissed again. She tasted of mint tea and the promise of an intimacy so deep a man would give his heart, his possessions, and his life to attain it. He shifted a breath away from her. "Cassie, life is so unpredictable. I've always tried to be an optimist, but there are so many things in my past that weigh down on me. Memories and scars and wounds so deep, I thought I'd never smile again.

And then you stepped into my life and made every moment so important. I love you."

Their tongues met, and they pressed into each other, becoming fully absorbed in the moment. She moaned and clasped his shirt to tug him toward her. As much as he wanted her, he wasn't convinced she was ready to be intimate again. At least not yet.

Her hands held his head. She pulled back for a moment and said with her lips still touching his, "I'm begging you. Now." Her breathing was heavy.

"Now?"

"Right now."

"Hands and knees begging?"

Her eyes widened. "You wouldn't dare."

"If you don't get on your hands and knees and beg me, I guess you're not emotionally healed enough to share such a mind blowing experience." The chair scraped the floor when he stood.

Her beautiful, sexy mouth dropped open, and the blue in her eyes darkened. "Wait."

He headed to the door.

"You better not leave this room," she called out after him.

He should have kept walking, given her something to ponder. Instead, he looked back at her. A tactical error. She'd slipped her shirt off when he was walking away. His body reacted instantly. There was no way he could leave this tall, blonde goddess standing before him in jeans and nothing else.

Trying to keep his own jaw from hitting the floor, he leaned against the doorframe and crossed his arms. "I'm waiting."

After a second of hesitation, she slipped her jeans off—still standing, but now she was wearing a minimal piece of red silk covering not much at all. He was tempted to ask her to turn around so he could see if it was a thong, but he didn't want to risk her changing her mind. The minx lowered herself to the floor and crawled toward him, slinking like a cat burglar and exposing the most amazing ass highlighted by, yes, a very thin red thong. Nice.

She stopped at his feet and lifted her eyes toward his. "Simon Dunn, I'm begging you to make love to me, right here and now."

A spider scuttled across the floor. He should have warned her, but he'd never had a near naked woman crawling toward him before. Then she noticed it. Jumping to her feet, she flung herself into his arms. He took advantage of her open mouth and possessed it with more passion and heat than he'd given to anyone in the past. He held her by her bare bottom, her long legs wrapped around his waist.

They made it to the bed in three steps. He was careful to avoid killing the spider, giving the arachnid full credit for getting Cassie into his arms quicker than he'd imagined.

He dropped her beneath him and stretched over her, careful to keep his weight from crushing her. His mouth pressed softly to her lips. "I saved your life. You owe me."

"I was the one begging. You owe me." She sucked in a few deep breaths and exhaled with a shudder.

One simple kiss and her sultry lips opened up to him. He could still taste the mint tea on her tongue—sweet mixed with Cassie's own brand of temptation. The thrust of her slender hips dared him to take her quickly. Patience, however, would create rewards far more satisfying than a quick release.

He lifted his head away from her, and she followed, trying to keep her mouth on his. She linked an arm around his neck and attempted to pull him back down. Her hunger for him began to crack his resolve. He lowered himself back over her for a moment, giving her the feeling of victory, and then he rolled off her.

A beautiful pout formed on her lips. "Come here."

"Not yet. If I owe you, I mean to pay up. Right now." His thumbs pulled her thong down past her thighs, her strong calves, and the red painted toenails.

He knelt between her legs. Her muscles tensed as he began to taste between her inner thighs. She moaned. Her legs opened wider. No matter what she claimed later, he definitely received the better part of this deal.

He moved to the center and continued his explorations, sampling her most sensitive area with his teeth. He felt her sharp exhalation, but his hand pressed her into the bed and kept her captive while he paid her back for making him crave a lifetime with her and the intense stress that came with it. With the precision of an expert, Simon controlled her ascent, higher and higher until she flew apart, head back, moaning his name.

# CHAPTER 18

───────────── ᏉᏉ ─────────────

The next morning, Cassie emerged from the farmhouse with her laptop and a pair of legs weakened from her marathon sex with Simon. She grinned. Definitely a control freak, but she'd easily persuaded him into positions that gave her maximum power and maximum pleasure. Plus, he smiled more.

And she loved him more than anything.

She found him in the barn with his four Israeli colleagues, all of them dressed in jeans and T-shirts. The wooden crates were open around them with a few drones sitting on plastic tarps. Simon introduced her to the men, who greeted her with guarded expressions, as expected when introduced to a stranger.

"Just the person we need. Can you hook up one of these into your computer?" Simon wore a business face. He saved his smiles for his personal life.

"After I check to make sure they all fly right. No use setting them up if the balance is off."

Pelican used a carbon fiber body to keep the weight to a minimum, combined with high tech components and a strong battery with another small backup that could withstand extreme hot and cold weather. She chose to work on four at a time. Pulling all twenty out would make it impossible to keep track of them all. She picked up a drone and inspected it. The hand control, the size of an iPhone, worked by a touch screen.

The men wanted to try their hand at flying them. It was all a game to them. She refused. Ben, their leader, helped her keep the frustration levels down by reminding them of the payment they'd receive in exchange for their handiwork. With a few grumbles, they backed off. Simon didn't bother to ask if he could fly one, smart man. As the head of the technological side of the mission, she controlled how the drones would be programmed and who played with them. If they wrecked one, it could take another two weeks to convince Dane to send another, and they didn't have two weeks. The North Koreans wanted the transaction to take place in only a week.

Flying each one with both a remote control and the GPS guidance system, she checked how long they each hovered without losing altitude. Almost all of them worked to perfection. She altered the controls on two of the drones to fix some problems with maintaining balance. Within a few hours, she'd adjusted the speed of the propellers and fixed the issues.

She remained in the barn through lunch and past the setting of the sun, completely in her element. The cameras mounted on the drones worked well. They had infrared technology and a color HD video system enabling them to obtain perfect visuals in both day and night time missions. The camera contained air vent systems to increase visibility when the infrared technology wasn't turned on.

For the first time since leaving the protection of her office, she enjoyed her job. Her work could help stop a war. If the drones detonated in North Korea and the traitors were caught, the South Koreans would have no cause for retaliation. The plan seemed too good to be true. Therefore, there had to be a flaw. She stared at the components set out across the table. The symbol of the Pelican along with an identification number had been carved into the body of the machines. U.S. designed and manufactured. U.S.

drones exploding in North Korea would be like poking the regime with a cattle prod. Her empty stomach was crushed under the realization that she could be starting a war anyway.

Simon approached her with a cup of tea and some bread. "Here. You're looking stressed." He handed it to her. "You need to eat and drink, or you'll be useless."

She placed the mug on the table next to a drone she'd been programming. "We have a problem."

Simon's forehead creased, as it often did when he was thinking about something. "Tell me."

"If the drones are detonated in North Korea, won't the North Korean government think it's under attack, examine any fragments found at the scene and learn they were manufactured in the United States?"

"We were going to detonate them in a remote, mountainous region. It was my understanding that the markings on the drones had been removed."

"They weren't removed. Look." She flipped over the drone to reveal the Pelican markings in the body. "Also, you can't remove certain technology markers. Pelican has a distinctive way of lining up the rotors. Even their landing gear is unique. If the North Korean army gets hold of even a fraction of one of these machines, they'll know where it came from, but maybe not the group that launched it." She paced back and forth across the barn, her breathing escalating, until Simon took her in his arms.

The strength of his embrace pulled some of the worry from her, but she couldn't shake the feeling that this mission was going to create more harm than good.

"I don't want to cause World War Three," she insisted.

"You won't." He kissed her gently and stared into her eyes. "Another dealer would supply drones with twice the explosive power and take out hundreds of people heading to a market or a school. Most guys in this game have no morals and no allegiances. You and I are charged with minimizing casualties and making it appear as though we are working diligently for our clients. Without our work, the world would be much more dangerous."

"You're right, but if this backfires–"

"If we don't handle this transaction, then someone else will. There's always someone who'll fulfill any contract for the right price. An international incident would escalate the sale of arms throughout the world. A win-win for dealers. Let me talk with the explosives team, maybe they can figure a way to destroy the drone so effectively, the origin will be untraceable."

"What are the chances of that?"

"I don't know, but I trust them. You should too." With another kiss, he walked out of the barn to locate his team.

Two hours after midnight, a tired crew had found the means to obliterate the drones. Acid.

---

NOTHING WAS SEXIER to Simon than a woman in her element. Cassie took control of the drones, the men, and the technical aspects of the project. Her intelligence and leadership abilities shined through.

They had three days to arm the drones and three days to deliver them. They'd easily make the deadline if Cassie continued to work nonstop to get the job done. Simon tended to stay away from the manufacture of arms, but Tucker had been adamant about the need for modifications on these drones to prevent the situation from escalating out of control.

In all the years he'd worked with Tucker, the man had been adept at infiltrating certain situations to control the playing field without anyone knowing of their involvement. What Tucker lacked in field skills, he made up for in strategic mission planning. Still, something was wrong with this particular assignment. Too many things could go wrong. The businessmen they were selling to were not normal customers, the drones had to be armed before the sale, and Cassie was not the best trained agent, although her inner strength made her better than average.

When he arrived in the bedroom, Cassie was already in bed asleep, dressed only in his T-shirt. Her limbs stretched out in four directions as though playing a grown-up version of Twister. He wanted to wake her, but she needed rest. Tomorrow, they'd be testing one of the drones. One more week and this assignment from hell would end.

If everything worked as it should, she could retire from the field and remain safe in the background. Keeping her safe was paramount.

In the morning, they ate quickly in the farmhouse, and then Cassie headed out to the barn. She wanted to go over the logistics of the acid core in the explosives. A frightening mix of chemicals, but necessary in this case. Transporting them would be tricky. Simon would have to hire a specialized cargo plane to bring the drones into South Korea. From there, the crates would cross the border through holes in the security of the Demilitarized Zone between the two enemy states. One of the more risky jobs he'd perform. Simon preferred his transactions to occur in a neutral location.

Standing on the front stairs of the farmhouse, he watched the team follow Cassie's directions. She had jeans and another T-shirt on, her ponytail flowing out the back of a San Diego Padres ball cap. She gestured for them to move a few crates out of the barn. She helped the men as they lined everything up for her to inspect. Their respect for her was obvious in the focused attention they gave as she spoke to them. She should be proud of how far she'd come.

He was certainly proud of her. There weren't many agents who could have done what she'd accomplished in the last few weeks. A far cry from the timid creature he'd frightened that first night, especially after going through a traumatic event. Soldiers had left active service for less hardship. If he didn't love her so much, and want to send her back to Oxford to live a quiet life with his family, she'd be his top pick as a partner in the future. Now, however, he wanted her as a different kind of partner.

Something moved in the woods behind him. He reached for his gun with his right hand and took a sip of coffee with his left. Son of a bitch. Dane, blending into the background in moss green and brown, leaned against a tree with his gun pointed directly at Simon.

"Nice place you've got here, Dunn." He moved closer, lowering the gun as he walked.

"Didn't you see the 'No Trespassing' signs? I put them up specifically for you." Simon put away his gun as well. Dane wouldn't shoot him, only torment him.

"Sorry, I can't read French."

"Might as well get you a cup of coffee."

"Thanks. I prefer walks on the beach to schlepping through damp wooded areas."

They clasped hands as old friends and headed into the kitchen before the team saw him.

"Did you follow the group I sent to pick up the drones?" Simon asked.

Dane shook his head. "Installed a GPS tracking device on one of the crates." He sat at the wooden table and stared through the lace curtain toward the barn.

"I should have repackaged them. Live and learn." Simon grabbed a chipped brown coffee mug that may have been in the farmhouse when it was built hundreds of years ago. With any luck, Dane would have lead poisoning and be stuck in bed for a few days. The man, however, had been granted more than nine lives, all healthy ones.

The American took the full mug and placed it on the table. "What the hell are you doing with my drones?"

"Making a sale. Same as I've always done. Jealous because the CIA demoted you to sales boy?"

A flash of irritation crossed Dane's brow. "You can do as you please unless it harms my existence. If those end up with the wrong group and I'm blamed, I'll hunt you down and destroy your operation."

"Go ahead. I'll be retired by then. After all this time, I'm surprised you didn't investigate my final buyer before you sold me such amazing pieces of technology."

"I thought you were selling them to the Serbians. You hid your tracks fairly well, except for one very beautiful partner."

"She's my girlfriend, and she stays out of this." Simon wouldn't reveal anything. Only Cassie could get hurt.

"Really? Then why was she flying the drones yesterday with a far more steady hand than the ditzy surfer girl in San Diego, who flew a drone on a suicide mission into the bay?"

So he'd been watching.

"Practice."

Dane took a slow, easy sip of the coffee. "You've never taken such an extreme interest in a woman before. You never cared if they shared my bed one night and yours the next. It's different with Cassie. You're downright possessive. Got me thinking. What if her value to you was outside the bed? I ran some searches for Ms. Cassie Watson. Not much to go on. Then I mentioned to one of our engineers that a leggy blonde from the San Diego area crashed one of the more expensive drones. He laughed and said there was a robotics expert in General Dynamics several years back who fit that description, Catherine Wallace. Sound familiar?"

"No. Are you saying there are no other blonde women on the planet who work in robotics?" Damn. She certainly was unforgettable, and figuring out her identity in such a small community would be inevitable.

"Nice try, but Catherine, aka Cassie, is one of a kind. In fact, from what I've found out about her, she'd be an asset to Homeland Security. And yet, she's not American at all. British with an American upbringing. As you boys would say, bloody brilliant. Convenient, too. You have an expert at your side all day, and a hot piece of ass in your bed at night."

"Enough," Simon growled.

"Since her passport says she's American, I'm assuming she's more my property than yours. Let's see how far she'll go to stay hidden in plain sight. I bet I can convince her to do anything to stay undercover. *Anything.*"

Simon pulled Dane off his chair by the front of his shirt. Just as quick, Dane's hand reached out and grabbed Simon's neck, squeezing hard enough to warn him off. Simon glared into his eyes, rage ripping apart his control. Dane needed to keep his distance from Cassie, because friendship or not, Simon would annihilate him and his career.

"Stay the hell away from Cassie or so help me God, I'll kill you."

A grin grew on Dane's face. "Even more interesting." He pushed off Simon, his breathing heavy. "Give my best to Catherine—I mean Cassie. I'll be in touch."

He waved back at Simon. The door closed and his cocky hide disappeared into the woods before Simon could fashion a comeback.

# CHAPTER 19

⟡

Three late nights, and limited meal breaks, caused Cassie's energy levels to plummet. Before she pulled the covers back to rise, Simon had run a few miles, showered, and was out of the house. His stamina never declined. While she felt feeble this morning compared to him, she'd appreciated his strength and energy the night before. She needed to keep moving, so she dragged herself out of bed, showered, and forced herself to return to the barn. Today they'd test their creation. If it didn't go well, they'd need to perfect the design over the next two days, potentially making them late for the drop off. An unacceptable conclusion to an already difficult assignment.

At least they'd found a way to minimize the possibility of tracing the drones to the U.S. The acid would be released backward into the drone as the explosive detonated outward. It should destroy as much of the carbon fiber frame and the software as possible, leaving a minimal amount of material for identification. Not a perfect solution, but better than nothing.

Seeing the test drone sitting in the field beside the barn, ready to launch, accelerated her pulse. Would it work? Would the local authorities be called after the explosion? Simon had assured her the location was an active blast site, but she'd never blown up anything before and had no idea the protocol involved.

"Good morning." Simon waved her over. He displayed an interesting mix of bad boy and protector. A very alluring mixture. He wouldn't touch her in front of the men, but they had to know where they both slept at night.

"Is everything ready?"

"Just waiting for the pilot. She looks fantastic today, by the way." He smiled at her, but something was different. It had been like that since lunch yesterday. He acted extra protective, rarely leaving her side when she was out of the farmhouse. Her instincts told her to be on guard, because no matter how protective he was, especially since Jordan, he'd never been the clingy type. That meant there might be danger lurking that he wasn't telling her about.

*Will there ever be a time when he won't have so many secrets?*

But she knew the answer.

She spun around like a model displaying a new dress. "Thanks. I'm feeling fantastic today," she lied.

She knelt beside the machine and looked it over. Making alterations on the model was tricky, raising the chance of a problem and delays. "I've been having so much fun playing with my expensive new toys, I didn't think about alternatives. Why are we altering these drones when we could have bought some Textron Battlehawks or Aerovironment Switchblades? They're already armed and ready to go."

"First, the battery packs won't allow for the distances that need to be covered to get over the DMZ. Second, they fly like a plane, and we need them to hover for a little while for maximum impact." He raised his eyebrow in a sexy manner, although he probably meant to look stern. "Finally, the U.S. government tracks the sale of armed drones more than they track the movement of large shipments of uranium."

"Ah. Makes sense." She made a few minor adjustments and

then walked over to the table to grab the remote and the glasses. When she had everything in place, she gave him a thumbs-up.

"See that cliff over there?" He pointed to an outcrop of stones on the side of fairly steep mountain.

"That's my target?"

"Just to the left of it is a small quarry."

"I've seen it from earlier flights. It's pretty active."

"It's closed today, due to a large payoff to the company president. They have a blasting permit and are scheduled to blast in about an hour."

"You are thorough."

"In everything I do."

She leaned in to whisper in his ear. "I'll appreciate your thoroughness even more tonight."

A grin lifted his face from gorgeous to decadent. "You're insatiable."

"And you're complaining?"

"Never." The spark of amusement continued to light up his face until one of the men turned the corner, then his expression fell back into a lighthearted scowl. Back to work.

Wearing the glasses that provided a view from the camera, she launched the test drone and flew it around for twenty minutes. The DMZ was approximately two and a half miles wide at the point where the businessmen wanted to stage the attack. She needed to ensure that the drones could travel at a low altitude for the requisite distance, even though it would never make the trip. She didn't understand how the team had managed to place acid in a sealed packet released only upon detonation by the explosives, but she appreciated how the weight increase to the drone was minimal.

The drone hovered in almost complete silence over a small field halfway up a mountain pass. A deer walking nearby through a forest clearing showed zero reaction until the UAV traveled within three feet, and then it bolted. At the twenty-seven minute mark, she flew to the quarry. Large boulders and piles of smaller rocks sat on the edge of the cuts into the mountain. A picnic table and small hut made of scrap wood and a metal roof became potential victims in the middle of the stone area.

"There's a small hut at the bottom of the quarry. I don't want to destroy it," she called out to Simon.

"Go ahead. I had one of the men check the site and remain nearby to keep anyone out. I'm curious to see the impact on a building. I'll reimburse the operator for it. Money tends to create a high degree of forgiveness."

She circled the area to make sure for herself that no one had entered the closed quarry without permission, and then lowered the machine a few feet to hover over the hut.

"Ready?" Simon asked.

She nodded.

The explosives team stood behind her, waiting to observe the fruit of their labor.

"In three. One, two, three."

She detonated the explosive. A bit more powerful than the usual blasts at the quarry, but nothing that should cause too much curiosity. The impact traveled all the way back to them. Trees swayed, birds launched into the air, and a cloud of white smoke rose above the forest. The control fell out of her hand. And Cassie collapsed.

She ended up on the ground as though the Earth had shifted, leaving her feet with no place to stand. Simon lifted her into his arms within seconds after the fall.

Being in his arms at that moment did nothing to calm her racing heart. She had always been a strong athlete, and losing her balance ticked her off. "I'm fine. I guess the blast knocked me over."

"No. The blast wasn't that powerful. You fainted. Did you eat today?" He tightened his grip on her and frowned. Being with Simon definitely had drawbacks—an overprotective man always ready to swoop in and handle things, when in reality she'd probably tripped.

"I had a banana and some orange slices."

"If I have to force feed you, you'll get adequate nutrition into that body of yours."

She glanced over at the explosive team. They had jumped into their car, ready to go check out the effects of the blast.

"Let me down. I want to go with them." She struggled against him, but he didn't relent. Simon headed to the farmhouse. "Have some water and a piece of bread first. They won't touch anything until we arrive."

———————— &o ————————

SIMON WATCHED Cassie drop and had to restrain himself from pulling the plug on the rest of the assignment. She'd been extra tired the past few days, and he feared she was putting too much into her work without adequately fueling herself. Any attempt to slow her down, however, would result in a fight he didn't want to have.

They drove out to see the results of their work in silence. The quarry was about twenty minutes away through winding dirt roads. Cassie sipped on a mug of tea and ate some Nutella spread over another piece of bread. When her tongue licked some of the chocolate from her lips, Simon almost swerved off the road. Damn, he craved her almost every minute, every second. She was a walking distraction and love was a major liability in the field.

The team hailed them over to a clearing near the quarry. Ben stepped up to the car before they opened the door. He gave them a thumbs-up. Good. Simon needed a success. After Dane's threats and Cassie's fainting spell, the mission's chance of success had decreased to unacceptable levels.

He escorted Cassie to the edge of the quarry. The drone had devastated the entire area. The hut was gone. All that was left was blackened stone and rubble from part of the collapsed wall. Brilliant.

The team had brought special suits to avoid coming into

contact with the acid. They dressed in white one-piece coveralls and put on gloves and a mask to shield their heads. Cassie searched the upper rim for residue, while he and the team dropped into the quarry to find anything useful they could examine for their post-blast analysis.

He climbed down the ledge using stone outcroppings as hand and foot grips because the ladder providing access to the area was on the ground, twisted into an interesting metal sculpture. The explosives contained more power than he'd anticipated. A quick glance at the team and their high fives told him they'd been surprised at the massive impact as well.

Four hours later, the team had only found three small pieces of the drone, all with untraceable markings melted into indistinguishable shapes. Mission accomplished.

Simon took several pictures of the site for the businessmen. This was exactly what they were looking for—a super powerful weapon that would force the South Korean government to retaliate. Allies would join them and soon North Korea would be a thing of the past. What the men didn't anticipate, however, was the Russian and Chinese governments' unwillingness to allow that country to become another casualty of the United States' need to help its friends and right wrongs. The consequences would be huge and unknown until after a major international incident. Men who looked at shortsighted profit margins could not understand the implications of the tsunami they were unleashing on the area and the world.

# CHAPTER 20

⟨⦿⟩

The drones had been transported early in the morning. The Israeli team had departed the previous night. That left Cassie alone with Simon for a day in the French country-side before meeting with the North Koreans in Hong Kong and then flying on to Daecheong Island, their departure point from South Korea into North Korea.

Cassie's fatigue continued to hamper her. She must have caught the flu along the way, because in addition to a general malaise, she didn't feel like eating. Simon had designated himself the food police and wouldn't let her alone without a bite of something every few hours. She lived on herbal teas and large amounts of baguettes.

"I'm ready to go." She carried her suitcase down the stairs and grinned to herself as Simon hopped up from his chair to grab her bags. "Relax. I'm perfectly capable of handling things myself."

"Since I had the unique opportunity of lifting you off the ground when you planted that cute ass of yours in the dirt, I have the right to assist you whenever I want. And I agree you are perfectly capable of handling things on your own. You're beauti-ful, intelligent, and completely competent. Now hand over the bags."

He wouldn't relent, no matter how hard she argued, so she gave him the luggage and followed him to the car. She sat in the passenger seat and watched him place the bags in the trunk and take a phone call.

His eyebrows furrowed as he spoke into the phone. He rarely showed anger, but now he paced back and forth while clutching his free hand into a fist. His tone intensified from businesslike to threatening.

Opening the door, she tried to listen to his conversation.

"Make it happen, I don't care how much you need to pay," Simon yelled into the phone.

She waved at him, wearing a sympathetic smile, but he shook his head and turned away.

He continued with a softer voice. "Three days at the most, then we need to find a new supplier...Call me back in an hour." He hung up on the person without a good-bye.

"Everything okay?" she asked.

"The crates are stuck in some bureaucratic nightmare with the French authorities. I need to know who tipped them off and what it will cost to get them moving again."

"You think someone ratted you out?"

He nodded and hopped into the driver seat of the car. "I have a gut feeling it's a jealous playboy from San Francisco who has suddenly gone under the radar. "

As he drove, he made phone calls to what seemed to be his suppliers and various government officials. His mood remained sour. Simon didn't trust the local airports, so he drove all day and into the night, through France and down into Italy. They stopped to sleep in a small hotel south of Milan. It would have been romantic, looking out into the fields and rolling hills, but Simon needed to keep the pressure on whoever was holding the drones.

After a brief dinner, Cassie took a walk down one of the small roads to refresh her mind and calm her nerves. Simon wouldn't notice—he was handling frantic calls to and from his associates all over the world.

Her energy levels had lifted since leaving France. Was she finally free of whatever was dragging her down? Her stomach sickness lessened as the day carried on. It tended to last through the morning and dissipate in the afternoon.

*Morning* sickness.

She froze on the side of the road. Her hand lifted to her chest to press on the ache of a heart beating too forcefully. How could she be so stupid? She quickly calculated backward to the only time they'd had unprotected sex and realized she was a week late with her period.

She continued walking into the village and found a pharmacy. A light was on in the back of the store, but the signs weren't illuminated and the main area was dark. Perhaps someone was still inside. She banged on the door. Nothing. Then she saw some movement. She banged on the door again. Slightly uncomfortable with her rude behavior, she carried on anyway. She needed to know.

"Please open, *per favore.*"

Nothing. She leaned her head against the door, willing herself not to cry. She'd find another way to figure out whether she was pregnant. Once she had a yes or no answer, she could plan. Facts first. No use panicking before she understood every angle of the problem.

Footsteps caught her attention. A figure moved toward her from the back of the store. The door opened. A beautiful woman, no older than forty, with long dark hair and a sympathetic smile, waved her inside and then shut and locked the door after her.

"*Si?* Can I help you?" Her English was slow and staccato, and the most beautiful sound Cassie had heard all day.

"I need a pregnancy test." Cassie's throat tightened while she attempted to tell the woman her embarrassing predicament. Her hand went to her stomach. The action told the storekeeper enough. With a subtle nod, she touched Cassie's arm and gave her a faint smile.

The woman appeared calm and non-judgmental. No overflowing happiness, no glance toward her finger for a wedding band. She simply entered the stacks behind the counter and returned with a box. Cassie assumed it was a pregnancy test.

"Go home or take here?" the woman asked.

She couldn't take it near Simon. He'd know something was going on the minute she walked in the door and would probably stand over her as she peed on the stick. "Could I take it here?"

"Yes, of course. Follow me."

She led Cassie through the back room, past rows of white boxes of medicines and medical supplies, into a house. An amazing house—white stucco walls, vibrant green curtains covering a large window that looked out into a courtyard not seen from the street. A small fountain provided the perfect acoustic backdrop to such a magical place.

In the privacy of the bathroom, she took the test and waited. Tears flowed down her cheeks. If it was positive, Simon might be angry. Would he help raise his child? If it was negative, however, Cassie would be heartbroken over the loss of a connection to Simon she never knew she wanted.

---

CASSIE HAD BEEN MISSING for an hour and a half. She'd left for a walk after dinner and damn well better be back in his sight in five minutes, or he'd handcuff her to him. He had the whole deal falling apart and didn't need to worry about Cassie's whereabouts as well.

She arrived with three seconds to spare. When she saw him, she nodded without expression and tried to walk past him into the house.

He grabbed her arm and whipped her around to face him. "You're grounded."

"Grounded?" She tried to pull away, but he wouldn't let her go until she understood his command. Her eyes focused on his, never dropping, never backing down. *Now she was the brave one?* She had no idea how much he needed her safe.

The tension of the past few days pushed through his calm and caused his words to come out harsher than planned. "You heard me. I don't need another international manhunt for your location. You remain with me or go back to London."

"You want me gone?" Her bravado faded.

"I want you in one piece, by my side." He released her. "Can you respect that?"

She nodded, relaxing into his arms. His hand swept through her hair, and he pulled her to him, as close as he could, tucking her head into his shoulder. *By my side, forever.*

After Cassie went to sleep, Simon confronted his biggest roadblock—the son of a bitch who had stopped the shipment of the drones. Some of his contacts in the French government notified him that a U.S. informant requested they look further into the origins of the crates Simon was shipping to South Korea. *Dane.* The bastard had warned him about using Pelican drones in something against U.S. interests, but he'd never sabotaged one of Simon's missions before. A few phone calls later and he had his answer. Dane wanted a meeting. They were to rendezvous in Hong Kong.

This was getting more and more complicated. The more players involved, the more could go wrong. He wanted Cassie as far from the action as possible. Since her return from her walk, she'd stayed hidden in their bedroom. Her emotions ranged high and low. It wasn't like her. She tended to be more stable and level headed.

The next morning, they drove through the Italian countryside to Rome. She'd dressed up for the trip, wearing a designer suit jacket and loose fitting trousers. Her high heels gave her a tactical advantage over most of the crowds in the airport. A supermodel, without the gaunt, smoker's face. Men froze as she breezed by, oblivious to their stares.

After the flight attendant provided water to Cassie and vodka for him, she stared out the window and then sank into a deep slumber. Her face relaxed while she was sleeping. The stress lines she'd worn between her eyebrows disappeared, and her lips fell into a soft pout.

If someone had asked him a few weeks ago if he'd trust her in the field, he would have said no without hesitation, but now he'd give an unqualified yes. He'd never seen a more miraculous transformation in a field agent. She wasn't perfect, far from it, but he could place his trust in her now. She used her intuition and stayed calm amid explosions and high-pressure deadlines. Too bad her trip had been hampered by whatever was ailing her—most likely her diet.

Thirteen hours later, they arrived at their destination. The Peninsula hotel in Hong Kong had the reputation and level of service Simon expected when he traveled. He booked a harbor view suite and enjoyed observing Cassie's reaction to the view of Victoria Harbor and the modern skyline, lit up with a million lights and bit of moonlight, too. But before Simon could persuade her to share strawberries and chocolate with him, she'd fallen asleep.

The next morning, she was up before him and practicing yoga in the living room. He'd take advantage of her flexibility later. When she saw him, she jumped up and gave him a kiss before pouring them each some orange juice. Damn, he'd love to wake up to that every morning.

"It's so beautiful here." Her hands pressed against the glass, and she stood still as though absorbing the view like a photograph.

"I'm glad you like it. We'll be here for a few days while I find a way to blackmail Dane into releasing our cargo."

"Dane stopped the shipment? I don't understand why he's being so difficult." She sounded surprised. Dane had been her hero in the past month, and it made sense she wouldn't see him as the jerk who was holding up the deal. She didn't know he was CIA.

Simon stared through the windows at the huge city in front of them. "If Pelican is listed as a supplier to a country that has an arms embargo imposed on it by the United Nations, the company could be fined heavily, and in some cases, officers of the company could be arrested."

"He'd get arrested?" Cassie approached him behind and slid her arms around his waist. She rested her head on his shoulder, the only woman he'd been with who was tall enough to do that in bare feet.

"No. He's not an officer, but his bosses could be interrogated, and the company doesn't need that kind of press."

He held her arms in place as he pivoted to face her. A lift of her chin and they were locked in a delicious kiss. A kiss from her morphed his screwed up world into heaven on Earth. Her lips opened, and her sweet breath took him to a place where a beautiful woman could reside with him forever, filling his life with comfort and passion. In his dream, he'd do the cooking, and she'd heat up his nights.

"I want you so badly, but I need to go downstairs to see someone who might be able to get the drones out of France." He pulled away with difficulty, his own body fighting his efforts, her body trying to seal itself to his.

Cassie's moan turned into a deep sigh. "Okay. But understand I'll be sitting next to you during the meeting with the North Koreans, completely horny and frustrated. And just maybe without my *knickers*."

He rested his head on hers and kissed her forehead, refusing to let himself become lost in her. Not right now. "I'm glad you told me that, because my job isn't difficult enough."

# CHAPTER 21

Simon slipped away from Cassie for his one-hour meeting. Dane opened the door to his room and gestured him inside before Simon could knock.

"Nice place. Remember back in 2010, meeting Miss Philippines and her sister? Good times." Dane's smile revealed nothing of his current mood.

Simon stepped closer to him without a smile. "I want the drones."

"I have conditions."

"If this deal falls through, you're out of a job."

"First, I want to know your purchaser."

"No."

"Second, I need to know how you plan to keep the weapons from detonating. Third..."

"There's acid located behind the explosives, it incinerates the drone upon detonation. In the test, we found only the smallest, unidentifiable fragments."

"And finally, is Cassie with you? Because I have need for a long legged blonde tonight."

Simon held back. Dane was goading him, and he wouldn't take the bait as he had in France.

"You've trusted me in the past. You need to do so right now," Simon replied.

"My gut tells me this one is different, and it's going to be my ass that will be burned."

"I'll give a few details in exchange for the release of the crates. But you can't interfere."

"I'll stay out of it unless I feel my interests are compromised. At that point, I can't promise anything."

"Deal." Simon sat on the couch and mapped out the basic plan in exchange for Dane's phone call to the French authorities.

An hour later, Simon and Cassie met their contacts at the restaurant called Above and Beyond. They had a private room and a very discrete waitstaff. Simon described the drones to the men, but he couldn't provide them the technical minutia without revealing gaps in his knowledge. He invited Cassie to go over some of the technological details, without revealing a few extra modifications they'd made to the machines. Their clients didn't need to know about the acid hidden under the explosives to eradicate the evidence.

Mr. Lee appeared to be the most technically minded and barraged Cassie with questions. "Ms. Watson, do you believe these drones can transmit payload imagery to a remote position?"

"The way they've been programmed, the only video interface is with the driver. If you want additional views broadcast to an isolated command center, I'll need a few additional days." Cassie explained. She seemed to have garnered the respect of the men in the room with her breadth of understanding.

Mr. Lee shook his head. "I don't think that will be necessary. We want the shipment within the week. Time is the enemy. What about the explosive materials? Can they be stored anywhere?"

"A typical munitions warehouse or storage unit would suffice for a few days, until you decide to engage in your mission." Simon tried to reaffirm their use of safe storage methods to minimize the loss of life.

"We cannot store them with the military units, as there are too many men willing to be bought off for better living conditions for their families, a promotion, and the gratitude of the government. We've identified twenty men who can carry out our objectives. The drones will stay with them in special backpacks until they are deployed."

"That's not optimal. Could you keep them in one location until the mission?" Simon pushed, but the businessmen were fairly stubborn about this point.

Mr. Lee shook his head and scowled as though Simon had asked him to blow up his own family. "No. Keeping them apart from each other ensures we will have enough to succeed in the mission, even losing a few."

Cassie sat stunned. Simon could see the lines on her forehead revealing her stress. She hadn't foreseen any casualties at all in this operation. She was still a pacifist, despite her employment with a hard-ass agency that justified murder when the need arose. He could feel her foot tapping in nervous waves against his leg. They'd figure out a solution when they returned to the hotel. After all, they didn't even have possession of the drones right now. Although according to Dane, they'd be shipped out of France to South Korea in a few hours.

The first thing Simon did upon arriving in their suite was to pour himself a drink. A vodka, no ice. Nirvana in a glass.

Cassie stretched out across the sofa and stared into the harbor lights. She didn't talk much at all during the ride to and from the meeting. Something was bothering her, and it wasn't the storage of the drones.

"Care for some wine?"

"No, thanks."

He moved a step closer to her and lifted his glass toward her. "Vodka?"

She laughed. "No. I'm fine."

"You're acting like something's wrong. As your boss, I need to be informed of everything that concerns me and the assignment."

"My issue has more to do with you than the assignment." She was no longer laughing.

"Am I too much for you in bed?"

"Not enough." She pulled on his arm so he was seated next to her on the couch. A smile emerged, but didn't engage all her facial muscles.

He placed his drink on the table and then nuzzled her neck until she purred. His hand dropped to her chest, and he paused at the intensity of her breathing. Too deep and erratic. Her heart was also beating at a speed much faster than it ought to be while snogging. Something more was going on. He sat up, pulled his hands off her, and took a swig of the vodka to prepare for whatever she needed to say. "Spill it, Watson. I hate puzzles and games."

"I'm pregnant." The hesitancy in her voice explained everything.

*Pregnant?* He could handle a lot of crap thrown at him, and anticipated all sorts of obstacles preventing him from completing missions, but he wasn't expecting that. Did she realize what this meant? He didn't.

Could he marry her? Should he marry her? Was the baby okay? Was she okay? No wonder she was so sick. Her body held an additional occupant. He'd be sick as hell if he had another being living within him, too. His brain spun around at a million miles an hour. Then he looked at her.

A deer in the headlights, waiting to see his response. He held his breath a moment, said a quick thank you to God for bringing Cassie into his life, and then smiled. He'd found his match, and she was more amazing than he'd ever imagined. And now she was carrying his child.

"You're good with this?" she asked. Tears streamed down her face, perhaps in relief.

"We're going to have the tallest child ever. I hope she has blonde hair and blue eyes like her mother."

"A girl?"

"I'll take a boy, but he has to promise to become a professor like his uncle."

She stared at him, and then her eyes lit up, "Henry's your brother."

"Half brother, on our father's side. So Alex's baby will have a cousin."

"I'm an only child, so I think that's wonderful." She sniffled.

He held her in his arms and listened to her heart beating slow and steady, as it should. Plans had to be changed, the assignment modified. The most important thing now was to keep her away from the crazy bastards who had just purchased the drones. She had no idea how ruthless these men could be. They wanted success at all costs and would throw anyone under the bus to prevent their exposure to their government. Too bad he might lose the heart of the woman he loved in the process of keeping her, and their child, safe.

---

CASSIE ENJOYED the afternoon at the spa at Simon's insistence, while he tried to needle Dane into freeing up the drones sooner rather than later. He'd told her about Dane's involvement in the CIA and most of the pieces of their friendly rivalry came into focus. No wonder Dane had tried to steal her away. They'd played this game over the course of the many assignments they'd shared. The outcome didn't matter because the women were willing and the men were horn dogs. The fact that Simon never stopped her from going to Dane's office to obtain the codes meant he trusted her to outfox a CIA operative, and she had. She smiled to herself. Simon did trust her as a field agent.

*Nice.*

When she arrived back at the room, a huge bouquet of red roses and a small wrapped box sat in the middle of the round glass table in the foyer of their suite. His true colors were revealed. He was a romantic. She opened the card next to the gift.

. . .

CASSIE (THAT'S *your name from now to the end of time, because I don't want our child being confused if someone calls you anything else),*

*I may seem heartless and cold at times, but I promise I will always protect you and take care of you and the little person you're carrying. Nothing is more important to me than your health and safety. When this assignment is over, I'd love it if you would become my wife. I'll understand if right now you refuse me, but the offer stands for as long as I'm alive.*

*With love and an apology,*
*Simon*

AN APOLOGY? Why would he have to apologize?

She opened the box and pulled out a ring. A huge square-cut aquamarine in a platinum setting. Her favorite stone. She slid the ring onto her finger. Of course she'd marry him. Why wouldn't she marry the man who made her feel beautiful and loved and intelligent and alive?

The flowers also contained a small note. She opened it.

STAY *in the hotel until I return from Korea. I should be back in a week. I've paid for your room and anything else you may need. Take care of yourself, angel.*

*Love, Simon*

HE JUST KICKED her off the assignment? That controlling jerk. He couldn't do that. She was essential. She grabbed her cell phone.

Simon answered and spoke in a straight-business voice. Not the best voice for a proposal, but perfect for an abandonment. "Cassie. How are you feeling after your spa day?"

"Where are you?"

"At the airport."

"No. Don't leave me. I need to be there." She ran back to the bedroom and noticed Simon's things were no longer there. She grabbed her bag. Her heart thudded into a gallop as she raced to get to him.

"It's my call. This is the last thing I want to do, but tensions are running high with all parties. If the businessmen suspect that I, or the team, are prepared to rat them out to their government, they could cut ties and try to eliminate the evidence. You've completed your job and can wait there safely until I return."

He sounded calm. He had no idea how much she hated being abandoned like this in a strange country. She needed to be with him. Pregnancy was not a disability. She could still use her mind. How dare he make that decision for her?

She threw her things from the closet into the suitcase in a huge pile of unfolded chaos. "I'm packing my things and meeting you at the airport. You have no right to leave me behind. You need me. If there's a malfunction, I can fix it on the spot."

"My flight leaves in ten minutes, you won't make it."

"I'll take the next one." She grabbed her toiletries and shoes with shaking hands.

"Not without your passport."

She paused. "You took my passport? Seriously."

"I'm dead serious. There's a problem. Nothing to do with you, but I don't want you to be here if this whole thing implodes. Something's not right. I can feel it, and I can't be worried about you and effectively perform my job."

"This is ridiculous. You can't hold me here against my will." She sat down on the edge of the bed. Heat rising through her body. "Someone needs to train the troops so they don't blow themselves up when using the drones. You don't understand the program well enough to keep people safe."

"I'm not as worried about them as I am about you. You're my responsibility, and now Junior is as well."

*This is about the baby.* He couldn't help being an overprotective jerk. It was part of his nature. But she wouldn't let him do this.

"What about the people who could die if something goes wrong? Don't they matter?" she yelled into the phone. Her hand shook at the realization that she couldn't help anyone if she was locked away. Simon would accept a certain amount of casualties— casualties that she could prevent.

"It's my mission, my call."

"Don't do this. I can help you," she pleaded.

"No."

"I hate you."

"That's okay. I love you enough to make up for that."

"That's the dumbest thing I've ever heard." She hit the wall and shuddered as pain shot through her palm. "Don't expect to come back and have everything good between us, because I don't take abandonment lightly."

"I'll wait."

"You'll be waiting forever." And forever after that as well.

"I have more patience than you do. Look, the doors are closing now. Stay safe. I love you."

"No, you don't," she screamed into the phone. "Don't do this."

"Goodbye, angel."

The call ended, and Cassie burst into tears.

# CHAPTER 22

—— ✐ ——

Cassie fell asleep on the couch and awoke several hours later. Now that the panic and anger had cleared from her mind, she could think rationally, so she called Tucker. He put her on this mission. He'd want her to complete it.

"Cassie Watson. You're not dead yet, so I assume you're faring well with your boy toy."

She tried to release the image of him pointing a gun at her in the flat and spoke with as much calm as could muster. "Simon left me in Hong Kong. I can't get out."

"Did he tie you down?"

"No. He took my passport."

"Stupid girl. Either you're having a lovers' quarrel, or Simon doesn't think you have what it takes to be on his team."

She held back what Simon had told her about Tucker's botched fieldwork.

"Where are you on the assignment? Were the drones armed successfully?" he continued.

She hesitated before answering. Simon didn't want her to contact the main office without his permission, but what choice did he leave her?

"Yes. Everything's set."

"Are they still going through Yonchon?"

"He only mentioned Daecheong Island."

"Excellent. I assume he's set up safeguards to prevent the detonation of the devices in the home villages of the soldiers."

"What do you mean *villages*?" Her voice climbed three octaves.

He laughed as though innocent children blown to smithereens was hysterical. "From what my sources tell me, the soldiers are taking the drones home at night for safekeeping. They don't want to risk losing the bunch in a mass explosion."

"Oh my God. They said that, but I didn't think they were taking them *home*."

"You met with the businessmen?"

"Yes. We can't let them harm those families. I need to disarm the drones."

His voice sobered. "I'm afraid I have no ability to get you out of the country. If only you knew an American with contacts."

"I think I know someone who could help."

"Do I know him or her?"

She paused again, a terrible habit when trying to conceal something. "No. I'll contact him and see if he can assist me."

He hung up before she could say good-bye.

Her anger and shattered nerves decreased after an hour of pacing back and forth. Tucker offered no help, as expected. He didn't help her out of jail, so why would he tick off Simon and assist her in following him? She needed Dane. Now that she knew his actual job, she understood how she left jail so quickly, without press or an international incident.

He'd programmed his cell phone number into her phone before they left Jordan, in case she needed anything. She did now. With a deep breath and false sense of bravado, she pushed the button. The phone rang several times before he answered. She heard a giggle in the background. This would have been her replacement if she'd decided to stay with him instead of Simon.

"Hi, gorgeous. Simon finally bore you in bed?" The giggles increased in the background. Were there two women with him?

"I need to speak with you…in private."

He paused. "Where are you?"

"I'm in Hong Kong."

"Good. Give me five minutes." He hung up the phone.

She placed the phone on the coffee table and poured herself some water while she waited for him to call back.

A few minutes later, someone knocked at the door. She looked through the hole in the door. *Dane?*

Why was he in Hong Kong? Did Simon know? She opened the door and backed up to let him in. His eyes roamed over her outfit, and he grinned. Not the best choice of clothes to keep Dane away.

When Cassie had arrived back from the spa, she'd been dressed to kill in a short red skirt, a low cut white blouse, and candy-apple-red heels that took her height to six feet five inches. Simon's height. Ready to seduce him. Now she was a wrinkled mess. All of her other clothes sat in a ball in her suitcase, ready to go nowhere except to the cleaners for some ironing.

"Hey there, beautiful. Don't I get a hug for old times sake?" He opened his arms for her, but she stood staring, still not understanding why he was in this particular part of the world.

Never one to be put off, he stepped closer. "You caught me at a bad time. Perhaps you can make it up to me."

She crossed her arms in front of her chest. "I know who you are."

"No loss. Simon shares everything with his partners. He always has. I also know a lot about you, Catherine Wallace."

Hearing her real name melted her brave facade. She wasn't sure how much he knew, or what she should tell him, but she needed to reprogram those drones before innocent children died.

His eyes narrowed in a predatory manner, and he moved beside her before she could get out of the way.

"Now that I know you're his partner and not his lover, we can make up for lost time."

She shook her head. "That's off the table. First, you have another woman's perfume all over you. Not the way to my heart.

And second, I'm not a toy. You and Simon will just need to find something else to compete over in the future."

He shrugged. "How can I help you, beautiful?"

"Simon and I had a fight, and he left me here."

"You're a big girl. Go back to London."

"I can't. He took my passport."

Dane laughed. "He's good. So what can I do for you? Hong Kong has closer ties to the U.K. than to the U.S."

"I'm still an American. And Tucker refuses to help me. And I can't go to the embassy. Not after Jordan."

"Tucker?" His expression changed to something dangerous. She shouldn't have mentioned his name. It tended to make the men around her angry. There were so many things about her new position that she still didn't understand.

She stayed silent for a second too long. He lifted her chin so her face was within an inch of his. The tension now showing in his neck caused her stomach to tighten.

"I need to know what Tucker's doing on this transaction, or I'm walking out of here."

The needs of the children in North Korea trumped Tucker's need to be anonymous. "He's the MI6 contact on this."

"Simon never told me Tucker worked this assignment. Who wanted you working with the drones? Simon or Tucker?"

"Tucker handpicked me for this assignment." Although she had no idea why Tucker had chosen her over a handful of others just as competent.

"Does Simon know this?"

"I think so."

His expression softened a tiny bit. "If Simon wants you in Hong Kong, I'd trust him. He has great instincts."

"I have to fix the drones. When I called Tucker about Simon leaving me here, he told me about the possibility of the drones detonating while they're being stored with families. Simon doesn't know that, but I'm sure he'll let me render them all useless to save lives."

Dane nodded, his focus fractured. "I'll help you on one condition."

She looked in those dark eyes. Devil or angel, it didn't matter. She'd do whatever he asked. She nodded her head.

"Good. I want all the drones back in my possession. If you can't do that, I'll hunt you down and kill you myself. Do you understand?" He placed his arm around her waist and kissed her on the lips as though sealing their bargain. She didn't kiss him back. Instead, her body remained stone-cold and motionless.

Dane directed her to the couch and sat next to her. He pulled out his phone and placed one of his fingers over Cassie's lips to keep her silent while he spoke to whomever he'd called.

"Greetings, my friend. I seem to have something you want."

She could hear Simon's voice in the background.

"Yes, she's a beauty. Very compliant too. Apparently, someone stranded her in Hong Kong without her passport. No problem. I can assist in getting her a temporary card to travel with me. We were thinking about taking a vacation to Daecheong Island. I hear it's very romantic."

Simon answered at such a high volume, Cassie could understand most of his words, which involved twisting off Dane's body parts and feeding them to wild dogs.

Dane snickered and pulled Cassie closer to him. "Here, he wants to say something you."

"Simon?"

"What the hell do you think you're doing? I gave you an order, and you need to follow it. Do not get on a plane."

She should have enabled full access to the drones from a distance. Instead, she'd left herself vulnerable. That wouldn't happen again if she could help it. "I have to. The drones are going to be stored in villagers' huts. Innocent families will be murdered —by us. I can't let that happen. I need access to them one more time. Please let me reprogram the drones and try to find a way to stop the massacre."

The curse Simon roared caused her body to flinch. Dane took the phone back.

"Don't bother, Simon. She's quite stubborn when she has a mind to be. We'll contact you when we arrive." He ended the call and returned the phone to his pocket.

Cassie's phone rang. She tried to get up to answer it, but Dane shook his head.

"Another condition is you forego contact with Simon until we arrive. I have no doubt he'll wait for you."

# CHAPTER 23

Simon hung up the phone and punched a wall in the house he'd rented. His fist went through and came back out with blood seeping from his knuckles. How could Cassie have contacted Dane? He didn't have her safety in mind, all he wanted was a bigger role in what Simon was doing.

He walked out of the small cottage to get the materials ready for the short boat ride from the South Korean island to the North Korean coastline. The businessmen would send someone to meet them and the transfer would take place just inside the border. He didn't like the information Cassie had relayed to him. If someone detonated the drones while they were in the villagers' houses, nothing would be able to roll back such an international disaster.

Perhaps all of this had gone too far. He considered contacting the South Korean authorities to raid his operation before he sent the weapons to North Korea. It might mean a few years in jail for him, but Cassie and the baby would stay safe and so would a bunch of villagers who had done nothing wrong. He tried to call her again, but she didn't pick up her phone. Dane probably forbid her to answer it so he could control the situation. He would have done the same thing.

A flight from Hong Kong to Seoul would only take three and a half hours, and they could charter a boat or helicopter to the island. He'd see her that afternoon.

The waiting was difficult, so he walked through the transfer details with his team. A few members of his most elite team had flown in after finishing a deal with a terrorist cell in Syria. These men had been through this many times and would make sure everything went as planned.

He sent them to rest in a house further in the village, leaving two men standing guard with the crates.

The only taxi on the island dropped Dane and Cassie off at ten minutes to midnight. Far later than he expected. Perhaps Dane had more trouble with the passport than anticipated.

Cassie, looking as though she'd walked all the way from Hong Kong, pulled her bag from the car at a slow rate. She was dressed in a tight red skirt, high red heels and blouse, and wasn't wearing the ring he'd given to her. He jumped up to assist her.

"Nice place you got here, buddy." Dane slapped him on the back.

"Fuck you."

"Right back at you."

"Cassie, follow me." Simon led her to a bedroom in the back of the hut. "I understand your inability to understand simple directions, but I'll try again. *Stay in here* until I come for you."

He didn't want her here, but now that she stood before him, he needed to hold her tight. He dropped her suitcase and pulled her into his arms. At first her muscles were tense, but after a few seconds, she relaxed and let out a heavy sigh. He kissed her with as much restraint as he could muster when all he really wanted to do was throw her over his knee and spank her for insubordination —and because she had an amazing ass.

Her body leaned into his for support. He couldn't convince himself to release the warmth she sent through him for another minute or two. Dane could wait.

She pulled her head back and stared at him with a strained expression. "I was wrong."

He held her tighter. "I wasn't. I want you, but I don't want you here. It's not safe and you need to trust me, or we have nothing."

She nodded. "I'm sorry. When Tucker told me about the villagers, I panicked. And I didn't know Dane would order me around so much."

"You spoke to Tucker?"

"I called him for help, but he refused."

"Back up a second. Tucker told you about where the drones would be stored? How did he know? He should have no contact with the buyers."

"I thought he arranged everything."

"No. I arrange my own deals. MI6 will send me in the right direction as they hear requests by target groups under their surveillance, and they'll occasionally bail me out, but the less people I work with, the less things tend to go wrong. This whole project is starting to smell."

His heartbeat pushed up three notches. Tucker should be in the dark on this assignment except for connecting him and Cassie to the contacts in Jordan. "How much did you tell him?"

"I told him the drones had been armed, and they were on the way to South Korea."

*Damn it.* "I told you not say *anything* to the prat. Don't you ever listen?"

Cassie pulled back from him as though he'd slapped her with his words. Shit. He shouldn't be taking out his anger on her.

"Sorry," he apologized. The stress she'd experienced couldn't be good for Junior. She needed forgiveness, and he needed her safe. He rubbed his thumb over her lips and dropped his mouth to taste her again. Her lips parted, allowing him to savor her intoxicating essence. She couldn't be that mad at him.

His work ethic stopped him from lowering her onto the bed. "I need to meet with Dane. *Stay here.* I intend to make you scream tonight."

She pressed further into his embrace. "In pleasure or pain?"

"Exactly."

————————— ❧ —————————

When Simon returned downstairs, Dane was sitting at a table thumbing through information Simon had left in plain sight. Nothing important. Timetables, flight schedules, and a list of materials needed to finish his preparation for the transfer.

The simple room decorated with a clean white design with black appliances and a wooden table felt crowded with the two large men in it. Simon grabbed two beers from the refrigerator and a box of Saewookkang.

Dane took one of the beers and a handful of the shrimp crackers. "I don't get it. She's crazy about you."

"She tell you that?"

"She didn't have to. Everything in her body language screamed *taken*. You're a lucky bastard. She's a terrific woman."

"I know. That's why I didn't want her here." He took a breath and shook his head to rid himself of the dread filling his psyche. "She's pregnant."

Dane's hand paused before the cracker hit his mouth. "Didn't see that coming. Yours?"

Simon nodded, and a slight smile lifted his expression. Definitely his.

"Congratulations, I guess. Are you ready for a shift in priorities?"

"More than ready. I asked her to marry me, after I left her in Hong Kong. She hinted that I had no chance in hell of marrying her. Although after she spent time with you, I think I can change her mind. I see myself retired and living a quiet life in the countryside somewhere, with a few hellions and a certain blonde bombshell."

"You better have a top-notch security system. I know several people who would love to pay you back for arms deals gone wrong."

Simon laughed. "I hear Iceland is nice."

"Enjoy, old man. I'm not ready for the farm yet."

"Trust me. When it's time, you'll know. I've been thinking about it since Nicola died."

"That was a huge loss. You had a great partner."

Simon nodded and took a large swig. He missed her competence, but she'd never have settled down with him. She'd lived and died for her job. Cassie was different.

"I still do. But I don't want Cassie to end up like Nicola, especially since she prefers playing with computer programs in an office."

Dane grabbed some paper and a pen. "Then let's get ourselves out of this mess. What do you know about Tucker handpicking Cassie for the job?"

Tension clamped his chest. Tucker handpicked her? "Nothing. Why would he put her in an impossible situation and then mock her when she failed?"

"Maybe he wants her to fail."

Simon paused as his brain unscrambled the puzzle that had twisted his thoughts since Cassie's arrival in his life. "No. Cassie's only collateral damage." Tucker's interest in the transaction suddenly made sense. "I can't believe I missed it. He's after blood. Yours and mine. He linked this assignment to your company to drag you in. This assignment is officially over."

Dane clenched his fist around the pen. "He's tangled me in this shit up to my eyebrows. When this is over, I'm seeking my own revenge. Tucker won't know what hit him."

"You'll need to beat me to it. He'll never work in the government again when I finish trashing his reputation and revealing his illegal collaboration with the North Koreans."

Dane drew out a timetable to provide the South Koreans with enough information to thwart the sale of the drones. The South Korean government would receive credit for stopping an anonymous plot against them and look like heroes, the North Korean businessmen would never be named, and the drones would stay in Dane's possession. Most important, the plan would enable

Simon to start his family life in peace. As much peace as he could find, always looking over his shoulder.

Dane tapped his pen on the table. "I recommend having an escape plan to pull you and Cassie off the island. If the authorities come, you don't want to spend your kid's first ten years in prison for selling arms to the wrong people. I'll arrive in time for clean up with the South Korean authorities. And I want the drones destroyed or returned."

That was fair. Dane didn't need to take the fall for Simon's lack of foresight.

"If you can get them out of here, they're yours." Simon leaned back in his chair, beer in hand. There had to be an easier way to handle this. "We might be able to make this go away without any government involvement. If the drones never enter North Korea, the businessmen will be unable to complain about the loss. They certainly won't complain to their own government. If they realize how close they came to being to ratted out, they may just fade back into the shadows."

Standing up and taking his phone out, Dane walked to the living room. "I need to make a few phone calls to obtain transport for the drones to a more secure location. If I can succeed without any government's involvement, we may be able to use them for retirement purposes sometime in the future, and I may avoid being demoted to mail boy."

"If you organize the transport, I'll give you the directions to my warehouse in Turkey. They should be safe there until we either disarm them or sell them."

"Perfect."

Simon heard the door close outside as Cassie peeked her head into the room. She looked tired, but gorgeous. Her typical appearance lately.

"I'm assuming you heard everything."

She walked up to him and rested her hands the table. "I didn't realize how dangerous this was. Could you really go to jail?"

"Occupational hazard. Let's hope everything gets cleaned up before that happens."

She paced back and forth, and Simon knew she had more on her mind than arms deals.

"Spill it, Watson. You suck at keeping issues to yourself."

"It's not about the assignment. It's about us."

"I'm listening."

"Do you really want to marry me, or are you just trying to make the baby legitimate?"

"My parents weren't married, since my father happened to be married to Henry's mother at the time. So I won't lie and tell you it's not a concern of mine. But I wouldn't marry just anyone. I've wanted you since you first pointed a gun at my head."

"That's the most romantic thing anyone's ever said to me." She laughed and her whole face lit up. She bent forward and kissed him. He needed to ship her away from this nightmare immediately. The next boat to the mainland was in ten hours, and she'd be on it. He pulled her onto his lap.

"If you won't include me in your little romantic interlude, then keep it behind bedroom doors." Dane strolled into the room and sat at the table next to them.

"You're definitely not included," Simon said.

"No loss. I wouldn't mess around with a pregnant woman, especially when her overprotective baby daddy is in the room."

"Keep it that way."

Dane nodded with a smirk. "Everything's set. We have fifteen hours to clean up and abandon ship. If we scrub everything thoroughly enough, the authorities don't need to be involved."

"Great. Let's get to work." He stood up, still holding Cassie. She slid down his body and stood nestled in his arms. "Cassie, there's no need to reprogram the drones since they aren't traveling to North Korea, so go get some rest. The ferry will be leaving in the morning and I'm asking you to get on it and travel back to Seoul."

"But…"

"Please. I'll follow you as soon as everything here is finished. If we get caught, we'll end up in prison. And we'll lose custody of our child. I couldn't bear that to happen."

Dane left the room, probably to avoid a possible battle between lovers. Cassie, however, had more sense than that.

"The drones are going with Dane?" she asked.

"Yes."

"And I'm not needed?"

"By me, yes, but not for the rest of the assignment."

She let out deep breath and then nodded. "Should I meet you in the penthouse suite at the nicest hotel in the city?"

"You read my mind."

# CHAPTER 24

———————————— ✆ ————————————

In the earliest hours of the morning, Cassie put on jeans and a shirt and walked out to see the drones. She waved to the guards and moved authoritatively from crate to crate. She added another safeguard to the drones, just in case. Then she needed to run to the bathroom. The little guy or girl inside her decided to create more havoc in her digestive system. If this lasted every day until the baby was born, she'd weigh only fifty pounds when she delivered.

She returned to an amazing sight—Simon sleeping. He was completely naked and sprawled out across the bed without any show of modesty. He didn't need any. Having a body like that would make most men confident. The long, thick muscles of a heavyweight boxer, the face that showcased masculine, hard features, and the ability to fulfill this woman's every sexual fantasy. What would it be like to wake every morning in his arms? She might know when this assignment is over. Would he ever regret asking her to marry him? Doubts bubbled up through her indigestion. She needed fresh air.

She slipped out of the house and began walking toward the ocean. The morning air was salty and cool. The path curved down the side of the small mountain for a mile or so to the village, a picturesque place sitting on the edge of the sea. The dark water moved slowly, in subtle waves that hit the wharf with a billowing exhalation followed by a deep inhalation. Several fishermen were preparing their boats for a long workday. They didn't speak, just moved heavy coolers into place and prepared their nets and lines. Otherwise, everything was silent.

She sat on the dock and returned the waves of several of the local men as their boats chugged away from the island. Her stomach growled, and she placed a hand over it. A sense of calm filled her. The doubts floated away with the early morning boats. She trusted Simon without question. He'd be there for her. Perhaps it was the hormones warping her intuition, but she would stake her life on his commitment to her.

The walk up to the house took longer than the descent. Simon and Dane stood outside directing men to load the crates into a helicopter. They needed to get the drones out of there to stop the mission.

"Good morning, beautiful." Dane waved her over.

Simon stood with his feet apart, and his hands fisted by his sides. He wore a frown held up by a clenched jaw. "You need to be down at the boat in half an hour. I'd appreciate you informing me when you take off on one of your long walks."

"Nervous I'll leave you?"

"No. Nervous someone will take you." He wrapped his arms around her and pulled her into a bear hug, kissing her temple. "Seriously, don't leave this area. It's not safe right now. I don't know who to trust, except Dane. And even he wants you in his bed."

A smile appeared on her face. Simon, the big threatening arms dealer, cared. He cared about her, he cared about his family, he cared about his friends, and he cared about complete strangers. How cool was that?

Dane stepped back and put up his hands in surrender. "I'm not ready to settle down and be a father. She's all yours."

One of the helicopter crew jogged over. "Mr. Dunn, several small crates are in the barn. Should we leave them?"

"Small crates?" Simon released her and stepped toward the man he'd introduced to her earlier as Greg, a four-year member of his security team. "The drones never left the large crates, so there shouldn't be anything left in the barn. Did the guards see anything last night?"

"I don't know," said Greg, "but the loading crew asked me to get you."

"I'll meet you back in the cottage," Simon said to Cassie before walking to the barn.

Dane turned away to take a phone call. Cassie's stomach told her it was time to find something to eat before Simon returned and forced her to eat dried fish or something else with extra protein.

---

SIMON MADE his way to the barn with Greg a few steps behind him. Why were there extra crates? He'd counted the freight himself when it arrived. He'd never worked with this particular helicopter crew. Another mistake. Another weak link. He signaled Greg to back him up.

The barn doors were propped open, and Simon strode past Greg. The place was empty, as it should be, with the large crates already loaded on the helicopter. Then he saw the massacre in the back corner of the barn. Regret erupted into pure rage.

All of his security team, except Greg, had been shot dead. This was a set up. Before Simon could reach his weapon, a member of the flight team shot Greg in the temple. The kid didn't stand a chance. The asshole who shot him would not die without serious pain inflicted upon him first, because Simon hated traitors more than he hated any other type of human. He reached for his gun and calmly pointed it the murderer.

"Put the gun down, Mr. Dunn." The man was already pointing a Browning handgun at his forehead.

*Where was Cassie?* Simon kept his pistol directed at the guy's face and stood completely still. The asshole smiled, too comfortable looking down the barrel of a gun aimed to kill.

"This doesn't bode well for your life expectancy." Simon shifted toward a wood column in the center of the room with a rigid precision meant to keep his enemy calm.

"I'll be compensated well for my work. Don't worry about me."

"Is your boss anyone I know?"

"I'm quite sure you know him." He glanced over his shoulder at the sound of a footstep by the door.

The man's knee exploded like a balloon filled with red paint. He fell to the ground, howling.

"Drop the weapon." Dane ran into the barn and kicked the gun from the man's hand as he screamed in pain. He turned to Simon. "Okay?"

"My crew, every one of them." He hissed the words through a snarl. "Where's Cassie?"

"She was heading to the house."

"Shit."

# CHAPTER 25

—————————————— ⌀ ——————————————

Before she could enter the house, a member of the flight team intercepted her quest for nourishment.

"Ms. Watson, the pilot needs you to look at the placement of the cargo prior to takeoff."

He clasped her by the arm and escorted her to the helicopter.

Why would the pilot need her? Simon handled transportation logistics. Maybe they wanted to ask her something about securing the drones. Since Dane had also disappeared into the barn with Simon, she walked with the man to find out the problem.

The rotors were already turning, blowing dirt and making a lot of noise. She ducked under to get to the side door, and away from the mini-sandstorm. The man who told her to go to the copter lifted her inside. The crates were all packed and ready to transport, but something wasn't right. Before she could ask anything, someone moved quickly from her right side and grabbed her shoulders, forcing her into a seat and restrained her in place with the safety harness.

She yelled, but the sound from the rotors accelerating into full velocity swallowed her screams. As she struggled to free herself, the men pulled her arms back and secured them with canvas straps. The noise increased. The intensity of the sound rung through her ears. Her eyes began to water in frustration.

Outside she watched Simon and Dane run full speed toward her. Simon sprinted ahead of Dane and pulled one of the men out of the helicopter before he could slam the door, but the helicopter continued to move. He grabbed for the helicopter a second too late. She was already flying above them.

Someone pulled the door closed, sat next to her, and secured himself to the bench. Within minutes, they were flying over the ocean. A few fishing boats could be seen in the distance and then nothing but water and sky.

---

THE DRAFT of the rotors kicked dirt in Simon's face and temporarily blinded him. When the air settled, he watched in horror as Cassie was spirited away from him.

"Cassie!" he yelled at the sky. Fury and anger shredded his last thread of control. His captive tried to move away from his side. A mistake. Simon dragged him back and proceeded to punch his face until blood spewed from his nose and mouth onto the ground. Dane pulled his arms back to stop him.

"Simon, enough. Get him into the kitchen. I'll drag in the other, if he hasn't bled out in the barn yet. We'll figure this out. Get a grip." Releasing his arms, he walked away.

Simon remained on the ground for a moment until he heard a moan. He pulled the injured man to his feet by squeezing his neck and yanking him up. He wanted to kill him, but Dane was right. They needed information, or he'd never get Cassie back. He forced the bastard into the house and tied him to the chair, making sure to break his humerus along the way. The man's eyes had swollen shut, and his nose was twisted and deformed. Blood coated his clothes and dripped onto the floor. Simon's clothes were also stained red.

Dane arrived a few minutes later dragging the man he'd shot.

The asshole's knee was missing and in its place was a gaping wound. Dane had pulled and secured his arms behind his back until his shoulders dislocated. The man's face had a few adjustments made since Simon had last seen him. His right eye was swollen shut, and a small amount of blood dripped from the corner of his mouth. Dane forced him into a chair near the other and secured him to it.

Simon rinsed off his hands and face in the sink to calm down. His anger needed to be channeled into a functional outlet. He'd be useless to Cassie if he panicked. His actions by the helicopter gave him pause. Never in his life did he want to destroy someone with such rage. If Dane hadn't pulled him off that son of a bitch, he'd have killed him. He had no doubt about it.

Dane, still facing the two men, typed into his phone. Simon pulled out his gun again, pointing it at the one without a knee.

"What the hell is going on?" He struck the wound of the nearest asshole with the butt of his gun.

The man flinched. His hands and legs shook in mini convulsions. "We were given orders to take the cargo and the girl."

"Who did you get your order from?"

"I don't know."

A gunshot rang out. The man screamed as blood poured from his shoe. Dane pulled back his weapon and stared him down, shouting over the man's screams. "I don't think you understood the question. Who are you taking orders from?"

Simon didn't react to the loud ringing in his ears from the gunshot. He wanted answers, and he and Dane would dismantle these men piece by piece if they didn't get them.

The man couldn't speak, until Dane lifted his gun again and pointed at his other foot.

He spit some blood out of his mouth and struggled to talk. "We don't know. The pilot, Sean, received a large amount of cash for the job. He promised to distribute half now and the other half after everything's complete."

His body began to shut down from the blood loss. Simon, however, needed more answers.

"What's the task?" Simon asked.

"The drones. Deliver them to North Korea. Train the soldiers. Leave the girl." His voice began to fade, and he passed out.

Simon's heart raced. He gripped the side of the table with his left hand to prevent himself from shooting the guy in the head. *Leave her in North Korea? She'd be gunned down as a spy. A U.S. spy.*

Dane moved closer to the traitor, his gun directed at his balls. "Who sent the money?"

"An English guy. He said Mr. Dunn worked for him." His words were muffled through the broken nose and teeth.

Dane turned to Simon. "Tucker."

The gun in Simon's hand grew warm. One bullet through the head of the nearest traitor would relieve his growing stress, but he needed to find an alternative method of keeping his cool. "We'll focus on his death later. We need to locate Cassie."

Dane nodded. "I'm on it. I put new tracers on the drones after I arrived last night. Not that I didn't trust you, old friend, but things happen."

"Trust is overrated. Stay here." Simon grabbed their bags from the bedroom and packed his essentials.

When he returned, the two traitors were dead. Simon would never question Dane about his methods. And his friend would never speak about them. That was how they'd both survived for so long.

Dane picked up his bag from next to the couch and dropped it by front door. He needed to remain behind to eliminate any trace of their encampment. Simon headed into town to charter a boat to North Korea. They'd chosen this location because of its proximity to their destination.

When he returned, Dane was sitting across from the two corpses, tapping into his phone. He never glanced up.

"Well?" Simon asked.

"They landed in Paechon County. Makes sense. It sits on the

Demilitarized Zone. I'm going to work on getting some assistance. You need to move quickly. I'll text you the exact coordinates. Let's get Cassie, and if we can, I want the drones as well."

Simon agreed, although at this moment, he didn't give a damn about the drones. Cassie's safety was everything.

He packed what he needed in a small backpack, slipped on a black knit hat, dressed in dark clothes, and started walking to the village. Dane would be traveling to the mainland on a U.S. Army helicopter from one of the local bases. Even years after he'd changed his name and transformed into a salesman, he still maintained the deepest connections in the government. Professional insurance. How he could mobilize military resources without informing his agency of the trouble brewing around him, Simon had no idea.

Halfway down the lane to the village, he saw the helicopter leave the island and then heard the explosives Dane had set in the house. A bright light flashed behind him. He ducked behind a car on the side of the road and watched several pieces of debris flutter past. No evidence of their time in the house remained, and no bodies would be recovered. Dane was always thorough.

# CHAPTER 26

⟳

She needed ear protection to shut out the extreme racket caused by the propellers, but no one cared about her health and safety. Could the loud noise hurt Junior? She refused to think about it. To keep sane, she focused on how to get away. A few minutes after take off, the ocean disappeared, and they flew over long stretches of rolling fields. After maybe an hour, they descended. Was this North Korea?

The men jumped into action when the craft touched down. They ignored her and unloaded the crates. Three men dressed in business suits watched from the ground. One or two of them looked familiar from the meeting in Hong Kong. The pilot was speaking to them and pointing in her direction. They all laughed.

She'd been a victim in Jordan. She refused to be one here. Every time they moved her to a new location, Simon would have more and more difficulty finding her. Escaping as soon as possible was the only solution. She tried to untie her hands, but they were bound together securely. To make matters worse, the area outside the helicopter appeared flat and rural. If she ran, she'd be an easy target for a high-powered rifle or even a handgun. Escape wouldn't be easy.

After the crates were unloaded and the helicopter was shut

down, they untied her. Her shoulders hurt from being propped in such an awkward position. She didn't have time to shake them out before the pilot pushed her to the ground. On hands and knees, she met the businessmen for the second time. She forced herself to stand. Her height, at least four inches taller than the buyers, provided her more confidence and a tactical advantage.

Mr. Lee stepped forward, wearing more ambition and greed in his demeanor than he had in Hong Kong. His gaze made an appreciative turn around her figure before returning to her face. "Ms. Watson, thank you for agreeing to train the men selected for this assignment. We will compensate you for your efforts."

"Thank you." Arguing would waste her energy and make them keep a closer watch on her actions.

They moved the crates into two large trucks. Mr. Lee escorted her to the backseat of a black sedan. He sat next to her, placing his hand on her knee. She remembered Dane's pursuit of her and how she'd made it through. *Keep my thoughts calm and my mind active.*

A rumble behind the car caught her attention. Her kidnappers had returned to the helicopter and were leaving. An icy chill spread through her, numbing her emotions. *I trained for this. Think.* Years of meditation needed to be unleashed. She couldn't lose it.

The car traveled only a few miles to a beautiful estate. A pond surrounded by topiaries and a curved bridge welcomed them. She'd lost sight of the drones and hoped they'd arrive soon. She needed a chance to disarm them.

Mr. Lee helped her from the car. "Come, you must be hungry."

She wasn't hungry any longer. Her stomach had turned to stone as she struggled to keep herself from sinking into despair. Despite her lack of appetite, however, she needed food to remain strong.

"I'm famished." Her smile relaxed the leer in his eyes. He appeared only mildly dangerous now. Perhaps she could take him off guard. She wouldn't kill him, but maybe she could slow him down so she could hide.

The Spartan surroundings of the Jordanian prison filled her thoughts. Mr. Lee, on the other hand, turned out to be a very generous host. His staff served a lunch of fruit, seafood, and kimchi. She ate as much as could, including the salmon. Energy for her escape. She pretended to drink the sweet liquor he provided. The roses in the center of the dining room table absorbed most of it when he turned to speak to a servant.

As soon as the meal was over, he led her back to the car, but didn't get in with her. The driver transported her to a small field where someone had lined up all the drones. They wanted a flight demonstration, but not a sample detonation. That worked for her. She'd programmed the drones that morning to include a remote detonation system she could use from a cell phone. Her phone, however, was back on the island with Simon.

For three hours, she taught the twenty soldiers, plus two back-ups, how to lift off, how to hover, and a sequence to detonate the explosives when they reached their targets. The men, with the help of a translator, took her instructions seriously. She neglected to mention that the detonation would only occur with a certain security code typed into each of the controllers. She remained tight lipped about the code. If she needed a bargaining chip, the code would give her something of value to negotiate with.

Mr. Lee's car returned after the training and brought her back to his house. At least, she assumed it was his house by the way he ordered the staff around. He was obviously one of the lucky North Koreans favored by the government and given privileges and freedoms normal citizens would never enjoy.

They shared another meal together, and she was led by one of the female servants to a beautiful bedroom overlooking the back gardens, more dramatic and extensive than the gardens in front. Curving pines added a whimsical element to the gardens. Iron herons, with wings raised, decorated the edge of a meandering stream. And there were flowers—reds, blues, and yellows throughout the entire area. If she hadn't been planning on an escape from this potential hell, she would have enjoyed its beauty.

When the sun dropped into the horizon, she fell into a sound sleep on top of the covers, her hand covering her stomach.

———————— ✺ ————————

SPEAKING the language of money and need, Simon located a fisherman willing to help him off the island. The owner of the wooden fishing boat would only take him so far toward the mainland. When the sky darkened, he paid the man and untied the small dingy that followed the boat. The water had turned choppy as the day turned into night, but he forced the oars through the waves and began his first move in his quest to find Cassie and bring her home.

The shore didn't offer too many places to hide, and the darkness didn't help his ability to navigate.

He tugged the boat up the beach and hid it in a row of bushes. He may need it for the return trip. Dane had provided him with a phone with the GPS coordinates of the crates. As the only person who understood how to detonate them, Cassie had to be within a certain distance. The signal beamed from a spot about twenty kilometers from his current location. He needed a car. He walked up the coast until he found a few small wooden huts and a house with both a car and a rundown Honda motorcycle. Within five minutes, he had the motorcycle humming down the road toward the signal. His black outfit worked well in the shadows. He hoped he'd only be in the country for one night, but he was prepared for a longer stay if necessary.

Potholes and caved in curbs made traveling slower than he wanted. At one point, headlights ahead forced him into a field to avoid detection. When he finally hit the road again, he was covered in dirt.

He found the crates in a warehouse about eight miles from the DMZ. Sneaking past the few men guarding the site, he confirmed all twenty drones had been assembled and flown recently. No sign of Cassie. He used Google Earth and found a few houses in a village about six kilometers from his location.

After an exhaustive search, peeking in windows and crawling across dirt yards, he came up with nothing. Three kilometers outside the village, a huge house, completely out of place in the impoverished region, stood like Versailles amid French peasants' hovels. Bingo. Probably part of the compensation package of one of the bigwigs of a North Korean corporation.

Simon left the bike behind a decorative bridge and slipped past a guard patrolling the grounds. The ground floor was dark, but the upper floors had a few rooms with lights on. He pulled himself up to the edge of one of the ground floor windows, grasped the trim and clipped his feet onto a balcony the next story up—the type of balcony one would have in a master bedroom. He stayed to the side of the open door and saw Mr. Lee curled up with a nude woman with black hair. Not Cassie. She had to be in the house though. Lee was the main player in this game.

Simon climbed onto the ledge and moved to the next window. Nothing but a dressing room. Step by step, he crossed window to window, gripping the edge of the house like a rock climber. Two rooms down, he saw her. Asleep in bed, still dressed as she'd been that morning. Part of that knotted feeling in his gut unraveled. She looked healthy.

He knocked on the window, but turned at the arrival of three helicopters and a distant convoy of trucks. Military, all of them. *Shit.* He lost his footing and reached out to grab hold of the sill, but missed. His body prepared to hit whatever was under him. He sucked in a breath to stop from bellowing his position to the entire compound. Falling arse over tit, he landed hard on the grass under him. His back ached as a warning of some serious pain that would arrive later. He needed to get to Cassie, before his problems quadrupled.

*Too late.* The helicopters landed in an adjacent field. He could hear the troops piling out of the trucks. He ducked behind some tall decorative grass and hid, body flat, face to the ground. There was no way he would win in this situation. Five minutes earlier, and he'd have rescued her and been on the motorcycle back to the beach.

He turned his head to the side without lifting it off the ground. His view improved, but not perfectly. The soldiers searching the house turned on lights, illuminating room after room as they moved through different areas. He held his breath when they reached the second floor. A flashlight added to the light in Cassie's room. They were with her.

Within ten minutes, the troops pulled Lee, the woman in his bed, Cassie, and a dozen staff members out into the yard. They must be holding Lee's security detail in a separate location. Everyone but Cassie was dressed to sleep. For several minutes the soldiers milled around and Lee argued with them. Cassie edged from the middle to the side of the group and remained silent. Several soldiers lifted their rifles toward the group of people, as if they were lined up for an execution.

Simon's heart pounded in his chest. He needed to calm down, make a plan. With slow, methodical movements, he reached for his gun. He couldn't do much against twenty-plus soldiers, but if Cassie went down, the bastard who shot her would too.

Shouts between one of the higher-ranking men and Lee grew more heated until a soldier moved to Lee's side and slammed him in the face with the butt of his rifle. Blood spewed from his mouth, and he fell to his knees. The man who'd struck him stood over him until he received an order from the officer. Then he aimed his rifle at the back of Lee's head and fired. The woman with him and members of the staff shrieked. Several tried to run to safety, but were gunned down too.

Cassie remained still, showing no emotion. If she'd cried over Lee, they may have shot her. Instead, they cuffed her and moved her apart from the household staff. Her height and blonde hair made her different enough to interest them. She might make it out alive. *Stay strong, angel.*

# CHAPTER 27

———————— ❧ ————————

Cassie had practiced yoga and meditation for years. She was not the best at it, but when pulled out of bed by the North Korean military and forced to watch Mr. Lee die, she'd reached deep inside and utilized every calming technique she knew. When they'd placed the gun above his ear, she'd shut her eyes and focused on a memory of the sunset at the beach. Peaceful and relaxing. She'd heard the shot, heard the screams, and then more shots. She looked at her feet and tried to keep her expression blank as her emotions flew around her in a vortex of horror and fright.

She held her screams inside. She'd save her nervous breakdown for later, or she'd be dead. Why waste a few moments losing control? Tucker had taken pride in making her squirm when he pointed a gun at her head. No longer. If these men wanted her to die, she'd do it with dignity.

A young man in a uniform cuffed her hands behind her back and escorted her to a military truck. He pushed her into the empty backseat. Her shoulders hurt, being wrenched back into an impossible position. Leaning her head on the headrest to try to alleviate some of the strain on her arms, she shut her eyes to keep her mind from being overloaded with images. They lined up Mr.

Lee's staff and would probably be gunning them down soon. There was no point in her witnessing a mass murder. Her thoughts fled again to the beach, a blue sky, and waves that crashed on the sea wall—the perfect day for cranking on her surfboard.

Her biggest worry before this incident had been whether Mr. Lee would rape her. That thought had constricted her chest with constant tension. Now her life was on the line. Stay calm. Don't panic. Simon and Dane couldn't rescue her. She needed to find the strength to survive on her own.

The car door opened again and a higher-ranking military officer—older, more confident—sat next to her. The door on the opposite side opened and a younger aide slid in and pushed her into the middle of the seat.

The younger man asked her something in Korean. She didn't answer. He then switched to English. "What is your name?"

She didn't answer. With her best composure, she reacted as though she didn't understand the question. If they thought she was American, they could kill her for being a spy. If she didn't speak, maybe they'd believe she was Russian or from another country that was remotely allied to North Korea.

After a few minutes, no one spoke to her. The two men discussed something of great importance, according to their tones and the expressions on their faces.

The car drove off over roads marred by potholes and inadequate upkeep. Cassie looked out the window and tried to memorize the route. It wouldn't be much help; it was more of a brain exercise. She'd been dropped in the middle of nowhere and had no idea how to get out.

They pulled into a base surrounded by barbed wire and filled with military personnel. The fortress plunged Cassie's emotions into a dark and miserable void. The younger man escorted Cassie to an office building and a small room. When he departed, slamming and locking the door behind him, she looked around. The room was stark except for a window with iron bars, a desk, three chairs, and a potted plant. Nothing she could use to escape. She needed more time and a plan: stay calm and don't talk, and look for opportunities.

Part of her problem was the homogeneity of the Korean people. If she escaped, her height and hair would be a beacon as to her whereabouts, like the Bat symbol.

The door opened, and three men walked in—the two men from the car and another older officer.

The younger man pulled out a chair for Cassie and forced her to sit. She bit back a cry of pain from the awkward position of her hands behind her as she slammed into the back of the chair.

"The drones were made in the United States, so we will assume, for now, you are American. It will be easier if you answer my questions."

Cassie stared at the wall and tried to stay in her surf daydream. If she didn't listen to the questions, she wouldn't have an urge to answer them. A soft rain began to fall outside. The rain on the concrete cast a light haze throughout the area. A wonderful night for a stroll to freedom.

Her interrogator spoke to the other men in Korean and then returned his attention to her. "Maybe you don't understand how serious this is. If you don't start talking, you will be convicted of espionage and sentenced to forty years of hard labor in a work camp. You will have a difficult time in the mines with your height."

They hadn't hurt her yet. She could hold out. The rain outside the window caught her attention again. The wind had picked up and was now blowing around like a monsoon. Most of the soldiers she'd seen lingering in groups at the edges of buildings must have found shelter. Her ears pulled the sound of the storm into focus and ignored the man speaking to her.

After what seemed like an hour, he gave up and spoke to the other two men. Good. Maybe they'd lock her in solitary confinement, and she'd be safe for a few hours. She'd survived prison before, even though it had been only two days. She knew she'd be able to keep her mind steady for a longer period of time if they left her alone. She ignored her body's need for food and sleep. And she ignored the small child growing inside of her. If she thought about Simon's baby, she'd break down and do whatever they asked of her.

———————— ❧ ————————

LETTING her go had been the hardest thing he'd ever done, but getting captured would have been a disaster. If they learned of Simon's love for Cassie, and vice versa, the enemy would be able break one or both of them to extract any information they wanted. Simon would have a hard time watching Cassie tortured. And they would most definitely torture one of them in front of the other, and eventually kill them both after they received all the information they needed. She stood a better chance of surviving if she was the only prisoner.

They must have killed everyone else, because not a sound came from the house. Only two military guards remained. They'd searched the house and disappeared around the back. The valuables Mr. Lee had acquired while propping up the North Korean economy would slowly disappear into the pockets of friends of the government. The two lucky guards stationed at the house would most likely spend the next few hours searching for jewelry and other small items to sell for a quick buck on the black market.

Simon remained hidden in the tall grass until the trucks departed and the birds began to chirp again, safe from human movement and interruption. He needed food and a disguise. The front door had been left open in the chaos of the evening. He eased into the house and located the kitchen. After refilling his water bottles, he located some kimchi and slices of beef from the refrigerator.

A long brown jacket and beat up straw hat from one of Mr. Lee's servants hung on a hook by the door to the back garden. He'd blend in as well as he could for a giant. Several minutes later, he crouched low while driving the motorcycle through the endless countryside. His backpack hid under the jacket like a beer belly. He was able to pass several cars without a second glance from the occupants. Then the rain fell. Slowly at first, then in heavy waves that slowed his movement and soaked his skin through his clothes and under his Kevlar vest.

The signal for the drones had moved east, further away from the coast and the small boat that could take them to safety. He passed through several small villages and down long stretches of farmland, pulling over three times to confirm the coordinates and once to change the battery on the phone.

The signal came to a rest in the middle of a small military base. Barbed wire on top of high fences, and the many men wandering between barracks and warehouses, confirmed his worst fears. How would he get her out of a military compound without a major international incident? He drove by twice within the span of an hour and began to access the logistics in the rescue mission.

He hid in an outcrop of bushes and watched the main gates open for merchants, soldiers, and visitors. A night rescue made the most sense. Too many people would be able to gun them down in natural light, even on such a rainy, overcast day. But that provided the bastards more time to hurt Cassie. He grimaced at the thought, and his temples pounded. Slipping into the woods about five kilometers from the camp, he called Dane.

"What's going on?" Dane asked.

"Cassie was taken by the military in a crackdown. The main buyer, his family, and staff were executed in front of her. I didn't see where his guards went. They may have been plants for the government. She's healthy, so far."

"Are you okay?"

"Just checking on everything. I can move in, extract her, and get out, but I may need some additional help to cross the border."

"I'm working on it. The South Koreans aren't too keen on infiltrating their neighbor to save someone else's ass. The agency won't help, so I'm alone. I'm trying to call in a few favors."

"Anything you can bring, I'd appreciate. This is Cassie were talking about."

"I understand. I'll do everything in my power to help her."

"Thanks."

"Don't thank me. I'm doing this so the great Simon Dunn owes me one."

"Say the word, mate. Say the word."

The sun dropped below the horizon, and Simon removed his disguise, hid the motorcycle and backpack, and armed himself for a mini-war. He slid through the shadows, doing work the SAS would do more efficiently. He preferred making deals and covering his ass.

Crawling around in the mud and digging a ditch under a hidden section of barbed wire fencing were not on his list of favorite activities, but he'd walk through a molten lava field to bring Cassie to safety. At least the rain helped muffle his movements. Huge gaps in the presence of North Korean military personnel also allowed Simon to move into the camp without being seen. They must be hiding from the weather. Once inside, he sat for an hour under the roof of a utility shed and waited for dark to completely surround the brightly lit base.

To succeed, two power sources had to be eliminated: the transformer moving electricity into the camp from an external source, and a large generator that provided back up in case a pissed off MI6 agent blew up the transformer to rescue the woman he loved. He'd take out the generator second.

The cold and miserable guards inspected the base with quick glances, never looking to see if anyone had infiltrated the perimeter. When they were satisfied they'd completed the task with a minimal level of competence, they turned back to shelter and their colleagues to discuss more interesting issues than protecting their own hides.

Dropping to the ground and inching his way along, Simon slithered to the generator, located beside a few dumpsters that smelled of rotting fish, and placed an explosive inside a panel that had nothing protecting it other than a rusty latch.

Moving back to the shed, he aligned the sight of his Smith and Wesson 500 on the center of the gray transformer sitting in the open, one hundred and fifty meters away. He didn't have a great shot, but didn't think he could place an explosive device without getting shot and killed in the process. He'd have two shots. Making the shot on the first try would be optimal.

The rain increased from a light shower to a downpour and blurred Simon's vision. He needed to have hawk eye capability to shoot out the transformer, and some assistance from Mother Nature, who was currently raging mad with a downpour and occasional lightening strikes. His brother Henry, a former Special Boat Service sniper, would have been the perfect man for the job. Simon tried to harness his brother's cool demeanor and accuracy.

He pulled the trigger and hit the upper corner of his target, creating a small fire. Shit. The sound of the gunshot caused the soldiers to stop what they were doing and act more professional. He aimed again and hit the bull's-eye. The transformer exploded. The fire he'd created with the first bullet helped to ignite the pole. The men would be working on fixing that for days. The lights went out for a minute and then powered back on, dimmer and with less coverage, thanks to the generator.

He pulled out the detonator on the explosive he'd placed and hit the switch. The blast lit up the back of the barracks and created havoc with the men in the yard as the lights died for good, and the darkness consumed them.

Showtime. He slid into the yard and headed to the main office building. A soldier stood sentry to the area, but everyone else had fled to their posts. Simon shot him in the head and took his assault weapon. He pushed through the halls and scanned room after room for Cassie, shooting whoever was in his sight. He found her a few doors down, tied to a chair, and completely emotionless. Now wasn't the time for heartfelt reunions, so he bottled up his relief and focused on getting them the hell out of there.

"Cassie? Are you all right?"

"Simon?" She spoke as though coming out of a trance.

He pulled out a knife, cut the rope that bound her, and guided her outside. They didn't speak. Her energy increased as she moved next to him. Thankfully she had on jeans and sneakers. They might have to hide in the woods for a few hours.

Simon kept his and Cassie's pace steady. A fast walk. Although he wanted to pull her out of this hell as quickly as possible, moving any faster would draw attention from the soldiers, now on full alert for anything different from the norm. They headed to a transport vehicle he'd seen earlier. Someone had parked it next to the office, probably to prevent the highest ranking officials from having to walk in the rain.

He pushed her though the driver's seat into the passenger side and climbed in after her. The keys sat ready in the ignition, waiting for a driver or a thief. North Koreans were efficient, and Simon appreciated it.

"Get down, all the way on the floor. Don't lift your head for anything until we reach the forest."

He turned the vehicle in a one eighty and proceeded toward the back, less heavily guarded, gate. Several soldiers had started yelling at him and then begun shooting. He pushed the gas to the floor and rammed the gate. The impact made a high-pitched scrapping sound as the fence bent outward to freedom. He flew down the road at top speed and refused to turn the headlights on as a beacon for his pursuers to follow. Five kilometers out, he pulled into the cut off, a small concrete area that shouldn't reveal their path. He parked the truck behind a group of trees and took a moment to look at Cassie. She'd sat up when the truck stopped.

"Are we safe?" she asked.

"Not yet."

They left the truck and moved farther back into the thick trees, hidden by the night and the heavy rain.

"Now what?" she asked.

He pulled out the motorcycle. "Transportation home. I hope."

"Are you serious?"

He was always serious when running for his life. "Get on."

She slid on the bike behind him and wrapped her arms around his waist. Her clothes had been soaked through, and she'd only get more drenched as they rode along. He would have put the large jacket over her to conceal them, but thought they'd have less drag and more agility without it.

They flew out of the trees and onto the roadway. A convoy of vehicles, illuminated by their headlights, closed in on their location.

Simon drove as fast as he could while ensuring the worn out wheels of the old bike held up on the slick roads. He glanced behind him and saw Cassie's long, wet hair blowing behind her like a surrender flag. They should have tied it back at the clearing. Not what they needed tonight. Tonight, they needed to blend in and be part of their environment.

# CHAPTER 28

C assie convinced her body that the man she was holding
tight on the back of a beat-up old motorcycle was not the
love of her life, but a mere stranger who had no
meaning to her. If she acknowledged that Simon had come for her,
blown up part of a military base, and entered enemy territory
with guns blazing to rescue her, she'd break down into a sobbing
mess of relief and complete and utter panic.

Was he crazy? He had to be to risk his life like that. But she
was so glad he did.

The bike rumbled and bounced over bumps and holes in the
street. She pulled herself more tightly into him so they could
rebalance their weight. She could feel his hips shift at each turn.
She leaned as he did to keep them balanced.

Without the headlights on, darkness blanketed the road in
front of them. She tucked her face into his back. Her eyes stayed
closed for most of the time, because rain pelted her face like a
barrage of pebbles. Her cheeks stung and her lips hurt, chapped
by the wind, swollen from the cold.

Just as her breathing decreased from the running-for-her-life
range to the almost-out-of-hot-water range, she noticed light on

the road before them. She turned to see how close their pursuers had come.

"Careful," he yelled. "You'll throw us both off balance."

"There are lights in front of us and behind us."

"We blew apart their electric transformer and stole a truck. They'll search every household and field in a thousand kilometer radius."

"They're getting closer."

"Hold on." He drove the bike off the road and into a small group of trees. "We'll hold out here until they pass."

She swung her leg off the bike and fell against one of the larger trees. It provided a bit of protection from the rain and helped her stand.

Simon pushed the bike into a hiding spot and came up beside her. The headlights continued closer, and Cassie's heart thumped hard in her chest again. The rain, the sopping clothes, the cold, her hunger, and her worry for Simon overwhelmed her. With a break in the get away, she took the opportunity to fall apart.

He held her close in his arms and brushed his hand over the wet hair. "It's going to be all right, angel. This is the fun part."

She couldn't help but laugh. "The *fun* part?"

"You and I traveling the world together on an adventure."

Before she could tell him how idiotic that sounded, his lips came down on hers, and he crushed her body against him.

His hands molded her sides, feeling her shoulders and arms, her back and her stomach. Rain fell around them and created a barrier from all of the bad things that had come before. He stopped, resting his forehead on hers. She could feel his inhalation. He was breathing her in, and she was hoping to be fully absorbed by the hero before her.

They remained locked in each other's arms as the trucks drove past.

"I prefer a boring life. Would you be able to handle that?" she whispered.

"I was thinking of starting a kitchen garden. Grow my own

herbs and vegetables to cook with. I intend to be every bit as boring as you."

—————————— ✺ ——————————

THRONGS OF TRUCKS passed their location in both directions, searching for them, but never coming close. As the silence returned, Simon's tense body eased. He had Cassie in his arms. They'd be fine.

"Come with me." He led her to a small group of bushes and crawled on his hands and knees, dragging his backpack.

"Where are we going?"

"No questions." He loved her curiosity. He loved her so much he couldn't get enough of her in this lifetime or a thousand others.

The branches hung to the ground, but underneath it was like a pop tent. A very dry pop tent.

"I thought you might like to get out of the rain for a few minutes before we continue."

"How far do we have to travel to get back to South Korea?"

"We're about ten kilometers from the border if we head due south, but the security is high and the terrain not conducive to a motorcycle. I took a small boat here on the coast. If we can make our way back there, which will take about two hours or so, we'll be back in time for a late dinner and a long and leisurely bath." He couldn't see her clearly through the darkness, but her silhouette made an appearance now and then as the clouds shifted in the sky and allowed the moonlight to dance among the branches. "We should stay for about an hour to let them move away from here. It'll also give us a chance to dry our clothes a bit."

He pulled out a Mylar blanket and wrapped it around her shoulders. She tried to cover him as well, but he refused. He had his own method of finding warmth, and it involved his fiancée, not metallic blankets.

"You rescued me, like a warrior from another time. Get under this blanket so I can take care of you."

"Get a grip, Watson. I'm not doing for this you, so don't get all high and mighty. It's for Junior. She's cold, and what kind of father would I be if I didn't provide warmth to my only child."

She sighed. "I wonder if this will be our only child."

"We'll stop having children when I say we're done and not a minute sooner. Remember, I'm the head of this family." He could see her with a whole gaggle of children.

She burst out laughing. "A thousand children, and I'm stuck working for you forever?"

"Exactly. You'll love it." And he'd love her challenging every decision he made. He'd win every argument, of course, but he wouldn't be offended by her attempts at control.

The rain became a drizzle, almost a soft humming in the background. A slight mist rose from the cool drops hitting the warmer ground.

He pulled off his shirt and his Kevlar vest, and then he reached over to bring her closer.

"Slow down, Tarzan. If you think we're having sex when we're running for our lives…"

"I could be quick."

"Tell me you didn't drag me under this bush for sex."

"As much as I crave your body constantly, I chose this spot to keep you dry for a few minutes. We need to wait a bit until the searching moves further afield. One more leg of the journey, and we'll be safe."

He reached into his backpack for a bottle of water and a few crackers.

"Drink and eat quickly. You'll need energy to make it through the night."

He refused to mention the baby on the way. The thought of her losing the baby would be unbearable.

———————— 🌀 ————————

# CHAPTER 29

Cassie remained under the blanket with one of Simon's arms wrapped around her shoulder waiting out the men who wanted to kill them. "I think it's time to go."

He shifted in place, but continued to hold her. "We have enough time for a fling in the foliage."

"Get up."

"It's now or never." He grinned, and some of the terror lifted off her shoulders. In the middle of hell, he was charming.

"That's a weak ultimatum. Never is a long time, and you wouldn't be able to hold out."

"I could last years longer than you, but I don't see the point when we could enjoy each other as much as possible in this lifetime. In my next life, I may end up with a very angry woman who hates sex and owns three ferrets." His words came out slow and relaxed, but he'd be at full alert within seconds of hearing her plans.

He lifted onto one elbow. "Put on the vest."

"It's yours."

"Have you forgotten who the boss is? It's not for you anyway, it's for Junior."

"You use that excuse for everything now."

"Exactly."

His eyes, lit up by the emerging moonlight, bore into her as though bending her will with a mere look. He won. He usually did. At this point, she didn't have the energy to argue. When she gave him a slight nod, he handed the vest to her. Her torso was almost as long as Simon's, but his chest was much thicker. She pulled the straps hard to tighten them. The stiff material hindered her ability to turn sideways, and weighed her down.

Simon watched her dress, but didn't move to help her. He couldn't have anyway. The space under the bush didn't allow too much room unless they shifted in tandem as they had minutes before. He took off his black knit hat and handed it to her.

"Cover your hair. It's beautiful, but not the right time to show it off to the world."

She tied her hair in a bun and pulled the hat down over it.

Would he be mad at her plans? Yes, but he'd go along with them. When his black shirt finally covered his perfect body, she took a deep breath and spoke.

"We have one thing left to do before we leave. I need to blow up the drones. I want to be within range to make sure the job is done right."

That caught his attention. His brows lifted. "I thought you already rendered them useless with the handheld controllers."

"I did, but they still have the Pelican markings on them. Do you have a phone that works?"

"Why?"

"I programmed codes into a system that uses remote satellite transmissions to activate a detonation sequence so I can destroy the drones." She understood the job now, and it didn't scare her. She'd save as many people as she could and work like hell to protect Simon and Junior's lives as well. Although if she had the choice, she'd rather bake vegan cookies for her children and leave the life and death stuff to people who preferred this line of work. "How many men, do you think are left at the base?"

"I'm not sure. Probably ten, although I'm sure reinforcements are on their way."

Reinforcements? More casualties. She had to do this as soon as possible. "I need your phone. Right now."

He hesitated, but after a solid moment of tension, he unlocked his phone. Good. Her attention veered away from their reconciliation and back to their job. She punched in several numbers. The service was spotty.

"Come on." She tapped the phone to log into the server.

She crawled back out into the rain, now more of faint drizzle. A branch pulled some of her hair out of the hat and the rain littered down from the leaves, sending a chill across her back.

Simon followed. He moved easily for such a large guy. He stared over her shoulder and watched her input the codes.

"Are you sure you know what you're doing?" He reached to take the phone away from her.

"Can you disarm a drone packed with explosives and acid with a computer program that will cease to exist if you make one faulty keystroke?"

"No."

"Then I have no need for you right now. Go check the motorcycle."

The stubborn male didn't move. He stood next to her being an intimidating force on her psyche. "Why did you do it?"

"I couldn't let them have such dangerous weapons, and I don't want to start a war, militarily or diplomatically. Give me a second." She had one shot to make this happen. They didn't have time for her to reprogram everything. "I won't leave here without some blood on my hands, but the families of those soldiers will survive."

He stood close, but didn't touch her. He understood her need for space. He understood so much about her. She shook her head to get back into the game. Three more buttons to lock the detonation for all twenty drones. Three, seven, four.

"Brace yourself." She tucked into his arms and dropped her head into his chest.

The explosion rang out and the earth moved. Simon's arms secured her to him. With the grace and strength of a panther, he rode the shockwaves and kept them upright.

The explosion could be heard for miles. She turned back in the direction of the camp and saw a white cloud rise over the horizon with flames stretching over the tallest buildings.

---

"HOLY SHIT. You blew up the whole bloody camp." He stared at the fireball erupting to the west.

"Dane will be happy to know the drones are gone." She spoke with a calm that unnerved him. *Where was the pacifist from a few weeks ago?* "People may have died, but a lot more would have if they'd declared war against South Korea. I'm hoping this is like the atomic bomb in Japan."

"You're now in favor of atomic bombs?"

"Simon, stop talking. I don't want to think about what I did until we're back in London. Okay?" A dark fog covered her emotions, but the sadness in her watery eyes and the tension in her neck revealed her understanding of her decision.

"Fine."

He went over to his backpack and pulled out a water bottle and a bottle of pills. He handed one to Cassie with the water.

"What's this?"

"Electrolytes. You need them. Eat one."

She didn't argue, which struck Simon as funny. She listened to him and followed orders better than most of the young new recruits now. Her obedience kept her alive most of the time. On the other hand, without asking for permission, she blew up a military base in a hostile territory, destroying millions of dollars of equipment and weapons, and killing more men than he'd led her to believe. She could survive without him. When she learned a skill, she took it to the expert level with a rapid assuredness unparalleled in other agents. The thought didn't make him upset, it made him proud.

"You need a gun." He rummaged through his pack for a Glock. It was heavy enough to keep from flying around in her hand and would kill on impact. If she needed to use it, she'd have her back up against a wall, and he probably wouldn't be with her.

"I hate guns."

"I don't have any extra explosives at present, so you need a gun."

She held it with an unsure grip and was about to slid it into her trousers.

"Take this." He handed her a clip holster from the backpack.

"Your bag is like the one in Mary Poppins."

"I don't have the flying umbrella, which would have worked real well both in the rain and in flying over the DMZ."

Before they left the clearing, he called Dane. His news wasn't promising. His contacts in the South Korean government had been notified, but were embroiled in politics and didn't want to send the troops out to play. He told Simon to try to reach the boat. There'd be no fancy rescue. They needed to rely on themselves.

The rain had slowed, leaving a light haze on the road, which made the darkness even darker. An occasional glimpse of the moon was the only light around them. Without the use of headlights, maneuvering the motorcycle around potholes was near impossible, especially at high speeds. They traveled slower than he wanted to avoid a blowout.

Ten kilometers into the trip to the coast, the rumble of a convoy caught Simon's ear. They were coming back. He needed to hide Cassie.

Several trucks sped closer toward them. He pulled off the road near a small broken-down farmhouse with crumbling concrete sides and a partially collapsed roof. The area seemed abandoned.

As they approached the old barn to take cover, a motion

detector light turned on, acting as a spotlight on their location for the troops following them.

*Why the hell would a remote barn have a motion detection system?* He couldn't spare the time to think about the answer.

The sound of brakes took their probability of success from near-sure-thing to no-fucking-way-in-hell. The vehicles turned off the road and moved toward them. He couldn't flee. There was no place to hide beside the barn and miles of open fields. They hid the motorcycle on the backside of the building.

He crouched behind a rotting wooden cart with Cassie close by. With a few minutes before the arrival of the soldiers, he pulled out a spare magazine and reloaded his gun. Four vehicles drove up, already shooting in the direction of the barn. He couldn't risk her getting hurt. His chest tightened at the possibility of her death. She had to live. He'd be her shield as long he was breathing.

"Get inside. I'll try to hold them off."

"There are too many. Come with me. We can hide together." She tugged at his arm and tried to move him. If he left his post, they'd be found and dragged into a heinous situation. He couldn't bear to watch her undergo a harsh interrogation.

With a strong shove, he forced her toward the barn entrance. "Go. That's an order."

She hesitated, but he ignored her to prepare for the battle. He heard her move away from him and said a quick prayer for a positive outcome. A dozen soldiers by his count, half of a platoon, exited the vehicles. Way too many.

He didn't have a chance to dial Dane's number again. The gunshots came too close. He ducked down behind the cart, but the wood didn't stop these caliber rounds. It didn't even slow them down. He aimed at the closest man and hit him in the neck. Three more men surrounded him and four men started around the back of the barn. He blanketed the area with rounds from the assault weapon he'd taken at the camp, the same weapon used against him by these men. He took a few more out, but the barrage heading his way overwhelmed him.

Cassie needed the best possibility of survival, so he held his position, taking down as many men as he could. His luck died on the impact of the first bullet. It struck him in the leg, near his ankle. The impact tore his leg apart. He wouldn't be able to run anywhere. He fell low to the ground to avoid being hit again. In the process, another bullet hit him. Clenching his teeth, he tried to stay coherent. The newest wound was high on his shoulder. Just a nick. He could still survive if his leg didn't bleed out.

The two wounds burned. The pain kept him alert. He lifted himself again and continued shooting. Six soldiers dead. He needed to take out six more before Cassie was safe. The stolen assault weapon would only last so long before it was out of ammunition. Ironic if he died because he ran out arms. His entire adulthood, he'd always had more ammunition than any one man needed.

Blood seeped through his trousers and dripped from his leg into a puddle next to him. Too much blood. He needed to protect Cassie's position in the barn, because it didn't look like he was going to have the chance to move her out. No regrets. He'd die a million times to keep her safe.

He maneuvered himself to the other side of the cart and shot at two men headed toward the barn. Ignoring the growing weakness in his leg, he dragged himself away from the cart. The two men refocused on him. Exactly as he'd planned. He opened fire on them again. A soldier to his left came into focus a second too late. A single shot hit him in the chest and stopped any chance of saving Cassie.

# CHAPTER 30

———————— ✆ ————————

Cassie hid in the back of the barn amid cobwebs and a musty smell. Her hands trembled when she pulled out the gun Simon had given to her. She knew how to use it and might be forced to aim it at another person, but she didn't want to. The sound of gunshots moved closer, accompanied by men shouting in Korean. Simon was alone facing all those soldiers, and she was hiding with a gun she didn't want to use. This was not where his partner should be. The numbers worked against him. He couldn't survive alone. She needed to help despite his order.

She headed to the back door, stepping over a pile of rubbish that smelled like rotting cabbages. Flies swarmed over the garbage. Using her gun hand to wave them away, she worked her way to the back entrance, stepping lightly. The shadows of two men crossed in front of the main door. They were coming too close now. Gunshots sounded again, and the men hustled away. She pushed open the back door as slowly as possible without making noise and drawing attention to herself. There was no one behind the barn. She crouched down and crept around the corner, avoiding puddles and areas of mud.

She stayed as tucked into the side of the barn as possible.

Focusing on helping Simon, she ignored the danger of running toward the soldiers instead of away from them. Then she saw him at the edge of the lit up area. Face down in the mud, twisted in an impossible position, with blood oozing from everywhere. He wasn't moving. Ice frosted her limbs. She needed to scream, but the sound caught in her throat.

A soldier standing over Simon held a gun to his head. He laughed as he spoke to his comrades. Cassie undid her safety and fired the handgun at the soldier. It missed, but drew his attention away from Simon. She aimed again and missed. All three men ran toward her, pointing their weapons. They screamed something in Korean. Ten feet from her, a soldier reached out to grab her. Her third shot was successful. She hit the man in the head. Directly in his forehead. He crumbled, but she caught him and used his bloody body as a shield.

The pistol wasn't working for her. She never aimed it accurately. Mr. Henley, her firearms instructor, had told her she'd do better with an assault weapon. Like the one the dead soldier carried. Spraying the bullets, she could increase her hits.

The weapon in the dead man's hand felt lighter than the ones she'd practiced with, but it fired the same. The other two men continued to charge.

She killed them. They lay in front of her with multiple gunshot wounds. She didn't care. Simon remained motionless on the ground. The silence scared her. Where were all the other soldiers? She placed the strap of the assault weapon over her shoulder in case she needed it again and thrust the dead man's body away from her.

She sprinted to Simon and knelt next to his mangled form. Her hand on his back picked up the faintest of movement in his chest. When she pulled her hand away, it was covered in blood. She rolled him over with great difficulty. His body, solid muscle, remained heavy and unresponsive. The blue eyes that sparkled when he laughed were sealed behind scratched eyelids covered in dirt. Sobs rocked her frame, but she fought through the horror in order to help him. She leaned over him and wiped the mud from his cheek, only to smear it from his nose to his temple.

"Don't leave me. Please, Simon. Don't leave me."

Her medical training didn't cover anything useful like gunshot wounds to the chest. She needed help. Jumping up, she ran to the backpack and carried it over to him. Simon had two phones in his pack. She tried to use them, but they had access blocks. Not even the ability to call 911. She pulled off the cover of the Android with a small toolkit she found in a side pocket of the bag. After a minute of reordering functions, she skipped the password and found the directory. Dane's number was the only one on this phone. She dialed it. Nothing. No answer. It went straight into voicemail.

"Dane, this is Cassie. Simon's been shot." Her uncontrollable crying cut into her message and garbled her words. She punched herself hard in the leg to give her body a little pain outside of her heart and to calm her nerves. "He needs help immediately. I don't know where we are or how you can find me, but please come."

What a useless message.

She stared at Simon's body, too weak, too bloody, too heavy. She held him and hated herself for not having enough medical training. What could she do?

Think, damn it. Blood was leeching from his leg and arm and everywhere. His heart still beat, but his lungs made strange noises as air entered and exited. First, stop the bleeding. She pulled out a T-shirt from his pack. Three rips provided four bandages. His ankle was shattered, bone fragments mixed into the inner layer of his skin. The bullet to the shoulder only grazed him. The wound was larger than a quarter, but manageable.

His chest. His heart continued a faint beat, but she didn't know what to do with that injury. It was beyond anything she'd ever seen. She heard a slight sucking noise as he struggled to breath. His lungs were leaking. How would she stop the air from escaping through his chest?

Hopefully, the bandages would help. The first one, she

wrapped around his leg. She tightened it as much as she could. The second bandage secured his shoulder. She used the longest strip there, because the wound on the shoulder was in such an awkward location. Finally she tried to blot the blood on his chest, but which side? It went through the front and out the back. The idiot gave her the vest, yet she was never hit. Anger and fury mixed with complete desolation.

The bandages didn't work to stop the air leaking from his chest. She rummaged through the bag again and found the Mylar blanket. It was easy to rip. She pressed a piece against his back and placed a white cloth bandage behind it and turned him over so the ground sealed the wound to the Mylar. Hopefully, it sealed his lungs successfully. She then did the same to the front of his chest. She used the final piece of the T-shirt to place over the Mylar seal and then pressed her hand into the bloody area and held it in place. His body was warm, and his heart thumped against her hand, struggling to maintain a steady heartbeat.

The moon peeked out from the clouds and brightened the area, illuminating the carnage. Simon must have killed at least eight men before being shot. He didn't have backup…and yet he did, and she'd failed him. Follow his orders? His orders sucked. By sacrificing himself, he could take away her future, the man she wanted to spend forever with.

Her voice rose up in a helpless howl. "You will not die, you bastard. Do you hear me? I need you to live so I can kick your ass for giving the worst orders ever."

She covered the rest of Simon's torso with the remnants of the Mylar blanket and made a pillow for his head with the pack. Then she waited.

———————— ✑ ————————

HOW MANY MINUTES could she sit in the wet mist in the middle of nowhere holding Simon as his life drifted away? If she'd left immediately with the motorcycle, she'd be a few miles away already, but she had no clue how to drive a motorcycle and no idea how to cross the border and find safety. *Too stupid to live.* It didn't matter. She refused to flee the area and leave him to die alone. And they were completely alone. No human being within sight. Not even the sound of a passing car on the road.

The breeze through the distant trees and the call of a bird in a low rumbled pitch calmed some of the savagery surrounding her. An occasional radio on the belt of a dead soldier came alive, spouting Korean questions and orders. No one was available to answer the call.

Her warrior, the man who wanted to marry her, remained helpless on the muddy ground in the middle of hostile territory. His head rested on the pillow she'd created from his backpack.

If she'd been more capable, he wouldn't be bleeding to death in front of her. Perhaps he would have trusted her to fight with him. Her hand stayed put on the Mylar cover pressed to the wound. She couldn't hear the sucking sound anymore, but could feel his weak heartbeat and the faint rise and fall of his injured chest.

A distant hum caught her attention. A helicopter? Without contact from their troops, the military would send out a search party. They might be able save him. Reality, however, was never that kind. They'd probably shoot him in the head. Brutal, remorseless. Like she'd been to the men she'd killed. Ironically, she felt nothing in her soul after killing all those people. They would have shot Simon and her without a second thought.

The helicopter continued toward her location. She'd have moved Simon's body into the barn, but he was too heavy. So she remained with him. Her free hand touched her stomach, where Simon's child grew.

The helicopter landed in a field a few hundred yards from the barn. The noise was deafening. A group of soldiers exited the doors. Two headed directly for her and Simon, two others examined the downed men. She raised her weapon and pointed it at someone coming too close.

"Cassie," another soldier yelled to her through the deafening sound of the helicopter. "Put the gun down. We're here to help."

She still held the gun, because she didn't trust anyone. The soldier who called her name approached her. She aimed the gun at his head. "Who are you?" she hollered over the noise of the helicopter.

He pulled his mask off. It was Dane. "Put the gun down, sweetheart."

*Dane?* The cold fear across her skin faded. She dropped her weapon and burst into tears. "Simon. He needs help."

Dane moved in closer to her. He rested his hand on Simon's neck. "We have a medic team that can help him. Back away. Let them do their work."

"No. I need to be with him," she shouted.

An extremely strong arm wrapped around her waist and pulled her away.

"Stop it. Let me go."

Dane wouldn't release her. "Let the team do their job. You finished yours. It's time to rest."

"I'm fine. Let me go." She fought him, but he held her from behind. She flailed around without striking any of his sensitive body parts. He lifted her off the ground and carried her toward the helicopter. He didn't appear that strong in his more casual clothes but looks were deceiving. He was built like a tank. There was nothing she could do but go along with him. The team carrying the backboard raced past them toward Simon. She couldn't see him anymore. He was surrounded by people. Would they hurt him? Would he die with strangers?

"I can't leave him." She struggled again, but Dane continued to walk away from Simon and toward the helicopter.

He dropped her to her feet and turned her around. Hugging her close and kissing her on the forehead, he let her cry and fight and completely break down. "There's a medic and a trauma nurse with him. They're his best chance."

He lifted her into the copter and motioned her to the back. Large black earphones provided a relief from the loud motor.

Cassie crouched by one of the windows and watched Simon being strapped to the board and lifted by two men. Soldiers with rifles flanked each side. Her vision diminished as the tears came down. He might survive. There was hope.

Dane caught her attention by lifting her chin and glancing at her. "What about you? Are you hurt?"

She squeezed his hand. "No. I'm fine."

He ignored her and began to examine her for injury. His hands proceeded to rub down her arms and legs, and he pulled at her clothing to see if she had any wounds.

"I'm fine. Stop." She swatted his hand away.

"Sit over here and strap in." He sent her to one of the back seats and took the seat next to hers.

The soldiers placed Simon in the helicopter, secured the backboard, and latched the door. They swarmed around him, cutting off his clothes, inserting tubes and, hopefully, saving his life. They acted as though he was alive. When the helicopter lifted off, Cassie took a deep breath, absorbed in their attempts to stop his bleeding.

# CHAPTER 31

───────────── ❧ ─────────────

The sand sparkled, reflecting the hot sun beaming down in the middle of the afternoon. Cassie, wearing a red bikini, escorted a little blonde girl carrying a yellow pail across an expanse of sand. Simon's daughter. Cassie smiled at her and pointed to a pink shell rotating counterclockwise and then clockwise as the rippling water offered it up to the shore and then pulled it away.

The sound of a helicopter chopped into the image, flying low and landing on the beach. Cassie's hair blew in all directions as the little girl tried to cover her face from the sand swirling in front of her. Fifty or more North Korean soldiers carrying Type 58 assault rifles flooded the beach. They all fit into the helicopter? It didn't make sense.

Cassie crouched to protect the little girl from the wind and the sand. She didn't tremble or quake in fear, but she had no weapon to defend herself. She needed a weapon. The soldiers surrounded them. Cassie screamed at them to stop, but they didn't listen. They aimed. She pushed the girl to the ground and covered her body completely. They fired.

His scream woke him. His eyes opened wide. Blinding light forced them shut again. *Cassie.* He needed to protect her.

Hands held his arms down. Their hold increased as he fought to escape. The more he struggled, the more hands forced him back. Who had captured him and why? And where was Cassie? Soon, restraints tied his body to the bed.

After the sting of the light receded, he opened his eyes again. His vision came into focus several pixels at a time. A hospital room. Several nurses and doctors, and Dane.

His friend's presence eased the panic. Simon opened his mouth to speak, but choked on a tube down his throat. His whole body convulsed in a deep pain, like knives and hot irons and scalding water combined.

The medical personnel buzzed around him fixing lines in his arms. He growled trying to get them away. Each intake of air was a struggle. He fought to get up. Fatigue pummeled him.

"Mr. Smith." The doctor, an older Asian man, stood next to him, holding an iPad, tapping the screen, and lifting his eyes to Simon every few taps. "You must calm down, or I will be forced to sedate you. The endotracheal tube can be removed, but I need your assurance that you will calm down."

Three younger doctors in lab coats remained one step behind him. They glanced between each other with fear etched in their expressions.

Simon tried to relax his mind and his muscles, no easy task with Dane smirking over him. After a moment, the doctor nodded to the other medical personnel. They had Simon lean his head back while they worked out the tube. It snaked its way past the gag reflex and out, leaving a horrid bile taste in his mouth. Someone placed a glass of water to his lips and helped him take a sip. The cool drink soothed his throat and calmed his nerves. Although pain intensified with each breath, there was air moving in and out of his lungs. The head doctor nodded to Dane and left the room with his entourage in tow.

"Welcome back, George." Dane, dressed for a board of directors meeting, was leaning against the wall, appearing amused with Simon's situation.

"Cassie?" The name crackled through his dry throat as he spoke. It hurt too much to say anything else.

"Your wife, Mrs. Sunny Smith, is doing just fine. And according to the medical staff here, so is the little Smith on the way. I forced her away from your side so she could sleep in a real bed in the hotel suite for a night. She'll return soon. For some reason, she likes being near you. Be nice to her. She thought you were dead."

Simon didn't want to talk, but he needed answers. He lifted an eyebrow.

Dane acknowledged his silent questions with a nod. "From what she told me, you'd been gunned down. Three bullets struck you, by the way. Impressive. She dodged a few rounds herself to get the assault rifle out of some dead soldier's hands and mowed the leftovers down. That lady of yours has brass balls." He shook his head with a grin.

*Cassie with a gun? Killing people?*

He had a hard time imagining it, but then he thought of the drones and Cassie blowing the base to smithereens. A pacifist unless crossed. He'd have to remember not to get on her bad side.

He glanced at the bandages across his chest and around his body and waited for Dane to continue.

"Where do I begin? You have a fracture in your ankle. You'll be out of commission for a little while. On a good note, you couldn't have been transported to a better place. These surgeons are the best. You'll be running marathons by next summer."

Simon tried to lift his leg, but the restraints held him back. The large cast covered something painful as hell. He nodded to Dane to continue.

"Skidmark over the shoulder. Loss of some blood, but nothing huge. And then there's your chest."

Simon's gaze dropped back to his sternum and the tubes and bandages and monitoring devices. His lungs refused to inhale more than a minimal amount of air. His ribs hurt with each breath he took.

"Your partner couldn't have handled the situation better. She sealed the wounds in the front and the back while keeping you protected and alive until we landed. Hell, she almost killed one of the members of the White Tigers who had arrived to rescue her. Although it wasn't really her fault. She had no idea the soldiers running at her with assault rifles were South Korean special forces. She thought she was still under attack."

Simon struggled to listen to Dane. He wanted to know the specifics, but his body wasn't cooperating. Every sector of his being hurt. He shut his eyes, and Dane mumbled a few things he didn't catch. He'd talk to him later when he could think. The darkness called him back, and he went willingly.

He woke up coughing in a dark room. A monitor continued to beep and display bright lights. Pain shot down his arm, up his leg, and across his chest, all congregating in a massive headache above his forehead. His throat still hurt, though not as much.

The door was open, and he could hear people wandering up and down the halls. He turned his head to look out the window and saw his heroine fast asleep in a vinyl chair. His Cassie stretched across the chair with one leg propped up on the windowsill to prevent her from sliding to the floor.

She looked beautiful. And he might have lost her. A tidal wave of pain reminded him why they were there. He groaned and tried to shift over—not a wise move. It hurt even more. His next groan woke Cassie up. At first, she seemed disoriented, but when she noticed his eyes open, she jumped to his side.

"Are you okay?" Her face was distressed, the creases in her forehead deep.

He nodded. His expression grew into a smile because nothing could be wrong in the world when she was next to him, alive and healthy.

"What are you so happy about? You almost died." Both hands caressed his face. "The doctor said you wouldn't have a hole in your chest if you'd been wearing the vest. The one you gave to me." Her composure broke, and tears streamed down her cheeks.

His smile lifted. "It was a gift."

Shaking her head, she brushed the tears from under her eyes. "It was a stupid gift. I was so worried about you."

"You had the vest. I have you." He lifted his hand to touch her face; a few tubes followed. The tears didn't detract from her beauty. He could only stare in wonder at the bravest, most intelligent, amazing woman he'd ever worked with. "Dane told me you saved my life."

"No. You rescued me from the military base, and then fought off a group of armed soldiers to protect me. You're the hero."

"I'm no hero. I just needed you safe."

Grabbing a tissue from the table beside her, she blew her nose and swallowed hard. "You scared me. You were facedown in the mud and completely still. Blood was everywhere. I don't think I could have gone on without you."

"You'd better be able to go on without me. Junior needs you." His reply came out strained, followed by a raspy cough.

She nodded. "Promise me you'll retire as soon as we get home. Junior and I need *you*."

He kissed her perfect lips and tried to imagine life without death threats and backstabbing traitors. "Soon, angel. I have a few loose ends to tie up."

---

TWO WEEKS LATER, Simon had nothing finished. At least his wounds had improved. He could stand on his leg, although the cast was still there, and he needed crutches. His chest wound, however, was healing more slowly. The constant effort to inhale made him crazy. And to make matters worse, the doctor forbade him from flying until his lungs gained strength. He was stuck in Korea in the hospital for a few more weeks. No privacy, no decent food, and Cassie's unwillingness to get naked for him increased his determination to get the hell out of there.

She sat on the corner of his bed and faced him. "The minute

they give you the okay, we're on a plane back to England. I promise."

"I'd rather be in a North Korean prison than in this little room."

"You'd piss off the guards and be dead in a week." Dane sauntered into the room, placing a dish of kimchi and large slices of tuna on a side table. His yawn escaped, despite his attempt to cover it with a devil-may-care smile. He'd flown back and forth from Seoul to San Francisco twice since Simon had been hospitalized. Simon suspected he visited partly to keep tabs on his competition, and partly because Dane felt the same bond of brotherhood with Simon as he did with him.

"Mind if I have some dinner with you?" He hugged Cassie and slapped Simon on his good shoulder.

"Only if you have what I'm looking for," Simon replied.

"I've found out some very useful information. My British sources have confirmed that Tucker directed the team to take Cassie and leave her in North Korea."

"I want him dead," Simon said with an eerie calm while helping himself to Dane's tuna.

"The only question is quick and effective, or long and drawn out for maximum pain." Dane seemed to consider both options.

Simon preferred long and painful.

Cassie frowned. She still held tight to her pacifist beliefs, despite her ability to take down armies single handedly. "Maybe he could suffer from an almost fatal accident, then live out his life in disgrace. Or we could talk to the authorities? They'll arrest him. We have three witnesses."

Dane and Simon glanced at each other, disappointed in her statement.

"He *is* the authorities, angel. You and I are poor witnesses, considering we don't exist, and Dane couldn't testify against someone in a rival agency."

"And that leads to my other news." Dane grinned. "Do you know some internal affairs guy named Keller Petch?"

"Keller Petch? Never heard of him." Simon glanced over at Cassie who shrugged.

"Funny how my sources are better than yours."

"Get to the point, O'Brien."

"He was the MI6 go-to guy for eliminating rogue agents. A few hotshots had found his name and tried to hire his services. Tucker, the only bureaucrat caught in the sting, had sent two or three analysts to their deaths, because they'd come close to fingering him in a number of rackets. Regrettably for Tucker, Petch simply moved the people to safe houses while gathering evidence to convict him."

Cassie stood up. "So they have Tucker in custody?"

"No. He disappeared. There are a lot of people searching for him right now, so Simon and I may never get to murder him as planned." Dane looked as disappointed as Simon felt.

# CHAPTER 32

⟋⟍

Time passed as though in a vacuum. One month after being rescued from North Korea, Cassie transferred Simon to a large suite at a hotel close to the hospital. The move away from the hourly monitoring lessened Simon's constant anger and agitation. He spoke on the phone with Dane every day, and she made plans for their return to England.

When the thrill of their new surroundings got old, they took short field trips to enjoy the summer weather and the lush parks in the area. One particularly beautiful morning, Simon escorted Cassie to the lobby of the hotel and slipped her into a limousine, but didn't get in himself. Instead, he left her with Dane, newly arrived from a ten-day business trip.

"Aren't you coming?"

"No. I'll catch up to you." Simon struck the side of the car to tell the driver to move.

*Would Simon send her away without him?* "What's going on?" She looked over at Dane.

"It's a surprise." He waved to Simon, standing at the hotel valet stand with a devious smirk on his face.

"For me?"

"From Simon."

The two men appeared too happy. She didn't trust either one of them.

High rises and huge apartment complexes created an urban view out her window for the first thirty minutes. Soon, however, they were traveling along a smaller road and up a mountain. The car stopped in front of what looked like a temple surrounded by an emerald forest. It was something out of a fairytale.

"We're going to a temple?" she asked.

"This is the Pavilion of the Three Purities. Pure water, mountains, and humanity."

"And Simon couldn't join us?"

A huge grin appeared on Dane's face, but he didn't answer her. He jumped out and instead of opening her door, trotted to the back and grabbed a large bag from the trunk. The driver helped Cassie out.

Dane, the bag hanging over his arm, clutched Cassie's hand and pulled her up the stairs.

A man dressed with a long white satin robe with a red scarf flowing over his shoulders stood at the entrance and greeted them.

Dane bowed to the man and then shook his hand. "Minister Jeong. Nice meeting you finally."

"Welcome Mr. O'Brian. This must be the bride. Congratulations, Ms. Watson."

"Bride?" *What the heck were they up to?*

She shot a look back at Dane. Why did he know her other alias and not Sunny Smith?

"Relax, Cassie. It's all good." Dane placed his arm around her. "Surprise. You're getting married."

"Today?"

"Right now. Hurry up and get dressed." He handed her the bag and pushed her into a small room to the right of the lobby of the main building.

She shut the door and stood in shock for a moment and then began to laugh. Simon wanted to marry her here in South Korea.

The control freak usurped the choice of the time, place, and the style of the gown. It didn't matter. For the chance to keep him in her life, she'd marry him anywhere, even if that meant letting him take complete control of her wedding day.

Inside the bag was a flowing gown in white silk organza with cap sleeves. She pulled it out. Simon had even purchased nylons and white heels to match. No veil? Maybe he wasn't as perfect as he liked to tell her.

She opened her purse and brushed her hair, leaving it long and unadorned. After fixing her makeup, she dressed in the outfit he'd chosen for her. It fit perfectly, as expected, including some extra room for Junior's growing little body.

Dane knocked on the door before opening it and paused when he saw her. "Damn, Simon's one lucky bastard."

"Thanks." She turned her back toward him and pointed at the zipper caught halfway up her spine. "Could you finish zipping me up?"

"With pleasure." He pulled it up and placed his hands on each shoulder. "I hope you don't mind if I'm the only witness."

"You're a perfect witness." She did like Dane around, but wished Henry and Alex had been able to visit them as well. But no one could know where they were, not even Simon's family.

Dane kissed her on the back of her head and turned her around. "I don't have much in the way of family, but I count Simon as my closest friend in the world. And now you. No matter what happens in the future, I'll always have your back. Always."

"I hope I never need anyone to watch my back in the future. I'd like to become a boring soccer mom with a desk job." She clasped his hands. "You should find someone to help you settle down as well."

He pulled back in mock horror. "How about helping me find a wild and willing woman in every city I land instead?"

"You don't need any help with that."

"I'm losing my touch. I couldn't steal a certain blonde beauty away from a brute of an Englishman." With a wink, he led her to the door.

He handed her a bouquet of white roses and Tiffany blue hydrangeas tied with white ribbons, and linked his arm in hers. They turned outside to a garden and a beautiful spot overlooking miles of scenery. The bright sun and the hundreds of white flowers decorating the area created a magical quality of space and air. The pure white dress billowed out from her waist and flowed several feet behind her. She wore three-inch heels, which lifted her to an inch taller than Dane. She wouldn't be taller than the groom, however.

Simon stood in a tuxedo, waiting for her. A glossy black cane with a brass handle leaned on a chair beside him. He'd cleaned up beautifully. Demanding, difficult, yet totally decadent. His grin dressed up his face with the confidence of a man who never lost.

Dane handed her over to Simon after helping himself to an innocent kiss on her lips. Simon's grin never faltered. He pulled her to his side and placed her flowers on his chair.

"I hope you're ready for this, because I couldn't wait to marry you." He brushed his lips over her ear. His warm breath and the feathery caress shot shivers down her back.

"Patience is the most important quality for a field agent," she whispered back.

"I've waited for you my whole life, that's long enough."

Clasping their hands together, the minister asked them to recite the vows they'd written to each other.

*Written vows?* She hadn't written anything.

Simon reached into his pocket, pulled out a piece of paper, and handed it to her. "I took the liberty of writing something for you to read."

"You wrote *my* vows?" She didn't mean to squeak, but seriously? He better not have written anything about obeying, because he already got his way more often than not.

He grasped her hands again. Those beautiful blue eyes of his deepened, and his face became stoic and firm. "I, Simon Dunn, promise to love you forever and be your protector. I give you all my worldly possessions, my future, and my heart. I will forfeit my life for yours without hesitation."

Cassie stood tongue-tied for a second, trying to understand exactly what he'd committed to her. Pretty much everything. She didn't want him to die for her. She'd already lived through that hell. She wanted him safe at home playing with a dozen children. Her mouth opened to protest, but he shook his head to stop her from speaking.

"There's more." He brought her fingers to his mouth and kissed them. As he lowered her hands, that adorable grin emerged. "I promise to help raise our children and to support you in every way I can. I promise to agree with you whenever your thoughts and opinions line up logically with my mine. And I promise to cook vegan as often as possible as long as it doesn't weaken my strength or the health of our children."

She burst out laughing.

The minister, his eyebrows raised, didn't seem to approve of the addendum, but nodded toward Cassie. "Go ahead."

She let go of Simon's hands and glanced down at the paper he'd given her. It was best not to see what he wrote before she read it, in order to remain calm. Her hands shook as she began. Two simple sentences:

"I, Cassie Watson, promise to love you forever. I promise to never risk my life for yours, because our children need their mother."

She stopped and looked at him. His expression, dead serious, caused tears to flow in her eyes.

Her head fell forward into his shoulder, and she remained there, trembling in his arms, until the minister said something about being husband and wife.

"I can't promise that," she mumbled.

"You just did."

He lifted her head and kissed his bride with a fierce possessiveness he rarely showed in public. He took everything he could as he deepened the kiss. Simon would always try to control every aspect of them as a couple. Cassie, however, held an equal amount of control in their relationship, because she held his heart.

And then she heard the gunshot.

———————— ❧ ————————

SIMON FORCED Cassie to the ground and shielded her body, while trying to free his gun from the holster. The minister collapsed behind them, and Dane dove behind a large stone.

"Stay," Simon ordered Cassie. "Do not leave this spot."

Her face had paled, and her lips pursed tight together. He forced himself to leave her side, his chest hurting from the pressure on the wound and the fear of leaving his wife without protection.

He followed the shadow of a man around the back of a small teahouse. When the shooter turned, Simon saw the deadly intent in Tucker's pretty boy features. He'd come to finish the job, to eradicate all evidence of his poorly implemented plan. They pointed their weapons at each other, neither backing down.

Dane ran around the corner into the middle of the standoff.

Simon yelled, "Duck!"

The window behind Dane shattered as he hit the ground. He was covered in glass, but not bloody. Tucker turned and retreated through a gate and toward the woods.

"You okay?" Simon called out to Dane, who carefully brushed off the glass debris.

"Pissed off," he yelled.

They continued their pursuit to the end of a garden path. Tucker was pulling himself over a tall stone wall. Dane stopped running, aimed his gun, and fired. He hit Tucker high on his thigh. A shot to slow him down, but not kill him. A strangled yell echoed across the garden. Simon continued toward him. Tucker flipped himself and his injured leg over the wall and tried to escape, leaving blood on the stone. Despite his wound, he was moving faster than Simon.

Simon's ankle burned as he ran. Sweat poured from his forehead. He'd tried to build up the strength and flexibility of his leg in the past few weeks, but his muscles cramped in response to the agony of inflaming his injuries. He wasn't ready for full throttle. His lungs weren't at top capacity either. The weeks spent convalescing screwed with his daily workouts. He had no energy.

"Where did he go?" Dane called out.

"Over the wall." Simon felt like shit for not being able to catch Tucker, but Dane could reach him, and they needed him alive and speaking.

"I got it, old man." Dane passed Simon and climbed the wall like a young recruit. Simon could hear shots fired, a few cries of pain, and then silence. He hobbled to the wall and pulled himself to the top. He'd assumed Dane would kick Tucker's ass. He'd assumed wrong.

"Fantastic agent you are." Tucker said, as he pointed his gun as Dane's head.

"You're still an idiot. You shot me in the arm after three tries." Dane taunted him. "Your aim sucks. You missed Simon as well and hit the minister in the chapel, you little shit."

"And you've been unable to handle anything larger than an observational role in covert activities unless Simon is tucked up to your side protecting your ass."

Dane's face hardened. "I'm more than capable of taking you down on my own."

Tucker laughed. "Certainly doesn't look like it."

Simon held onto the wall with one arm, watching the men argue. His gun targeted Tucker's head, but he was unsure if he could hit him at such a distance. If he missed, Dane would be finished.

"This is for Valeriya." Tucker stepped closer to Dane.

"Since when have you been a Russian sympathizer?" Dane asked.

"She was a student, nothing more. The intelligence was wrong."

"Her best friend Marta, disappeared after meeting with U.S. recruiters. The poor woman's family received one finger at a time. Ironic that Marta's ex-boyfriend graduated Langley with me. Last I heard, he was in a prison north of St. Petersburg. All your beautiful fiancée's handiwork. I did you a favor. She would have had you arrested within weeks if I hadn't terminated her."

Tucker straightened his arm and let out a huff of air. "You're wrong."

Simon tossed a loose stone into the woods behind Tucker. He took the bait, idiot that he was, and turned his head a fraction. His gun moved away from Dane. Simon fired and missed. Tucker's body, however, flinched back and collapsed to the ground. Dane jumped up and took his gun. Tucker appeared to be breathing, but blood spilled from a knife in his throat. The one Dane always hid near his ankle.

"Still need work on your aim," Dane called to Simon. "But thanks for the distraction."

"It was payback for helping Cassie in North Korea." The image of Cassie on the ground in the chapel rushed into his mind, and he turned back up the path. "Take care of Tucker."

It took all of his energy and a lifetime of effort to get back inside. He limped down the path, holding himself up by the back of random chairs. Cassie was crouched over the minister. When she turned around, he noticed blood all over her gown. Everything else blurred.

He fought his pain to get to her side. "What's wrong? Were you shot?"

Her hair was damp with sweat, and a streak of blood marred her perfect face. "I'm fine. The minister was shot in the shoulder. I'm trying to minimize his blood loss until the ambulance arrives. Where's Dane?"

"He's keeping vigil with the shooter." Simon strode two steps closer to her and collapsed to the floor. One hand reached out to touch the blood on her cheek.

"Are you hurt?" she asked.

"I'm fine." And he would be, as long as Cassie was nearby.

Two hours later, Tucker was dead, and the minister, Simon, and Dane were hospitalized. Simon, stuck in bed again, wrapped an arm around Cassie to keep her next to him, but away from the newly opened wounds in his chest.

"I can't believe you brought a gun to our wedding." Her head rested on his shoulder, her blonde hair drifting across his arm.

"Aren't you glad I did?"

She shrugged. "We'll never stop looking over our shoulders, will we?"

"I have plans to slow down."

Simon wanted to retire from his strange placement at MI6, but it would be safer if he stayed in the arms field. Retired, he'd be considered weak and a target. If he remained in the game, he'd be able to keep tabs on all the players. Having a second-in-command as competent and loyal as Dane would keep him even safer. Dane, however, wasn't ready to give up his cushy sales job in California. But Simon could be persuasive when he wanted to be. He just needed the right bait.

Cassie had clearance to return to her old job. He'd already spoken to his contacts at HQ, and they'd agreed to allow her to work remotely from the farmhouse near Oxford he'd purchased for her wedding present. Living close to Henry and Alex would also be a benefit.

"So I stay home, and you run around the world making arms deals?" Cassie asked after hearing the details of their future life together.

"We can switch positions, but your knowledge about the arms trade is weak, and I'm not quite as advanced as you are in computers. Besides, I'll do all the cooking when I'm home."

"Vegan meals?" With a twist of her neck, she faced him nose to nose.

He kissed her. Long, hard, deep, and intense. She should know better than to come so close. If only he could lock the door. She pulled back first, breathing deep and looking a bit flustered. Man, he loved her.

"We can be vegan on Mondays, Wednesdays, and an occasional Friday."

She lifted her eyebrows. "I bet you'll be in London on those days."

"That's what I love about you, angel. Analytical skills galore."

---

LIFE MOVED EXACTLY as Simon had envisioned. He scaled down his business, Cassie happily worked from a home office, and Junior continued to grow inside her mother. She'd be arriving into the world in a matter of weeks.

At that exact moment, however, Simon dedicated himself to Cassie's physical needs. She looked amazing under him, as though she had been placed there for his dinner, dessert, and tomorrow's breakfast as well. By the time they had finished the first three courses, Cassie's eyes were beginning to close, but Simon was still hungry. He began to explore her expanding curves. He started with her breasts and moved to her rounded stomach.

Her pregnant body fascinated him. He caressed down her side until his fingers detoured over her thigh. "Don't move. I want to see if you can remain perfectly silent as I torture you."

She laughed, and her body shook, but she said nothing.

"You're failing. Stop moving."

The phone on the bedside table rang.

"Ignore it," he called out before descending further.

His cell phone rang.

"Don't move," he ordered.

Cassie, always one to follow orders, lifted his cell phone. "It's Dane."

"He can talk to my voicemail."

Dane's refusal to become his partner pissed him off. They'd be perfect together, and Simon wouldn't have to worry about the CIA breathing down his throat. Dane, however, didn't want the hassle.

"You better answer it."

"You'll be asleep if talk I on the phone."

"Exactly. I need a break. You're insatiable."

"You need more sex to improve your stamina."

She handed him the phone, kissed him on the cheek, and rolled over. "Good night, Simon."

He hit the speaker function. He didn't have secrets anymore where Cassie was concerned. "Dunn."

"We have a problem. How quickly can you get to Columbia?"

*We?* He glanced at his almost sleeping wife. "I can't. I no longer have a death wish, and my wife will kill me if I leave her before Junior arrives."

"A rebel group took my sister. I need backup from outside the agency." The strain in Dane's voice changed Simon's mind.

Cassie turned to face him. "Go. We owe him our lives. You might as well pay him back before the baby's born." She sat against the headboard, completely alert. She still showed fear on her face without any attempt to conceal it, but the strength bubbling up through her inner core created a steel wall that would protect her in the future.

Simon gave Cassie a slight nod and spoke into the phone. "I'll be at Heathrow in two hours. Text me the specifics."

Dane let a relieved laugh. "I love that woman of yours. Give Cassie a huge kiss for me, but nothing more. We don't have the time."

The phone call ended, and the prospect of Dane joining his organization just improved one hundred percent.

He grabbed his suitcase and threw in a few necessities for the trip. After he finished, he walked over to Cassie. She should have put her clothes back on, because her naked breasts were seducing him back into bed. He kissed her with a blaze that would never extinguish, no matter how much he tried to satiate himself in her.

"I'll be home soon."

"I know you will."

"You do?"

A smile lifted the corners of her mouth, more like a skilled operative than a seductive wife. "If you aren't back within two weeks, I'm coming to get you."

"You wouldn't dare."

She raised her eyebrows, fierce and proud as a lioness. *Damn, she would.*

*Turn the page for a sneak peek of True Peril, Danes's story.*

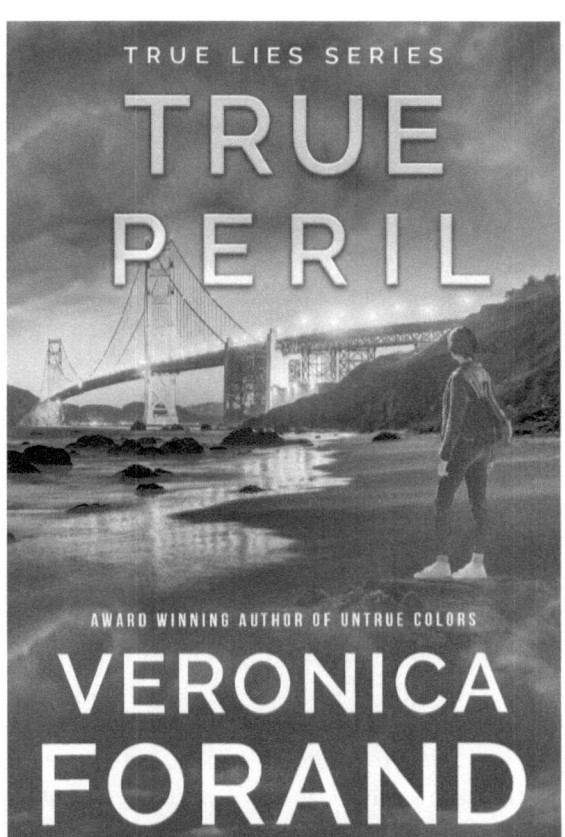

TRUE LIES SERIES

# TRUE
# PERIL

AWARD WINNING AUTHOR OF UNTRUE COLORS

# VERONICA
# FORAND

# CHAPTER 1

———————— ❧ ————————

A beat-up Land Cruiser, bald tires, and a dirt road complete with potholes and gullies made for one shitty way to travel to San Stefano, a tiny nothing of a village. Drug cartels and rogue militias ruled these mountains of Columbia. Dane O'Brien, however, had a mission to complete—retrieve Jenny Bloom and send her back home to the States—so he'd snagged the first transportation available to get the job done. The mission was as close to impossible as any Dane had been on in the past. This woman, full of crazy intelligence and insane compassion for the poor and underserved communities of the world, preferred living in war zones to the suburbs of Maryland.

When he'd discovered where she was, he'd called and tried to convince her to leave. The pain in the ass do-gooder, however, refused to stop risking her life for people she didn't know. He played a similar game and absorbed the risk as a means to an end, but Jenny's situation was different.

She was his baby sister.

He drove into the small, colorful village expecting the slow rhythms of a mountain farm community. The tension across the crowded marketplace put him on instant alert. Something foul had soiled the atmosphere. A crowd of people milled about in the town square. Several men stood together wearing stress and fear as part of their wardrobe. A group of women conversed with arms waving and eyes blazing.

He parked at the schoolhouse, a new two-floor building made through contributions from the international organization that had hired Jenny. The few villagers outside the school quieted as the stranger arrived. He showed his empty hands in a gesture of good faith, nodded briefly, and headed into the building.

"Jenny?" he called into the large empty classroom on the first floor.

A door opened and closed above him, and footsteps pattered down the stairs. Jenny flew around the corner and jumped into his arms, looking like the freckle-faced teenager of their youth. Her hair was still short and flyaway with no recognizable style to it, and her face was red and blotchy as though she'd been crying all night. His happiness in seeing her faded to a deep concern. Jenny was not the type to whine, complain, or cry without major cause.

"You made it. Thank God." She hugged him tighter.

"What's wrong?" His hands automatically moved across her shoulders and down her back to check for injuries. She'd sounded happy when he'd spoken to her the day before.

"I'm fine." She shook him off and paced to the window, looking into the marketplace. Her breathing slowed and mixed with an occasional sob. "Rebels came here last night and killed the barkeeper. They took Trista, my roommate. She hasn't returned."

Rebels? This wasn't a FARC controlled area. The Revolutionary Armed Forces of Columbia, otherwise known as the People's Army, had moved out of this area years ago, and the major leftist groups had relocated closer to the coal mines. "Which group?"

"The Red Hawks. They're a small rebel faction more interested in making money than causing government reform. Once or twice a month, a few men come down from their base to buy supplies. These two were barely out of their teenage years. Their uniforms and guns gave them the confidence to do anything."

"And they kidnapped her?"

Jenny looked at her feet. "They were kidnapping Natalia, but she wouldn't have stood a chance, so Trista said she would take her place."

"She volunteered to leave with them?" *Is the woman crazy?*

"Natalia, the barkeeper's daughter, is only fourteen. She'd just watched her father gunned down. She was crying uncontrollably and the murderers decided why not completely blacken their souls by raping and possibly killing their victim's daughter. They pulled her out of the bar to their Jeep. They would have destroyed her. I wish I'd had the guts to do something, but I honestly had no idea how to handle it. Trista's different. She works with the rehabilitation arm of the ICFP."

"The what?"

"The International Children's Protection Fund. The group that set me up here. As a rehabilitation specialist, Trista has helped hundreds of children leave military groups. She's also rescued girls forced into marriage. She must have thought she could talk to the rebels and escape. At least, that's what I think she'd intended."

Did Jenny realize that Trista's job would invite death threats and retaliation?

"She wanted to negotiate with horny adolescents with guns, drunk on their power? Shit. She may never return."

"No. I don't believe that. She's smart and prepared and has been in a bunch of war zones." Jenny paced around the room and told him everything that had occurred in the bar. Her friend Trista sounded like a martyr. Dane was grateful Jenny didn't have that same heroic instinct. He'd take down entire countries if something ever happened to her.

"And no one stood up to stop them?"

Jenny shook her head. "The Red Hawks burned a nearby village about five years ago. Most people died. Everyone here is terrified."

The more she told him, the grimmer Trista's future appeared.

Even if she escaped, she'd be stranded in the middle of the jungle with no food or clean water.

Part of the crowd gathering outside the school had circled his SUV and were peering in the windows of the schoolhouse. They had reason to be cautious, although from Jenny's descriptions, the whole village was more fearful than confrontational.

"Can we go somewhere more private?"

"Come upstairs." She grasped him by the hand and led him to her apartment on the second floor. The apartment had a kitchenette, a couch, and two chairs, with a bunch of doors probably leading to bedrooms and a bathroom. The only color came from the bright blue curtains. Not much of a living space, but probably larger than many of the homes in this area. A collage of photos lined the corkboard on the wall. A picture of him as a new college graduate ready to conquer the world sat among ones of a smiling Jenny on various assignments.

He focused on the photos of Trista. She had an athletic body, with feminine curves, and she wore her brown hair long. A wayward strand partially covered her hazel eyes. In every photo, her expression appeared as though she was waiting for rain or a zombie apocalypse. To a man who read faces and body language as part of his job, she appeared not to trust most people.

He guided Jenny to the couch. "We have to get you out of here. It'll only get worse if the soldiers come back."

"Leave?" Jenny stared at him with wide, wet eyes. "I can't leave the children. They won't have a teacher if I run away. Three of them live with us and have no one else in their lives. And what about Trista? I can't take off without her. She risked her life to help Natalia. I owe her. The whole village owes her a debt."

"The Columbian army won't protect you in this inkblot of a town. Even if they did, it would take two days to travel here."

Jenny stood in her jeans and gray T-shirt with her hands on her hips, ready to fight her older brother, as she'd done again and again in the past. "I have responsibilities. Erika is only five, and little Juan and Sergio depend on me. Hell, Natalia lost her father last night—she needs someone to care for her. ICPF support should be here in a few days. They're bringing supplies and a few extra people." After Jenny's husband, a Peace Corps volunteer, died a few years ago while building a bridge in Madagascar, she poured her heartache into her assignments. A tribute to the late Fred Bloom. Only Fred would probably not have been so supportive of her trekking to the most remote and dangerous areas of the world.

"I only have two days, and then I have to return to San Francisco." He'd wanted to spend the time convincing his sister to come home, but her roommate dominated his thoughts. *Is she going to make it back?* He shouldn't get involved, but those damn hazel eyes were embedded in his brain, and her bravado in saving that girl made him curious about her and…shit. He couldn't leave a woman alone with a bunch of punks.

"You can take a longer vacation. You're a salesman. Who cares if you don't show up for work?"

He wasn't exactly a salesman. He was a CIA operative who monitored arms deals throughout the world. His access to the major players in the field came from being embedded with a California drone technology company. Jenny didn't know his real employer, and he preferred to keep it that way for her own protection.

He glanced at the photos of Trista again. Staying here was stupid and a risk to both him and Jenny, but after seeing Trista and feeling the inevitable pull of his conscience, he wanted her safe as much as Jenny did. Work would have to wait.

"We can drive up the mountain and search for her," Jenny said, reaching for a jacket.

"We? You're staying in the village. I'll take a drive. I'm limiting my search to thirty miles, and then I turn around." Dane had his own doubts about the safety of the village as well, but alone he could move faster, and old skills he'd tried to bury could be resurrected to pull Trista out safely, if she was still alive.

"Why can't I go with you?"

"You're safer here." Whoever took Trista wouldn't let her go so easily, and Jenny was not going to head into a potential shootout. On this, he wouldn't budge.

His biggest concern centered on finding Trista in an unfamiliar and dangerous jungle he knew nothing about. He couldn't call for backup because the CIA wouldn't acknowledge his employment. If he was discovered, his cover could be blown, and Pelican would go into a media frenzy, accusing the government of inserting government informants into corporations. Not exactly the public relations the intelligence community needed right now.

His current assignment required him to gain access to corporations to steal information, and wine and dine presidents of small countries in order to locate holes in their defense systems. In the past, however, he infiltrated countries and took out individuals hostile to American interests. He preferred his expense account to his rifle. And yet he kept falling back into situations where his old skills were necessary. Perhaps this wouldn't be one of those times. The increased tension in the back of his neck told him otherwise. He sure as hell wouldn't be smoking cigars and drinking Scotch on this rescue mission.

Four hours later, he'd changed from corporate flunky in khaki pants and a button down shirt into a lost tourist in worn jeans and a T-shirt. After talking with a few of the villagers, he located enough supplies for a brief drive into the jungle. His only weapon, a Glock he carried on him at all times, rested in his shoulder holster, covered by a worn flannel shirt he'd bought off one of the local farmers.

Leaving the village, he followed the dirt road into the higher elevations of the mountains. Remote didn't begin to describe this place. Little to no electricity, and the only gas station around was in the back of his SUV in the form of a twenty-gallon red plastic jug. The density of the jungle encroaching on each side of the road made him wish he had access to a team of Navy SEALs. Those badasses would extricate Trista in under an hour and still have time for a drink at the local bar. He'd have to go it alone.

The road forked in several locations, but the few sets of new tire tracks in the mud all followed the same route. A rutted pull-out next to an old broken down hut caught his attention. He drove past the hut and parked his car about a mile down an old walking path, wide enough to fit the SUV and far enough away from the road to avoid detection if anyone returned, and used a small shovel to shift the mud across his tracks at the entrance to the path.

No sound came from the building, but there was evidence of recent activity that indicated something had gone down at that spot within the past twelve hours. Gun in hand, he pushed the door open with his foot.

The stench hit him first. Blood pooled across the ground in large brown stains, exposing a recent, probably fatal, injury. Was it from Trista? The thought made his chest hurt. She'd risked her life for someone else. A stupid but brave action.

He searched for a sign she'd been there, hoping he didn't find her body. A few sets of heavy footprints going to and from the road dug into the ground. Dane was no tracker, but those were made by combat boots. He'd bet his life on it.

Every bird that flew near the hut added three more gray hairs to Dane's mostly brown-haired head. He had solid instincts in the field, but in today's technological world, the smallest camera could be beaming his location and description to anyone, and he'd be none the wiser. He headed to the door and noticed a lighter and smaller set of footprints in the dirt leading to the jungle. Sneakers?

He followed the tracks to the edge of the clearing. Thick vegetation hid from view anything farther than fifty yards into the jungle. If she was in there, she could stay hidden forever.

"Trista?" he called out through the trees.

No answer.

"I'm Jenny's brother. It's safe."

He called to her several more times and then started back to his car to gather supplies to hike a mile or two farther to try to find more evidence of her presence. The swish of a branch behind him caught his attention. Whoever was hiding had emerged.

Relief turned to caution as Trista walked out of the jungle with a layer of mud covering her and a handgun aimed at his head.

"Trista?"

She didn't speak. Her eyes stayed focused on him, and her legs seemed poised to take off at the slightest threat.

"Are you hurt?" he asked.

Hovering in the area between the road and the forest, she shook her head. "You're Jenny's brother?"

Her voice sounded stronger than her faltering body appeared. Some of the mud that covered her looked more like blood that had dried on her shirtsleeves and part of her pants.

"Yes. I'm Dane O'Brien."

"What's Jenny's middle name?" Her eyebrows furrowed as they had in the pictures.

"She doesn't have one."

She took a tentative step forward. She observed Dane's movements and fixed her eyes on his like a panther ready to pounce. "What's her favorite drink?"

"Chocolate milkshakes. Or a margarita if the bar carries fresh limes."

Her frown remained, but she pointed the gun to the ground and walked over to him. His arms opened automatically—after all, the woman had been through hell. She probably needed a hug or a shoulder to cry on.

She crossed her arms over her chest, the gun dangling from her hand. Her breathing pattern switched from a heavy sigh to a shivery exhale. He put his arms down and observed her.

"Are you okay?"

She nodded. "I'll survive."

"Let me rephrase. Do you need medical attention?"

"No."

"Where are the men who took you from the village?"

"Dead."

"You killed them?"

She nodded. Her gaze dropped to the ground. Most people never recovered from such a nightmare. Yet she'd not only lived through the ordeal, she emerged from the jungle healthy and armed.

Impressive.

He'd placed the odds against her, but now that he saw her in person, he'd have changed his bet. He approached her with caution. Her finger rested just outside the trigger, in a position a skilled shooter would feel comfortable with.

She peered up at him. "I'm glad you're here. I didn't know how I'd get down from the mountain. Is Jenny all right?"

"Worried about you."

"What about Natalia?"

"I don't know anything about her, except she's probably alive thanks to you. Did they hurt you?" He placed a calming hand on her shoulder and slipped the gun out of her hand.

"No." She eyed the weapon, but didn't reach for it. Not that she'd be capable of taking it back from him.

"I've been listening to the group's radio all night. They're coming back. For me." A tear rolled down her cheek. She ignored it and looked toward the hut. "I didn't mean to kill them."

"Kill or be killed." He urged her toward the Land Cruiser with a soft hand still on her shoulder, trying to ease the wretched emotions that would brand her view of the world forever—the same emotions that tortured his soul every night. "You survived a kidnapping by two moronic men. Don't feel guilty."

"You'd have killed them?"

More than killed them. That's why he hid away in an office now. If anyone had threatened to rape a young girl in his presence, he would have flayed their skin and stuffed it down their throats before ripping their hearts out. "I wouldn't have been as merciful as you."

# CHAPTER 2

Trista followed Dane to a dusty black SUV hidden a few hundred yards from the hut. Her steps were not exactly bouncing. Could more fighters catch up to them? The men from the Red Hawks had been so brutal, killing Natalia's father, almost raping her. She had no choice but to kill them. The spray of their blood, the cries of agony played over and over in her head, a continuous loop guaranteed to destroy her mind. Nothing would ever be the same. Ever. The night in the jungle had wiped out the rest of her sanity.

She studied the confident man rummaging through the bags in the back of the vehicle. Jenny's brother? She'd mentioned that he sold UAVs—Unmanned Aerial Vehicles, or drones—and that he was over protective. Perhaps it was the night she'd just spent warding off insects in the jungle, but she'd never been so glad to see a person in her life. His looks were an added benefit.

He pulled out a bottle and handed it to her. Water rushed down her throat and relieved the dryness she'd experienced after finishing her supply the night before. She then poured some over her face to remove the awful smelling mud and dirt she'd coated herself with to blend into the jungle.

"You traveled all the way up here to see Jenny? I'm

impressed." She dried off with the bottom edge of her shirt. The fabric caught on a scab on her arm. Blood dripped to the ground. She pressed her fingers over the wound and handed him back the water.

He ignored her offer and, instead, lifted each of her arms and inspected the wounds on her elbows. His light brown eyes narrowed—really intense brown eyes. "I try to check on her as much as I can."

"It's a pretty dangerous region with rebels sneaking around and law enforcement rarely making a visit."

"That makes it even more important I visit." His words hit her in the most sensitive area of her heart. Someone who cared. She'd give her right arm to have even one of her four siblings care enough about her to send a Christmas card.

He picked up her pack from the ground and pulled out the other gun and the radio she'd taken from the men to monitor their comrades' movements.

"Yours?" he asked.

"Not really."

"We'll need to get rid of them." He slipped everything back inside, including the other gun.

He grabbed another backpack from his truck and rummaged through it for a few moments. He held out a moss green sundress she recognized from Jenny's closet. "Throw this on. We need to bury your clothes as well."

No use arguing. She did need to lose the blood stained clothes. "Can I have some extra water to clean up with?"

"Only use one bottle in case we're delayed driving back. And hurry up."

He stepped away so she had a moment of privacy. A very short moment—within a minute, he was telling her to hurry up. Exhausted from the ordeal, she almost told him to leave her alone, but the water invigorated her. It motivated her. It brought back her immediate need to leave the area.

By the time she'd changed, she felt a hundred times better.

One drive down the mountain and she could take a long, hot shower and fall into her bed.

In the distance, a new rumble echoed up the mountain—the sound of a truck. Shit. Her body tensed. They wouldn't have time to drive away without announcing their presence.

He placed his finger to her lips to stop her movements and then motioned toward the jungle. "We need to get out of here."

"Where are you going?" She didn't want to hike back into the jungle. Too muddy, not enough food, and way too many insects. Too bad she'd soaked her jeans while washing up. A clean sundress was not optimal for this type of journey.

"I'm assuming the rebel group found the bodies in the hut. If they've radioed their base already, no one will be moving in a vehicle for fifty miles in either direction without a fighter searching every crevice for anyone who might have killed the two punks. I don't want to take that chance. We'll stay in the jungle tonight and then drive down in the morning. And if we still can't then, we'll walk."

Walk? Her body wouldn't budge. The blisters on her heels told her to stay put. Dane's arm, however, prodded her forward, forcing her to move.

They traveled in silence for a few minutes. His pace was quick, but not too fast. She could keep up if she didn't think about sleep or food.

"Trista's a pretty name." He walked ahead of her, his voice floating back and luring her forward with the smooth, husky sound.

"Trista means sad. Not exactly inspiring."

"Is that why you never smile, because of your name?"

"I smile—"

"Liar. I saw the pictures on the wall at the schoolhouse." He glanced over his shoulder and grinned.

Trista rolled her eyes. "Maybe I don't have much to smile about. What about Dane?" she asked. "Were you named after a dog?"

"A great dog." He turned toward her again, and his insanely sexy grin grew bigger.

"Lucky you." She held back her own grin so he didn't think he was getting to her, because he was really getting to her, in a weird attracted-to-the-rescuer kind of way.

At one point Dane stopped and placed the bag with her old clothes, the two guns, and the radio under the root of a large tree. Then he covered it with dirt and debris. The loss of her weapons didn't make her feel any safer, but if caught with rebel firearms, they'd have to explain how they got them.

They continued a mile or two into the forest. Her steps slowed, and she fell farther behind Dane.

"Are you okay?" he called back.

"Better now that I have company, but I need some sleep, some water, and something to eat or I won't have the energy to walk more than a few miles."

He lifted his pack off his shoulder and pulled out more water and a few bananas. "Keep these with you."

His kindness strengthened her will. She stored the supplies in the small pack he'd given to her, and picked up her pace. "I'll try, but it's been hard forcing food down with the bloody images of those men haunting me."

Her thoughts flashed back to the expression in Mateo's eyes when he realized she'd shot him in the chest. The kid, no older than eighteen, died without ever really living. He'd been brainwashed into a life of murder, probably before he'd turned ten years old. And then her mind jumped to the other fighter. Pedro. He'd roughed her up, but he didn't have to die, especially by a bullet to the head. She was supposed to rescue these guys, not gun them down.

*They would have raped and killed me. I didn't have a choice.*

A tear fell down her cheek, and she lost her appetite again. Her feet slowed until she stood still and stared through a blurry haze at the ground.

Dane walked toward her. "Come here."

She wiped her damp face and sniffled. "What are you doing?"

"How can I help you get through this?" He spoke with a seriousness bordering on military.

"You've already solved all my problems," she said with sarcasm. "I feel perfectly fine now that my prince has rescued me."

His frown actually cheered her up some more.

"So I'm your prince? I can accept that."

"Actually, you're not my type." Although he'd be perfect for a lazy weekend at the beach, indulging in fantasies.

He threw up his arms in mock horror. "Is that a rejection? Damn, I'm losing my touch."

He wasn't losing his touch, he just had the wrong target. She was one's damsel. From Jenny's description, Dane seemed country club perfect, like her own family. Possessed of pretty boy looks, rarely away from his office, rarely in anything but a suit or golf shirt. He probably had fashion models calling him all the time to go out. Men like that never interested her. They could offer her nothing she desired. Yet, here he was in the middle of a forest helping her. And the golf shirt had been replaced by a flannel shirt that rocked his muscles. That was a type she could appreciate.

They walked farther into the thick trees and located a narrow path. He stopped for a moment and stared at her.

"What's wrong?" she asked.

"Come closer?"

"Why?"

He stepped behind her and clasped her by the shoulders. "I'm sorry."

"For what?" Before she could react, he pulled a blade out of nowhere, grabbed her ponytail, and cut it off.

"What the hell?" She yanked away from him. "Are you insane? You come one step closer to me, and I'll do the same thing to your throat."

"You killed two men. Someone besides me knows this as well.

You need a disguise. I can't color it, but at least it will be shorter. Come here so I can even it out."

She stayed a few feet from his reach. "And the reason you couldn't tell me your intentions?"

"I figured it would be easier." He shrugged as though severing a ponytail from another person was not a big deal.

"I'm not an idiot. And I don't appreciate being treated like one. If we're going to be traveling together, we're equals."

The right side of his mouth lifted in a half smile, as though he was trying to hold back a full grin. "I don't usually work in a team, but I'll try to respect your opinion. Now come here so I can fix your hair to look like a style someone would actually want."

Trista allowed it because it was already too late to stop the assault on her formerly nice hair. She didn't want to know what he was doing, because clumps fell on the ground around her, and she couldn't imagine losing that much hair without going bald. Yet, this low didn't affect her as much as it might have the day before. Her feelings had been numbed so much in the past few hours that the loss of her hair didn't matter as long as she was alive.

He shoved the pieces he'd cut off into a hole and covered it with dirt and leaves. Her hands rubbed through the finished style. It felt like Jenny's short and wispy hair, but probably not as cute.

They walked side by side for a while. The heat made the hike more difficult. At least she had company now.

Dane paused for a moment. His muscles seemed tense. Before she could ask him what was wrong, he shoved her off the edge of the trail. She plunged down the muddy ridge. Several rocks rose up out of nowhere and struck her in the hip, on her back, and once in the head behind her ear. Her yell was absorbed by the flight of a flock of birds surprised by her crashing through their environment. She landed at the edge of a stream, unable to catch her breath and aching from the impact.

Dazed and confused, she opened her mouth to demand an apology and a rope. Before she uttered a word, she saw Dane up on top of the ridge, faced away from her, his arms raised in the air as a man in camouflage clothing searched him and forced him to the ground.

He'd saved her life.

And sacrificed his.

Covered in dirt and as still as the stone that had bruised her back, she blended into the forest floor and waited for the men to leave. She remained unmoving and silent until she could no longer hear the soldiers pushing Dane farther away. Step by step, she climbed back up the hill to the path. Without a thought to her body's need for rest, she followed their tracks through the jungle.

---

*How the hell did this go so bad, so quickly?* Dane struggled to keep his gaze away from the bottom of the ridge, where Trista was no doubt cursing him out. If she had a brain, she'd refrain from screaming out his name. People, however, rarely did what they should. After several minutes with his face in the dirt and no woman charging up the hill, Dane realized she must have seen the other men.

The three rebels took his backpack, phone, and his gun, leaving him with nothing but the knife in his boot and a feeling of dread. He didn't want to play Rambo today. He just wanted to return to San Francisco, sit in his office overlooking the bay, and spend the night with a beautiful woman by his side. Instead, he was stranded in Columbia under armed guard, worrying about a traumatized woman who needed a hot shower. Dumping her off in the middle of the jungle wouldn't endear him to her, but she'd be better off away from anyone who could connect her to the murders. And he wanted her safe above all else. Damn morals.

After what seemed like a two-hour march straight uphill, they arrived at an active compound hidden in the low clouds of the mountains. Soldiers were everywhere. Mostly young, all male. He needed to wait for more secluded terrain to make his move.

He surveyed the area, looking for an opportunity to escape. Small houses created a neighborhood atmosphere tucked under some trees on the edge of the fields. Two men and a woman worked in a poppy field, a crop studied extensively at Quantico by new recruits. The plants had not yet matured, so there was no sign of flowers or the pods where the milky sap would ooze out after being sliced by a sharp knife. In a few months, the field would be full of rebel fighters turned farm workers. They'd harvest the crop for heroin to be sold for a fortune in the United States or Mexico.

His escorts pushed him into the largest building, a glass and cement structure that appeared to be part home, part fortress. The extravagant decor and furnishings appeared out of place in the harsh mountainous region. A mini palace, funded by drugs. An older man, mid-fifties, wearing a loose linen shirt and black tailored pants, sat next to a breathtakingly beautiful woman. The man appeared arrogant and untouchable, Dane's favorite personality. Men like him were predictable, with the right incentives.

"Liliana, leave us," the man told his companion in Spanish.

She stood and peered over her shoulder at Dane. The man cleared his throat, and she sauntered away, her white skirt swaying in the same rhythm as her long dark hair.

Dane, accompanied by two armed guards, walked with the calm facade he'd developed for unpleasant situations. After a nod from their leader, his escorts backed up against the wall and watched in silence.

"You are in my territory. Are you lost?" the man asked in Spanish.

A businessman would fetch a high ransom as a kidnap victim, although both of Dane's employers, Pelican and the U.S. government, would refuse to pay. His status, if revealed, as a CIA operative guaranteed Dane would be tortured and then murdered. He had one more option—an identity that would assure him safe passage and allow him to find Trista again.

"I was checking out the area," he answered in his best Spanish, his American accent laced throughout. "I have an order to deliver some goods through Ecuador, and this seemed the safest route."

"Order?" The man shifted in his seat.

This could backfire, but Dane had to use the biggest weapon in his arsenal. He kept his expression unreadable and stared straight into the man's soul. If he hesitated, the guy would know he was bluffing.

"I work for Simon Dunn."

His captor took a moment and then reacted with widened eyes. "And you are?"

"Dane O'Brien, his assistant."

He nodded. "Welcome, Mr. O'Brien. I am Juan Carlos Gomez. It's an honor to have someone from Mr. Dunn's operation here. How may I assist you?"

Simon Dunn, Dane's best friend, acted as one of the most notorious arms dealers in the world. He was credited with burning to the ground a mansion on the Right Bank of Paris with the occupants in it. The U.S. and U.K. governments also linked him to an explosion that blew up a military base in North Korea, killing an unknown number of soldiers. His legacy made him one of the most feared men on Earth. Dane was one of only a handful of people who knew the real Simon Dunn, an embedded operative attached to MI6. Simon used every means available to keep arms from flowing to enemies of the U.K. His tactics were so fine-tuned, his targets often called him to commiserate over the loss of guns and ammunition in government raids arranged by Dunn himself.

Simon and Dane had spent their early careers assisting each other on international assignments and competing with each other for the foreign beauties who often crossed their paths. Simon, now married with a baby on the way, wanted Dane to leave his observational role and become active in his operation. Dane, however, preferred his easy assignment cataloguing drone shipments to third world countries. Killing had been too easy for him in the past. He feared that part of him that would kill anyone or anything when pushed to the wall.

"I can't divulge our clients, but I need a route by which to run a shipment to a spot about two hundred miles from here."

"I understand. And if I offer my territory for your operation?"

"I'm sure Mr. Dunn will reward your kindness." And it would be taken out of Dane's hide for involving him in Columbia, a location he preferred staying out of. Linking his old friend to this mess would complicate their already messed up relationship, putting Dane in Simon's debt, a place he never wanted to be.

"And you have no problem if I confirm this information?"

"Not at all. Can I have my phone back so I can call him?"

Carlos nodded to one his minions who handed the phone to Dane. He hit speaker, and called Simon. He placed the phone on a teak table beside a porcelain vase of flowers and a gold letter opener.

Simon answered on the second ring. "What the fuck do you want, O'Brien?"

Juan Carlos moved to the table and took over before Dane could say a word. He spoke in slow broken English. "Mr. Dunn, I am Juan Carlos Gomez. Your man, Mr. O'Brien, has crossed into my territory from Ecuador. I need confirmation he is with your operation."

"Where are you calling from?" Simon spoke in perfect Castilian Spanish.

The tension across his captor's face relaxed, and he slipped back into his mother tongue. "The Southern Andes in Columbia."

"He's exactly where he's supposed to be. I hope you're not delaying him. I need him in London in two days." Simon's message to Dane was clear. He wanted to personally kick his ass, and he wanted him in London to do it.

"My only issue is payment for using my land to travel through."

Son of a bitch. No one tried to blackmail Simon. This could only get worse.

"Fifty thousand pounds for a single cross over. That's my only offer," Simon responded.

"And if—"

"And if you don't take it, I'll flatten your house, burn your fields, and take the arms through the area for free. Put Dane on the phone."

Juan Carlos, his breathing more rapid, but otherwise in control, stepped back for Dane to approach the phone on the table.

"I'm here." Dane spoke in English, because his Spanish was lousy.

Simon's English accent shot through the phone and stabbed Dane in the gut. "Get your bloody arse on the next plane out of Bogota."

He hung up before Dane could respond.

A young soldier interrupted the awkward silence. "Sir, a woman has been spotted on the periphery of our property. She's following the trail straight into the compound."

*Trista.* Why did he risk himself to save her if she was stupid enough to waltz right into the camp? If they linked her to the murder of the two soldiers, she'd be executed, and Dane wouldn't be able to stop it.

*Damn. Damn. Damn.*

He raised his eyebrows in feigned surprise. "Short brown hair, a green dress, body to die for?"

The soldier nodded.

"That's my wife, Eve. I'm glad you located her." Inside, he seethed at her stupidity. Outside, he smiled.

Juan Carlos pinched his lips in surprise. "You travel with your wife?"

"Always. I prefer keeping her with me. She usually shops while I work, and I have the benefit of a clean companion at night. She wanted to come with me this afternoon to find an orchid that grows in this area. Your men didn't seem so welcoming when they escorted me here, so I left her."

"Interesting." He shooed the soldier out the door. "Would you like some lunch while you wait? I'm sure I can find something you'll like."

"Yes. Can I clean up a little first?"

"Absolutely."

He followed Juan Carlos toward a hallway and a clean bathroom with a majestic view of the Andes. Trista better be a good actress, or they were both dead.

# CHAPTER 3

———————— ✑ ————————

Trista pushed through her fatigue and followed the path out of the jungle. She'd known Dane only a few hours, and he'd risked his life for her. *Who does that for people?* Well…she did. But she wasn't going to let him die for her. She had to at least try to save him.

He'd have no clue how to deal with subversive groups. Neither did she, although after working with about a half dozen international aid groups to provide child fighters a way back to a normal family life, she'd lived through some pretty scary situations. If she could convince the fighters that Dane was harmless and without economic worth, she might be able to help him. Her last attempt at negotiating with hostile forces, however, had ended up with two dead men. The tension knotting her gut tightened with each step.

As she climbed, she spotted some fields through the clumps of trees. Dirty white houses with metal roofs stood by the road leading to more houses and buildings. This had to be the Red Hawks camp. Ironically, she'd been planning to meet with the Red Hawks' leader to discuss educating the boys in his group. Ignorance, however, made for better followers, so her attempts would probably not have gone well.

A faint acidic odor, like paint thinner and rotten eggs, stung her nasal passages. She circled the area, pausing to observe soldiers on patrol and a few people working in a field on the far side of the mountain. The pungent smell came from one of the buildings on the outskirts of the little community. A drug lab. She'd worked near one in Bolivia and would never forget the smell. That would be the most heavily guarded area. A path between the fields and the houses protected her from notice for a mile or two, but then her luck ran out.

Two fighters, armed and young, approached her. She tried to meander along the path like a local, but they didn't give her a chance.

"Your husband is waiting," a fighter called out in weak English, as though she couldn't speak Spanish. Trista did speak Spanish, though. Fluently. Maybe they thought she was someone else. She kept quiet, just in case.

One of them took her pack, while the other grasped one of her arms. He forced her to walk into the heart of the compound. Fear coiled throughout her body and slowed her steps. Had Dane already been executed?

Brilliant idea trying to save him. Now they'd both be killed.

The headline in the Greenwich Post would read, *Philanthropist socialite murdered in Columbia while trying to rescue salesman.*

The men led her to the largest building. Crossing the threshold pulled her away from the poverty of the Andes into a luxurious mansion overlooking a beautiful mountain range. The wealth in these surroundings heightened her fear. People didn't become rich in these parts unless engaged in something illegal. Most likely heroin.

The scene in the dining room caused her even more confusion. A man, dressed for a day at a beach resort, sat next to Dane, who appeared sophisticated, sexy, and clean in a black T-shirt cut to make the most of his strong shoulders and thin waist. Both men wore huge smiles and smoked cigars.

When Dane saw her, his expression morphed from contentment to concern.

"*Eve*, where have you been?" he asked in English, emphasizing the name. He shot out of his chair and clasped her shoulders.

"I—"

"I told you to wait near the car. God, I've been worried about you."

Before Trista could move, he covered her dry lips with a warm, deep kiss. The emotion and power of his kiss made her feel as though she'd been his for a long, long time. Wow. That was one hell of a welcome. When he pulled back from the kiss, his forehead stayed touching hers. She dropped her gaze to the floor, because looking into his tender eyes was overwhelming. His hands gently held her cheeks, and he sighed as though he hadn't just thrown her down a hill.

He turned her around in his arms so her back rested against a rock hard chest and she faced their host. "Juan Carlos, I'd like to introduce my wife Eve."

The man took her hand and kissed it. "Beautiful."

"Thank you. I'm a lucky man." Dane wrapped his arms tighter around her shoulders. He kissed the top of her head, never loosening his grip.

Trista could only nod as her heart fluttered against her will.

"What happened?" His voice was low and calming. He checked her arms as he had a few hours before.

"When you didn't come back, I followed the trail here. I tripped over a root and fell during the hike." She shrugged as if were no big deal.

"Sit and have something to drink." He pointed to the chair beside him then picked up a glass of water from the elaborately set table and handed it to her. Her parched throat and her body thanked her.

"Mr. O'Brien, would your wife care for some food?" Juan Carlos asked Dane in Spanish.

Yes. His *wife* did care for some food. Blue and yellow thick pottery filled with fresh fruit, a salad, bread, and a pile of empanadas sent sweet and savory aromas into the air. Her stomach grumbled its request for nourishment.

A woman in a simple blue dress, who looked like a house-keeper, prepared Trista a plate and placed it along with some silverware on the table in front of her. She dug in, ignoring their conversation. Survival instincts took precedence. After devouring an empanada and some pineapple slices, she observed Dane.

He'd turned back to face the man and resumed speaking in Spanish. "As I was saying, the scene at the hut was a bloodbath. I searched the area behind the hut, but found no evidence of anyone else around. I'm not sure we can use this route if there are active hostilities between groups. Too much of a risk. My boss is very careful in the locations where he sells his goods."

*Is he offering to sell this man a drone?*

He seemed perfectly comfortable in this world, despite the men with AK-47s standing behind them. Juan Carlos, a man who appeared to be a drug lord, enjoyed a drink that looked like cognac from a snifter as he and Dane discussed the easiest route to Ecuador. Dane had to be the best salesman in the world to have been captured by hostile rebels and then treated like royalty while perhaps obtaining a sale and maybe a large commission.

"I will have my men investigate. I can assure you this has never happened before."

"We'll need at least another month or two of no violence in the area before we send the couriers." Dane puffed on his cigar and blew a long stream of smoke as though he'd always enjoyed cigars. Maybe he did. "I think my wife needs to clean up."

Dane spoke directly to their host, and never once looked at her when he spoke Spanish. She, in return, didn't acknowledge that she understood his poor Spanish pronunciations. If they searched for a woman fluent in Spanish, they wouldn't find one here.

The gentleman rose and called out to someone. "Liliana."

An elegant woman in her mid-thirties appeared a few minutes later. The woman tried to speak to her in Spanish, but Trista spoke only in English, making sure she didn't answer any of Liliana's questions. Despite the language barrier, the woman treated her as a treasured guest. Liliana's mumblings referred to strangers in the forest and her husband's limitless kindness to others. She led Trista to a marble bathroom where she laid out towels.

"Thank you." Trista reached out her hands and clasped Liliana's in a gesture of friendship.

Her hostess wore a radiant smile and squeezed Trista's fingers and then left her to clean up.

The warm water melted away her tension. Rose scented soaps and shampoos further improved her mood. She dressed quickly in a new sundress provided by the hosts, towel-drying her new short hair into something stylish. It actually wasn't that bad. There was a layering effect around her face and the pieces fell shorter than her shoulder.

After strolling through the house admiring the beautiful furnishings, she found Dane and Juan Carlos outside on a terrace overlooking the mountains. When Dane noticed her, he beckoned her over. His arm wrapped around her waist, and she rested her head on his shoulder. He smelled of cigars. She wasn't a huge fan of cigars, but if that was the way he bonded with their captor, she'd happily breathe in the smoke.

"You clean up well," he whispered in her ear.

"So do you."

"How long have you been married?" Juan Carlos asked in English.

Trista turned to Dane and allowed him to answer. "Three months, but we haven't gone on our honeymoon yet. Too much work." He clasped her hand. "I know I promised you a trip to Fiji, but we need to fly to London first. Is that okay?"

She pretended to be put out. "I guess it'll have to be."

---

True Peril on Amazon

# ACKNOWLEDGMENTS

Thanks to Jim, Sophia, and Vivienne. Being the family of a writer is not easy. I tend to ignore the dishes, the laundry, and meal preparation while I'm struggling with a story, and my thoughts are often in another dimension thinking about fictional people and events. I love you guys more than words can say.

Thanks to Candace Havens, my editor, for your amazing assistance in polishing this manuscript from a good story into a great one.

Kate Forest, Betty Bolté, and Susan Scott Shelley are the best critique partners ever. Thanks for the support.

A shout out to my agent Michelle Grajkowski for guiding me through this crazy business.

And a special thanks to all the fans who loved Simon in "Untrue Colors" and asked for his story to be told.

# ABOUT THE AUTHOR

Veronica Forand is the award-winning writer of romantic suspense. Among her many awards, she won the Golden Pen Award and the Bookseller's Best.

Her experience includes: attorney, international corporate tax manager, college professor, university track and field coach, United Nations intern, homeschool mom, barista, waitress, and road crew. When she isn't writing, she's a canine search and rescue handler with her dog Max.

———————— ✍ ————————

*If you enjoyed True Deceptions I encourage you to leave a review so others will be encouraged to read it.*

*Sign up for my* newsletter *and be the first to receive information about new releases, sales, and bonus materials.*

*Check out more of my titles here!*
*www.veronicaforand.com*

*Thank you for reading.*

www.ingramcontent.com/pod-product-compliance
Lightning Source LLC
Chambersburg PA
CBHW020909200626
46814CB00001BA/248